THE LAST SUPPER

THE LAST SUPPER

_____

SEAN HARDIE

MICHAEL JOSEPH

LONDON

MICHAEL JOSEPH LTD

Published by the Penguin Group
27 Wrights Lane, London W8 5TZ, England
Viking Penguin Inc., 40 West 23rd Street, New York, New York 10010, USA
Penguin Books Australia Ltd, Ringwood, Victoria, Australia
Penguin Books Canada Ltd, 2801 John Street, Markham, Ontario, Canada L3R 1B4
Penguin Books (NZ) Ltd, 182–190 Wairau Road, Auckland 10, New Zealand

Penguin Books Ltd, Registered Offices: Harmondsworth, Middlesex, England

First published 1990

Typeset, printed and bound in Great Britain by
Butler & Tanner, Frome, Somerset
Set in Monophoto Sabon 11/12½ Sabon

A CIP catalogue record for this book is available from the British Library

ISBN 0 7181 3290 4

The extract from 'These Foolish Things' by Noel Coward (pp. 109–10), © 1936 by Boosey
and Company Ltd, is reprinted by permission of Boosey and Hawkes Music Publishers Ltd

For Bill
and
Sheelagh,
and for
Kerry

I

THE MOMENT CHARLIE SAW Julia he wanted to sleep with her. He wouldn't, of course – what would a sexy, pearl-toothed, athletic young blonde like Julia Cornwall see in a shop-soiled old hack like Charlie Kavanagh?

But she fancied him, there was no mistaking the signs.

He'd been drunk when she'd phoned the previous evening.

'You don't sound like a Julia to me.'

'Don't I? Maybe there's more than one kind.'

'You could hardly be worse than the last one.'

'What was wrong with her?'

'I married her. What can I do for you, Julia?'

'I'd like you to go to Israel.'

'The food's awful. You ever eaten Israeli food, Julia?'

'The money's good.'

'They do things like Chicken Stomachs, Lungs in Gravy, Stuffed Spleen, all that Yiddisher crap. Does this have to be Israel?'

'Afraid so, Charlie.'

'And what do you want me to do when I get there?'

'Make a television programme. You do still make programmes, don't you?'

'When asked nicely.' When asked at all – these days he made programmes about *anything*. The habit of taking any job he was offered had started out as a road to somewhere particular, but he'd long since forgotten where.

She'd laughed, and he'd wondered what she looked like.

'How am I doing?'

'I'm not sure. What do you look like?'

'Caucasian female, twenty-six, five foot nine, eyes blue, hair currently blonde.'

'What are you wearing?'

'Nothing.'

'In this weather?'

'Business is slow. How will I recognise you?'

'Easy, I have dandruff.'

Charlie was forty-two. He had curly brown hair, blue eyes, freckles, wrinkles at the corner of his eyes, a face that had laughed a lot, laughed when it should have been listening, not noticing that life was passing him.

He was about to get a lot more wrinkles.

'Hold on, when are you going to see me?'

'Tomorrow, of course. The Golden Calf in Charlotte Street. One o'clock.'

It was now one-fifteen. They sat in a corner of the murmuring restaurant, fiddling with their wine-glasses and pretending to study the menus. God but she was beautiful.

'I'd try the fried cheese, if I were you,' Julia suggested.

'How did you recognise me?'

'I have your photograph. If you don't like cheese try the crab.'

'What photograph?'

'None of your business. You weren't making much sense, so I thought I'd better be sure. You were drunk, weren't you? Let's order.'

'Was I?'

'Crab or Camembert?'

'Neither. I got drunk because I had a premonition of danger. I dreamed I was going to meet a blonde stranger in a café and she'd ruin my life. I'll have soup, any soup. Who are you, Julia Cornwall?'

She sat back and blew a column of cigarette smoke towards the ceiling.

'I'm a TV production company.'

'Just you?'

'Just me. How do you like the café?'

'But you call yourself Cornwall Associates,' he guessed.

2

She blinked.

'You checked?'

Charlie was looking at her mouth. A perfect mouth, near to perfect as he'd ever seen, playful, gossamer, dangerous, perfect white teeth poised to bite. Good neck too, long and elegant over an open-necked silk shirt and a string of what looked like Mexican beads. No bra, but enough to fill a B-cup if she'd wanted to.

'I'm just curious.'

'People take you seriously if you put "Associates" after your name. Where did you check?'

'Same place you got my photo.'

This is crazy, Charlie decided, the woman's a headcase. Lovely, but a headcase, first division. Does she know what she's doing? Of course she knows. Then why's she doing it? Who cares.

'So what's happening in Israel?' he asked her.

'You finished the foreplay already?'

'Just a practice run.'

'Money. And not only in Israel. You've heard of the Harry Greenbaum Foundation?'

'Nope.'

'Nor had I. They're American, they're extremely rich and philanthropic, and they're about to get into television. They have a contract with the Global Village Network in the States and satellite and cable in Europe to produce a live one-hour current affairs programme each month about a person or people behind that month's big news story.'

'Person or people behind the news.'

'Yes.'

'As opposed to the furniture, or the weather. Smart angle.'

Julia rubbed her thumb avariciously against her middle finger.

'A lot?' asked Charlie.

'A lot.'

'OK, I'm sorry. It's a brilliant idea. Go on.'

'The series is called *The Last Supper*. A variation on *This is Your Life*, except it's done as a dinner party. The subject himself and half a dozen guests. Only he or she doesn't know who else is going to be there. And they interview him, only

3

unlike a normal interview the questioners know their victim intimately.'

'What kind of hour? In this business there are all sorts of hours. An American hour is about thirty-eight minutes – the rest is commercials and promos. ITV and Channel Four come in somewhere around fifty minutes, the BBC does fifty-nine.'

'American. Three commercial breaks. It's a rush job. They screwed up, there was meant to be a pilot but the network just pulled another show. They want this now or never.'

'When's now?'

She looked him straight in the eye and smiled.

'Eight days' time.'

'Shit.'

'Is that impossible?' asked Julia.

'Not impossible. But bloody tight. What's the big story in Israel?'

'You know the new Foreign Minister?'

'David Bermant? Do you mean do I know him professionally? Of course. Anyone who's ever made a film in Israel knows David Bermant, he's in the Berlitz Guide to Interviewees. He's been the resident liberal rentaquote for twenty years. Everything the outside world wants to hear about Israel. Wildly unrealistic, but terribly impressive on camera – all those wise wrinkles and compassionate eyebrows. Nice man. At least he used to be. I don't know what's happened since he got into office.'

'He's due to address the UN on Tuesday week. It's going to be a major speech. We transmit the night before.'

'Live?'

'Live.'

'Dinner-time in Israel is lunch-time in New York. Hardly prime-time.'

'It goes out live to European satellite and cable stations. The Americans tape it and run it eight hours later.'

'And he doesn't mind us making a film about him now he's a World Statesman?'

'He's agreed, and we've fixed to do it on the Monday.'

'We have?' Charlie drummed his fingers on the edge of the table. 'You ever made a TV programme before?'

'No.' She gave him a broad smile and ran the tip of her tongue

4

along her teeth. 'But I've read a book about it. And I'm a quick learner.'

'OK. First question. How come Harry thingummy got this series sold without so much as a producer or director on his books?'

'He knows people. And he's got a business reputation for delivering. If he hasn't got what he wants, he hires it in.'

Also, Global Village and the satellite boys aren't the fussiest of clients, Charlie refrained from saying.

'And of all the producers in all the joints in all the world he hired ...'

'That's another story.'

'I'd like to hear it.'

'You will. Not yet.'

'Second question. Are you Jewish?'

'-ish.'

'Third question. How do you know it's going to be a major speech?'

'I know. He's told us.'

'Ever meet a politician who told you he was about to make an unimportant speech?'

'This one's important. A new initiative.'

'Says who?'

'Reliable sources. That's the phrase, isn't it?' She bared her teeth again. Charlie needed dark glasses to handle this sort of stuff.

'OK. Last question. Why me?'

'Because I like your work.'

Charlie choked on his aperitif. Nobody liked his work. Nobody disliked it much either, but certainly no one got excited about it. He was, he hoped, a tolerable human being. People liked him, they wanted to like his films. But it was a struggle to find anything positive to say about them, except that they weren't bad. And that about summed it up: they were never bad, just as they were never really good. Ten years at the BBC making unexceptionable films for a succession of unexceptionable late-night current affairs programmes, and then came the cutbacks. In the six years since he'd been making anything that was offered him on the free-lance market. The anything was mostly corporate videos, parochial documentaries for the ITV regional opt-outs, very occasionally a low-budget commercial. Charlie must have been responsible for hundreds of hours of television – there couldn't be more than a handful of people in the country who hadn't seen one of his films at some stage or other. But they didn't remember them – why should they? Any more than they remembered the music they heard in lifts, or old weather forecasts. And yet the beautiful, intelligent, smart-arsed Julia not only remembered them, she liked them.

'Did I say something wrong?' she asked, biting the tip of her little finger.

Charlie liked the look of her fingers, long and thin and restless, nails painted blood-red. Aesthetically he didn't give a damn about red fingernails, but he liked the intention. You don't paint your nails that colour if you mind going to bed with people. Not unless you're Nancy Reagan.

'No, no, not at all.' He wiped his mouth on his napkin. 'What have you seen?'

'A lot of the old *Midweek* stuff, the film you made for Thames in Berlin . . .'

'The history of the catering corps?'

'No, the one about Hess.'

Just checking. His film on army cooking had been shot in Catterick.

'And I've seen most of the things you did in Israel – the Black Hebrews, the Red Mayor of Nazareth, the Topol profile . . .'

And on she went. The food came; she reminded him of forgotten triumphs on the West Bank and in southern Lebanon. Charlie was amazed.

'You're good, Charlie Kavanagh.'

'No I'm not. I'm competent.'

'That too. And you've worked in Israel before.'

'Not for years.'

'Doesn't matter. Do you want the job?'

'Can we talk about it over dinner?'

'Sure. But you have to say yes first.'

'Yes.'

'Tomorrow?'

'Why not. I'll pick you up.'

'Where?'

'Your flat.'

'You know the address?'

Stupid question. Of course she knew his address. Julia seemed to know an awful lot about Charlie.

He found the contract waiting for him on the mat when he got home. Twenty pages of legal gobbledegook in six languages, including Hebrew and Arabic. He skimmed through the English: two and a half weeks' work; five thousand pounds, half in advance, half on completion; standard residuals on overseas sales. He went upstairs to the flat and rang the number on the Cornwall Associates compliments slip.

'Seven. Plus expenses.'

'You're kidding,' said Julia.

'One of us is. I'm not sure which.'

'How about six and a half grand.'

'Done.'

'Who's paying for dinner?'

'Harry Greenbaum, of course.'

Six and a half grand. Near enough three grand a week. Six hundred quid a day for a five-day week. Seventy-five quid an hour for an eight-hour day. Not that there were likely to be any five-day weeks or eight-hour days. With luck there'd be a lot of night work on a job like this.

Julia put down the phone, checked her address book, and dialled New York.

'He'll do it.'

'What's he like?'

'Much as I expected. Pleasantly undistinguished.'

'Keep him happy. But not too happy. I'm flying over tomorrow night. I'll call when I get to town.'

Charlie went out to celebrate. Never could resist spreading good news, could Charlie. He phoned his old mate Dougie Thomas at London Weekend Television and fixed to meet him in the Duke of York in Notting Hill Gate. Dougie brought Simon

Macari and a pretty PA called Sally and two friends from a German TV station. They drank pints until the noise from the jukebox got on their nerves, then adjourned to the Redan in Westbourne Grove, where Charlie bought champagne.

'What's her name?' asked Simon.

'Julia.' He kissed the tips of his fingers. 'Julia Cornwall.'

'Never heard of her. What's she paying you?'

'Three grand,' Charlie lied. 'For two weeks' work.'

'Shit,' said Dougie, 'why?'

'It's the only way she could figure to get to meet me.'

Sally and the Germans left at eight. The others stayed drinking for another hour, then moved across the street to the Khyber and ordered more lagers and a curry.

'How's the divorce?' asked Dougie while they waited for the food.

'It'd be easier if we had kids,' said Charlie, removing a white carnation from the table decoration and sticking it behind his ear. 'There'd be some dignity if we had kids to argue over. Maybe we should adopt some while there's still time.'

Later they bought a bottle of Bushmills at Oddbins and walked the half-mile back to Charlie's flat. Simon rolled a joint while Charlie doodled his usual four chords on the guitar. The flat was home but no home, borrowed from a friend now debunked to America, under-furnished, draughty and grey with dust. No matter how hard you cleaned and hoovered, it was always dirty, and Charlie never tried that hard. Its grimy south windows looked down on the nervous clatter of Westbourne Grove, but the entrance was round the corner in Monmouth Place, a narrow verminous alley littered with refuse sacks and empty cartons from the Lebanese all-night supermarket.

'Someone up there loves me, you know, Dougie.' Charlie put down the guitar and sucked on Simon's joint. 'Israel's a doddle as long as you do what they want. God's own photo-opportunity. Pick up the press pass, tell them what you have in mind, sit back by the pool while they fix it up, then off you go on the guided tour. "Welcome to our industrious kibbutz, let me introduce Yitzak, the war hero who runs homes for the handicapped. Be sure to film our happy infant school and the Russian emigrants' Ukrainian folk choir. Tomorrow a bus trip to the war, bring your bathers." '

Dougie laughed and helped himself to more whiskey.

'Last time I was there,' he told them, 'was the first time the Israelis invaded Lebanon in 1978. The place was crawling with American TV crews, you never saw anything like it. There weren't enough editing machines, so the guy who runs the film studios in Petah Tiqwa flew in his own, but he didn't have anywhere to put them. He'd just finished shooting a Kosher Western on the lot, he had this Arizona main-street built in the car park, and he moved us all on to the set – NBC had the saloon, CBS were in the jail, the Japanese shared the barber's shop with a bunch of Canadians. He had his own satellite dish, and when the deadline for the US news shows was coming up he auctioned off his satellite time to the highest bidder. Cash on the spot – it was like Black Monday on Wall Street, all these senior network execs shouting and screaming and waving wads of dollars. Then they'd all drive back into Tel Aviv and sit around in the Hilton bar waiting for the calls from New York to find out how much they'd got on the bulletin. Thirty seconds was champagne time, a minute and they passed out on the spot. We were on much later, so we never had any trouble getting on the bird. I was producing quiet little nightly studio discussions for *Newsnight*, three politicians round a table nattering about this or that for fifteen or twenty minutes. The Yanks couldn't believe it. "Get much on tonight?" ABC would ask you. "Oh, about half an hour. How about you?" Wonderful.'

Outside in Westbourne Grove two Arabs were arguing with a mini-cab driver, cheered on by the waiters from the Lotus Flower. A police car hurried towards Ladbroke Grove, siren wailing, off to search some poor Rasta's window box. Charlie was thinking about Julia Cornwall.

'You serious about the three grand?' asked Simon.

'Absolutely.'

'For what?'

'Haven't a clue. Producing, I suppose. Carrying the can if it goes wrong.'

He realized he had no idea who was going to do the research, fix the interviews, look after the logistics. But he hoped it wasn't him. Producing was easy: you just told people what to do and sat back and waited while they did it. Research bordered on real work.

'I've hired a kid called Walter Azeff in Tel Aviv,' Julia told him when he called her the next morning. 'I'll send you round what we've done so far.'

Her research arrived by taxi, in three boxes. Cuttings on Bermant, books on Israel, maps, research notes – and a programme treatment. She'd done it all, chosen the contributors, roughed out a structure, suggested what they should talk about, even checked out the facilities. He glanced through it quickly, and picked up the phone again.

'You did this yourself?'

'Nothing's immovable,' Julia explained. 'It's just a skeleton waiting for the flesh.'

'You make me sound like Frankenstein. Where'd you learn all this stuff?'

'I told you, I read a book. You like it?'

'I like it.'

'What are you doing on Monday?'

'As in tomorrow?'

'As in tomorrow.'

What Charlie was doing on Monday was visiting the laundromat, drinking coffee, maybe taking the bus down to Twickenham in the evening to argue with his estranged wife about who got custody of the chaise-longue and the Bokhara rug her father had given him for Christmas two years before.

'Invading Poland.'

'Harry Greenbaum's over from the States, he wants to buy you lunch.'

'Does that preclude dinner tonight?'

'Not at all.'

He'd hoped for a Porsche, and was frankly disappointed when she arrived to collect him in a humble Ford Sierra, which she parked, hazard lights needlessly flashing and two wheels on the pavement, among the Monmouth Place garbage.

'Do you want to come up?' he asked her, hoping she'd say no

in case the squalor above changed her mind about the class of director she was hiring.

'Not yet,' she promised, 'I'm hungry.'

She lifted her clutchbag off the passenger seat to let him get in.

The car smelled new, salesman-fresh, polythene valet-sheets still on the seats. But there was another smell, Nina Ricci, the cologne he used to buy the other Julia in duty-free shops on his way back from overseas trips. He resisted the reflex to lean across and lick her nape.

'Where are we going?' he asked.

'Italian, if that's OK with you.'

She had her hair up, showing off her long swan's neck and the swinging silver pendants in her ears; she wore a black silk blouse that followed the shape of her unsupported breasts, then a cream linen skirt that ended just above her knees. After that it was all black-stockinged leg down to the dangerously high heels. I bet she plays tennis, thought Charlie, I bet she likes to wrestle. His own choice of evening wear was restricted these days to the grey double-breasted office suit or the Donegal tweed jacket with the shaggy smoke-blue corduroy trousers and the loose Italian shirt, rakishly rounded off with a snake-buckle belt and a new pair of plimsolls. No choice at all, since the suit was at the cleaners for its annual service. He still didn't know if this was a date or a script conference. Maybe she didn't either. He couldn't believe how much he wanted to touch her.

The Italian was in Waterloo, round the corner from the Festival Hall and the National Theatre. Tuscan tiles on the floor, smilingly insubordinate waiters, a sideboard groaning with fresh fruit and soft cheese, white walls lined with framed and signed photographs of actors, not all of them famous.

'He has crates of them,' Julia explained, nodding towards the pictures. 'Someone rings up and books a table, he gets their portrait out of the box, makes sure it's up on the wall to impress their friends. Costs him nothing, earns him plenty.'

Charlie laughed, and twirled the stem of his wine-glass, wondering who she'd like him to be – dry and cynical, cheerful and extrovert, well-travelled but moodily modest? Keep your options open, kid. As far as he was concerned she was fine as she was.

'Listen, I'm not really hungry,' he wanted to say. 'Why don't we just have a sandwich and go to bed?'

'Tell me about Harry,' he offered instead.

'Harry? He's sweet. Made a bomb out of pharmaceuticals, I think it was. Terribly generous and romantic, loves sentimental gestures. If there's anything you've always wanted let it drop and it'll be on the doorstep next morning with the milk.'

'Like a car?'

She snapped a Vienna roll between her fingers, took a bite, brushed the crumbs off her lips and then giggled.

'Like a car. Only I wanted a Scirocco and he thought I said Sierra. He'd be completely mortified if he knew. He doesn't drive himself.'

'I like your earrings.'

'Do you? Thanks. I paid for those myself.'

'I guessed. And how did you meet Harry?'

'By mistake – I rang him up. I was trying to contact a Professor of International Relations called Hilda Greenbaum for an article I was writing, and they're both listed in the New York phone book as H. Greenbaum. He asked me to tea – Harry, that is. And I went. I've no idea why, it's not my style at all.'

'And how was the breakfast?'

'Go to hell, Kavanagh.' And be careful. But she didn't seem offended. 'He'd be terribly entertained if people thought he was up to anything like that. There's a Mrs Greenbaum, by the way. She wouldn't be. Have you ever seen a turtle with its shell off?'

'In Bayswater we eat little else.'

'That's Sarah. Very determined lady. "Don't make trouble, Harry," ' she mimicked Sarah Greenbaum's Bronx, ' "That's my job." Mercifully between religion, hypochondria and improving Harry she hasn't much time left for the rest of us.'

'So back to afternoon tea. Over the cucumber sandwiches he confessed he was in desperate trouble, he was looking for someone to make a TV programme ...'

'More or less. I –' she flickered and blushed and reached for her wine-glass. 'You don't believe me, do you.'

'Journalists are bred not to believe in anything. Complicates the job. But I'd like to believe you.' Careful, Charlie, careful. 'Of course I believe you. At least I'm prepared to believe you rang him up and asked for a job. But I'm not entirely convinced by the business with the phone book.'

She smiled, and filled her mouth with wine.

'Nor am I, to be honest.'

'So what did you do for a living before Harry's tea-cakes?'

'I was an academic. Honestly, I've a thesis to prove it. Heard of Tomas Masaryk?'

She stretched across and filled her fork with salad from his plate. The Nina Ricci made his balls tingle.

'The celebrated defenestrator?'

'No, that was Jan. Tomas was his father. First president of Czechoslovakia. My father was Czech, it was an excuse to explore my roots.'

'And your mother?'

'Much less exotic. She was from Golders Green. She's dead now – they both are.'

'Brothers and sisters?'

'A sister in Australia, married to a town planner. Two cars and three children: one of each and a spare. Next question?'

'What was your most unforgettable moment?'

'You really want to know?'

'Yup.'

'Discovering television isn't as full of mystique as it thinks it is. At least I hope it's not. What did you think of the treatment?'

'Great.'

'Seriously.'

'I'm serious. I think you've done a very good job.'

He'd hardly glanced at it. He didn't need to: anyone could make a programme like that. Falling off a log. Charlie wasn't thinking about the programme: he was hopelessly in love. If she'd asked him to run away with her to Doncaster and live down a coal mine he'd have said yes and sold his soul to pay for the train fare.

She lived in a well-bred single-girl's garden flat in Maida Vale, very tasteful and self-contained, walls of books that looked as though they'd been read, Afghan rugs on the polished pine floor, a desk by the window, dried flowers in the fireplace, framed pictures of her family propped against the over-mantel mirror.

13

Charlie took off his jacket, stretched out on the sofa and studied the ceiling. It was half-past eleven.

'Sugar?' Julia called through the open door of the snow-white kitchenette.

She was making coffee. Through another door he could see her half-darkened bedroom, freshly ironed navy-blue cover on the undented duvet, moody lighting from the white glass lamp beside the daffodils on the low bedside table.

'No thanks. Write it down in case you ever need to know again.'

'Fuck off. Help yourself to music.'

Two questions. First, what does she like? Second, what does she hope I like? He seesawed to his feet, crossed the room and crouched down to inspect her albums. A lot of Mozart, always a safe fall-back. No one minds you liking Mozart. The Police, Blondie, Van The Man, Eric Clapton, The Clash, all somewhat battered, probably a time-capsule from student days, unplayed since. A mint copy of Cats, never opened, unwanted gift from an unwanted suitor. Bessie Smith – more hopeful. Lyle Lovett, Randy Newman. Or Tom Waits, better still.

'How about "Heart Attack and Vine"?' he called back, but she was already behind him, coffee mugs in one hand, wine bottle in the other.

'Thank God, for a moment I thought we were in for the bloody horn concertos.'

Her leg rested against his shoulder as she put the mugs down on the bookcase. He put his hand on her knee, resisting for the moment the temptation to move higher. This was a dream, things like this didn't happen to Charlie Kavanagh. Last knee he put his hand on belonged to an overweight vodka-sipping secretary with a serious skin disease, and he got slapped for his trouble.

'What's the catch, Julia?' he wondered out loud.

'There isn't one, Charlie.'

'Come on. There's no such thing as a free fuck.'

'Don't worry. I'm paying.'

2

THE HILTON LIFT HUMMED a melody that might once have been 'Trains and Boats and Planes' or possibly 'Lara's Theme'.

'What are you thinking about?' asked Julia.

It was noon, and they were on their way to meet Harry. Charlie had dropped in and picked up his suit from the cleaners on his way home from Julia's, and brushed his hair. He was all adrenalin.

'I'm wondering what to ask him for for my birthday.'

'Won't I do?'

'You don't count, you have to want me anyway. I was toying with His and Hers islands. Inishmore and Inishmaan, Coll and Tiree, Trinidad and Tobago . . .'

'Real estate's out. Harry never buys anything he can't move if he has to.'

'How about a statue?'

'Movable?'

'With difficulty, but I'm sure it could be done. It's in Sri Lanka. A hugely fat, benign, slumbering stone god who looks as though he's had a good lunch and then fallen fast asleep. I've never seen anything quite so well-fed and contented. Always been a role-model for me. Or perhaps it's vice versa.'

'And Man created God in his own image,' said Julia, lifting a hair off the shoulder of his jacket.

'Precisely. Has he seen your treatment yet?'

'Yes, except that I told him it was yours. He was quite excited.'

'Why?'

'Why what?'

'Why did you tell him it was mine?'

'Because I wanted you to do the job. I know what he wants, you don't.'

Harry's aide, Eric, met them outside the lift. Eric was small, maybe five foot four, Mormon crew cut, shining shoes, off-the-peg suit, buttoned-up waistcoat, button-down shirt: the sort of rig that Hertz would rent out if Hertz rented out clothing. Eighteen going on fifty, slim build, choir-boy good looks, eyes a startling, ice-cold blue, well-cleaned teeth. He spoke earnestly, like a man who'd learned his manners from a phrase-book.

'How was your journey?'

'Rough' said Charlie, 'but we broke it overnight at the third floor.'

Little Eric switched on the nervous smile civic dignitaries wear when introduced to the inmates of old people's homes.

This guy's going to be fun, Charlie decided.

'If you would follow me, please. Mr Greenbaum will be with us in a minute.'

It was a suite like any Hilton suite: hoovered to within an inch of its life, removables bolted to the walls, filtered air, filtered coffee on the table, cellophane wraps on the fresh fruit and flowers. Two chintz sofas faced each other across a glass-topped occasional table. On a point of principle Charlie pocketed a cigarette lighter. He had something of a collection at home – Rex Harrison's corkscrew, a toothbrush from George Bush's bathroom, the gold-plate scissors the Queen had used to cut the ribbon when she opened the Humber Bridge.

'Coffee?' offered Eric.

'Ice and no lemon,' Charlie suggested hopefully, then watched in wonder as Eric solemnly fetched cubes from the fridge and spooned them into his coffee cup. The aide tightened his civic smile from geriatric home to nut-house.

'Sugar, Mr Kavanagh?'

'No thanks, I'm driving.' He picked up the cup. 'Would you do something for me, Eric?'

A look of alarm came across Eric's face. He scratched nervously at the stubble on the crown of his head. Julia looked out of the window to hide her giggles.

'Of course, Mr Kavanagh?'

'Please, call me Charlie.'

'Of course. What is it you'd like me to do for you, Charlie?'

'That was it. Call me Charlie.'

'Oh. Right. Thank you, that's very kind of you. Charlie.'

At that moment the door from the bedroom opened, and in waddled Harry Greenbaum. Harry was an overfed duck, short and fat, his waist entirely circular, like one of those hoops clowns wear to hold up their trousers, except that Harry's bulk hung pregnantly forward from his frame, placing his centre of gravity some distance in front of his feet – a physique the Australians call 'a veranda over your toyshop'. He was in his mid-fifties, with a very obvious hairpiece and a dyed moustache. Compensatory thickets of greying black hair sprouting from the backs of his hands and the base of his neck. He wore an immense blue blazer and a wide tartan tie which ran out half-way down his shirt-front.

'Julia! And you must be the famous Charlie Kavanagh.'

His handshake hit Charlie like a well-timed forehand smash.

'Pleased to meet you, Charlie. Julia's told me such a lot about you. Too much, if you want my honest opinion. I'd begun to feel quite intimidated.' A chuckle rippled through his body. 'So here we all are. Sit down, make yourselves at home, have another drink.'

He poured generous whiskeys, handed them round and balanced himself on the edge of the sofa, knees wide open to make room for his collapsing stomach. Eric brought peanuts from the fridge.

'Cheers. Tell me, Charlie, do you like pictures?'

'Yes. Very much,' said Charlie enthusiastically, true to Kavanagh's Sixth Law of Journalism: *always pretend a lifelong interest in important people's hobbies*. He'd have said the same if he'd been asked about ferret breeding or beer-mats.

'You do? I'd value your opinion on something I bought this morning. Eric, could you . . .?'

The Mormon vanished into the bedroom, and returned with a large gilt-framed seascape of extraordinary ugliness, misshapen purple fishing boats against a marmalade orange sunset, painted in oils so thick they looked edible.

'Stunning,' said Charlie politely.

'I think so,' said Harry, putting on his spectacles to study the canvas more closely. 'It's a woman called Margaret Williams, lives in Corn Wall. One of the undiscovered geniuses of her generation. At least, I think so. You really like it?'

'Stunning,' Charlie repeated, fingers crossed behind his back. Harry took a handful of nuts, chewing them as he talked.

'Have it.'

'I'm sorry?'

'I'd like you to have it.'

'But I . . .'

'If you're being polite, Charlie, say so.'

'No, no, I think it's beautiful, it's just that I . . .'

'Just nothing. Take it. I can get another.'

Charlie swallowed a mouthful of Eric's cocktail to show the scale of his appreciation.

'Thank you very much,' he said at last. 'I'm very touched.'

'Don't be. Just enjoy it. Let's get us some lunch. The roof restaurant, I'm afraid – the only way to eat in this town is to be strictly functional about it. A place like this doesn't have the imagination to poison you.'

He finished his drink and ushered them out of the room and down the corridor towards the lift. Harry moved improbably fast for a man of his size, like a hound on a scent, talking as he went, poking the air in front of him to emphasise a point. Two steps behind him Julia let her hand brush lightly against Charlie's arse, and he tingled.

'See that woman?' Harry asked as a Filipino maid ducked out of their way into a vacant bedroom. 'What does she earn – fifty pounds a week? Whatever, a lot less than we're about to spend on lunch. That's how my grandmother lived when she came to America, Charlie. My grandmother was a Russian Yid, from the *stetl*. For a thousand years they'd lived off cabbage and religion, cowering in a corner waiting to get hit. They lived in the *stetl*, but really they lived nowhere, a world of their own. In Biblical times the Jews prayed for rain in summer – in Israel you needed it. They moved to London or Berlin, they still prayed for rain every summer. Why would anyone in London pray for rain? Because they weren't really in London at all, they were in the desert. Or their brains were. When she got to New York the only language she spoke was Yiddish; every time there was noise in the street she thought it was the *pogromshchiki* coming to get her again. She was eighty-nine when she died, she was living in a luxury home in Palm Springs, still living off cabbage and religion, still worried about the *pogromshchiki*. You have to remember these things, know what to change, know what not to change. I still study the Torah and I still eat cabbage every day. To remember.'

And he did: a modest side-order of coleslaw, which he left till last, after the quail terrine and toast and the eighteen-ounce steak, the corncob and zucchini, the onion rings and mushrooms and jacket potatoes. He swallowed the coleslaw like foul but necessary medicine, a fork-full at a time, winced at the taste, then washed it down with a full glass of Macon, and smeared his wet lips on his napkin.

Charlie asked him about his business.

'I'll tell you how I make my money: from other people's misfortune. That's what pharmaceuticals is about, Charlie – the price the sick will pay for the slenderest hope of better health. No one ever went broke underestimating the frailty of the human body. I don't feel guilty about it. I think our drugs work, if they didn't I wouldn't sell them. And most of the money goes back into research. The guys who should feel guilty are the ones who make money selling the things that make people ill in the first place.'

'Mmm,' said Charlie.

Harry reached across the table and filled up their glasses.

'I'm lying, of course. I do feel guilty. Guilty enough to feel guilty but not guilty enough to give it up. You may be as hard on me as you wish, it's not a thing I would hold against you. But at least I try to spend my money constructively.'

When the sweet trolley arrived Harry ordered profiteroles, his eyes following the waiter's spoon to and from the plate like a tennis fan watching a rally.

'That's a very interesting treatment you've done for us, Charlie. I appreciate how much work you must have put in.'

'Thanks,' said Charlie, trying not to catch Julia's maliciously smiling eyes. 'It was only meant as a discussion document.'

Harry stuck his finger in his ear.

'What do you think of it, Julia?'

'I think it's good. Provided he can deliver what he promises, of course. We haven't got a lot of time.'

Charlie bit his lower lip to abort a smile.

'Can you deliver?' asked Harry.

'More or less. These things always change a bit as you go along.'

'Sure.' His hand reached out and patted Charlie's knee. 'But make it good. This project means a lot to me.'

'We'll do our best.'

'I know you will. When are you off?'

Charlie looked at Julia.

'Tomorrow,' she announced.

'Of course I'm serious,' she told him in the car.

'Jesus.' He shook his head and pushed his fingers back over his scalp. 'I've been on this job exactly three days, Julia. I haven't even had time to worry about it properly. Why tomorrow? Aren't we meant to do some pre-production, dither over the programme title, print stationery, have a few unnecessary lunches – Christ, we haven't even had a decent argument yet.'

'We have seven days, Charlie. Seven days to get out there, set it up and shoot it. We can do the pre-production afterwards.'

'What happens if I have something else planned for tomorrow?'

'Like what?'

'I have to wash my hair.'

'Wash it in Tel Aviv.'

'I have a headache.'

'Bring it with you.'

Fair enough, he decided. This is a wonderful dream as dreams go, why spoil it now? It'll end itself in its own good time.

'Oh, and there's a seminar on in the morning,' Julia added, 'I thought you should go to. Yaakov Tyler's in town. He's holding court at the Royal Garden Hotel, round the corner from the Israeli Embassy. He's one of Walter Azeff's suggestions for the dinner.'

'Walter's our researcher, right?'

'Right. I thought it might be an idea to get a preview of what Tyler has to say. The flight's not till two, shouldn't be a problem.'

Yaakov Tyler, Charlie half-remembered. The Man In Black. Religious Fundamentalist, Businessman, Crown Prince of the Zionist Right. He's coming to the dinner? If she says so. It was probably in the treatment somewhere. The lion shall sit down with the lamb, live on TV.

'Sure. You coming too?'

'I'd love to, Charlie, but I can't. I have things to do. Get money, arrange tape stock, fix a crew.'

'Which crew?'

She hesitated.

'I'm not sure.'

'Do me a favour, will you Julia? See if Goliath's free?'

'This is a camera person?'

'This is Rafi Katz, if he's still alive.'

'Right,' said Julia, very cautiously. 'You have a number for him?'

'Sure.'

They'd reached the corner of Westbourne Grove and Monmouth Road. Julia had a mercy-mission appointment with a depressive girl-friend in the western suburbs. Charlie was due in Highgate at four for tea with his ancient mother.

'Will I see you tonight?' he asked.

Question expecting the answer yes, as his Latin master used to say.

'Of course. I'll be back around ten.' She took a spare key from her bag. 'Let yourself in if I'm late.'

He got out of the car, collected his painting from the boot, and stood on the pavement for a moment watching her drive off. He was in a trance: his flesh tingled to the slightest touch, his hand brushed against his face like the wing of a bird. He gathered up the picture and walked slowly round the corner into Monmouth Place, protecting himself from any intrusion that might destroy the delicate envelope of sensation. These waves of sudden pleasure broke over Charlie rarely, normally when pretty women spoke to him in a whisper, or when a hairdresser accidentally nudged him with her thigh. Julia didn't even need to whisper. He fumbled for his keys and let himself in.

Charlie hated coming home on his own, opening the door and finding everything just as he'd left it, only dustier. The solitary dirty dish in the sink, the bachelor's half-made bed, Friday's *Evening Standard* still open on the kitchen table by the half-drunk mug of cold coffee. If you could see me now, Harry ... what the hell, he reminded himself, next week in Jerusalem. And tonight in Maida Vale.

He propped the fishing boats against a wall, switched on the radio and tried to think of something to do in the meantime. Being alone in a house used to give him a secret pleasure that reminded him of childhood, sneaking downstairs after his parents had gone to bed and searching through drawers and cupboards for unmentionable adult secrets. And now too he wanted to misbehave, but couldn't think of anything to do, except perhaps masturbate. Pathetic, really. But there weren't any secrets any more. It was his flat, he knew what was in the cupboards. In the early months of his marriage, searching through the first Julia's private places had been a dangerous, exciting voyage into the mysteries of femininity – he'd never lived with a woman before, never known what they kept in the depths of their handbags or hidden among their crumpled tights and bras and knickers in their dressing-table drawers, drawers that smelled deliciously of perfumes and illicit sex. He didn't even know what he was looking for, except that it had to be something less mundane than hair-slides and old lipsticks and empty cosmetic jars. Whatever it was he never found it.

Being alone now unsettled him. He turned off the radio, left his coffee half-drunk on the table, and took the Tube to Covent Garden. For the first time in months he had real money to spend. And someone to spend it on.

Harry took off his hairpiece and poured himself a Scotch.

'How'd I do?'

Eric was in the bedroom, packing. He didn't answer.

Harry was sweating. Adrenalin made his right eyelid flicker like a car indicator. He rubbed his eye with the heel of his hand.

'Was I nervous? I thought maybe I was a bit nervous. I never rehearsed a part this way before.'

Eric appeared at the bedroom door. He carried the suitcases lightly, as though they contained almost nothing.

'Keep your hairpiece on,' he ordered. 'We're checking out.'

'Sure.' Harry put the wig back on and checked himself in the mirror. 'You know, it's great though, getting to do some improv acting again. We did a lot of it in college. Stretches you. I mean, I've done plenty of conventional theatre work, TV, commercials, movies . . .'

'What movies?' Eric had a cloth from the bathroom and was wiping the surface of the coffee table. His voice was flat and disbelieving.

'Uh,' Harry gave a nervous chuckle, 'You didn't read my, huh, curriculum vitae yet? No. Right. Well for starters, I went to the same college as Marty Scorcese.'

'What movies?' Eric repeated.

He rubbed over the doorknobs and window-sills.

'OK.' Harry sipped his whiskey and wiped his lips with his tongue. 'You ever see *Midnight Run*? Bobby De Niro? What a nice fella. Remember the scene outside the bondsman's office, when the clerk goes across the street to make a phone call? I drove the truck . . .'

Eric took his whiskey glass off him.

'And before that I was in *Beverly Hills Cop*, with Ed Murphy and Stevie Berkoff.'

'Let's go.'

'I was the police clerk.'

They were in the corridor now, Eric carrying the bags.

'Which police clerk?'

'Three desks back, next to the rubber plant. Where we going now?'

'Heathrow. Curtain call.'

They took the lift to reception. Eric paid the bill in cash, and they walked across Park Lane to the underground car park.

'Did you ever see a TV Movie called *Icicle Blues* with Sophia Loren's niece in it?' Harry loaded the cases into the boot of the rented BMW. 'I played a male nurse . . .'

He heard the click as Eric released the safety catch behind

23

him, and half-turned, so that the bullet entered his face from the side instead of the back. He fell forwards into the boot. Eric lifted his legs in after him, closed the boot and walked back upstairs into Hyde Park.

It was January, the sky clear, the air cold. A bunch of American students were playing football, noisy and healthy, full of harmless, cheerful aggression. Beyond them well-groomed *au pairs* in navy cashmere frog-marched their charges round the Serpentine.

Julia was waiting for him on a park bench, ducks at her feet.

'The painting was cruel,' she said as he sat down beside her.

Eric smiled a thin Mormon smile, and opened his briefcase and took out a banker's draft.

'There's two and half grand there to be going on with,' he explained. 'Make sure it's in his account before you leave.'

She slipped the draft into her bag.

'Is that all?'

'For now.'

'Thank Harry for the lunch.'

'I will.'

'You off tomorrow?'

Julia got up.

'Midday flight.'

'Don't I get a kiss?' asked Eric.

'Always a mistake to mix business and pain,' said Julia. 'And anyway, I'm spoken for.'

Betty Kavanagh balanced on the edge of the chaise-longue, cutting a supermarket money-off voucher out of the local paper. Hanging plants and lace curtains the colour of skimmed milk obscured what should have been a view over Highgate Hill. The air was hot and heavy with the smell of proprietary cleansers. She sipped her tonic wine, leaving a vivid purple lip-print on the crystal. She was an incompetently vain old trout, the folds of her face caked in cosmetics, her steel-rinsed hair spun upwards like candyfloss. Not for the first time Charlie tried to imagine this painted cod of a woman as a girl, when she'd been famous for her beauty. Or so she claimed.

'Israel?' She folded the paper and put it on the marble coffee table beside a vase of bloodless hydrangeas. 'What an extra-ordinary place to want to go on holiday.'

'It's not holiday, mother, it's work.'

'Still, you need a holiday, you don't look right. I wish you had my health.'

'Mother, your health is bad, you're always telling me how bad your health is.'

'It's better than it might be. So who's the woman?'

'What woman?'

'Didn't you say you were going with a woman?'

'No.' He hadn't, either.

'Don't tell me, that secretary of yours at the BBC. Miranda something. The one with the painted nails.'

'Barbara? That was years ago. She's married, with twins. Anyway, we never went out together, she was just my secretary.'

'She's after your money, Charles. You're the only one who can't see it.'

They moved through to the dining-room. The prow of Betty's cantilevered bosom rested on the glass table-top as she poured tea.

'I made beetroot sandwiches for you, you look tired.' She paused and wiped her wet prune lips on a damask napkin. 'The *Reader's Digest* says we're all meant to be eating beetroot now, but of course it's in the Bible, you don't need doctors to tell you that. No Charles, you go off to Egypt or Abyssinia or wherever it is, don't worry about me, I'm sure I'll be all right. Things are different these days, you have your own life to live.' She lifted a sandwich off the plate with a silver shovel. 'I'm sure Doctor McLennan will look after me. He's not able to get out as much as he used to, but I know he's looking for a student to help him out. It's just that I'd like to see your children before I die. Did Julia phone Mrs Stirling's friend at the clinic?'

'Mother, Julia and I are getting divorced, you know that. And I'm only going away for a couple of weeks. You have the alarm if anything goes wrong.' Charlie had seen it in the cloakroom when he arrived, still in its box. Six months ago he'd given it to her. 'Wear it round your neck. If anything happens all you do is press the button and it phones for help.'

'What happens if I'm in the bathroom?'

25

'It works in the bathroom.'

'It doesn't seem decent, taking it to the bathroom.' She was having trouble with her dentures. 'Have some junket, it's your favourite.'

Junket. Charlie had always hated junket, he didn't know where this misunderstanding about him and junket came from. Maybe she did it on purpose.

He left at six and went home and packed, and then took a taxi to Maida Vale. He toyed with the idea of doing some work on the treatment, but instead spent the evening watching Julia's television and reading the Sunday papers. By the time she got back at midnight he was lying naked on the bed in the darkness blowing smoke rings at the ceiling. He heard the car door close, a rattle of keys, soft footsteps in the hall, a shower running in the bathroom. Then a cistern flushing, the brushing of teeth, more footsteps, and the bedroom door opened.

'How was your mercy mission?' he asked.

Julia turned on the light. He looked up: she was naked too.

'Take your socks off, Charlie,' she giggled. 'You look ridiculous.'

'Not till you close your eyes. I'm shy about my feet. Incidentally you have the least interesting desk drawers I've ever ransacked.'

'You read my diary?'

'All of them. That's what I was meant to do, wasn't it? What kept you?'

'The time it takes to remind yourself why you haven't seen someone in five years.'

She took the cigarette out of his mouth and stubbed it in the ashtray. Her body smelled soft and fresh from the shower.

'What's wrong with your feet, anyway?'

'They're ugly.'

'Of course they're ugly. All men have ugly feet. Move over.'

And then she saw the parcel on her pillow.

'What's that?'

Charlie bent down and took off his socks.

'I couldn't manage a Scirocco at this notice.'

She undid the gold foil. Inside was a pair of earrings, two

26

hanging fuchsia blossoms worked in delicate silver, and a book. She took one of the earrings and dangled it in her fingers.

'Oh, Charlie!'

And then she looked at the book, Martin Gilbert's history of the Holocaust. She froze, mouth open. Her hands were suddenly shaking. She stared at the cover.

'Is this a joke, Charlie?'

It wasn't a joke, it was a present.

'I'll change it if you don't want it.'

'Why? Why the Holocaust?'

'I'm sorry, I thought it might be useful. Every time something in Israel gets to you you open a page and read it. Helps you understand.'

'That's all?'

'That's all.' Charlie pulled himself up on his elbow. 'What's the matter? Don't you like surprises?'

Suddenly she melted into his arms. 'I'm sorry, Charlie, I ... I thought ...'

'Yes?'

'It's a lovely present. I'm sorry. I find all that holocaust stuff hard to cope with.'

She was beside him now, her long lean body curling itself around him, her mouth at his ear.

'I love you,' she whispered.

'Moi non plus,' Charlie whispered back.

3

DAVID BERMANT HAD NEVER wanted to be Foreign Minister: he
felt too old, too tired, too pessimistic. The man who had persuaded him to take the job was his old friend and Labour
Party rival Chaim Ezra, Minister of Finance and Deputy Prime
Minister in the coalition government.

Chaim had driven up from Jerusalem to see him on a dry hot
December day, a little over three weeks before. It was the
Sabbath. David was not a religious man, but he enjoyed the day
of rest, communing with his vegetable garden, talking to old
friends and constituents, clearing the angry bedlam of Jerusalem
out of his head. In Jerusalem the talk was always of wars and
rumours of wars, trouble on the West Bank, trouble in Gaza,
the collapsing shekel, the unbalanceable budget. That morning
the army had shot a three-year-old child near Jericho; in Gaza
the stone-throwers were beginning to retaliate with petrol
bombs; Beirut was in flames; the PLO's diplomatic siege of Israel
was tightening by the hour while the coalition government
watched like a hypnotised rabbit. Here on the kibbutz, although
the shadow of violence was never far away, the problems seemed
more direct, more human. David's house was modest and solitary, a flat-roofed concrete bungalow set aside from the main
kibbutz, perched on a bare rocky ridge like a shipwrecked ferry,
looking out across the patchwork of green fields and orchards
etched into the barren landscape, north to Lebanon and Mount
Hermon, east to the Golan Heights and Syria. Now green: once,
lives ago, when he and Ruth first hoed the soil together, a Lee
Enfield hanging awkwardly from his shoulder, the fields had

28

been a malarial swamp, the hills bare and rocky, full of danger-ous shadows at dusk among the olive trees. He could see it still, without closing his eyes, and people the landscape with long-dead faces and passionate conversations. He was an unsen-timental man, but he thought a lot about the past. Somehow these things seemed to draw nearer just when they should be receding entirely from what was left of his memory.

Chaim had arrived late in the afternoon. The favour-seekers had been and gone, and the two men sat on hard wooden chairs, sleeves rolled back to the elbow, sharing their beers with the flies in the shade of the vine-encrusted bamboo awning. They were both in their seventies, had known and argued with each other for half a century or more, from the time they fought side by side in the Haganah before Independence.

David looked ill, but he always had, since childhood; skull-faced and so thin that the mechanics of his bones and joints were quite visible when he moved: you felt you could snap him over your knee. His skin was the colour of cigar ash, and his cotton suit hung from his shoulders like a sheet on a hook. But his face was still full of life and humour, the famous eyebrows lengthening with the years.

He'd come to politics late in life, after an army career that spanned the battles of '56 and '67; a popular, self-effacing war hero. Finally, in '73, after the fiasco of the Yom Kippur war, he'd been persuaded to stand for election – quite why he no longer remembered. He won a seat easily, but he'd always refused to join the government, preferring his role as philosopher in the wings.

That December afternoon Chaim – not for the first time – had pressed him to change his mind. The Deputy Prime Minister was a professional politician, brown and wizened as a walnut, but a varnished, well-cared-for walnut in expensive tailor-cut clothes and good Italian shoes. He'd entered the Knesset in the fifties, rising slowly and carefully first to the leadership of the Labour Party, and ultimately the job of Deputy Prime Minister in the present coalition. Now he wanted David to join him in the government.

'Na!' David dismissed the idea. 'Coalitions are like bad mar-riages. It's a way of keeping up appearances when you've got

29

nothing in common. Less than nothing. Parties in coalition don't share objectives, they don't share common means or common ends, just common enemies. You lot sit there like a basket of hang-dog basset-hounds, pretending you're doing your reluctant duty, hanging on in to stop the others doing something really unspeakable. That's your only motive, the desire to frustrate each other. You're none of you for anything, you're just against the other lot. So no one does anything. You're handcuffed to each other.'

David waved his boney, age-freckled hand loosely in front of his face to disperse the flies. Chaim sat in silence, drinking his beer, picking specks of dust off his sleeve.

'On second thoughts, that's not true,' Bermant continued. 'There's something else you've got in common: you'd rather be in office than out of office. What does it take to make someone resign these days – scandal? Incompetence? Moral bankruptcy? A better-paid job, that's all people resign for now. Listen, Chaim. You and I have our disagreements, but we share ideals. At least we used to. We wanted a state, a secure state, that's all. It didn't have to be Eretz Israel, the whole enchilada, every stone a prophet ever stubbed his toe on. Originally it was Galilee and the coastal plain, now it's Judea and Samaria – why stop there? Why not Lebanon? Syria? Jordan? Why not? Call it a pre-emptive strike, call it Secure Borders. The Nile would make a Secure Border. Or the Euphrates, for that matter. We're in the Lebensraum business, Chaim. 'Lebanon is historically a part of Israel.' Don't laugh, it's happening. Look at the army maps now, they mark Beirut as Be-erot. On the orders of your friend General Gad Navon. He's right, it used to be called Be-erot. A mere three thousand years ago, when it belonged briefly to the tribe of Asher. A great game, trying to turn the map of the world back three millennia. What's happening to us, Chaim? We set out to build Hampstead Garden Suburb and we've ended up with Sparta. You want me to go and explain all this to the Americans?'

'You finished yet?' asked Chaim. 'You want to hear what I have to say?'

'No.' David took a sip of beer and wiped his mouth on the back of his hand. 'I know what you have to say. I'm more interested in the things you won't say. For example: it's a fall-guy you're after, isn't it? Things are going badly, about to go worse, you want a sacrificial lamb.'

'Libschitz is the fall-guy, David. You're the new broom.'

Simon Libschitz was at that time the incumbent Foreign Minister.

'What's wrong with the old broom?' David objected. 'And does Libschitz know he's taking the fall?'

'Yes. He's resigning. Health grounds.'

'His health's a lot better than mine. Political resignations are like those signs on the buses, "Please vacate your seat for someone less able to stand than yourself." '

Below them in the valley an overloaded truck climbed out of the fields on to the main road and accelerated painfully up the hill, throwing clouds of dust and diesel fumes into the hot heavy air. Even in winter this was a hard, harsh landscape, a place of sharp rocks and thorn scrub, lizards and snakes. The kids with the uzi sub-machine-guns at the end of the unpaved track to the house stood back to let it pass.

'Tell me something, Chaim. You ever see a movie called *Easy Rider*?'

'Last film I saw,' Chaim admitted, 'was *The Sound of Music*. *The Sound of Music* is a film about a Nazi with a heart of gold. Once I seen that I decided I'd seen it all. Unless perhaps one day they make a film about a whore with the heart of a Nazi, which come to think about it they probably did.'

David tapped a cigarette from a carton of Marlboro and put the pack back in his shirt pocket.

'Ruth took me to the movies. Every week, didn't matter what was on: cowboys, cartoons, war films, English comedies, any kind of rubbish. She watched, I slept; she'd wake me up when she got scared or when something upset her. She didn't scare easily, and mostly what upset her was sex: she always woke me tut-tutting when anyone was getting undressed. All I remember about most films is the lingerie. *Easy Rider* didn't have a lot of lingerie, but I woke up anyway because there were insects on the sound track. I dreamed I was being eaten by insects. And when I opened my eyes there was a drunk lawyer sitting by a camp-fire, talking about old times, trying to make himself heard above the cicadas. "This used to be a hell of a country," he says. And so on. A dream that turned into nightmares. Powerful stuff.'

He lit his cigarette, took it out of his mouth and studied the smoking tip.

'This was going to be a hell of a country too. And what was going to make it a hell of a country was that we all believed in it, we knew what the problems were and we knew how we wanted to solve them. Not any more. None of us can remember what the dream was any more. I don't want power, Chaim, because if I had it I wouldn't know what to do with it. I've forgotten the dream. I've done too much, seen too much; nothing's simple any more. I've stopped believing. Candide was right: all is for the worst in this worst of all possible worlds. *Il faut cultiver votre jardin.*'

'*Cardin*,' Chaim corrected him. 'Or that's what the wags say nowadays. *Il faut cultiver votre cardin.* It's a kind of French shirt, I think. Whatever, you just want to cultivate something, keep out of people's way, is that right? General Bermant had a farm, ey-ay-ey-ay-o. Why? *Pour décourager les autres?*'

'Not at all. To let them do it their way. They could hardly make a worse job of it than we did. Anyway, old men are a nuisance.'

'It's too easy, David. What's worse, you know it's too easy. Sitting here like a village elder, messing with tomato plants, petitioning for road repairs and playing fields, avoiding the outside world.'

David shifted in his seat to ease the arthritis in his hip.

'I'm not avoiding the world. I just don't have anything very interesting to say to anyone. You think about things too much, it paralyses you. I'm not being modest – I mean it. I know too much. Not a lot, but too much. You need to be ignorant to be a good politician, you need to believe things are possible. And you need convictions. I haven't got any anymore. Luckily there are other people around who have – we have a national surfeit of convictions, the place is crawling with people who know what should be done. I'm not one of them.'

He paused to dig a fig-seed out of his back teeth with his little finger, then nodded down the hill towards the sentries.

'And I'm sick of all this security, it's bad enough as it is. Already you guard me like a virgin daughter, Chaim. I have security barriers at my gate, spies on the hillside, floodlights outside my windows, soldiers patrolling the garden. What am I, some zoological treasure? A genuine *maskil*. Maybe you should breed from me, we're an endangered species.'

Chaim hit the side of his hand against the table in a karate chop for emphasis.

'We guard you because you're a symbol of something the world admires about this country. We need that kind of symbol, not just for the outside world, but for ourselves.'

'We? Who's this we?'

'Israel.'

'My country needs me. You sound like that fat fool Kitchener. Which bit of my country? Our Labour Party friends? Likud? The NRP? Gush Emunim? Peace Now? Organised Crime? The Brooklyn Blue Rinse Legion of Zion?'

'All of us. You should be flattered.'

'I should? I should be flattered that I'm so much a nothing that I'm acceptable to everyone?'

Chaim gave him a weary smile.

'Another thing, before I forget. They're planning a ceremony in your honour at the University, I was asked to sound you out. A doctorate, a gala concert, something of that sort.'

David laughed.

'God forbid. You know they named a street after me once? Not just a street, a dual carriageway. In one of those terrible high-rise settlements on the hill outside Nazareth, full of miserable homesick Russians. They took an olive grove and covered it in concrete, and called it after General Bermant. With honours like that who needs insults. No more, please, I beg you.' He finished his beer and put down his glass. 'Anyway, back to the main business. Why me?'

'Because there's nothing you want any more, no personal ambitions, you have nothing to lose. You do things because you think they're right, not because you want to out-manoeuvre your rivals. And most of all because you believe peace is possible.'

'No I don't. But I think we have to try, because otherwise it's all been for nothing. I'd go mad if I thought it was all for nothing. So when do I have to decide?'

'Soon.'

David sat very still, scratching his neck with the back of his hand, saying nothing. The Deputy Prime Minister got up to leave.

'Think about it.'

'If I think about it I'll say no.'

'Then don't think. You're right, it's like the other business, makes you blind.'

'I'll ring you tonight.'

And later that evening, after drinking two glasses of brandy and smoking half a pack of untipped cigarettes, he'd picked up the old black Bakelite phone in the hall and rung Chaim and said yes, but give me a little time. He wanted three or four days to collect his thoughts, and say private goodbyes to his life on the hillside, because he knew that from now on there would be no coming back. It was like a death, trying to hold as much as he could of the sounds and smells and the solitude before it left him for ever.

He wished Ruth was there with him. His wife had been dead for fifteen years now, but he still missed her every day, the way a prisoner misses freedom, or a blind man his sight. He missed her angry indignation, the urgent way she sucked her soup at table, the constant noise of her routines around the house, her suddenly defenceless, vulnerable presence beside him in sleep. Most of all he missed their arguments, the constant scheming and wrestling of wills, their elaborate attempts to bully or seduce each other into accepting the other's plans and arrangements. While she was still alive he'd often longed to be single again, craved the private intimacy of his own unaccountable company; but now she was gone he felt redundant, a soldier in peacetime. He'd learned to put so much of his time and emotional energy into battling with her that without her he was lost, could find no outlet for the devious skills and cunning anger that forty years of marriage had bred in him. Ruth had defined his sense of who he was and what his life was about – he was too old now to invent a new self, choose a new wine for what was left

34

of his battered old leather-bottle of a body. Ruth in death seemed so much more alive to him than any of his fellow politicians, the squabbling, ambitious, self-righteous men and women with whom he spent his working days.

And such a death. Someone you love asks you to kill them, what do you do? And after it's done, who do you tell? Who can you talk to about a thing like that?

Chaim had been right: what happened to him now didn't matter, he had nothing to lose that he minded losing.

4

CHARLIE WALKED ACROSS THE lobby of the Royal Garden Hotel to the porter's desk, picked up his suitcase and ordered a taxi to Heathrow. Outside the hotel, Kensington High Street was busy with late-morning traffic. Forty minutes to the airport – he'd just about make the flight.

He felt ridiculously cheerful. This was like the old days, when plenty of weeks started with a taxi to the airport, a wallet of traveller's cheques and a round ticket to Miami or Jo'burg in your pocket, a folder of newspaper cuttings and a sheet of contact numbers in your briefcase. Only this was better than the old days: better paid, better company, and less worry. A rush job, but there was nothing like a bit of adrenalin to keep the mind focused. And a tight timetable meant you had no time to worry much, you just got on and did it. Any fool could do what he was about to do if he kept his nerve. Do it, and enjoy it: a week in Israel, lavish salary, lavish expenses, someone else to do the research. And Julia. The job would be over in a week, but not Julia. She must be mad, messing around with him when she could have anyone she wanted. Anyone. Wasn't it odd the way really beautiful women so often wound up with spectacularly dull men? And never the other way round. He wondered if the fact that he was with Julia made him dull too.

Press briefings would turn anyone into a dullard. Charlie had spent the previous two hours sitting on an upright chair in an overheated hotel conference room studying the chandelier and listening to Yaakov Tyler lecture twenty journalists and a handful of strategic-studies academics from the government-funded institutes on the inherent anti-Semitism of the British Foreign Office. Tyler was in his mid-fifties, a bull of a man, square across the shoulders, with a greying black beard and big hands. He wore a loose black three-piece suit and a white shirt open at the neck and size twelve sandals over plain grey socks. Sarcasm, wit and indignation were the hallmarks of his oratory, rising to towering crescendos of bile. Just as each rant reached its climax, he would fix his deep black eyes on individual members of his audience, drop his voice to a whisper and slide in his final stiletto. Yaakov Tyler was the sort of man who made the Orange Order look like a bunch of liberal-minded appeasers. There was no room for compromise or negotiation in his beliefs: the land of Israel belonged to the Jews by divine right, full stop. What the outside world thought didn't concern him: this was a matter between God and his chosen people. In front of a crowd his apocalyptic hyperbole could have a certain charisma; but in a warm, comfortable conference room the effect was merely soporific. Hence Charlie's new-found interest in chandeliers.

The briefing lasted two hours twelve minutes: Charlie timed it, and did the sums. Harry was paying him seventy-five quid an hour, one pound twenty five a minute, two point zero eight recurring p per second. Net profit one hundred and thirty-two pounds, plus three cups of coffee, two custard creams, and enough Zionist tracts to line a dozen cat-trays. He had a quick word with Tyler afterwards, rode down with him in the lift, shook hands, and wandered over to the porter's desk to order his taxi. Tyler put on his trench-coat, made for the doors, stepped outside, hesitated, remembered he'd forgotten his umbrella and walked back into the hotel.

The big Israeli was half-way back across the lobby when the bomb went off in the forecourt. The explosives had been set inside a concrete flowerpot ten feet beyond the hotel doors: if Tyler had kept going the blast would have killed him instantly. Glass from the windows flew across the lobby: there was a rush of wind, the air filled with dust and debris. And then came silence. The smoke hung in the air, hardly moving: everything seemed to be happening in slow motion. Charlie saw an American woman fall to the ground, her blouse soaked in blood. One of the porters lay on the carpet, curled in a foetal ball, rocking slowly to and fro. A display case of tourist brochures toppled to the ground, scattering theatre handbills like leaves in an autumn wind.

And then the mayhem started. People started screaming, alarms went off. The duty manager stood in the middle of the foyer, the sleeve of his jacket hanging loose at the shoulder, shouting orders. Police appeared in the forecourt – singly at first, then a dozen, Diplomatic Protection Squad officers on duty round the corner at the Israeli Embassy. Charlie was choking: he felt his chest, arms, legs, scalp, searching for damage, found none. A small splinter of concrete had ricocheted off the wall behind him and landed on his suitcase. He picked it up and dropped it in his pocket. Guests and staff were rushing past him towards the street.

Fuck me, he realised, I could have been killed.

The next thing he knew he was outside on the pavement, still holding his suitcase. Two fire engines were pulling out of the station behind what used to be York House Barracks, and more police were directing traffic and erecting cordons to keep the onlookers away. A crowd of survivors had gathered on the pavement across the street. Charlie scanned their faces. Dorothy Dale from Chatham House was there, and Bernard Wiggins from the *Sun*, and the *Guardian* diplomatic correspondent. But no Tyler.

He reached into his wallet for his out-of-date NUJ Press Card, put his thumb over the year, and waved it at a policeman on the barrier.

'Press,' he announced.

'Police,' said the constable coldly.

And then Charlie saw Tyler. The big trench-coated Israeli was standing by the foyer doors, stroking his beard with one hand, holding his trilby on with the other, and talking to a senior policeman. The image stuck in Charlie's mind like a photograph: Tyler talking to the policeman without looking at him. When the policeman talked back Tyler shifted his gaze, but not to the policeman.

'Anyone hurt?' Charlie asked his constable.

'Two dead, we think. A couple of tourists cut about a bit, a porter with a broken leg.'

Charlie did a quick time-sum in his head. He could forget the flight, stay where he was, offer himself as a witness. Or catch his plane. He fought his way through the crowds towards Barkers department store and waved down a taxi.

'Irish,' the driver announced, nodding back towards the hotel. 'Or Arabs.'

'Probably,' said Charlie.

'Animals.'

'We are, aren't we.'

He was sweating. If the bomb had gone off a minute later he'd have caught it. He thought of those people you meet at parties after an air crash who claim they were booked on the flight but changed their plans at the last minute, and how you never believed them.

They cut down Young Street to avoid the traffic. The cabbie leaned back closer to the partition to make sure he could be heard.

'Odd people, Arabs. You know what happened to me the other week?'

'Probably,' said Charlie, lighting a cigarette. His hands were shaking.

'Picked up this Persian bird in Chiswick,' the driver continued. 'Some kind of princess, all fur and gold, wants me to take her to Chelsea. When we get there she says she hasn't the money on her, will I come up to the flat to collect it. A fancy high-rise off the river, in behind Cheyne Walk. Up in the lift, down the corridor, opens the door and soon as we're inside she pops her tits out, kicks her shoes off, unzips her skirt. We're in the bedroom now. "Do me a favour," she says, "would you mind terribly tying me to my bed?" And she tosses me a length of rope. You think I'm having you on, don't you.'

'Yes,' said Charlie. They were past Earls Court now, heading for the Cromwell Road.

'But I'm not. I set to tying the old knots, all the while she's lying there helpless saying don't I find it terribly hot in all those clothes. Which as a matter of fact I do. So as soon as she's safely strapped down I start to undo my shirt, then I remember the motor's still running outside on the pavement. "Hold on a minute, darling," I says. "Back in a tick." "Quick as you can," she tells me. And I nip out the flat, down in the lift, fix the cab, and set off back to the lift. Then you know what happened?'

'You realized you couldn't remember which flat she lived in.'

'Not a clue. There's maybe two hundred flats in that block, all I know is that she's in one of . . . here, hold on, how did you know that?'

Charlie stubbed out his cigarette and immediately lit another.

'Same thing happened to a policeman I met in San Francisco.'

'Blimey. You serious?'

'And you hung around for a while trying to think what to do, but in the end you just drove home, leaving her tied to the bed.'

'That's right . . .'

'A couple of weeks later you met her again in the street, and you thought she was going to go for you, but instead she gave you a lecherous smile and told you she'd never been so turned on in her life.'

'More or less.'

'Small world.'

'I suppose it is.'

In the silence that followed Charlie settled back in his seat. His heart was still running fast. To distract himself he opened his briefcase, and started reading Julia's treatment.

'Going anywhere interesting then?' the cabbie tried again as they swung round Hogarth Corner.

'Alma Ata,' said Charlie.

Someone had told Julia the rules. The stationery was immaculate: top-of-the-range binder, well-spaced black type on heavyweight, watermarked vellum, a scattering of well-drawn charts and maps, enough but not too many. Ten out of ten for presentation. Which should have made him wary first time round. Kavanagh's Third Law of Television: *the quality of an idea is in inverse proportion to the cost of the paper it's written on.*

'Alma wotsit. That's in Spain, isn't it?'

'Not exactly.'

The cast-list was solid and intelligently chosen – two politicians, a soldier, a businessman, a diplomat, an academic, all distinguished in their own fields. What was less clear was which if any of these sages had agreed to take part. Anyone could write a list like that. Hyperbole by the pint, possibilities by the gallon. But nothing definite. And all this had to happen in less than a week.

He thumbed on until he reached what purported to be his CV.

'Charlie Kavanagh,' she'd written, 'is one of the outstanding documentary makers of his generation, sensitive but single-minded, with a strong visual imagination and a rare talent for observation . . .'

Spurious garbage, but at least it was only a subjective judgement. What followed, however, were straightforward lies. First there were the awards – BAFTA, The Royal Television Society, The Broadcasting Press Guild, even an American Emmy. Charlie had never won a pot in his life, unless you counted the third form spelling prize. Then came four pages of reviews, all entirely fictitious. His dismal little report on the Icelandic Cod War was allegedly described by *The Times* as 'Deeply moving, a film Grierson himself would have been proud of.' The shameful series of promotional plugs for the National Nursing Awards which he'd directed in a drunken stupor for BBC *Nationwide* struck *The Guardian*'s critic as 'A unique view of the Health Service, quite unlike anything television has attempted before.' And on and on. Why? Why the lies? Why the pretence? Why the hurry? And in particular, why me? Too much was happening too fast.

He was still shivering from the sound of the explosion as they passed Brentford and headed out on to the M4 towards the airport.

Julia was waiting for him in the coffee shop, looking wonderful, her only luggage a light canvas shoulder-bag from which he knew she'd somehow produce more changes of clothes than he could fit in a cabin trunk. She smiled when she saw him, put down her paper and offered him a kiss. Charlie declined. He pulled out a chair and sat down.

An unsmiling Pakistani cleaning lady hurried in and wiped the table between them.

'We've got to talk,' Charlie announced.

'Sure. Can I get you a coffee?'

He dropped the treatment in front of her.

'This is a heap of shit.'

'I know, Charlie.' She filled her cup from the stainless-steel jug, took a sip and wiped her lips on the back of her hand. 'I told you it was. You're the one who liked it.'

'It's full of lies.'

'Is it?'

'Lies and misleading information. How many of these people have you actually spoken to?'

'The dinner guests? All of them. At least, Walter has.'

Charlie hesitated. God but she was lovely. Long cotton skirt, bare ankles, espadrilles, white blouse open at the neck, navy jumper slung casually round her shoulders. This was a woman he'd kill for.

'*All* of them?'

'Of course.'

'And they've agreed?'

'With a few reservations. Liel wants to know the subject-matter in advance, Eli Kaufman won't talk about his family because he's recently changed wives, Kimche has to clear himself with the IDF. Otherwise they're all willing and able.'

'OK. My CV.'

'Creative writing.'

'I know it's creative writing. What I don't know is why.'

And then she laughed. She laughed so loudly that people at neighbouring tables looked up to see what the joke was. She laughed so hard she couldn't hold her coffee-cup steady. She was still laughing as she got a tissue out of her bag and mopped her skirt.

'Oh, Charlie,' she said at last, drying her eyes on her sleeve. 'Has no one ever fallen in love with you before?'

He scratched the back of his head.

'But you'd never met me.'

'You have a terrible memory.'

'Have I?'

'Remember Dick and Liz's wedding?'

He did remember: a famous wet weekend in Wales, three months before, when he and two hundred other guests had been bussed down from London, accommodated in slate-walled

42

farmhouses and half-timbered climbers' hotels, and the thin winter sun had shone and the tops of the peaks were powdered with snow like icing-sugar, and the little church in a field in the scree-walled valley near Llanberis had been decorated with branches of laurel and ropes of ivy, because it was November and there were no flowers. At least he remembered that much, and the start of the reception in an out-of-season Bangor hotel, where Liz Davies's teetotal Methodist relatives sat in rows round the edge of the ballroom like so many granite tombstones while the rest of them got drunk. After that his recollection was a little vague.

'You wore a bottle-green velvet suit,' she reminded him, 'going thin at the elbows, a cream shirt and silk tie with pale pink stripes on it.'

'And what did I do?' he asked cautiously.

She could well have been there, he could even have talked to her. It had been a long and eventful night.

'You talked – not to me, to everyone. I was just part of the audience. You were very funny.'

He looked at her, searching his memory drawer by drawer. The Pakistani was back, scrubbing the spotless table with her J-cloth.

'It's clean,' Charlie objected.

'Thank you,' she said, and kept polishing.

'You don't remember, do you,' Julia sighed. 'And I tried so hard.'

'Your hair,' he guessed. 'What colour was it?'

'No clues.'

And then, suddenly, he *did* remember – looking across the hotel bar and seeing a pretty woman and realising she was looking at him too, although it was obvious she was with someone else. And he was too drunk to do anything about it even if she wasn't.

'Red,' he announced. 'And a lot shorter than it is now. And you were with someone who looked as though he'd just come from an Arnold Schwarzenegger Look-Alike Convention.'

'That was Nick. Sad case. Steroids leave you limp for life, did you know that?'

'And what happened to him?'

43

'I moved out.' She took another sip of coffee. 'All this is quite out of character, by the way, not my style at all. But I didn't have much choice. I knew if I chased you you'd run away. At least, I would have if it had been the other way round. I had to find a project.'

'You're crazy.'

'No, just single-minded. And anyway, it's an interesting project. The programme, I mean.'

'Hold on, let me get this straight. You set up this whole circus just to . . .'

'Not entirely. I was working on it anyway. I do have to work, you know.' She looked at her watch, and put her hand on his shoulder. 'We should check in, Charlie. If you're coming.'

Above in the gallery, Eric watched them walk through International Departures and phoned Tel Aviv to confirm they were on their way.

'By the way,' said Charlie as they manoeuvred their way through the security checks, 'someone tried to blow up Yaakov Tyler.'

Julia stopped dead.

'*What?*'

'Someone tried to blow him up. At the hotel, just as I left.'

He told her what had happened. Her face went pale.

'You're joking.'

'No I'm not. At least two dead, maybe more, I didn't hang around to find out. Tyler's OK, I saw him afterwards.'

'Bloody hell, Charlie. Are you all right?'

'More or less. It's only just beginning to sink in.'

Getting through security to Gate 23 at Heathrow isn't that difficult: passport control, an X-ray for hold luggage, a hand-baggage and body search, and a long, long walk to the end of the terminal spur – the British Airports Authority likes El Al, in common with the South Africans, to park their aircraft as far as possible from the centre of things. Getting from Gate 23 on to the El Al aircraft is another matter altogether. Here British security ends and Israeli security begins. The searchers are young and intense. They only get to do the job for six months, at the end of which they're thought to be in danger of going stale, and a new batch is flown in. Getting past them and on to the plane

44

is a bit like applying for a job as the Queen's private detective. They ask you a lot of questions – where you come from, where you spent last night, who you know in Israel, whether you know any Arabs in London, who packed your suitcase, who paid for your ticket, where the receipt is, on and on. Then they go and check the information you've given them; and while they're gone someone else comes over and asks you all the same questions all over again, and they too go off and check your answers.

'You understand why we have to do all this,' said a polite ginger-haired youth with a clipboard. He wore jeans and trainers and a bomber jacket, not at all the standard Heathrow uniform. This wasn't Middlesex any more, this was Israel.

'Yes, of course,' said Charlie. I was at the Royal Garden this morning, he was about to add, but decided against it: they'd be there another hour at least. Even though the last thing anyone who'd just tried to blow up an Israeli would do would be to jump a plane to Tel Aviv.

Finally they boarded the 757. As they fastened their seat-belts a security man in a padded jacket came down the aisle with a video camera taping them all for the Mossad family album. Julia leaned across and kissed Charlie on the mouth as he passed.

The flight was crowded with rabbis and tourists and a party of Church of Ireland clergy on a pilgrimage.

'Tell me about my namesake,' Julia asked as the Hounslow reservoirs drifted away beneath them.

'Do I have to?' Charlie complained. 'I'd rather talk about what the steroids did to Schwarzenegger.'

'Later. What does she look like?'

'Thin. She's not actually all that thin, she just seems it. And brittle. Like those miniature animals they make out of glass – poodles and flamingos and giraffes and so on. The sort pre-pubescent girls line their bedroom shelves with. Takes life very seriously. Wishes her eyesight was worse so she could have the excuse to wear specs. Plays the oboe. She's very into thrift, steals plastic cutlery off aeroplanes and takes it home and uses it – we had a very nice twelve-place stainless cutlery set we got for a wedding present, but she'd rather use the plastic ones, because

45

they're free, something for nothing, never touched the good stuff in eight years. That enough?'

'More.'

'Finds me very immature.'

'Are you?'

'I don't know. Honestly, I don't. I worry about it.'

'Where did you meet?'

'University. I was a demo-organiser for the North Vietnam Support Group, she helped run a Catering Cadre for the Provisional Wing of the Harold-Wilson-Sold-Out-To-The-Establishment Brigade. We met throwing eggs at the Foreign Secretary outside Cambridge Town Hall.'

'You were a revolutionary?'

'Sure, who wasn't? Great gas, we knew the answers to everything. The weird thing was, people took us seriously. Grown men wrote Colour Supplement articles about students then as if we were important. You threw an egg at George Brown and instead of getting arrested you got interviewed by Anglia TV. You old enough to remember George Brown?'

'Just about.'

The hostess brought drinks. Charlie took a beer, Julia a Bloody Mary.

'Anyway, that was how we met. After that we became a Couple, you know the kind? Everyone else is worried sick because they're twenty-one and not living with anyone, we were worried sick because we were. His and Hers lecture notes, stilted hotel lunches to meet each other's parents, taking turns at the laundromat, all my friends watching enviously as I shoved her bra in with my Y-fronts – these things were extraordinary in those days. Other way round nowadays, I suspect. Or maybe not, maybe it's gone full circle again. You'd know more about that than I do.'

'Would I?'

'You're twenty-six, I'm forty-two. I'm old enough to have kids going to college. I'm at that awful stage where I've begun complaining about Youth and getting cautiously sentimental about Old Times. I went to a memorial service the other day, some old cameraman, and it was full of contemptuaries I hadn't seen for fifteen years. And they all looked so old, fat, balding,

46

grey, deflated, and I'd say "Heh! Mike – I didn't recognise you, you've got so . . ." and shut up because he was looking at me in just the same way. Twenty-six is the essence of Tir na n-Og, Julia. Stay twenty-six as long as you possibly can. I managed to stretch it out into my mid-thirties.'

'And you went straight into the BBC?'

'I was a graduate trainee. Very prestigious. They only took on half a dozen out of seven hundred applicants. I was lucky. This was 1968, the Beeb was under a lot of pressure to broaden its recruitment base and shake off its establishment image – the previous three years every single one of their trainees had come from Oxford. So they decided to make a gesture to democracy and take one from Cambridge. That was me.'

'And why did you go into television?'

'I wanted to be a journalist, but I couldn't spell. You don't need to be able to spell in television.'

'And why did you get married?'

'Sex, I think. Not that it was ever that great, but I had rather a tidy mind in those days. I thought – marry her and you'll never have to worry about going without. Hideous how naïve you can be at that age. And I think she reckoned the way to stop men pestering you all the time was to get a permanent one – I was her anti-man serum. Also, everyone expected us to, it was part of the conveyor-belt: school, university, marriage, job, they came along like buses, and you just got on, didn't think about it. Like most of the big decisions in life, they just sort of happen. You spend weeks worrying about the little ones, but the big ones swallow you up without you noticing. You ever been married?'

'Nope. I told you, I'm saving myself. So why did you wait so long to get divorced?'

'We wanted to wait till the children were dead.'

'You haven't any.'

'Then I don't know. I suppose we must have been happy enough for a time. The trouble is happiness is like pain, you can't remember what it feels like after it's gone.'

There was a disturbance behind them: Heathrow had failed to load enough Kosher food, and a crows' parliament of indignant orthodox Jews was gathering in the aisle. A harassed flight

47

attendant offered to take them back to the galley to see if they could find anything for them.

'What you got in the galley, eh? I tell you: peanuts is what you got in the galley. You call that an in-flight meal? You want rid of your peanuts you take them to the zoo, lady. I want to talk to the Captain.'

Charlie wanted another drink.

'Great floor show,' he told the hostess, nodding backwards towards the catering dispute. 'What time's the band on?'

'Shouldn't be long, sir. We're waiting until we hit the iceberg.'

Brussels would have been visible to their left but for the cloud.

Charlie got out his papers and read through Walter's biography of Bermant. Born in Germany, came to Palestine with his parents at the age of four, grew up under the Mandate in the thirties and forties, joined the Haganah resistance when he was sixteen, fought in the Kiryati Brigade during the War of Independence, and stayed on in the newly-founded Israeli Defence Forces afterwards. In 1955 he took part in the Israeli raids against the Egyptians in Gaza, and the invasion of the Sinai in '56. Later he served with the Israeli military missions in London and Washington, spent three years behind a desk in Tel Aviv, returning to active service in 1965. He was a colonel at thirty-eight, a lieutenant-general at forty-two, a full general at forty-five. In the Six Day War he was wounded in the leg, and put back behind a desk. He retired from the army in '73, after Yom Kippur, and went into politics on the left of the Labour Party, active in civil rights and liberal causes, but shy of taking office. Until now. Married 1942 Ruth Ethel Cohen, now deceased. No children. Hobbies gardening and talking to the press.

He pencilled in the names of the dinner guests against the chronology, fitting them to the important periods in Bermant's life – sometimes just one, sometimes two or three together. Then he began listing sequences, archive film they'd put together for a brief biography of Bermant at the start of the programme.

It was mid-evening when they made their final approach to Lod, coming in low over the coast, while the devout among the passengers closed their eyes and hummed patriotic songs, and the rest of them puzzled over their immigration forms.

'Which hotel are we at, by the way?' asked Charlie, briefcase on his knee, documents in both hands, pen between his teeth.

'I booked us into the Dan in Tel Aviv to start off with. Walter's suggestion.'

'Oh,' said Charlie.

He finished filling in the form, put away his pen, stuck his face against the window and looked down on the night lights of Tel Aviv and the darkened plain beyond, remembering the smells, petrol and dust, and the honey-wagons spraying recycled shit across the melon fields. Long way from Westbourne Grove.

As the aircraft banked for its final approach the old man across the aisle started shaking, his head in his hands, convinced they were about to crash – there's always one on every flight. His wife put her arms round him and stroked his forehead.

'At least you die now, you die in Israel.'

The pilot lowered the undercarriage, the cabin lights dimmed, and they were on the ground.

Six years since Charlie was here – more, seven. The air outside was warm and soft, somewhere in the low seventies. A light wind blew in from the Mediterranean. Still the arc-lights, still the date palms, the smell of petrol, still the military everywhere, wary eyes following you at every turn, while you wait to get down the aircraft steps, and wait again to board the buses to the terminal; watching you as you stand inside the swaying bus with your eyes on your feet, listening to the coughing of radios and hissing of hydraulic brakes; still watching as you pick up your bag and climb down from the bus and queue to get in the terminal door, eyes narrowing suspiciously and the boy's hairy hand gripping the Uzi as you reach into your jacket, but it's only to take a packet of cigarettes out of your shirt pocket. On and on, from queue to queue, like slaves in the auction ring. And never a smile from the watchers. Almost the only smiles you see in Israel these days are on the faces of visitors determined to like what they see. This is a country which dropped out of charm school in the first semester, never worried too much about cosmetics. But then why would it? And Charlie was excited to be back, enjoying the bickering energy, the chronic indignation, the utter disrespect with which its citizens treated

49

each other. If you want passive, smiling natives, go to Samoa. If you want an argument, welcome to Israel.

Julia stood beside Charlie as they queued to get inside the terminal, one finger twisted in his. She'd refreshed her cologne before landing, and brushed out her hair, and Charlie wouldn't have minded where they were, though on further reflection he'd rather it wasn't Ben Gurion airport.

'What you do?' demanded the immigration man, without looking up from his blue-lit shelf.

'Director,' said Charlie pleasantly, leaning over and pointing helpfully to the entry on his passport. His interrogator pushed his hand away.

'I said: what you do? Director means nothing. Director means: I don't want to say what I do.'

'I make television programmes,' Charlie smiled, a word at a time.

The official looked up at last, and nodded towards Julia.

'She with you?'

'Yes. We're business partners.'

'Married?'

'No.'

'Who works for who?'

'Does it matter?'

'Everything matters.'

And so it went on, through baggage reclaim and customs, where they found the Dean of Limerick steaming like a forgotten kettle while his suitcases were tipped upside down on the bench.

'They once found explosives on a Greek archbishop,' Charlie explained to Julia in a stage whisper, 'years ago. Now they do it to anyone in a dog-collar. Habit.'

Not entirely habit. The death toll in Israel in December had been forty-one. Twenty-three Arab youths, the youngest a girl of seven; four Palestinian commandos, drowned when their inflatable boat was hit by machine-gun fire off Rosh Haniqra; six Israeli soldiers, burned alive when a petrol bomb went off under their APC near Hebron; and two Jewish settlers who blew themselves up outside a mosque in Nablus. In the first three weeks of January twenty-seven more people had died, the latest an old man of seventy hit in the face by a Palestinian rock while

50

driving to see his wife in hospital in Nazareth. One reason the death toll was so heavily weighted towards the Palestinians was that Arabs weren't allowed to carry arms: most Israeli settlers were obliged to by law.

At last they emerged into the seething bedlam of cabs and tour buses. By now Charlie was hanging on to his even temper by his teeth, but Julia seemed utterly calm, almost to be enjoying it.

'I thought you did this for a living, Charlie.'

'I told you, I'm getting old.'

But he handled the haggling cabbies like a pro, fixed a rate in advance, inspected the vehicles, made sure the driver knew the way, while Julia waited on the sidewalk in the shelter of an army policeman.

'Hold on, where are we going?' she asked as the swaying old Mercedes ignored the Tel Aviv signs at the airport perimeter and swung left, inland, towards Jerusalem.

'To bed. I've got a surprise for you.'

'But –'

'No buts.'

For a moment there was panic in her eyes.

5

CHARLIE WOKE NOT LONG AFTER dawn, with the first rays of sunlight slanting through the shutters. He raised himself on one elbow and looked down at Julia's sleeping face breathing softly and evenly on the pillow beside him. She looked beautiful, warm and tender and trusting. He wondered what was going on inside her head, what secrets and worries were there, what public front her subconscious was dreaming up for the day ahead. And he wondered what the hell he'd done to deserve a moment like this.

The bedroom was large and simple and elegant, its walls whitewashed, a single faded Turkish rug on the bare pine floor, a washbasin in the corner, two upright wooden chairs with woven raffia seats. A lazy ceiling fan idled overhead, and there were roses in a vase beside the brass bedstead. In one corner of the room, as an afterthought, someone had balanced an old black-and-white portable television on top of the rough-carved chest of drawers.

Each time he came back to the Hotel Anani he was convinced it would have changed, but somehow it never did, or not much. The Anani was tucked away in a quiet corner of what had, before the Six Day War, been Arab East Jerusalem, ruled by the Jordanians. Its courtesy and simple comforts belonged to the days of the great British Arabists – Burton and Lawrence, Thessinger and Stark and St John Philby, travellers of modest, almost ascetic tastes, whose works filled the book-lined library on the ground floor, and it remained an oasis of calm in a city which elsewhere seemed perpetually on the verge of a municipal nervous breakdown. Three blonde sandstone storeys and a pantiled roof hedged in by eucalyptus formed a pallisade round a serene, vine-encrusted courtyard, at the centre of which stood an ancient citrus tree grafted to produce both oranges and lemons. There was no air conditioning, but even in high summer the white-vaulted, stone-floored public rooms were as pleasantly cool as a catacomb. Now, in winter, the hotel was kept warm by an ancient but efficient central heating system. The staff were mostly male and elderly, and wore white cotton jackets and baggy trousers held up by elasticated snake-buckle belts. The food was simple and unpretentious, with a polite bow to the English, who were served Twinings tea in silver pots and bacon and eggs with their breakfast. And there was no piped music, none, not even in the bar.

The day was blue, and cooler than the coast: Jerusalem is a hill town, and this was February. But the air was warm and fresh and invigorating, like an English May, scented with pine and mimosa. The room looked south, through the pine trees and TV aerials and across the mushroom mosaics of the stone-domed rooftops, towards the Old City.

Charlie slipped out of bed, wrapped a towel round his waist, crossed to the balcony and opened the shutters. He felt full of energy – everything told him this was going to be a memorable trip. And he wanted this job to be special. You don't make the best programmes for money, you make them for people, often just one or two. Earning Harry's cheque was neither here nor there: all that Charlie wanted to do now was please Julia. And maybe surprise her a little.

They'd arrived late the night before, almost midnight. The taxi had dropped them off under the trees, and they'd crossed the floodlit courtyard to the flagstoned reception.

'Hallo,' said Charlie, willing Salam Anani to remember him. Heaven knew why, but he did.

'Mr Kavanagh! How are you!'

Salam was English-educated, thin with age and stiff and upright as a heron. His clothes were immaculate: a well-cut suit, white shirt, silk tie and dustless black shoes. His was the sixth generation of his family to run the hotel.

'Tired. Salam, this is Julia.'

They shook hands.

'Do you have a room?'

Salam smiled sadly.

'You didn't book?'

'I'm sorry. We came straight from the airport.'

He pulled out the register.

'How many rooms you want?'

'It's that bad?' asked Charlie.

'I'm afraid so,' said Salam. The register was almost empty. 'The season is a little quiet. Better for us than for some, but yes, quiet.'

An elderly porter in an equally elderly but spotless uniform picked up their bags and led them up the wide stone stairs.

Julia was silent, almost cross. But then it had been a long day.

'I'm sorry,' said Charlie when they were alone. 'It was meant to be a surprise.'

'Don't be sorry, it's not your fault. I'm the one who should be sorry. This is wonderful.' She ran her fingers along the top of the pine dresser. 'I don't know why I was thrown, Charlie. I have a stupid fear of ending up in strange towns with nowhere to stay. And I told Walter we'd be in Tel Aviv.'

'Ring him in the morning and tell him to come here.'

'Sure. I'm sorry, I'm being ridiculous.'

She gave him a tired smile and started to undress.

And now it was morning. Life seemed full of infinite promise. Their balcony was on the outside of the hotel, overhanging a narrow alley lined with trees, pine and eucalyptus. Already the wailing had begun from the muezzins, *Allahu akbar, La ilaha illa Allah, Al – salat Khayr min al-naum.*

'What does it mean?' asked Julia, resting her chin on his shoulder. He could feel her breath on his neck, the gentle pressure of her breasts against his back. He reached back and put his arm round her waist, and felt her body, naked under a thin cotton robe, still warm from the bed.

'God is great, there is no God but God, prayer is better than sleep. Have you been here before?'

54

'Mmm.' She bit gently into his ear, and nodded across the tree tops towards the Old City. 'There. But not here. Where are we?'

'Do you need to know?'

'Not really.'

'The land of unlimited impossibilities.'

'Who said that?'

'Barbara Tuchman. An American historian. Fine writer. We're in Arab East Jerusalem, about half a mile north of the old City Walls, midway between the Tomb of the Kings, and the Sheikh Jarrah mosque. Over there's the Mandelbaum Gate – used to be the main crossing point between the two halves of the city until the Six Day War. That's what's left of the old border, the Green Line.'

He gestured towards a corridor of wasteland maybe a quarter of a mile wide. The area looked as though a bomb had dropped a long time ago, and people had made a half hearted attempt to camp out in it, plant a few trees, lay roads on the bare earth. Half-way up the slope someone had made a modest attempt at a municipal park. Modest because unendowed: almost everything that had money spent on it in modern Israel – parks, benches, trees, ambulances, synagogues, theatres and concert halls, even the impressionist paintings in the National Museum – was named after someone, normally a recently-dead American. Not many American widows donated park benches to East Jerusalem, any more than the Saudis queued up to donate ornamental fountains to Tel Aviv.

Looking down, he realised they weren't alone. Below them two lovers stood under a eucalyptus. The girl was pretty but almost anorexic, lean and thin and thinner still at the waist. She had pale pre-Raphaelite skin, like white marble, the delicate blue veins showing at her wrists and the back of her hands; a long neck, and long red curls down to her shoulders. She wore glasses. The boy was tall and athletic, a body-builder, his hair long and blond, the colour of corn. He stood very close to her, talking, pausing sometimes to flick his head and clear the hair from his eyes. Their hands moved constantly against each other, and you could tell he was pleased that she loved him. Charlie sensed that she wasn't even listening to what he was saying, she

55

just wanted to laugh and make him happy, and be whoever he wanted her to be.

And then the girl looked up.

'Shalom aleichem,' said Charlie cheerfully.

She blushed, and smiled back at him.

'Aleichem shalom.'

Charlie gave her a wave, and turned back into the room, but Julia lingered a moment, and the boy looked up too, and gave her a brief nod of recognition. Then the lovers looked away, and Julia went inside. Charlie was lying face down on the bed, rereading her treatment. Julia climbed astride him, and began massaging his spine.

He pushed away the folder.

'I had a friend once, a journalist who'd been in Vietnam for three months covering the war. He flew out to Bangkok, knackered. And he wanted a massage – just that, no sex, all he wanted was a rub. And he couldn't get one. Every time he asked a taxi driver or a hotel porter or the tourist office where he could get a massage they gave him a knowing smile and sent him to a brothel. And each time he got to a brothel, and the girls started in on him, he'd stop them, and try to explain. And then they'd get upset, and feel insulted, so he'd give in. And the more he got laid, the more the idea of a simple massage became an obsession, and he kept trying.'

'Did he get one?'

'Nope. He got the clap, gave it to his wife when he got back, and she divorced him. Moral little tale.'

'What's the moral?'

'Never sleep with your wife.'

She laughed, and moved on to his neck.

'You hungry?'

'Yup. What time is it?'

Julia glanced across at the alarm clock beside the bed.

'Ten-past seven.'

'Shouldn't you ring Walter?'

'In a minute.' Her tongue was on his ear now. 'You want the fixed menu or the à la carte?'

'Who's paying this time?'

'Harry. Harry pays for everything.'

56

Room service brought them breakfast – croissants, honey, fresh orange juice, a pot of coffee and a basket of fruit. While they ate Julia phoned Walter Azeff in Tel Aviv and told him where they were. The drive up from the coast to Jerusalem would take him a little over an hour. It was half-past eight: they arranged to meet at the Anani at ten. In the meantime they had work to do, car hire to arrange, press passes to collect.

Jerusalem is built on hills. At its heart, on a long thin ridge, is the walled Old City, a labyrinthine souk a mile square, centred around the Temple Mount, where Abraham prepared to sacrifice Isaac, and Solomon built the First Temple, and from where Allah ascended into the Seven Heavens. A hundred yards away are the Via Dolorosa, Golgotha and the Holy Sepulchre – the scale is more that of a village than a city. In the nineteenth century the cramped and seething community finally overflowed the city walls, and new settlements grew up in all directions, Jewish and Christian, Ottoman and Arab. With the partition of Palestine in 1948 the Jordanians got the Old City and the East of the new town, and the Israelis got the West, splitting the town in half. During the Six Day War the Jordanians were driven out and Jerusalem was again united, this time under Israeli administration. Since then the population had expanded across the neighbouring hill-tops in a chain of modern high-rise settlements, all – like the Old City – built from the honey sandstone which makes Jerusalem The Golden. The municipality, like the British administration before them, insisted on stone: you could build monstrosities, but they had to be stone monstrosities. Almost half a million lived there now, less than twenty thousand of them inside the Old City.

Charlie and Julia walked down the slope from the Anani to the Old City in the morning sunshine, a brief indulgence before the imperatives of the programme took over their lives entirely.

Charlie loved the place, always had. It made him laugh a lot: the way the whole city, Old and New, stubbornly refused to get on with life, eat, breed, work, sleep and be civil to its neighbours like the rest of the world. Here it was a virtue *not* to eat, or sleep, or work, and a cardinal sin to listen to, let alone see, another man's point of view. Jerusalem was a religious asylum, a place where the impracticalities of life were elevated to an art

57

form and discomfort celebrated in temples and shrines with names like Our Lady of the Spasm, the Church of Flagellation, the Dome of the Chain. He loved the intensity of it all, the way the Jews scurried like homburged ants up and down the stony hills, hunched under the weight of their theological burdens, squabbling about the small print of their Destiny, ploughing head-down into oncoming pedestrians, stepping blindly off pavements in front of the traffic, rushing nowhere in particular. Not just one kind of Jew, but seventy, eighty different national-ities of them, Jews from Europe, North America, Morocco, Egypt, Turkey, Brazil, South Africa, Russia, Iraq, Yemen, Ethi-opia, India, Bokhara, Argentina, Australia, almost any country you cared to mention. It's a great city for hats: embroidered skull-caps, fur-trimmed *streimel*, pork-pies from Germany, trilb-ies from England and America, Neville Chamberlain homburgs, Uzbek astrakhans, felt hats, plastic hats, wool hats and leather hats, turbans and caps and knitted bonnets with bobbles on – a millinery Babel. A man who wears a skull-cap will often wear another hat on top of it, so that if he were to lift his trilby to you (not a likely event in this least courteous of societies) a second hat would be revealed underneath, like a Russian doll. When it rains in Jerusalem people take off their hats, put them in plastic bags, then put the hats and bags back on their heads again. Hats are important to men's dignity in Israel.

But not in Arab East Jerusalem. In East Jerusalem some women wear veils, and some men wear *keffiyahs*, and groups of Christian pilgrims occasionally wear cotton sun-hats with the name of their tour-company on the front, and that's about that. No one seems to be in too much of a hurry.

Half-way along Salah-Ed-Din, between the Alhambra Cinema and the Al Nahar Liberrary (gifts and school articles) and opposite the blue-and-white Israeli flags on the gates of the District Courthouse, a defunct clothes shop had been converted into an emergency hotline centre for victims of violence.

'Should we be nervous?' asked Julia.

'Yes,' said Charlie. 'I mean not really. Just careful.'

In ten minutes they reached the walls of the Old City. Last time Charlie was here the place had been seething with life –

tourists, monks, hawkers filling the narrow lanes. Now everything was quiet, the atmosphere tense. Daily strikes reduced the bazaar's selling season to four hours a day. A few nervous Arab merchants approached them with bargains – jewellery, woodwork, bedouin dresses.

'Buy for your wife and she give you good time in bed to thank you,' suggested a shopkeeper.

'I'm gay and she's my sister,' said Charlie.

'You have no wife? I get you one.'

'Is she pretty?'

'Frankly no. But these are difficult times, you must take what God offers.'

In less than a mile they met three Israeli army foot-patrols, bands of dishevelled, gun-toting teenagers, loitering around the pavements like street-gangs in an after-the-bomb movie. Jerusalem always had its quota of soldiers and police on the streets, but now they were everywhere, an iron fist in an iron glove. Most days there were strikes, and most days there was rioting, young Palestinians who'd lived their whole lives under military occupation exchanging stones for rubber bullets with the grown-up children of Holocaust survivors.

They left the souk and crossed the rubble of the Green Line into the New City, through the scruffy woodland of Independence Park to the International Press Centre, a flat-roofed white-stone blockhouse next door to the Italian Synagogue, to get their passes and accreditation.

'Who you work for?' asked the bored woman behind the desk.

'Julia Cornwall Associates,' Charlie told her.

'Who are they?'

'They're us. She's Julia, I'm the Associate.'

He scoured her face for a smile, but there was none, not a hint.

'And who are you?' he tried.

'Sharon.'

She made it sound like a swear word.

Charlie picked up Julia's passport while they waited. Brand new, no stamps or endorsements. Occupation Academic, born Calne, Wilts, 4 March 1964, no distinguishing features, no children, no clues. Bleached-out black-and-white photobooth picture in a cotton raincoat with the collar up, could be anyone.

They filled in their forms, collected their passes and walked back down to the park. Charlie went to the shop on the corner of Hillel Street to buy cigarettes. Julia looked down the street. The blond youth from the alley was perched on a low wall, hiding behind a motor-cycling magazine. He was on his own now, in a khaki shirt and army boots, a forage cap pulled low over his brow, drinking coke from a can. She strolled over to the wall, and stood with her back to the boy, trying not to move her lips.

'Hi. I'm Julia.'

'I know,' said the blond. 'I'm Shimon.'

She kept her eyes on the park. A cat was stalking wagtails. There were crested hoopoes there too, poking for insects in the hard soil. She could hear a woodpecker in the distance.

'And the girl?' asked Julia.

'Tina. She'll be around too.'

'How did you manage to find us this morning?'

'He always stays there. When you didn't show at the Dan we guessed.'

'You with us all the time?'

'Only when you need us.'

'The Tyler bomb, was that to do with you?'

'Ask Tyler, he'd be the one to know. You need to contact us, ring any time.'

He passed her a slip of paper with a phone number on it. Julia slipped it in her bag.

Charlie was coming out of the shop, a copy of the *Jerusalem Post* under his arm. BUSH TO MEET PLO, announced the headline.

'Where to next?' asked Julia.

'Hertz. And tell me about Walter.'

They crossed the park and headed up King David towards the YMCA building and the car-hire office.

'He's sweet, you'll like him. He's a mature student of politics, his father was a member of the Knesset.'

'He's Moses Azeff's son?'

'Correct. You know him?'

'I met his father. We interviewed him once, ten years ago. I think he's dead now. Go on with Walter.'

'He's a slut. Baths once a month, owns two shirts and three socks, the sort of man who uses a slice of salami as a bookmark. He speaks good English and he costs two hundred dollars a week including expenses.'

'Who hired him?'

'I did.'

Julia wanted a Merc, but Charlie insisted on a Subaru. He'd driven lawn-mowers with bigger engines, but he liked the toys on the Japanese estate, which was a Fisher Price for grown-ups, full of LED displays and switches and gadgets and multicoloured flashing lights, the sort of car that probably has a microwave oven somewhere in the dash if you could ever find it. A cheerful yellow sticker inside the driver's door reminded them that damage from landmines was not covered by insurance. Charlie didn't mind: the car went, he went too.

Julia was right – Walter was a shambles. He arrived at the hotel an hour late, looking like an old armchair with the stuffing hanging out. He was curiously built – arms too long, legs too short, a barrel chest and enormous feet, swathed in the remains of a black two-piece suit. A nervous, friendly mouth, uncertain which expression to offer, big wet cow's eyes, and terrible skin, a pock-marked complexion that looked as though it had been sandblasted with rough gravel. His thick black hair was matted at an angle as though it had been knitted in place by a toddler, and he carried two supermarket carrier-bags crammed with files and a roll of toilet paper from which he intermittently ripped off sheets to blow his nose. Walter had a cold.

'Hi,' said Charlie. 'I'm Charlie.'

'How did you recognise me?'

Charlie and Julia were seated at a wrought-iron table in the courtyard of the Anani, shaded by boughs of laburnum from the heat of the sun. Walter dumped the carrier bags on a chair and held out a porky hand. He was out of breath but talking fast.

'Always happens to me, when I was a kid my mother used to send me across Tel Aviv by bus to people I'd never met; the

61

moment I got to the bus door they knew who they were looking for.' He shrugged his shoulders. 'I'd make a terrible spy.'

'I just sort of knew you weren't a tourist.'

'You're very kind. Hallo, Julia.'

'Hallo, Walter.'

He called over the waiter and they ordered beers and sandwiches. Walter stopped the waiter as he was leaving and asked for cake as well.

'Cake or cakes?' asked the waiter.

'Everything you've got,' said Walter. 'This is an emergency.'

When Charlie congratulated him on his research, he blushed and fiddled with his glasses.

'I'm glad you like it. It's a bit of a cheat, though. I mean, it's all true, but I knew it all already, if you know what I mean. We met before, by the way. You interviewed my father at our apartment in Netanya, in seventy-eight. I was ten at the time, you won't remember me. You had a bald Australian cameraman who wore aftershave, and a little Scots sound recordist who let my kid sister play with his tape recorder.'

And the film was junked, Charlie recalled. A piece on the economy, which they'd tried to tag on at the end of a *Newsnight* special to celebrate the thirtieth anniversary of Israeli Independence, only they ran out of time before they could finish it.

'Of course I remember. The cameraman was Butch Calderwood, the soundman was Freddie Downton. Freddie died too. You lived in a block of flats on top of the cliff, above the beach. Always reminds me of Bournemouth, Netanya. Our electrician broke one of the aluminium struts of your balcony door putting up a light. When did your father die?'

'Three years ago. Big funeral, plenty of speeches.'

'I'm sorry to hear it. If you're Moses Azeff's son, you must know Bermant anyway. They were colleagues, weren't they?'

'Sure. Though I wouldn't exactly call him a family friend. He and my father were in dispute at the time he died. You know how the Left is, always eating its own. But he's a civil man, doesn't seem to hold a grudge.'

'Do you?'

'Me? No, it all seems a long time ago. And I don't think you can blame someone if they happen to be having a row when the

Julia was back, and ordered brandy sours for them all.

'Goliath'll see us at somewhere called Finkles at five,' she announced. 'You know where that is?'

Charlie nodded. Walter looked at his watch.

'I have to go make some calls.'

'Use the phone in our room,' Julia offered.

'Thanks, but I'm shy. What if you need to use the bed in a hurry when I'm on a call? I get all inhibited when I think other people can hear me. Also I shout sometimes, people think I've been taken ill. And I draw on the furniture when I'm on the phone, I've wrecked a lot of good woodwork in my time. I can go to my sister's, she lives across town, she's used to me. You want to meet these people beforehand?'

'Sure,' said Charlie. 'If we've got time. Are they all in Jerusalem?'

'Most of them. Benny's down on the Red Sea at this time of year, ogling topless schoolgirls on the beach. Liel's kibbutz is about half-way between here and Tel Aviv. Kaufman's usually in Beersheba, you could drop in on the way down to Eilat.'

'How about Bermant?'

'He wants to do it cold. He says he'll turn up, eat his supper, talk to anyone we throw at him.'

Charlie looked dubious.

'How do we know what he'll say?'

'You ever heard him say anything surprising?'

Charlie supposed not. But he'd be happier if he'd talked the whole thing through with their star beforehand.

'Not a hope, I'm afraid,' said Walter. 'His timetable's solid. I've done a lot of notes on him, though.'

He took another armful of papers out of his bag. Charlie picked them up and walked him back to his ancient Volkswagen, once pillar-box red, now faded to cream-of-tomato soup. Significant parts of the car were missing – a bumper, a door-handle, a rear window taped over with cardboard.

They shook hands.

'Nice meeting you again,' said Charlie. He liked Walter.

'You too. I'll see you at Finkles. With a schedule.'

Walter took a teaspoon from his pocket and unlocked the driver's door.

'By the way, have you known Julia long?' Charlie asked.

'What day is it today?'

'Wednesday.'

Walter counted.

'Ten days. And you?'

'Five.'

'She's a fast worker, kid,' said Walter.

Bloody unbelievable, Charlie realised as he watched the beetle weave down the lane towards the main road, Walter hunched myopically over the wheel. Less than a week ago he was in Monmouth Place doing the ironing, minding his own business. And here he was, staying at the Anani with a beautiful blonde, earning six hundred notes a day, with a tame leg-man to do all the work. Making a programme for a man he'd met once and knew fuck all about, except that he was rich and had desperate taste in art.

Hard to find anything to complain about, though. And he wanted another drink.

6

JULIA WAS STILL at the table.

'You're right, he's sweet,' Charlie told her as he sat down. 'Where did you find him?'

'Pot luck. I phoned the TV station and asked them to recommend someone. They gave me four names. He was the only one who could do it.'

'When? I mean when did you phone them? How long was this circus on the road before I joined up?'

She bent forward, ran her finger round the rim of her glass, and looked him straight in the eyes.

'About a fortnight.'

'And you did it blind from London?'

She was smiling, but her eyes kept staring, daring him.

'I didn't say that.'

'So how long since you were last here?'

Her eyes still hadn't moved.

'Ten days.'

And yet there's no stamp in your passport. But then a lot of people ask not to have their passports stamped when they come to Israel, causes problems elsewhere afterwards.

The courtyard was empty, the sun high in the sky. They sat leaning forward towards each other across the wrought iron table, so that in profile they looked like two griffins crowning a coat of arms.

'Who are you really, Julia Cornwall?' asked Charlie.

She tapped her fingernail against her front teeth.

'Whoever you want me to be.'

'I'm bored with the footloose academic. Try something else.'

'OK.' She took out a cigarette. 'My mother was German, from Hamburg. She was seventeen when the war ended. All her family were dead or missing. Nowadays we forget how it was in Germany after the war – people were starving, living off rats and insects and tree-bark. For months, years even. Nowhere to live, no clothes, no work, nothing. The winters in Hamburg are hard. My father was much older, a bachelor Major in the British Pay Corps. He caught her stealing slops from the pig pails outside the barracks. She told him she was twenty. They got married – not at first, because she was a Defeated Alien and the Brits weren't meant to have any contact with them. But later, in forty-seven, after he'd been discharged. He didn't dare bring her back to England to start off with, so he got a job with the British Council in Rome . . . am I boring you?'

Charlie shook his head. He could spend a week listening to her reading out a telephone directory without getting bored.

'No, but you're not convincing me either. Why this urge to have a foreign parent? First a Czech father, now a German mother. And the dates don't add up. They met in forty-five, married in forty-seven, you weren't born until sixty-four . . .'

'I was a late mistake. Not that late, even – she was only thirty-six when I was born.'

'Did she love him?'

'She'd have married him anyway, he was her only hope. Strangely enough, though, I think she did.'

'Did you?'

'I never really knew him. He died when I was four. In the pictures he looks a bit pompous, waistcoats and cravats and stout brogues.'

'And you were brought up by your mother?'

'In Calne, where the sausages come from. Went to school there, too. And then I worked abroad for a year, in Switzerland, teaching. You really want to know all this?'

Charlie was making notes on a serviette. He looked up.

'Sure. It's my version of *Call My Bluff*. You get to give me three life stories, and then I choose which one to believe.' He folded the serviette. 'Enough of this shit, we have work to do. We don't have a location, no one's signed a contract, we haven't

70

finalised lights or cameras or sound, we haven't confirmed the transmission and satellite bookings – am I getting this right?'

'Absolutely. I'm trying to make you panic, I haven't seen that yet. Do you panic, Charlie?'

She gave him a dangerous smile, moistening her lips with the tip of her tongue.

'What's the deal with Goliath?' he asked her.

'Whatever we want. He'll hire the gear and crew it. Do you know what you'll need?'

'I won't know about lights until we have a location. The rest's fairly straightforward. Four cameras, a mixer, three tape machines – master, back-up and one to play in the archive material.' Julia took notes as he talked. 'Three on sound should do us. Radio mike on Bermant, the rest can have personals, and a boom-swinger to cover in an emergency. Floor manager, couple of AFMs. Make-up. Someone to look after props and so on, doesn't have to be a set designer. A PA of sorts. I'll do the vision mixing myself. Transport in case they need picking up and taking home.'

'And that's all?'

'For the shoot. There are some other bits and pieces we'll need beforehand when we edit together the introductory film, opening and closing titles. Captions, music, credits. Does this series have a signature tune yet?'

' "Also Sprach Zarathustra".'

'Oh dear,' said Charlie. 'The disco version?'

'The one Kubrick used in *2001*. You don't like it?'

'When I worked on *Nationwide* we kept four records permanently in the cutting rooms to brighten up dull films. Anything on the economy we used either "Money, Money, Money" or "Big Spender". Anything to do with showbiz or sex we got out "The Stripper". Space or new technology got "Also Sprach". Oh, and I think there was a copy of Vivaldi's *Four Seasons* for countryside sequences.'

They ran on through the logistics of the week ahead. Julia's face tensed with concentration as she worried at the lists. But Charlie wasn't worried about lists: he was worried about the programme. He leaned back in his chair to let the waiter deliver more drinks, then lit a cigarette.

'Dumb question. But – does this have to be Bermant?'

Julia's glass paused half-way to her mouth.

'You serious?'

He flicked out the match and tossed it into the flowerbed.

'Absolutely. Everyone's made a programme about him. I'm sure he's even been on *Blue Peter*. Everyone knows what he stands for, we don't need to say it all again. And it's misleading. What he stands for is Western wish-fulfilment. People at home think that Israel's full of David Bermants. Is it hell. Israel's full of angry, disillusioned Joe Soapovitches who are sick of the whole business, sick of being called up into the army, sick of the rest of the world expecting them to behave like angels, who don't understand why Westerners crucify Israel every time an Arab gets hurt but keep their eyes and mouths shut about every other regime in the Middle East. Some crazed IDF squaddy beats up a couple of Palestinians in front of an American film crew, it leads the US network news. But the Syrians can do what they want. Assad wants to knock off a couple of thousand of his political opponents, no one breathes a word. Not a mention anywhere. You know how Hussein runs Jordan? No, you don't. No one does, no one's interested. Hussein's a pro-western moderate, that's all you need to know. Ask anyone on the West Bank what life was like under the Jordanians, you get some very revealing answers.'

'It has to be Bermant. Harry has to have this thing on air next Monday, Charlie. That's five days' time.'

'He can have it. He can have it about Israel, he can have something that ties in to Bermant's speech. He can even have Bermant's dinner party. But let's at least get some interesting guests for him. The conscripts we saw in the Old City this morning. The boys who are cracking the skulls. Shoot the dinner in their canteen, find out what it's like in a riot having metal bolts and half-bricks rained on you. Find out how they live, what they think, what they believe in. Their family histories, where they came from before Israel.' Charlie was getting enthusiastic. 'Hold on. Do it the other way round. Start with an old man who emigrated here forty or fifty years ago, a homeless refugee from Poland or Germany or wherever. Get him to tell his story, about the early years, before Independence, what life was like then, what his hopes were for the future. Then pick up on one of his children across the table, a generation down, someone who lived through the sixties and seventies, fought in the Six Day War, Yom Kippur and so on. And finally we get to the grandson, here and now, one of this lot, or those IDF kids with the uzis knocking people's doors down in the middle of the night in Hebron and Ramallah.'

Julia was shaking her head. Charlie took another mouthful of brandy.

'No? OK, let's get a table-full of settlers, Gush Emunim, the Hassidic Revolutionaries. Who emigrates to Israel nowadays? Orthodox Jews, yeshiva students. Who leaves? Secular Jews, people with skills. That's the big trade nowadays, exporting moderates, importing bigots. Which lot is least likely to favour compromise with the Arabs?

Charlie mimed a beard and a skullcap.

Julia was still shaking her head.

'I'm sorry, Charlie. It has to be the way it is.'

'It does? Why?'

'Because that's what Harry wants.'

'He does?'

'He does. And he signs the cheques.'

'OK,' Charlie sighed. 'I give in. I'm sorry, I'm making a fuss. It's just that you get terrible feelings of *déjà vu* in this business, you keep asking the same interviewees the same questions, year in and year out. It's a curious sort of television law, you never put anyone on the box unless you already know what they're going to say. In which case why put them on in the first place?'

'Because –' Julia started.

'I know,' Charlie interrupted. 'I know all the excuses, I even believe a lot of them. But it still worries me. Tell me something else – does Harry run this thing on his own? Just you and him?'

'And Eric.'

'The three of you.'

'As far as I know.'

'So who's looking after the next one?'

'The next what?'

'Programme. The one that goes out in March, presumably. And the one after that.'

'I don't know, Charlie. Maybe we are. I'm in the same boat as you, I was just hired for this job.'

'Good money?'

'Yup.'

'You know you're over-paying me, by the way.'

'Sure. It's Harry's philosophy.' She took a toothpick out of the glass jar on the table. 'The interview over yet?'

Her expression had changed, as though her mind had moved into another plane. He realised he was making her nervous.

'I'm sorry. I'm only trying to earn my fee.'

He offered her a smile, and got one back. Not a grin, but a smile of sorts.

Julia puzzled Charlie. Most of the time she was all carefree confidence, game for anything, daring him on. He loved that in her, the danger, the recklessness. And then the next moment she was a jobsworth; Harry wants it done this way, that's how we'll do it. The two halves didn't seem to fit.

And then it occurred to him what she must be going through. She was in charge, she had a show to deliver. And she'd never done this before in her life. Even for Charlie the days before a shoot were always hell: you had to exude confidence and conviction to the outside world, while inside your guts were knotted tighter than a whalebone corset. Once you were on location, necessity took over. There wasn't time to worry much. But the build-up was a nightmare. Charlie was always convinced the crew wouldn't like him, interviewees wouldn't show up and would say the wrong things when they did, it would rain, he'd lose his notes, he'd be late for everything and everyone, the sparks would complain about the call time and directions, he'd have forgotten to ask for the right equipment, he wouldn't have done his research, still not know what the programme was about. Year in year out he went through the same ridiculous ritual, unable to eat, scared to drink, convinced his alarm wouldn't go off, unable to talk to anyone about anything because he was so ashamed of his insecurity in a profession where confidence counts for ten times more than talent. He'd worried on the eve of every show he'd ever made, and there must have been two or three hundred of them.

Except this time. The prospect of next Monday's shoot didn't give him so much as a twitch. Ever since the first phone call from Julia the whole thing had run with effortless military precision. No fuck-ups, no panics, anything he needed delivered to his door. He was sure that if he asked for a chauffeur-driven limo to pick him up and take him to location, and a furnished trailer with a cocktail cabinet and jacuzzi to rest in between takes, he'd get that too. This time he wasn't worried at all, because he wasn't in charge. Julia was in charge, a woman who'd never produced a TV programme before in her life. No wonder she was nervous. He felt a sudden rush of guilt and affection.

The waiter was at his shoulder.

'Phone call for you, Mr Kavanagh.'

'For me?'

'In the lobby.'

On his way across the reception Charlie noticed the pre-Raphaelite girl with the marble skin sitting in a wicker chair reading Len Deighton, the way you sit when you're waiting for someone you know is always late.

'The defector's wife turns out to be lesbian.' Charlie stopped off to tell her. 'She elopes to Moscow with the hero's girl-friend.'

The girl gave him a shy, embarrassed smile. He picked up the phone on the desk.

'Charlie Kavanagh.'

'Hallo,' said a soft seductive female voice. 'Do you speak English, Mr. Kavanagh?'

Charlie thought of his actress friend Shirley, who did the sexy voice-overs for Hawaiian nymphs in TV chocolate commercials. Shirley was forty-three, weighed over two hundred pounds and dressed like a canteen cleaning lady. Charlie never trusted sexy voices on the phone.

'Un peu,' he told her.

'My name is Tanya,' the voice continued, speaking more slowly now to make sure she was understood, 'I'm phoning from the Jerusalem Diamond Exchange and I wondered if I might interest you in a visit. We can pick you up at your hotel and bring you here at your convenience. Are you married, Mr Kavanagh?'

Telephone selling – everywhere you went now they were at

it, offering you things you didn't want and couldn't afford. They get a list of names off someone at the hotel, ring them up one by one to make it sound personal. There was a time when phones were for talking to friends on, or doing business you wanted to do. Not any more.

'Not actively,' said Charlie.

'Oh,' said Tanya.

'And you?'

'My husband is away with the army in Samaria until Monday. Listen, forget the Diamond Exchange, maybe we could make jig-jig at my place. You have your own manacles?'

'Hallo Walter,' sighed Charlie. 'What can I do for you?'

Walter chuckled.

'You want to see Bermant? He has a briefing this afternoon at the Foreign Press Association. It's at the Foreign Ministry, across the mound from the Knesset, starts in half an hour's time. I'll ring and let them know you're coming. I doubt he'll have time to talk about the programme, but it might fill you in on what he's thinking these days.'

'Thanks,' said Charlie. 'Does this preclude the jig-jig?'

'Not at all.'

David Bermant was alone in his office. The Argentinian Ambassador had just left: in five minutes he was due downstairs to brief the foreign press. After the journalists he had a meeting with his staff to discuss International Maritime Law, then a chamber concert at the Hilton, and finally dinner with a delegation of visiting Spanish socialists. Civil Servants know how to keep their political masters busy.

It was a wide, square room: wood-panelled walls hung with portraits of Hertzl and Weizmann and Ben-Gurion, beige and pink patterned carpet and pale-green curtains, a big leather-topped desk with an array of intercoms, two chintz sofas arranged around a low occasional table. Move the desk out and bring in a bed and it would make a handy hotel suite – there was even a washbasin and shower in a side-room behind the panelling.

Even after three weeks David still found it hard to think of it as his office. For twenty, thirty years he'd known this room, and

76

the tenants who'd occupied it before him: if he closed his eyes he could still see Golda Meir, Abba Eban, Moshe Dayan or Shimon Peres holding court, aides busying in and out, the air thick with cigarette smoke, politicians and ambassadors standing with their backs to the room muttering at the windows. So many ghosts, so many dead voices.

He sat down at his desk and pulled a sheet of paper out of the top drawer, the letter Ben Libschitz had left behind for him the day Ben resigned. A brief and affectionate note, wishing him well, and ending with a friendly reminder of the realpolitik of Israeli foreign policy:

One: Express a willingness to talk to anyone, but lay down conditions which you know they'll never agree to.

Two: Tell the press at least once a month that you're about to launch a new initiative.

Three: Never launch a new initiative.

Four: Remember that all United States pronouncements on the Middle East are for domestic consumption only, but that they will almost never treat your own remarks with the same courtesy.

Five: The European Community feels a strong obligation to have an independent world view, almost regardless of what that view is. Confine yourself to shaking hands with their representatives at airports.

Six: Any suggestion you make in cabinet will be undermined by either the Prime Minister or the Defence Minister. When they both support you you're in serious trouble.

Best wishes and good luck,
Benjamin.

David smiled, slipped the paper back in the drawer, walked across to the fridge and poured himself a glass of iced water. Imported water, from France. No wonder the economy was in the state it was. He picked up the framed photo of his wife from the bookcase and studied it for the thousandth time.

The intercom buzzed, summoning him downstairs.

Charlie and Julia made it with two minutes to spare. The

conference room was filled to the walls with journalists and cameramen. The television people had turned off the air conditioning, and the air was hot and stuffy. Bermant sat at a long table covered with a green baize cloth and cluttered with microphones, flanked by two civil servants from the Ministry. He made a few opening remarks, urbane, low-key, enough to indicate to his audience that nothing of note was about to be said.

A Canadian correspondent asked the Foreign Minister about a recent CIA analysis which questioned Israel's long-term military superiority in the Middle East.

Bermant scratched his neck with the back of his hand.

'First, I don't accept the analysis. Nor, I might add, does the American government. Secondly, armies are not the only means by which a country defends itself.'

'Does that mean ...'

'It means nothing very much. It means we must always be prepared to meet might with might. But military strength doesn't necessarily bring peace. We've fought a lot of wars these past forty years, and none of them has brought us peace. We don't want superiority, we want parity.'

Charlie scribbled 'Waffle' on his notepad and passed it across to Julia. Bloody briefings. He'd been at a briefing at the British Embassy in Moscow once when David Owen was Foreign Secretary. Loads of journalists there – Moscow in those days was light on news. Owen got up, said hallo, and asked for questions. No one could think of anything to ask him. In the end the Foreign Secretary had been obliged to interview himself. Bermant was doing better, but not much.

The old man took a hostile question from the *Jewish Chronicle*, pausing to fill his glass with water from the carafe before answering.

'I've only ever advocated talks under certain conditions. And you have to remember that the PLO are victims too. They're victims of all the nations and politicians who told them they could win a war with Israel. Doesn't justify their actions against us, but we have to understand the enemy's situation if we're to make any progress at all.'

More competing voices from the floor. Bermant had to lean

forward and cup his hands behind his ears to hear what was being said. Someone asked him about Israel's image abroad.

'It's a problem. We want to appear invincible to the Arabs, vulnerable to the West. The more we succeed in the former, the more we alienate Europe and America. We win a war, the West says "pick on someone bigger than yourself, you little bully". But there's more to it than that – we have to offer the West something they can admire. We used to, in the early days. Not any more. This country doesn't even like itself. How do you expect people to like us when we don't like ourselves?'

Charlie looked at the old man behind the desk, the Ministry apparatchiks flanking him on either side, and thought of his father. He must have been about Bermant's age when he died, maybe a little older. Same physique – flesh shrinking off the bone, legs beginning to bow, bladder giving him trouble, hearing dodgy, memory and reflexes shot to hell. Bermant didn't look in much better shape. Wise enough in what he said, gentle in his emotions, but too tired of the old arguments, too weary to listen to new ideas. Why was it that politicians never retired? Most men are reckoned past it at sixty-five: politicians keep going until they drop. And judges: senility's considered a virtue in the courts.

The conference went on for an hour. Charlie looked around the room for familiar faces, but found few he knew – a couple of long-serving British and American newspapermen, a Reuter's woman he'd met once in Vienna. No one he wanted to talk to. Finally one of the civil servants looked at his watch and brought the session to a close.

'He looked ill,' Julia remarked as they queued for the lift.

'Weak heart,' explained the man from the *Jewish Chronicle*. 'Also he has gall stones, emphysema, maybe shingles. And a bad conscience.'

'Why?' asked Charlie.

'The heart I think is hereditary, the emphysema from too many cigarettes. The shingles I don't know about, maybe someone gave him measles.'

'And the conscience?'

'Who knows?'

7

ERIC STEERED THE BIG BLACK BMW down the slip road and filtered across into the outer lane of the M4, heading back into London. Harry had gone from the boot, weighted down and dropped in the Hounslow reservoirs the previous evening. He'd spent the night at a motel in Reading, out of sight and mind.

'Nobody love you when you rich', sang the radio, the coloured girls singing high and giving it plenty of vibrato.

In place of his Brooks Brothers' suit he wore jeans and sneakers, a black sweatshirt and a beret to hide the Mormon stubble. He drove like a professional, fast but not too fast, flicking his cigarette as he fiddled with the Blaupunkt.

'Poetry in motion', sang another station. Only for Eric it would always be 'Show a tree in motion', the way mis-heard lines from songs always stuck permanently in his head. Like 'Love grows where my rosary goes', 'In the gateaux', 'I'd like to teach the world to sin'.

He turned north off the motorway at Hammersmith, and in another ten minutes was in Bayswater. He left the BMW in the underground car park at the corner of Bishop Bridge Road and Porchester Road and killed a couple of hours shopping.

Shopping was Eric's real appetite in life, above sex, above eating. He went to shops the way art-buffs visit museums. But while the art-buff looks for beauty, Eric looked to find out what was new, how models had been adapted, specifications altered, ranges replaced. Hi-fi and electrical were his speciality, then cars, cameras, domestic gadgets – anything mass-produced, because what was being mass-produced told you what was happening, what the world aspired to, what the future held in store. The concept of the one-off – the Great Picture, the Limited Edition – had always seemed to him absurd. If something's any good, they make a lot of them. Volkswagens, Sony Trinitrons, Black and Decker Workmates, Samsonite briefcases. If a picture's any good, it gets mass-produced too, knitted into carpets, printed on biscuit tins, etched into copper ash-trays. But not many make the grade. A Michelangelo may pass the test of time better than a Duracell flashlight, but much good it does Michelangelo. 'I would not like to be Mozart', as Bob Dylan once said, 'he's dead'.

He looked, but he bought little, and then only after days of thought and comparison. Buying a radio or a set of speakers could take him a week. Clothes were worse, nobody made good clothes in sizes that would fit a guy Eric's size. They had special shops now for tall people, and fat people, and people with one foot bigger than the other. But not for small people. If you were small you wound up shopping in the teen sections of department stores, getting funny looks from the staff.

The staff in the Bayswater shops didn't give you any looks at all, just took your money and got on with talking to each other or reading their magazines. The area was a fly-trap for tourists from the hot countries, better-off Africans and Arabs in town to spend their precious pounds on something to impress the neighbours back home in Lagos or Dubai. They wanted ghetto-blasters with plenty of chrome and flashing lights, leather jackets with pads in the shoulders, machines to line up on their kitchen worktops to make the neighbours go agh! That or porn videos, 'Big Swedish girls do it with goats'. He bought a postcard of a purple-haired punk sticking his tongue out at Buckingham Palace to send the man who fixed his cars in New York, and a clockwork dog that pissed against people's legs for his nephew in Syracuse. Then he picked up his suitcase from the car and walked round the corner to Monmouth Place.

It was drizzling. He sidestepped the piles of garbage in front of 2b, pulled on his gloves and examined the lock. Eric hated this moment, ever since someone loosed off a shotgun at him through a door-panel in Philadelphia.

This time there was no reception committee.

But someone had beaten him to it. Not just burglars, but twisted toss-it-everywhere burglars, the kind who piss on the carpet and shit in the drawers. He cursed as he tripped over a pile of clothing in the hall, and moved on to the sitting room. It was light outside, but the curtains were drawn, and he could barely make out the cardboard boxes, scattered papers, the empty whiskey bottle on its side on the coffee table. He moved cautiously across the room and turned on the standard lamp.

'Jesus,' he hissed.

And then he relaxed. No burglars: Charlie's flat was always like this.

The room was painted chocolate brown, with bookcases along one wall. There were three unmatched armchairs, an old sofa upholstered in sixties' William Morris, now faded and threadbare, and bean-bags scattered across the floor. Charlie's desk was in the corner, crowned by two half-drunk cups of coffee, a tin of dead biros and a dusty clipframe containing family photos. Two were of Charlie's father. The first must have been taken half a century ago, in the thirties. It showed a handsome student in corduroy shorts and a white shirt rolled back at the elbows, standing on a rock in the Alps, apparently yodelling. The second seemed recent, an old man, stubble-chinned and stiff in the limbs, but with a ghost of a twinkle in his milky eyes, sitting on a bench in what looked like Regent's Park. Between them was jammed a polaroid of his mother, a brightly painted woman in a voluminous silk blouse, wincing into the flashlight at a Christmas dinner.

Eric lifted the suitcase on to the sofa and started work. Busy week he was having: and another busy week to come. He started with the books, stuffing fistfuls of Marxist and Maoist tracts into the bookcases, then moved on to the posters. Che Guevara replaced Degas above the kitchen sink, Bobbie Sands and Gerry Adams moved into the bedroom, Arafat grinned mischievously out of the alcove in the hall. Next he took a folder of documents out of his case – receipts, invitations, maps, lists of names and phone numbers. Charlie didn't seem to have a filing system, just drawers full of random papers and stationery, a jumble of old letters, insurance policies, broken staplers, foreign book-matches, hotel soaps, old airline tickets. Eric added his own papers to the chaos, blending them in like a dealer shuffling his pack. Next he took a small plastic bag of white powder and sprinkled it lightly on the kitchen table. Last of all he pinned a newspaper photo of Yaakov Tyler to the wall behind Charlie's desk.

Finkles was in the heart of the new city, a vaulted cellar in a side street off Ben Yehuda, half bar half restaurant. Walter and Goliath arrived together. They made a bizarre couple, Goliath's six and a half feet towering over the squat, Neanderthal figure of the researcher, scurrying to keep up with him through the restaurant tables. They were laughing.

Charlie had known Goliath a long time, and liked him a lot. The big cameraman embodied many of the Israeli virtues – directness, intelligence, passion, fiercely democratic instincts, a minimum of cant, plus a very un-Israeli appetite for carnal excess. Also, Goliath was very good at his job. He couldn't handle money, drink or women, but he took good pictures, even in the most unpromising situations. He was the man who taught Charlie to carry a couple of bottles of blood when filming wars and disasters, so that when seats on planes and helicopters were hard to find you could claim to be carrying medical supplies. Worked miracles getting in places other camera crews weren't allowed. Charlie had worked with him maybe a dozen times, often in uncomfortable places. The most recent was eight years ago.

'You know what this kid just told me?' Goliath asked Charlie. 'A joke. Hold on, let me get this right. "Doctor, doctor, I can't feel my hands." '

Walter shook his head despairingly.

'Try again.'

Goliath concentrated.

'OK. "Doctor, doctor, I can't feel my legs." '

Another pause. Walter nodded.

' "I know," says the doctor,' Goliath continued. ' "We just amputated your hands." '

He turned to Walter.

'Right?'

'Right.'

'And you must be Julia.' He gave her a little bow, and turned back to Charlie. 'How you doing, kid?'

Charlie was doing fine. His hand disappeared into Goliath's massive palm.

'Just fine? Don't talk bullshit, Kavanagh. You're alive, you're in Jerusalem, someone else is paying for the wine. This bastard,' he told Julia, 'saved my life, you know that? Lebanon, June seventy-eight, we were caught in a fire-fight outside Sidon, the car went up in smoke. I was trapped inside, lead flying everywhere, he pulled me out. Real Sly Stallone stuff. Lord knows why he bothered.'

'You owed me money,' said Charlie.

'Lies.' Goliath looked him up and down. 'God, how you've aged.'

'You too.'

'You know how old I am, arsehole? Fifty-seven.'

'Are you fuck.'

'OK, forty-nine, what's the difference?' He pulled up a chair. 'I tell you what the difference is. The difference is that at our age people are more impressed if you add a few years on. All those celebrity birthday lists they print in the papers – "Jane Fonda will be sixty-three on Thursday", and a picture of her in leg-warmers looking ten years younger. Everyone says "Isn't amazing for her age, how does she do it?" She does it by being ten years younger than she tells the papers she is. Smart girl. How old are you, Julia?'

'Sixteen,' said Charlie.

'And you two . . .?'

'Every night,' said Julia.

'I need a drink,' complained Goliath, wiping his hands on his T-shirt and reaching for the bottle. 'And tell me about this fiasco we're shooting next week.'

'Piss off, cack.'

'I beg your pardon?'

'Piss off, cack. French cameraman called Grossjean I worked with, anything you asked him to do, he said "piss off, cack". Took me a week to work out what he was saying.'

Goliath shook his head.

'Piece of cake,' Charlie explained. 'We're here to do The

Wonderful World of David Bermant. For the Americans. It's a dinner party, seven talking heads. Four cameras.'

'This is a remote?'

'We call them OB's in England.'

'OK. Live?'

'Live.'

'Where?'

'A restaurant.'

'Any particular restaurant?'

'Still to be arranged,' said Charlie.

'You want me to supply the gear?'

'That's the plan.'

'Piece of bread,' said Goliath. 'Tell me what you want.'

Julia got out her pad and read out the list. Goliath listened, nodding, scribbling notes on the back of a cigarette packet.

'You paying dollars or local?'

'Dollars,' said Charlie. 'Used notes.'

'I love you. Doesn't sound too much of a problem. I'll need to make calls. Who's handling the transmission?'

'Israeli Broadcasting Authority. Bezeq will provide the land-lines from the OB to the satellite dish.'

Walter grabbed a waiter.

'Excuse me, do you sell food here?'

The researcher ordered kebabs: the others stuck to their liquor.

Two hours later they were still there, Julia and Walter examining their coffee-cups, Charlie with his legs out straight and his chair tilted back, Goliath by now in full song. It was like old times, except that this time Charlie was cheating at the drink, taking small sips of wine and plenty of mineral water. Goliath drank deep and often.

' "They ain't making Jews like Jesus any more," ' he roared. ' "They don't turn the other cheek the way they did before" – shit, what time is it?'

'Seven-fifteen.'

'Fuck your mother, I'm meant to be babysitting. Where you staying?'

'The Anani,' said Charlie.

'Flash bastards,' said Goliath. 'I'll call you tomorrow.'

'Is he really that good?' asked Julia when he'd left.

'Brilliant. Even when he's sober.'

Walter had brought more notes and cuttings and a provisional schedule. Tomorrow morning they'd meet Chaim Ezra at his office. In the afternoon they were due at Kefar Sharon, Reuven Liel's kibbutz, ten miles north of the Tel Aviv-Jerusalem highway. Friday, they were in Jerusalem all day: in the morning they'd talk to Danny Feinberg, after lunch they'd cross to the Old City and meet Tyler at home in the Jewish Quarter. Saturday they'd travel south to Eilat on the Red Sea to meet Kimche, stopping off on Kaufman in Beersheba on the way. Sunday they'd drive back to Jerusalem, finalise a shooting script, edit together the archive and titles, get ready for the big day.

'Sounds like a bus tour,' Charlie complained. 'Six geriatrics in four days.'

It was eight o'clock by the time Charlie and Julia got back to the Anani.

The hotel was full of cops. They met three of them in the car park on their way in, surly young men with tired, angry faces loitering by the line of blue and white Ford Transits with mesh on the windows and aerials on the roof. Charlie gave them a smile and got nothing back, not even a nod. These cops didn't look like cops, but they didn't look much like hotel guests either. Two wore blue nylon tracksuits and carried sports grips, the third wore cheap Cypriot jeans and a white shirt and carried a leather jacket on a hanger in a dry-cleaner's bag.

Inside it was worse. The lobby was packed with them, maybe thirty or forty, sitting around five to a sofa drinking coffee from thermoses, smoking acrid cigarettes and reading the sports pages of the tabloid papers. These weren't teenage IDF conscripts, the kind they'd seen idling loutishly around town the day before: these were full-timers, professionals. They reminded Charlie of the sort of hulks you'd find in a gym off Belfast's Shankhill Road, young, confident, fit but overweight, shirt-sleeves rolled back over thick ham-hock forearms, bellies showing between their tracksuit tops and trousers, average age maybe twenty-four. In a fight they'd know how to handle themselves, but no discipline, it would be every man for himself. Some were in mufti, some in riot gear, some coming off duty, others about to start. There were guns everywhere, Uzis and M16's and Galils, shields and helmets and long thin batons, the kind the British used during the Mandate. The Brits left a lot behind after the Mandate, including the red GVIR letterboxes and the laws which allowed the Israelis to brick up or bulldoze houses and deport their occupants without trial.

'Good evening,' Charlie tried again as he and Julia made their way across the lobby.

No one looked up.

'Jesus,' said Julia quietly. 'What happened?'

'He forgot to buy a TV licence,' Charlie explained.

Salam was full of apologies.

'It's temporary, I promise. They bring them in from out of town, we have not much choice. They'll stay a few days, maybe a week.'

'They pay you?' asked Charlie.

'Corporate rates.'

Another patrol came in, dressed in one-piece navy-blue body suits, helmets under their arms. Charlie and Julia fled to the bar, only to find three tables occupied by NCOs and officers, briefcases out, doing their paperwork.

'This happen often?' Charlie asked the waiter.

'Since last year.'

Twenty years Charlie had been coming to the Anani, off and on, and now when he thought of it this was what he'd remember.

'No you won't,' said Julia. 'We'll laugh about it, that's all.'

The future tense put him at ease again. They found a quiet corner and ordered drinks. They were both tired. Charlie pulled his unread copy of the *Jerusalem Post* out of his shoulder bag and started reading.

'What's new?' asked Julia.

'Scotland Yard picked up two Arab students for the Yaakov bombing. The British Foreign Secretary says it's the Libyans, the Libyans say the Israelis set up their own man. Settlers' leaders have established a protest camp in the park opposite the Prime Minister's office to demand tougher action in the Territories. Again – they do it about once a quarter, provided the weather's reasonable. Ariel Sharon joined them for the photo-call. The Syrians deny they're building a chemical weapons plant at Duma.' He turned over to the inside back page. 'The national basketball team beat Fiji eighty-six/eighty-five in the quarter-finals of the World Cup in Mexico City. You want more?'

Charlie looked up, winced, and hid his head in the paper.

'Don't look round,' he hissed.

But it was too late.

'Kavanagh!'

Charlie swallowed a quick mouthful of whiskey and choked.

'Hello Vincent,' he spluttered, rising to his feet. 'What the hell are you doing here?'

Vincent Fallop was plump and scrofulous. His clothes smelt of old sweat and tobacco, his stomach hung over his belt, and his greying hair was lank and oily and too long for his age, which must have been around fifty. He wore a lightweight suit, dandruffed at the collar and slightly stained and crumpled around the crotch.

'Freebie. There's a UK trade delegation in town, hungry for sympathetic exposure. Rest of the posse are staying at the Sheraton, I told them I had an allergy to Muzak. That was before I knew Anani had called in the military. Spare bed over there, if you don't mind sharing a room with a halitosis victim from the *Glasgow Herald*. Mind if I join you?'

Charlie minded a lot.

'No, of course not. Vincent, this is Julia. Julia, this is Vincent Fallop. Investigative reporter, fashion model and amateur piss-artist . . .'

'Do you work in television too?' asked Julia as he sat down.

'Not any more, dear. I'm a *Sunday Telegraph* man now, very respectable. What are you two up to?'

'Adultery,' Charlie announced.

Dear old Vincent. He was one of those friends you couldn't begin to explain or justify to the outside world. You could spend a week trying to think of a nice thing to say about him and still come up with nothing. He was idle, dishonest, unreliable, pompous, mean, insensitive – and yet, and yet . . . dear old Vincent. Maybe it was just that Charlie had known him so long, spent so many hours with him running with the hack pack, watching minor riots and demonstrations, waiting around on damp pavements for union meetings to break up, watching government Ministers nodding sympathetically at confused pensioners in community centre cafeterias. And wherever he went you knew he'd behave grossly, randomly insulting anyone who crossed his path: bishops, waitresses, accident victims in their hospital beds, widows with the tears still wet on their cheeks. No one who knew Vincent ever consciously arranged to meet him again, but you knew he'd crop up sooner or later.

Vincent helped himself to one of Charlie's cigarettes, stretched over and picked up Julia's lighter.

'Haven't seen you in ages, Charlie. Thought you'd retired.'

'I have. Moved down to Worthing, bought a nice little bungalow near the golf course, taken up evening classes ...'

'Fuck off and buy me a drink.'

Charlie cringed. She'll hate him. She'll despise me for even knowing him. The scales will fall from her eyes and she'll see me for what I am, another noisy opinionated arrogant journo.

'What can I get you, Vincent?'

'Same as ever, Pernod and pop. Large.'

'Julia?'

He looked at her miserably across the candlelight. She gave him a kick under the table, and looked at her watch.

'Have we time?'

'Shit. When are we due there?'

'Ten-thirty. A quick one.'

'Due where?' asked Vincent.

'The Wailing Wall,' Charlie improvised. 'To see a man about a dog.'

'I checked, it's sold. You eaten yet?'

'He's serious,' Julia interrupted. 'We do have to meet someone. Get the drinks, Charlie, and I'll call a cab.'

Charlie walked with her as far as the bar.

'I'm sorry,' he whispered.

'Why?' She took hold of his hand. 'He's magnificent. I'm just not sure if I can face a whole evening.'

The cab took fifteen minutes to arrive, during which Vincent subjected them to his overview of the Middle East situation. Vincent suffered strong obligations to omniscience, and could produce an opinion on any subject you cared to mention at the pop of a wine-cork. He'd been to so many places that he often imagined he'd been everywhere. And it was like much-talked about books or films – after a while you genuinely convince yourself you've read or seen them. He hated admitting to people that he didn't know about Somalia, or Finland, or even Lincolnshire. And anyway so much of life was generic these days – what was true of one country was like as not true of another. Charlie remembered meeting him at Heathrow once on his way to Bhutan. 'Bhutan?' Vincent had said. 'You lucky bastard, can't think of anywhere I'd rather be right now. Mind you they've ruined the coast, used to be beautiful before they built all those hotels.'

Bhutan, of course, doesn't have a coastline.

Israel's fundamental problem, he told them, was birth control. 'To solve a problem like this you need a certain intelligence, plus the muscle to impose your solution. And there's less and less intelligence around. More and more muscle, less and less IQ. Give us another fag, Charlie.'

He lit up and slipped Julia's lighter into his pocket.

'The reason there's less and less IQ around is because smart-arses like us look at the world and see it's overpopulated, which it clearly is. So we stop breeding. But no one else does, the rest of the planet's podding away like gerbils. The stupider they are, the more they breed, and bleeding-heart Western liberals keep shipping them plane-loads of antibiotics and EC-surplus milk to make sure none of their progeny snuff it. Net result, the world gets proportionately stupider by the hour. And the problems get worse. So what do we do about it? We feel guilty. We think it's our fault that idiots with thirteen children can't be bothered to use a condom. You don't need to win wars or elections any more, you just up tools and make babies, out-breed the opposition. Sorry, I'm not offending you am I dear?'

Julia sucked on her cigarette, gave Charlie's shin another surreptitious tap, and shook her head.

'Not at all.'

'Good. Where was I. The numbers game, yes. This country was originally set up by intellectuals – Europe's finest. Full of good practical idealism – kibbutzes, free health service, no shirkers, all that stuff. And the first thing they do is throw their

90

gates open to all-comers, any Jew who fancies a change of scene. Very altruistic. Except that these all-comers aren't Nobel Laureates or Booker Prize winners, they're peasants – Moroccans, Iraquis, Yemenis, even Ethiopians. Not an O-Level in sight; most of them can't even tie their shoe laces, let alone perform a lobotomy. But what they can do is reproduce, bloody brilliant at it – apparently the climate helps too. And before you can say Yom Kippur they're in the majority, voting the founding fathers out the window, replacing them with a lot of hot-blooded illiterate rabble-rousers. Same goes for the Arabs. In the days of the British Protectorate they had village elders and headmen – devious lot, but at least you could do business with them. Look at them now. The Palestinian camps have one of the highest birth rates in the world, churning out trigger-happy little guerrillas by the thousand, year in, year out. Do you know what the average age on the West Bank is? The *average*? *Fifteen.* Can you believe that, Kavanagh? Half the Arabs on the West Bank are under fifteen. Eat your heart out, Dr. Malthus. That must be your cab now.'

'Maybe we'll see you later,' Charlie offered.

'Doubt it, I'm for an early night. Picked up *Memoirs of a Victorian Maid* at the airport this morning, thought I might give it a whirl, get the problems of export/import off my mind. And an early start, they're taking us on The Tour. Beersheba and Dimona tomorrow, then on to the Dead Sea salt works.' He pocketed Charlie's cigarettes. 'Tell you what – you're not going to be in Tel Aviv tomorrow, are you?'

They weren't sure.

'The Embassy's throwing a thrash for the delegation. Free Pimms, all the Twiglets you can eat. Starts at around six, I think. Just show your NUJ card, tell them you're working for *The Economist.* I'll warn them to expect you.'

'Where did you find him?' asked Julia as they sat back in the safety of the taxi.

'I lifted up a stone,' said Charlie, 'and he was sticking to the bottom.'

8

THE NEXT MORNING THE weather broke. Milky curtains of rain lashed across the hillsides, and torrents of water overflowed the gutters and rattled down the storm drains, washing building materials into the streets, causing traffic chaos as commuters battled the one-way systems. Low cloud enveloped the tops of the high-rise buildings like a wet duvet, and in the parks trees bent like grass before the gate.

Charlie and Julia went to see Chaim Ezra. They went alone: Walter was face-down in the viewing theatre all day, looking at archive film.

The Deputy Prime Minister's time was tight, and they'd been allocated a quarter of an hour at ten o'clock, provided that Chaim's meeting with the head of the Bank of Israel didn't over-run. The Ministry of Finance is the first of three long rectangular office-blocks built into the side of the hill on Eliezer Kaplan. Number two houses the Ministry of the Interior, number three the Prime Minister's office. All around is open parkland, which the Ministries share with the Israel Museum, the Hebrew University, the Wise Auditorium and the Knesset itself.

A friend of Charlie's once made the mistake of wearing a sports jacket to interview the Shah of Iran, and wound up on the secret police files as a dangerous subversive. Ezra wasn't the Shah, but he was a powerful man, and likely to get more so. Charlie had got out the suit and tie again. A little tact costs you nothing. Julia produced an elegant, crushproof jersey dress from her hold-all, worn with a simple stainless-steel necklace, silver earrings, black stockings and high heels.

They checked in at the reception desk at quarter to ten.

'Good luck,' Charlie whispered while the clerk made a phone call.

Julia lit a cigarette and sucked on it hard.

'Thanks. And you.'

A junior PR man arrived and guided them through the security checks to the lift.

'You're from NBC?'

'Wrong, I'm afraid,' said Julia. 'We're just us.'

The PR consulted his clipboard.

'My mistake. You're Cornwall Associates. Come on up. Can I get you coffee?'

They waited for Chaim among the pot-plants and celebrity photos in his outer office. Chaim with Ben Gurion, Chaim with Jimmy Carter, Chaim with Topol and Barbra Streisand and Danny Kaye.

'This is Monday night we're talking about,' the PR checked again. 'You have a location?'

'Not yet.'

'And who else will be taking part?'

'It's a secret.'

'Not to us it isn't. We need all the participants, crew names, everyone who'll be in the building on the night.'

'Oh,' said Julia. 'The crew won't be a problem. But we'd rather the participants didn't know in advance who else will be there.'

'I'm afraid we'll need to know.'

'I don't suppose there's any way we could tell you without the Minister knowing, is there?' asked Charlie.

'Maybe. I'll need to talk to security. Where can I reach you – you have an office?'

'Only a bedroom, I'm afraid,' said Julia.

The PR smiled.

'Does it have a phone?'

And then Chaim arrived through the double doors. Julia and Charlie stood up and shook hands, then Chaim spoke in Hebrew with the aide, briefing himself on the identity of the strangers in his office. As soon as he had the facts he turned on his beaming politician's smile.

'This is in honour of David, right?' His manner was charming, that of a man well used to ingratiating himself with the Press. 'A pre-emptive strike at America. I like it.'

Charlie explained the programme format, and Chaim nodded thoughtfully.

'I shouldn't do it, of course,' he said when Charlie had finished. 'I'll look like I'm a disciple sitting at the feet of the great Bermant. I'm meant to be his boss.'

'But you'll do it?' asked Julia.

'Of course, my dear. There are a lot of things I'd like the old fox to admit to. How many of them are transmittable is another question. You going much into his background?'

'A bit.'

'You dare ask him what happened with him and me and the two blonde youth delegates the last night of the sixty-two Labour Party Conference in Tiberias, I have alibis, several alibis. And a good lawyer.' And then his expression turned serious. 'Be gentle with him, he's a good man. You dig too deep in anyone's life you find things they're not too proud of.'

Charlie wondered what he was hinting at. And why.

Outside the window a helicopter hovered over the Wohl Rose Garden.

'Excuse me,' Chaim waved at the helipad, 'My taxi's here. I look forward to seeing you on Tuesday.'

'Monday,' the PR corrected him.

'Whenever. Meanwhile enjoy your stay.'

And then he was gone, pausing to give them both a double-fisted handshake.

'One up and five to go,' said Charlie as they handed their passes back in at the desk.

They had lunch in town, and by two were on the road again, headlights on and windscreen wipers slashing at the downpour, negotiating the one-way systems towards the Jaffa Road. Charlie had the radio tuned to Abie Nathan's Voice of Peace, anchored somewhere off Tel Aviv.

'No More War,' grunted Abie, followed by a soft-drink commercial. Then Dobie Grey sang 'Drift Away'. Always had good taste in music did Abie, even if his record collection was a bit dusty.

After the Central Bus Station the traffic thinned, and they joined the main Tel Aviv highway, twisting down the rugged pine-clad valley towards the coastal plain. At Latrun they turned right towards Petah Tiqwa, and drove north for fifteen miles, along the fringes of the foothills. The countryside was gentler now, and green, wide unfenced fields of spring wheat dotted with citrus orchards and groves of eucalyptus. Kibbutz Kefar Sharon was signposted at a point where the old Jerusalem-Haifa railway line recrossed the road for the third time.

The kibbutz movement has never been as big as the outside world assumes – at the height of its pioneering strength it never accounted for more than seven per cent of the population. But historically its influence always far outweighed its size, and for the first forty years of the State, politicians with kibbutz connections, from Ben Gurion on, were a major force in the Labour Party. 'From each according to his ability, to each according to his needs' is an appealing philosophy, and the image of the kibbutz, its communal living and democratic decision-making, gave Israel a sense of idealism and social experiment.

Kefar Sharon was founded in 1938 by a small group of Jews fleeing from Hitler's Germany. They arrived in the summer, forty of them, in the middle of a June night, and built watch-towers and a wooden stockade on a low hill, finished and secure by the time the sun rose the following morning. Initially relations with the inhabitants of the neighbouring Arab village had been reasonably amicable, but it didn't last. In 1948, in the midst of the fighting, with the Arab Legion less than fifteen miles away to the east, the Haganah surrounded the village, and the Arabs left.

The kibbutz had by then grown to a community of two hundred. In the following decade it doubled its population, and by the mid-sixties there were over five hundred people living in Kefar Sharon, augmented by short-term volunteers from Europe, by no means all Jews. They cultivated citrus fruit and avocados, cattle and poultry. A school was built, and a swimming pool, and an administration building with a theatre and health clinic. The children lived in the school house, visiting their parents on the Sabbath.

Some time in the early eighties things started to go wrong. The volunteers were fewer, the young started to leave, the numbers fell. Parents wanted to keep their children at home and not send them to live in the school house. A decision in principle was made, but there were practical problems: the houses were built for couples on their own, and they couldn't afford to add bedrooms for the children. A sharp frost destroyed the avocado crop, and the next year they found that their customers in Europe had found alternative suppliers in Latin America. The fruit was left to rot. Two years later the same happened with the citrus, and the orchards were dug up. A young Danish volunteer started a pottery, but her thick brown domestic ware was awkward and fragile, and the pottery closed after a year. Then they thought of opening a tourist guest-house, but there was nothing much for tourists to do: they were too far from the sea, too close to Jerusalem. Some people advocated a light industry, plastics or packaging; but they had no knowledge of commerce, no skills in marketing or distribution, and no money to build a factory anyway. Only government intervention saved Kefar Sharon from bankruptcy. One reason the Labour Party kept going into coalition was to keep its fingers on the state purse-strings so that it could continue to subsidise its supports in the kibbutz and the Histradut, the country's powerful but bankrupt union organisation.

Charlie and Julia had reached the entrance, where a sentry box and a blue and white Israeli flag guarded an eight-foot double gate in the perimeter fence. Beyond, up a slight rise, they could see rows of single-storey chalets among the trees, a water tower, corrugated iron sheds and what looked like a sawmill. The air smelled of chicken sheds and cow pens and diesel.

The gate guard was a bearded youth, who spoke rudimentary English.

'We're early, I'm afraid,' Julia apologised.

It was still only twenty to three.

'No matter.'

He wrote their names down in phonetic Hebrew, phoned through to the administration, and gave them directions. A Hercules transport flew in over the tree tops, tail lights flashing, heading for the military airfield across the hill. The rain had stopped, but the cloud was low and grey, and the light an ominous yellow, promising more storms later.

They reached a T-junction; Charlie turned left, towards a

96

two-storey concrete building with a flat roof and ornamental palms outside. There was red mud everywhere, on the road, under the trees, in the flower beds.

'I wonder what it's like to live in a place like this,' asked Charlie. 'I mean I can see the attraction, but the claustrophobia must be desperate. Can you imagine it? Being born somewhere, living your whole life there, with the same people, the same landscape, same problems? That's all there is to your entire existence.'

'I'd love it,' said Julia. 'Perpetual school.'

'You *liked* school?'

'I'm afraid so. I couldn't wait to leave, but I loved it while I was there.'

'You're not meant to admit things like that,' said Charlie.

They were met by the kibbutz secretary, a pear-bottomed woman of sixty with very short grey hair. She took a dying cigarette butt out of her mouth, dropped it and ground it under her shoe.

'Sarah Kaplan,' she introduced herself, with a bony hand-shake. 'The Committee will be here at three o'clock, perhaps you'd like some coffee?'

'The Committee?' asked Charlie innocently.

'To discuss the programme, there are some things some people are not happy with. We can talk about them.'

'What sort of things?'

'The interviews, what things we would like you to film.'

'I see,' said Charlie, catching Julia's eye. 'Perhaps I should explain. We're not planning to film or do any interviews here, we've come to talk to Reuven Liel about a programme which we're making in Jerusalem next week.'

'I know. Walter Azeff explained it to me. He's not coming today?'

'Walter? No. You know him?'

'I grew up with his father. And his sister lived with us for a while, she'd been ill and came here to convalesce. This programme is Walter's idea?'

'No, he's just researching it.'

'It's quite an interesting idea. Quite, but not very. I think maybe we have something better.'

97

'Oh,' said Charlie. 'Well yes, then coffee would be nice.'

They walked across to the dining block, Charlie trying to make light conversation. Sarah Kaplan didn't have much light conversation. He pointed to an arrangement of concrete blocks decorated with orange ceramic tiles.

'Who does your sculpture?'

'A Roumanian woman. You like it?'

'Yes,' said Charlie. 'I do.'

'I think it's hideous.'

At last Sarah smiled, and suddenly Charlie realised she wasn't being rude. There was no hostility here, just a certain wry, sad diffidence.

The dining block was huge and echoing, the size of a gymnasium, and contained maybe thirty rectangular tables arranged in ranks down the length of a glass wall. It was empty except for a solitary cat asleep beside a radiator. They collected cups from a rack and filled them from a thermos jug on the self-service counter. Julia picked a table at random and sat down.

'Not this one, please, there is one reserved for us,' said Sarah, and marched them the length of the hall, where another table had been decorated with a jam-jar of plastic flowers and two foil ashtrays.

'Do you take it in turns to do the cooking?' asked Julia.

'No. The cooks take it in turn to do the cooking.'

'I see.'

The Committee arrived and were introduced one by one.

'I don't wish to appear ungrateful,' Charlie told them, 'but I think we may be wasting your time. Unfortunately this isn't a programme about Kefar Sharon, or the kibbutz movement: it's a programme in which one particular member of your kibbutz may, if he agrees, take part, along with a number of other Israelis.'

'Twenty-five years ago, when you thought we made interesting television, you people couldn't make enough programmes about us,' objected Ephraim, a bearded *sabra* in his forties. 'Every week there were crews here, from England, France, Scandinavia, Germany, North America. Now we need you, and you don't want to know. Unless you tell the world about us, no one tells them. We don't have money to make our ideas known.'

'You're right,' said Julia.

'Then do something about it.'

'We can't, not this time.'

'Then when?'

'Another time. But you still haven't told us your idea.'

'You have to realise, we don't understand television. We're not qualified to produce ideas. What we are offering is a subject: we hope you might have the idea.'

The meeting lasted an hour.

'OK,' said Sarah finally, 'you understand us, we understand you, thank you for listening. Maybe you'll come back some time anyway.'

'I hope so,' said Charlie.

At moments like this he hated himself and hated the business, the smiling half-truths with which he'd learned to brush off ordinary decent people who didn't fit in to a programme, the patronising assumption that they didn't matter, that his job was somehow more important than theirs. Hated it, and kept doing it.

'I'll take you to meet Reuven Liel,' said Sarah, finishing her coffee.

They left the administration building, and walked along a concrete path between the trees. The rest of the Committee wandered back off to the kindergarten and the chicken sheds and workshops.

'How does a man like Reuven fit in to the kibbutz?' asked Julia.

'You mean how does he fit himself in, or how do we fit him in?'

'Both, I suppose.'

'To be honest, with some difficulty. He's still a member. He still lives here, still belongs. When he was an ambassador he had a life outside and to an extent that was his choice, but it can be useful to a community to have a foot in the outside world. It happens quite a lot: we have a teacher's wife who works as a hostess for El Al, for example, and an engineer who does three days a week with a firm in Tel Aviv, and others too. They're still members, their families are still kibbutz families.

With Reuven it has always been a little difficult, but I think that's to do with him as much as us. You've met him?'

'No.'

'He was a good ambassador in Paris, I'm told, also in Montreal. Washington, I gather, was not such a success. But then it's a difficult job, there are too many Jews in America.' She put her hand on Charlie's arm. 'It's all right, it's a joke. It's what they always say about Israel, the Jews own all the best businesses.'

Another Hercules flew in overhead, so low that Charlie could see the crew's faces. They'd reached a line of low, single-storey three-room chalets, yellow breeze-block shoeboxes which their occupants had tried to make individual with little gardens and ornaments. Not primitive, but simple, their balconies crowded with bicycles, garden chairs with rotted seats, half-dead geraniums in improvised pots.

Reuven's was the last house in the row, and different from the others. The garden was neat and well-tended, a small lawn and miniature flowerbeds laid out around a tamarisk tree, hedged in by rose bushes and dwarf juniper. In place of the bicycles and geranium-pots, the balcony was furnished with urns and amphorae and broken-off chunks of marble pediments. Reuven Liel's hobby was archaeology.

'He was a friend of Moshe Dayan,' Sarah explained. 'Whenever someone started excavating a new site, they'd show up together as an official delegation and pocket a few souvenirs. He has rather a fine collection.'

Inside, the house was like a museum, every inch of wall-space crammed with shelves and display cabinets, the floor crowded with pots and sculpture. There was just room among the exhibits in the living room for a small two-seater sofa, a coffee table and two upright chairs. Sarah made the introductions, shook hands and left them to it.

'You'll not forget to come back,' she told Charlie.

'Of course not.'

Down by the chicken sheds a rooster crowed.

The old man had an almost full head of curly hair, which made him look younger than his seventy-five years. Hair also sprouted from his ears and nostrils, and his skin looked as thick and grey as a rhino's. He wore an old brown corduroy jacket over a green and blue check shirt, flannel trousers and sandals.

Before they got down to business he showed Charlie and Julia round the rooms, display case by display case. You didn't need to know much about archaeology to realise you were in the presence of a remarkable collection. Liel was no amateur magpie, but a professional, precise and obsessive. Piece after piece was described and compared favourably with similar exhibits in the Israel Museum in Jerusalem: Nabataean vases from Avdat, crusader brooches from Acre, Roman pottery from Caesarea, Mesolithic tools from Jericho, Canaanite baskets, Jewish ritual bowls from Capernaum and Hebron, all lovingly labelled and catalogued.

'You found all these yourself?' asked Charlie innocently.

'Na,' Reuven shook his head. 'Some, most even. Some I get from friends, people who know they'll have a safe home. Sending precious artifacts to a museum is like putting your children in an institution. No one to love and understand them. Some I buy, very occasionally. But not at auction. Privately.'

He made herb tea in the little back kitchen, and sat them down side by side on the sofa.

'Did Walter Azeff explain what this programme's about, Mr Liel?' Charlie asked him.

'A little. As I understand it we all have supper with David Bermant, and ask him awkward questions, and you film us and show it to the Americans, who don't understand a word.' He smiled. 'A novel idea. How long is this programme to be?'

'An hour,' said Charlie.

More lies. But if he told him thirty-eight minutes the ambassador might cry off. An hour was bad enough.

'And there are six interrogators? That means he will answer each of us for ten minutes.'

'More or less.'

'About what? About the past, or about now?'

'A bit of both.'

'OK, I'll tell you about the past.' He sat down. 'The Bermants and my parents came to Palestine together, it was in thirty-three, thirty-four perhaps. After Hitler became Chancellor, but before everyone realised what would happen. I think old man Bermant maybe realised. When we arrived we were living up North, near Haifa. David and I were the same age, we used to talk to each other in Hebrew because our parents couldn't understand, it was like a private code between us. His family came from Magdeburg, I think. We were from Berlin, they met on the journey out here and became friends. The Bermants were wealthy when they arrived, but they knew nothing of agriculture, nothing. The father had been a businessman, a banker, something like that. When they came they had money, they bought land, and tried all sorts of things, cattle, citrus fruit, vegetables, cheesemaking. None of it worked, and they ran out of money. The same with a lot of people, a lot died of malaria, a lot gave up and went home. My own father was a doctor, so for us it was easier, people always need a doctor. But the Bermants were not so lucky. Before they had been used to luxury, a big house, servants, now they lived like peasants. But they decided to stay anyway. I remember very clearly in the thirties, a family of their relatives came from Posnan for a visit, wealthy people. They were shocked at how the family was living, the clothes they wore, what they ate, seeing David's father milking cows and digging latrines. They begged the Bermants to come home to Germany with them. But they wouldn't go, and their relatives went home alone.' Reuven shrugged his shoulders. 'Back to the gas chambers. That was David's family, that was how it began for him, I suppose.'

They talked for an hour and a half, about growing up in Palestine under the Mandate, about the war and the British and the struggle for independence.

'I think David's a bitter man now, he thinks the country didn't work out the way it should have done. Myself I'm not so sure, I think we've done OK. Not perfect, but better than it might be.'

'Are you sad your children have left Israel?' asked Julia.

Reuven had two sons, both now in America. His wife was there now, visiting them.

'A little. It's more difficult for my wife. I have my other children, you see.' He waved at his cabinets. 'So. You want me on Monday evening, am I right? Is there anything special I should wear? I have an evening suit, but it's a long time since it was worn. Maybe I've shrunk a little, maybe the moths have had it by now.'

'Come as you want,' said Charlie. 'Nothing too formal, just be comfortable.'

'And you won't tell me who else will be there?'

'No, no one knows. Not even the host.'

They left at six.

'How far's Tel Aviv from here?' Julia wondered out loud to Charlie.

'Thirty miles, I'd guess. Why?'

'Vincent's party. Had you forgotten?'

9

BUSINESS WAS QUIET IN Business Class: Eric was the only passenger in the front cabin. The hostess liked Eric, very quiet and considerate. A couple of hours into the flight she decided to stop being a hostess, collected a bottle from the galley and sat down beside him to watch the movie.

'More champagne?' she offered.

Eric took off his headphones.

'Can I ask you something?'

'Sure.'

'Is it your experience that people *like* champagne? I know they drink it, but did you ever meet anyone who *liked* it?'

She thought for a moment.

'The President's wife. James Mason used to. And kids. Once in a while someone uses it to dope a kid that's crying, seems to work.'

'That's all?'

Another pause while she thought some more.

'That's all.'

'Then why do you serve it?'

'You travel back there in steerage you pay maybe five hundred dollars for your ticket. You travel up here in Business Class you pay a thousand. Or your company does. Champagne costs the airline four dollars a bottle. I never made college but I can do sums.'

'Doesn't mean they have to drink it.'

'They drink it because they think that's how you behave in Business Class.'

'Do you know what I like about Israel?' Eric said. 'You never get held up by air traffic problems. New York, Washington, London, Frankfurt, Amsterdam, it's chronic these days. Twelve hours hanging round the terminal waiting to take off, an hour or two getting someplace, three hours stacking overhead, another half hour while the pilot finds a place to park the thing once he's landed. At Tel Aviv you have the airport to yourselves.'

'That's because no one wants to come here any more,' said the hostess. ' "Visit Israel, Land of a Thousand Roadblocks". Even the Christians are staying away.'

'Do you mind? I mean, you know what they say, it's nice to have visitors, but the best part is when they leave.'

'You know the difference between being an air hostess and being a waitress? Waitresses get tips. In this job the fewer passengers you have the happier you are.'

'That's what I figured,' said Eric.

'Kavanagh and Cornwall, *Economist*', said Charlie confidently.

The gate guard checked their passports against a list, double checked, shook his head. It was half-past six.

'Vincent Fallop said he'd leave word,' Charlie tried again, holding out his Press card.

The guard flicked through his clipboard.

'Can you spell that for me, sir?'

'F for effort, a for aitch, el for elephant, o as in Wateau, P –'

Julia kicked his shin. Charlie was panting for a drink.

'Ellerman, Emerson, Evans, Fairfax, Falconer – here we are, Fallop. Plus two. Right you are.'

They moved in through the gates and joined the polite queue of businessmen and diplomats that stretched round the side of the Residence, past groves of oleander and mimosa, to the fresh-shaved lawns where Sir Piers and Lady Wasson had taken up their welcoming positions under a white canvas awning. Chinese lanterns hung from the trees. The rain had cleared, and a warm damp wind blew in from the Mediterranean. The temperature was in the upper sixties.

'Nice to meet you, splendid, so glad you could make it, good, good, excellent, ha ha ha,' Sir Piers parrotted to all comers, while to his right his floral-frocked, over-powdered wife flashed her weary smile on and off like a lighthouse, hoping perfume and toothpaste had smothered the gin on her breath. A small brass band played light classics on the balcony.

'Ever been to one of these before?' Charlie asked Julia as they bent together towards a tray of fishpaste sandwiches.

'My father was in the British Council, remember?' She took a pack of cigarettes out of her handbag. 'Where's the drink?'

All around them loud Anglo-Saxon voices ricocheted across the turf.

'I'm a great believer in feminism,' bellowed the Military attaché.

'Don't you mean femininity, Hugh?'

'Do I? Perhaps I do.'

'Poor old Guy,' hooted someone else, 'set off to discover himself and wound up discovering Ulan Bator, ha ha ha!'

There was no sign of Vincent, but Charlie spotted another familiar figure, standing with his back to the herbaceous border, dispensing thin smiles to passing acquaintances and fingering his wine-glass.

'Good God. It's Hogarth.'

'How do you do,' interrupted a short fat woman in a cheap purple sari. 'My name's Golda, I'm Jewish, I'm Lesbian, I'm a Socialist and I've had a hysterectomy. What do you do?'

'I'm Basil,' said Charlie, 'I'm heterosexual and I work for the SAS. This,' he introduced Julia, 'is my mother. She's drunk.'

By the time he looked round again Roger Hogarth had vanished from the flowerbed. He thought he caught sight of him in the thick of a flock of grey-suited trade delegates, and then he was gone again. Meanwhile Susan, a tall toothy woman with large feet and a silk scarf round her neck, wanted to find someone who'd drunk Russian milk. Susan – she pronounced it Soosan, with the lips in a gaping scarlet sphincter – was Someone's Wife.

'They water it, you know,' she brayed. Her voice must have been clearly audible in Damascus. 'It's quite impossible to drink. Heaven knows what it does to the children, their bones must be soft as pilchards'. When we were in Moscow Brian arranged to have all ours brought in on the overnight train from Helsinki.'

Her husband, trousers braced so his waist came half-way up his shirt front, called out from a neighbouring conversation.

'Still, it was a damn sight better than Tegucigalpa, darling.'

'Tegoose?' She threw her eyes to heaven. 'Good God, *nothing* worked in Tegoose!'

Charlie and Julia mingled with the crowd, trying not to giggle.

'I've always wanted to be an ambassador,' said Charlie. 'Not a very important one, somewhere like Nepal, or the Cook Islands. Pleasant house, plenty of servants, reasonable clothing allowance, your own drinks cabinet, *Daily Telegraph* delivered a week late in the diplomatic bag.'

'You'd get bored.'

'Nonsense. I get bored when I'm working sometimes, but I never get bored when I have nothing to do. Ambassadors in small countries have all the spare time in the world. Must be bliss. Monday morning, woke up, had a shit, got dressed, suggested to Perkins he update his report on the prospects for the yam harvest – then what? On a bad day you might issue a visa or spend half an hour drinking coffee with the Prime Minister, give him some advice on English public schools for his pampered offspring. Go to cocktails with the Belgian Ambassador, again. Offer to sell some secrets to the Chinese, haggle over the price a bit. I don't know what the hell else they do.'

'Behave themselves. You'd hate it.'

'You're right. I'd hate it.'

'Anyway,' Soosan's husband was telling anyone who cared to listen, 'the Colonel finally got round to sending me a reference for the man. "Re Captain Dale: I would hesitate to breed from this officer." Haw haw.'

The band came to the end of 'Yellow Submarine'. From somewhere among the roses an unseen Australian voice filled the sudden silence:

'Do you know what really causes wet dreams, Margaret?'

The crowd was enthralled.

'Fuck all to do with sex, if you'll pardon my Croat. Gluttony, pressure of a full stomach on the prostate. So much for Siggie Freud, eh?'

In the confusion Julia palmed two more glasses of Pimms off

a passing waiter. Charlie took a sip, swallowed, grabbed Julia by the hand and navigated her through the crowd.

'Someone I want you to meet. Roger!'

'Kavanagh! Dear boy! How extraordinary!'

Roger Hogarth bounced robotically towards them, left foot and arm advancing together, then the right, so that his tie swung to and from across his chest like a pendulum. Roger had a face like pinched Plasticine, and his hair was flattened in patches, like corn after a storm. He wore an ill-fitting stockbroker's suit with a tired rose in the buttonhole, and stout black brogues: a Morris Oxford of a man.

'Julia, this is Roger. Her Majesty's leading gay diplomat.'

'Shh,' said Roger, blushing. 'All that's long gone. I have a wife.'

'So I've heard. Do I get to meet him?'

'She went back to UK last week.'

'*The* UK,' Charlie corrected him.

'Bugger off, Charles,' said Roger.

'So what are you these days? Last report I had you were doing something with sugar beet in Brussels.'

'I was. Got posted here eighteen months ago.'

'Still trade?'

'Still trade.'

'Enjoying it?'

'It's OK, I suppose.'

Bloody English middle class, always underselling what they're doing – a job's OK, or a bit boring, or curate's eggish. When do you ever hear a public school voice say it likes its work, that it's exciting, or even well paid? Only Americans have the decency to admit when life's treating them well.

'And you?' asked Roger.

'Organised crime, officially. But that's only the cover.' He leaned forward, tapped his nose and whispered in Roger's ear. 'We're making a television programme.'

'For the *Economist*,' interrupted Vincent. 'Hope you don't mind, Roger. Ran into him in Jerusalem last night. Didn't know you knew each other.'

'We were at Cambridge together,' Charlie explained.

Julia went looking for the Ladies.

'So what *are* you up to?' Roger asked.

'Well may you ask.' Charlie scratched the back of his neck. 'She works for something called the Greenbaum Foundation, rang me up out of the blue a week ago and asked me to direct a programme on David Bermant. And here I am.'

'Interesting time to be here,' said Roger. 'A lot hinges on old Bermant.'

'We're seeing him on Monday.'

'Really? Put in a word for our exporters will you, old boy? How's the other Julia?'

'Mrs Kavanagh? In clover. Vitriolic, bitter, foul-mouthing me to the world – hasn't enjoyed herself so much in years. I prefer this one.'

'You going to marry her?'

'Probably. At the moment she's still under warranty. But no complaints so far. Except that she cries in her sleep sometimes. And yours?'

'Mary? Very understanding. Can I interest you in some family photos?'

'Please,' said Vincent.

The voice beyond the bathroom door was still singing in a thin, wobbly soprano:

A tinkling piah-no in the next apartment,
Those stumbling words that told you what my heart-
meant.
And still my heart has wings –
These foolish things, remind me of you . . .

Julia had been waiting ten minutes, and her bladder was in crisis. She knocked on the door. The singing continued:

Gardenia perfume lingering on a pillow
Wild strawbrees only seven francs a-kill-o
And still my heart has wings
These foolish things . . .

'Hallo?' asked Julia, and knocked again.

The singing stopped.

'Go away, Piers.'

'Hallo?' Julia repeated.

'Is that you Piers?'

'No,' Julia shifted her weight to the other foot. 'I'm sorry, I need to use the toilet.'

'Oh. You'd better come in. It's not locked.'

Lady Wasson was lying fully clothed in the empty bath, glass in hand, sentimental tears running down her cheeks. A gin bottle nestled among the sponges and loofahs in the soap basket. She resumed:

> *The smile of Garbo and the scent of roses,*
> *The waiters whistling as the last bar closes,*
> *The song that Crosby sings – these foolish things ...*

The Ambassador's wife dabbed her eyes with a flannel and waved towards the cistern.

'Don't mind me, go ahead.'

'It's a lovely song,' said Julia, wondering what to do.

'Is it?' She sat up in the bath and poured herself another gin, singing between sips.

> *These things are dear to meee*
> *That seem to bring you*
> *so near to meee ...*

... I suppose it is, in a way. Reminds me of a summer in Corfu, years ago. I was only twenty-one. He was married, of course. Ran into him once, long time later, he didn't remember me at all. Who does it remind you of?'

'My father,' said Julia without thinking.

'Mine was a Henry, he's dead now. So tell me about your father, dear. What happened to him?'

'Not a lot. I think whatever happened happened to me.'

By the time she rejoined the party the Ambassador had launched into his speech.

'Tell you a story, Julia,' Vincent insisted when Sir Piers had finished. 'True one, saw it happen myself. In Riyadh, at a dinner for the Saudi Foreign Minister. British Ambassador gets up to make a speech and tells a joke. When he gets to the end of the joke the Brits all piss themselves laughing, which they would, of course, being proper diplomats. But the Foreign Minister doesn't react at all. The First Secretary or Head of Chancery or somesuch realises there's a language problem, leans over politely and starts explaining the joke to Prince wotsit. The Prince raises his hand to stop him. 'Forgive me,' he says, 'Understand joke perfectly. But joke not funny.'

Roger snorted his Pimms.

'What *was* the joke?' asked Charlie.

'There's these two buckets of sick walking down the pavement, and one turns to the other ... no, hold on ... a Welshman, a Pekinese and a Transvestite walk into a sperm bank ...'

They were joined by a drab, bespectacled woman from the Consulate. Roger did the introductions.

'Joan Willis, Vincent Fallop.'

Joan stood with her feet firmly apart, swaying slightly, hands together across her stomach, grasping her handbag. Her bottom stuck out at right angles, as though she'd been kicked in the stomach. When Roger got to Charlie, she blinked.

'Did you say Kavanagh?'

'Yes,' Roger scratched his nose. 'Charlie's a journalist.'

'How extraordinary. We've been looking everywhere for you. A wire came through yesterday. No one knew where you were.'

Charlie sobered up.

'A wire? Who from?'

'London. I think it's about your mother.'

They waited in the Ambassador's study while Roger put the call through to the hospital. The room was so meticulously English that in London it could only have belonged to a foreigner – chintz furnishings, oak bookshelves, hunting prints and watercolours of the Lake District, a bust of Shakespeare and a gilt-framed reproduction of the Queen above the fake-log fireplace. Comfortable, but with that slight air of impermanence that characterises expatriate residences all over the world.

'What's she like?' asked Julia.

'Betty?' Charlie tapped his fingers against the side of the desk. 'How the hell do you start to describe your own mother? She's seventy-five. An odd woman, I suppose. I love her, but she's odd. Like a blindfold crow on speed, can't sit still, abhors a conversational vacuum. I think she's always been terrified of stopping and looking around, or listening, or coming to terms with herself.'

'Is your father still alive?'

'No, he died three years ago. He was her clutch, the only thing that kept her engaged with reality. It's astonishing that anyone could reach seventy-five and have so little under-standing of the outside world. Or maybe she does understand it, and rejects it, I don't know. Either way she's a passionate evangelist of ignorance. She relies entirely on subjective infor-mation – she meets someone who has a niece who once visited New York for a day, and that's all she needs to know about the country. Angela Billow's niece has *been* there and she says it snows on Fifth Avenue in June. Maybe it did the day Angela's niece was there, but for Betty now all North America is snow-bound throughout the summer months. Her friends' random experiences become definitive gospel. The first person she met who used the word cholesterol pronounced it sholestol, and that's it, engraved in marble for all time. She can hear the word pronounced correctly a million times afterwards, but all the dictionaries and etymologists in the world won't get her to change her mind. Her senses all face inwards.'

'I have an aunt like that,' said Roger.

Charlie tapped the top of his head with his index finger.

'It's like the Chinese water torture, lunatic opinions and mispronunciations dripping relentlessly on to your raw skull at all times of day and night. It was fine when Ken was alive because he loved her, and went along with it all, and that was all the confirmation she ever needed. Since he died she's got like a mad dog.'

'Did she work?'

'Not for money. She was a Hospital Visitor, if you call that a job. She had her own views on patient care. If the doctor prescribed something she didn't approve of she'd sabotage them. I don't think she ever knew much about medicine, but she knew what she liked. Starting with fresh air, or what she assumed was fresh air, though what comes in an open window in North London is not exactly fresh. Give her a patient suffering from ingrowing toenails and she'd open every window in the ward. Within the hour he'd be half-dead of pneumonia. And diet, she had a thing about diet. She used to bring Tupperware boxes of food into the hospital and force-feed the patients when no one was looking. Spinach, mostly, and beetroot, and raw eggs. She gave up when she was sixty.'

Joan asked Charlie if he had any other family.

'No, I was as far as they got. I'm a one-off, the object of all her fantasies. Somehow I'm meant to be rich, starving in a garret, successful, unambitious, stable, quixotic, responsible, carefree, humble but a household name, a world traveller who's always at home when he's needed. Which latter I have been, for ages. She'll have been standing up in that bath for a year waiting for me to leave the country before she fell over.'

Bloody Betty. And now she was two thousand miles away, probably dying, and years of irritation dissolved into hopeless guilt.

The switchboard operator at the hospital was Bengali and new to the job.

'Kavanagh,' Charlie shouted again down the echoing line.

'And what is your boy's surname please?'

'He's a she. A geriatric she.'

'OK OK, keep your hairs on.'

Julia and the others withdrew across the study while he got the news. He sat on the corner of the desk, nodding, biting his lip, tapping the desktop with the side of his hand. London did most of the talking, until the end when Charlie gave them the number of his hotel in Jerusalem, thanked them and rang off.

'She fell downstairs,' he told them when he'd finished. 'She's in intensive care. I'll have to go home.'

He lit a cigarette. Julia crossed the room and put her arm round his shoulder and gave him a squeeze.

'I'll get you a drink. Do you want to send flowers?'

'I suppose I'd better. Spinach would be more appropriate.'

But it was Vincent who proved most practical. Under the thick veneer of yob he could rise to a real crisis with astonishing speed and sensitivity.

'I'll check the flights. Probably won't be anything until the morning, but I'll try. There may be a charter.'

'Shit,' said Charlie. He stubbed out his unfinished cigarette and rubbed the back of his head. 'I'm sorry about all this.'

'Don't be so bloody public school,' said Vincent.

Charlie got up from the desk and pushed his hand back over his scalp.

'I wonder if she used it.'

'Used what?' asked Roger.

'The alarm. She had one of those granny alarms, the kind you always see advertised in the colour supplements.'

Vincent put the phone down.

'Nothing tonight, I'm afraid. You're booked on the two-thirty BA flight tomorrow afternoon. Check-in's at twelve.'

Julia bit the tip of her thumb and looked away. She needed to get to a phone, fast.

10

BLOND SHIMON AND pre-Raphaelite Tina shared a modern apartment on the second floor of a low-rise block in Nayot, in West Jerusalem, a stone's throw from the Hebrew University and the Israel Museum, across the park from the flattened pagoda of the Knesset. It was Shimon's apartment, with a veneer of Tina on top; his sporting trinkets and equipment, framed photos of athletes in flight and mountaineers on glaciers, cheap trophies on the mantelpiece, tracksuits and trainers in the closets; and Tina's nature remedies on the bathroom shelf and a Tibetan mantra on the wall in the bedroom.

Shimon had his feet up on the kitchen table, one hand in his pocket, the other holding a can of beer.

'I really can't understand why you poison your body,' said Tina.

He smiled.

'That beer,' she started counting on her fingers, 'contains sugar, alcohol, carbon monoxide, yeast, toxins, colouring. And aluminium from the can. Plus whatever's in the water in the first place. Uranium, for example.'

Most of the time Shimon went along with this stuff, but sometimes he pulled her up short, just for the hell of it.

'Uranium or plutonium?'

'The one they use in power stations.'

'Which one is that?'

'Plutonium. I think. What time is it?'

Shimon looked at his watch.

'Half-ten. They'll be in bed soon.'

Downstairs someone turned on a television, cartoon rocks bouncing off indestructible rodents.

'I wonder how she does it,' asked Tina.

'Does what?'

'Screws him. In cold blood.'

'Lies back and thinks of Israel, I suppose,' said Shimon. 'No big deal, hookers do it all the time, on the hour, every hour. Or so I'm told.'

'But she's no hooker. And she's not Israeli.'

'Maybe she thinks of someplace else. Hell, we all do things we don't feel like doing. Perhaps she fancies him, who knows?' He took another mouthful of beer. 'Where did you find him, by the way?'

'Kavanagh? I didn't find him, Julia did,' Tina explained. 'With a little help from friends in the Embassy. They have files on journalists who've worked here, his profile fitted. Maybe she got lucky, maybe when she met him she decided she fancied him anyway.'

The phone rang. Shimon put down his beer, walked across to the door, and picked the receiver off the wall. It was Mrs Weizman, the downstairs neighbour. She had to shout over the sound of her television.

'You're in,' she told him.

'Sounds like it,' said Shimon.

'Someone just rang my entryphone and said they were a friend of yours, they couldn't get any answer from your bell, must be broken.'

'And you let them in?'

'Of course. What else are neighbours for?'

Eric climbed the stairs two at a time, but silently, pausing occasionally to listen to the sounds in the building.

Odd to be back in Israel, smelling the smells, hearing the voices: reminded him of when he was a kid, before America, before his father decided there was more money to be made selling hardware in Brooklyn than there'd ever be running the family business in Nahariyya, if he ever got to run the family business. And there was money in hardware in the States, particularly if the goods in question had blue-steel barrels and hardwood handles. Israel gave you a good education in that sort of hardware. It was fifteen years since they'd moved to New York, fifteen years since he smelled Israel. But Eric had always had a very good memory for smells, particularly childhood smells.

He reached the top of the stairs and eased open the swing-door to the third-floor landing a little. It was dark: the landing light had gone.

The trouble with flying to Israel was that you couldn't carry a gun. You couldn't carry a gun, but you could carry something that looked like a gun and didn't show up on X-rays and metal detectors. But the trouble with a gun that wasn't a gun was that people only respected it if they could see it. Dummy guns don't impress anyone when the light's not working.

He waited for a moment, getting used to the sound from inside the apartments, printing them on his mind so that he'd notice if they changed, or if something that wasn't moving decided to move. He took a coin from his pocket, tossed it blindly through the air down the corridor, listened as it rattled to the ground twenty feet away. Nothing stirred. He stepped through the door and edged his way down the corridor. He was still adjusting his eyes to the darkness when the voice spoke, quietly but firmly.

'Turn round.'

And then the light went on.

'And drop it.'

He let go his shoulder-bag.

'Against the wall. Legs apart,' the voice still hardly more than a whisper.

'Hands behind your head.'

He felt gun-metal in the nape of his neck, and hands running over his body until they found the Beretta replica tucked in his waist-band.

'It's plastic,' Eric explained. The cold steel left his neck. He wondered who owned it.

'I'm Eric,' he gambled.

'Maybe you are. A lot of Erics in this world. Most of them are taller.'

Eric relaxed.

'You must be Shimon.'

'Maybe.'

'You finished yet?' asked Eric.

'For the moment.'

Eric lowered his arms and turned round. Shimon was leaning sideways against the wall, tucking his pistol back in his shoulder-holster.

'What the hell was all the cat-burglar stuff about?' Shimon wanted to know.

'Safety first,' Eric explained. 'Suppose this place was staked out?'

'If this place was staked out you'd be dead by now. We weren't expecting you until tomorrow.'

'I switched flights.'

'Thanks for letting us know.'

The first thing Eric noticed about Shimon was that his hair and eyebrows were blond but his pupils were black, black as ebony. Easier to dye your hair than your eyes, though they could do a lot with contact lenses these days. Shimon wore a lightweight suit over his bulging biceps, and brown leather shoes with supple rubber soles. Shin Beth regulation issue, like the holster – Eric had met Israeli government security men before. Imagine wearing your work clothes on holiday. But then Shimon's leave was almost up.

'Come on through,' Shimon told him.

Tina was still seated at the table.

'Hi,' said Eric.

Shimon offered Eric a cigarette. The only reason a man like that offers you a cigarette is because he needs a match. Eric took a Marlboro and lit up for them both.

'You guys are killing yourselves, you know that?' Tina complained. 'Cancer sticks. Not only that, you poison the air for other people. Passive smoking kills hundreds of thousands of innocent people in this country every year.'

'How many hundreds of thousands?' asked Shimon.

'A lot,' said Tina.

Eric liked the look of Tina, the red hair and the clean white skin with the freckles, the tight jeans on thin legs, the high shoulders and little fried-egg breasts under her blouse. He'd never been to bed with someone as thin as that, wondered what it was like. He wondered if it was possible to want someone enough to become a vegetarian. Not for ever, just an evening, or maybe a day or two. He looked back up from her breasts to her face and saw she was looking at him too. He didn't blush, but his ears turned pink.

Shimon tossed him a beer.

'Everything on course?' asked Eric.

'So far,' said Tina.

'You got my rod?'

'What you need a gun for?' asked Shimon.

'You ever have a security blanket when you were a kid? Some old piece of cloth you liked to suck?'

'Not that I remember. I heard of people like that, though. That kid in the Peanuts strip has one, right?'

Eric gripped his Marlboro between his teeth.

'Well, I like to have a gun.'

'How many men you killed?' asked Shimon. His smile was cut into his face as if by a knife.

'That something you need to know?'

'I reckon.'

'Then you know the answer already, don't you?'

Shimon blew smoke out of nostrils and examined his cigarette.

'Maybe.' He looked up. 'But I'd like to hear you talk about it. That way I learn something about you. Who was the first?'

This place is wired, Eric decided: this is the confession tape. They need an American, they hire one in. But they don't trust him. Maybe they plan to get rid of me anyway.

'President Kennedy,' he began, ticking the names off his fingers. 'Then Luther King, Bobby Kennedy, Jimmy Hoffa, Lord Lucan, John Paul I, Indira Ghandi, John Lennon, Tina Onassis. Oh, and Elvis. Interesting job, that one, we used an exploding nappy. How about you?'

Shimon smiled again, lips thin as wire across his teeth. He liked a joke, did Shimon, almost as much as he liked putting a second slug in a stiff.

'Only gentiles.'

'Check beforehand, do you?'

'Of course.'

'Then I'm safe.'

'There's always a first time.'

'Shit,' said Tina, 'what is all this? We're meant to be on the same side.'

'Sure,' said Eric. 'Nothing personal. I just like to know who I'm working with.' He held out his hand to Shimon. 'No offence meant.'

'None taken,' said Shimon, and completed the handshake.

Eric took a mouthful of beer, then pointed the can at Shimon.

'Oh – one more question, if it's not too personal. Do you dye it all? The hair, I mean.' He pointed a finger at Shimon's crotch. 'I've always been curious. I knew a variety dancer once who had a whole collection of pubic wigs to match her hair – red, brown, yellow, anything she needed. They sell them in New York, I gather, I could mail you one when I get back. But I'd need your measurements.'

Eric had a thing about peroxide blonds who pulled guns on him in dark corridors.

And then the phone rang again. It was Julia.

They were at Latrun, half-way from Tel Aviv to Jerusalem. They needed petrol, and Julia said she'd better phone Walter and tell him what had happened, start unscrambling arrangements. Charlie watched her behind the glass of the payphone, searching in her bag for coins and her address book, tapping her fingers nervously against the wall while she waited for the connection. He wondered what she'd do, whether she'd carry on on her own or hire someone else.

'I'm sorry about this,' he apologized again as she got back into the driver's seat.

'It's not your fault.'

But something in the way she said it suggested that it was. This was a new Julia, with a shifted focus. Three times he'd seen her like this before: when he gave her the book in London, when he switched hotels on her the night they arrived, and when he suggested they drop Bermant from the programme. Evidently she didn't like surprises. Women rarely did: advertisements were always full of girls responding rapturously to spontaneous gestures, nancy-boy strangers who gave them bunches of flowers in the street, flat-chested male models in restaurants who sent unsolicited bottles of mineral water to their tables. In real life Charlie found spontaneity with women almost always got you into trouble. But then people in advertisements did a lot of things no one did in real life, like talking to each other about detergents or finding vacant places to park their new mini-cars outside Harrods.

'What will you do?' he asked her.

She blew cigarette smoke at the windscreen and started the ignition.

'I don't know.'

And that was that, no comment. He could sense her tension getting worse as the road began to climb. It was a clear night, and a full moon hung like a silver shilling over the black silhouette of the mountains. This narrow boulder-strewn valley was where they fought in '48, the Arab Legion against the new state, gnawing away at the precarious highway that connected Jerusalem with the coast. They passed a wrecked tank, left on an outcrop among the pines, overhanging the road as a reminder of that desperate battle.

'Are you really going?' she asked eventually.

'I don't have a lot of choice.'

'I suppose not. It's just that – people always seem about to die on you until you drop everything and fly back to see them. My brother was in a car crash in Australia. The moment I heard I drove straight to Heathrow and took the first plane to Sydney, walked out the airport and grabbed a cab. When I got to the house he was out of hospital, messing around in the garden with the kids. He looked at me as if I was mad.'

'Sod's Law. If I go, she'll be fine. If I don't, she won't.'

'Sure,' she said bitterly. 'If you want to go I can't stop you.'

Charlie winced.

'It's not a question of wanting.'

'Then go.'

'For heaven's sake. Listen, Julia. I'm sorry that my mother's been so bloody inconsiderate as to fall down stairs, but she has. Bad timing, in future I'll make sure she checks with my employers beforehand. But it's happened. She's seventy-five years old, I'm her only child. I haven't got much choice.'

'You don't even like her much.'

'Is it the money? Is that what's bugging you?'

'What money?'

'If you have to hire someone else. It's expensive, rescheduling.'

She turned and looked at him, and let out a nervous laugh.

'No. No, money's the last thing I'm worried about.'

They'd reached the outskirts of the city. Half Jaffa Road was dug up for repairs, and they crawled through the late-night traffic towards Zion Square.

Charlie tried a reconciliation.

'It's only Thursday. With a bit of luck I could be back by Monday.'

'Don't bother.'

They turned left up Heleni Hamalka, heading for the Anani, and came to a halt at the traffic lights on Shivtei Yisrael. Julia tightened her grip on the steering-wheel.

'Listen, Charlie ...'

And then she shut up. The lights changed, and they drove on in silence to the hotel. As they turned in off the main road Charlie looked back over his shoulder.

'Someone's following us.'

'Who is?'

'Look.'

She stopped the car, and turned in time to see a khaki pick-up idle past the gates. The driver was male, and there was a girl in the passenger seat. The pick-up slowed to a halt for a moment, then continued up the road.

'What makes you think so?' asked Julia, with a telling half-chuckle.

'Remember them? French-kissing under the balcony the other morning. Bloody funny time of day to be exercising your tongue. They've been behind us since the bus station.'

Julia opened the car door.

'Don't be ridiculous, Charlie. They probably live round here, that's all. Why would anyone follow us?'

'Habit. They do it all the time. Phone bugs, Shin Beth gophers on the switchboards. God knows why. Keeping up with the Syrians, I suppose.'

'Who's Shin Beth?'

'Internal security. Checking to make sure we're not plotting to assassinate the Deputy Prime Minister.'

Charlie got his shoulder-bag out of the boot. They were standing close together in the darkness, sheltered from the street lights by a line of pines, the shadows of the branches dancing in the breeze.

'What is the matter, Julia?'

She brushed the hair back off her forehead.

'Nothing. If you want to go home, go.'

They went upstairs, and Charlie began to pack. He picked up Walter's research papers and began leafing through them. Julia filled two tooth-mugs with Bushmills, handed him one and sat down on the bed. She was relaxing a little.

'Did I tell you about the ambassador's wife?' She giggled. 'I went for a pee, she was in the bath, fully clothed, singing a song and reminiscing about her youth. I shouldn't laugh, it was rather sad.'

Charlie froze.

'What the hell's this doing in here?'

He lifted a booklet off Walter's stack.

'What is it?'

'*The Freedom Fighter's Handbook*. The Compleate Terrorist. Jesus. I haven't seen one of these in years.' He sat down on the bed beside her, and opened the book at random. A diagram explained how to booby-trap a briefcase. 'Probably quite a collector's item. You used to come across them in Belfast in the early seventies. And London – some Scots anarchist got sent down for owning one.'

'Show me,' she said, a little reluctantly.

'It's a cookbook,' Charlie explained. 'Everything you ever wanted to know about the tricks of the trade. Explosives, timers, letter-bombs, poisons – is there something you haven't told me about Walter?'

'No. I mean, not that I know of. Maybe it's a joke.'

'In this country? He must have a pretty bizarre sense of humour.'

'Leave it with me, I'll burn it.'

Charlie took a swig of Bushmills and put his mug down on the bedside table.

'Burn it, and swallow the ashes. If I didn't know better I'd say someone was trying to set us up. I'd better pack.'

He took his suitcase down off the top of the wardrobe and began taking his clothes out of drawers. Julia stayed on the bed, smoking nervously.

'This is a final decision, is it?' she asked.

'Listen, love. It's only a film. Just because you're losing a director doesn't mean you're losing a lover.' He looked up. 'Does it?'

She gave him a bitter smile.

'It's your decision.'

'I'm not going to be hard to replace. For this kind of money you could probably get George Lucas. Or Jean Luc Godard, for that matter.'

He looked across at her, and realised she was crying.

'I'm scared of losing you, Charlie.'

He put down his shirts and sat down on the bed beside her, arm around her shoulder, fingers resting on the bare skin of her arm. The tears came slowly, like a dripping tap. He reached across and handed her a tissue.

She wiped her eyes.

'This programme has to happen, Charlie. I'm not sure I can do it on my own.'

'Of course you can. All you need to do is find someone to direct the cameras on the night. Goliath must know people.'

'That's not the point.'

'What's not the point?'

She got up from the bed without answering and went through to the bathroom.

None of this was making any sense. Charlie crammed the rest of his clothes into his suitcase and went out on to the balcony. The alley was empty. He crossed the room, opened the door and walked down the corridor until he reached a window looking out over the car park. There were a dozen cars there, none of them a khaki pick-up. He retraced his footsteps to the bedroom. Julia was looking at Walter's handbook.

'Let's get something to eat,' Charlie decided.

'It's gone midnight. I doubt if ...'

'Trust me.'

She put down the book and looked at the floor for a moment, tapping the palm of her hand against the edge of the bed.

'Why would I do that?'

'Bring the bottle. And something warm.'

Charlie drove the Subaru towards the city centre, watching the mirror. A hundred yards from the Anani he stopped and pulled over to the kerb. The road was almost empty: a taxi passed them, then the pick-up. As soon as it was clear of the front of the car he pulled the wheel hard to the left, and did a rapid U-turn. He kept his foot on the accelerator, tyres screaming against the tarmac, until they were over the crown of the hill. Then, just as abruptly, he slowed and turned right down a side street.

Julia was bent forward, shielding her face with both arms.

'Charlie! What the hell's going on?'

But it was his turn not to answer questions. He stopped again, turned off the headlights and backed the car into an alley, his eyes on the main road. They waited less than a minute before the pick-up overshot the junction, slowed and reversed. The driver glanced past them down the empty street, threw his cigarette out of the car, reversed, and turned slowly down towards them.

Charlie waited until they'd passed, taking a good look at the driver.

'Blondie and Miss Marble.'

'What the hell's this about?' Julia repeated.

'You can't make a marriage with three in the bed.' Charlie turned the headlights on, started the ignition and accelerated back up to the main road. 'And I've a suspicion there's a lot more than three in this bed.' He gestured towards the other car. 'Are they friends of yours?'

'You're crazy.'

'Not crazy, dumb.' He took a right, racing the gears, and then almost immediately turned off again. The pick-up matched them turn for turn. Eventually Charlie slowed up and drove north towards French Hill. If they want to come along for the ride, why not? After all, it's quite a free country.

Julia smoothed her skirt. Her hands were shaking. She reached into her handbag for a cigarette. Charlie held out his lighter for her. He was beginning to enjoy this Philip Marlowe stuff. Not a lot, but enough to keep his mind off the real world until he'd had time to think.

Julia looked straight ahead through the windscreen and made a careful speech.

'Listen, Charlie. I'm sorry I went wobbly on you up there. No excuses. I'm new to all this – believe it or not I've been living on a wing and prayer all through this whole business. Outwardly calm, inside all panic. Like a swan in a current, serene on the surface, feet thrashing away dementedly under the surface. And tonight I cracked, that's all. I didn't know what to do, and I cracked. I'll be OK soon, I just need time.'

He looked in the mirror. The pick-up was back.

'And those two?'

She shrugged and looked back nervously over her shoulder.

'How would I know? They follow all sorts of people here. You said it yourself – they have to.'

They'd come to a dual carriageway. Charlie pulled into the outside lane and cruised the car up to fifty.

'You ever been to Massada?'

'Is that a restaurant?'

'People go there for picnics sometimes.' Charlie checked his mirror. They were fifty yards behind him now, headlights dipped. 'No, it's not a restaurant. It's a fortress. Herod The Great built it as a temple to paranoia, on top of a mountain in the Judean wilderness, miles from anywhere. It's a thousand feet up, surrounded by cliffs, more or less impregnable. He had permanent grain stores and water cisterns there, enough for a long siege. Only he never used it. But a thousand Zealots retreated there from the Romans after the fall of Jerusalem. The Tenth Legion surrounded it and camped out around the bottom, and got Jewish slaves to build a ramp. Vast thing, the size of a slag heap. It took eight months: all the time the Zealots could see and hear what was going on, watching the ramp get higher and higher, closer and closer. Outnumbered fifteen to one. When the ramp was finally finished and the Romans lined up to storm the citadel, they killed themselves and their families. Very tidily, in rows, almost a thousand of them. No suicides, that's against Jewish law, they had to do it to each other. When there were

only nine of them left, they drew lots. The lucky winner knifed
the other eight and fell on his sword. All the Romans found
were bodies, and two women with their children hiding in a
water pipe. Very symbolic place. Reminds me of the British
Labour Party's performance in the eighty-three election.'

'Yes, I know that Massada,' Julia said quietly. 'I thought you
were hungry.'

'That was just for the listeners. At least I assume there are
listeners in that room. But you'd know more about that than I
would.'

'Charlie, I haven't a clue what you're talking about.'

'I'd love to believe you, Julia. I haven't a clue what's happening either. But I have to be at Ben Gurion airport at twelve
o'clock tomorrow morning to catch an aeroplane. And before
I go I'd like to know what I'm leaving behind.'

They'd reached the outskirts of the city now, heading down
through the wilderness towards Jericho. Charlie drove with one
hand, the other hanging loose out the window, patting the
bodywork, the way the kids did in *American Graffiti*. The radio
was on, tuned to The Voice of Peace, Scott McKenzie still on
his way to San Francisco. Julia started humming. Neither of
them wanted this row, neither of them could avoid it.

'What were you doing in August sixty-seven?' she asked him.

'You really want to know? Wearing flannel trousers and a
sports jacket and going to history tutorials. We all were. Just
don't tell anyone, it wrecks the image.'

They were ten miles from Jerusalem now, coasting down the
long steep empty wadi to the Dead Sea. The countryside was
bare and treeless in the moonlight. Occasionally they passed a
Bedouin camp by the roadside, lights showing under the black
canvas and plastic sheeting.

'You're serious about Massada, aren't you?'

'Yup.'

'Won't it be closed?'

'Probably. But not as closed as the Tenth Legion found it,
and they got in. Do you really love me, Julia? I need to know.'

'Charlie . . .'

'Say yes. You don't have to mean it.'

'You need to know but you don't mind if I lie?'

'Something like that.'

'Yes. But ...'

'That's enough. No buts. Let's do this together.'

The pick-up was half a mile behind them as they passed the sea-level sign beside the road.

'Glug,' said Julia.

Another eight hundred feet down and they'd be at the Dead Sea.

II

'How much further is it?' asked Julia.

She'd put on a sweater against the chill, and her arms were folded tight across her chest. In front of them the mirrored surface of the Dead Sea stretched flat and shining in the moonlight. Beyond lay Jordan, a high ridge of bare black mountains rising sheer from the water's edge.

'About thirty miles.'

Charlie sat beside her on the bonnet of the car, smoking a cigarette.

'Have you ever tried swimming in it?' he asked her.

'No.'

'It's desperate – lukewarm porridge. Very healthy, I'm told. The Emperor Vespasian used to throw manacled slaves in to test the buoyancy. I always wanted to spend a night in it, floating, see what it's like to sleep in. I suppose you must be able to float and sleep at the same time. If you're drunk enough. Who do you reckon they are?'

He nodded back down the road. Somewhere in the shadows behind them lurked the pick-up.

'I honestly don't know.'

'Honestly?'

'Honestly.'

He butted his cigarette under his heel.

'Tell me more about Harry. The bits you didn't want to tell me before. Were you lovers?'

She laughed awkwardly, and shook her head.

'No. You don't think he's ...'

'I don't think anything. I'm blindfold. You'll have to be my white stick. How did you first meet him?'

'I told you, Charlie.'

'Tell me again.'

She waited a moment before answering.

'Just because I lied to you about this doesn't mean I lied about the rest.'

'OK. And vice versa. Tell me anyway.'

'He was a friend of my father's. He rang me up, he was looking for someone who knew about television.'

'Which father was that?'

She fidgeted with the car aerial.

'The real one. He was a minor industrialist. Nothing glamorous at all, he worked for British Steel.'

'And he's dead?'

'Yes.'

'So there was no way of knowing if Harry was a friend of his or not?'

'I suppose not.'

They got back into the car and drove on, towards the distant lights of Qumran to the south. Qumran, where they found the Dead Sea Scrolls.

Julia rubbed her eyes. It was two in the morning.

'Aren't you tired, Charlie? Don't you need sleep?'

'I need a minimum of eight hours. Given the chance I'll take eleven. But not tonight. Tonight lasts as long as it takes, Julia. I want to get you so tired you stop thinking. If you're tired enough there's some chance you'll start making sense. If Massada doesn't do it, we'll drive on to Sodom, Sharm El-Sheikh – Cairo, if need be.'

The late-night radio played 'You've lost that loving feeling'. Charlie turned it up loud, singing along with the harmonies.

'You were born in sixty-four, weren't you?' he asked her. 'Great year. "House of the Rising Sun", "It's All Over Now", "Hard Day's Night", "Pretty Woman" – perfect music to be conceived to.'

'I was conceived in sixty-three.'

'Oh. Yes, I suppose you must have been. Pity. Not a lot to

130

get excited about in sixty-three. "Wayward Wind", "Summer Holiday", "Telstar" . . .'

' "Telstar" was sixty-two.'

Charlie looked at her.

'How the hell did you know that?'

'Just guessing. You're an easy man to double-guess. Bluffers always are.'

The road cut through a rocky outcrop, turned a bend, then straightened out. The shore was somewhere in the darkness on their left, the water beyond still glistening in the moonlight.

'Uh huh,' said Charlie.

There was a road block ahead, two jeeps parked at right angles across the tarmac. Someone waved a flashlight at them. Charlie dipped the lights, slowed, and stopped the car. A reservist in battle fatigues came across, unshaven, cigarette on his lips, Uzi slung from his shoulder, flashlight in hand.

'How you doing,' said Charlie.

The soldier shone the lamp on Julia, then on the empty back seat. He gestured at the boot. Charlie took the keys out of the ignition, got out and walked round to the back of the car.

'Open, please.'

He pointed his torch at the lock while Charlie fiddled with the keys, then examined the empty boot.

'Where you going?'

To Eilat, Charlie was about to say. Been up visiting friends in Jerusalem, driving back overnight to Eilat, the Red Sea Hotel, room 357. We're tourists, enjoying a happy stay in your fertile, friendly country.

But he knew these guys were too smart for that. The radio operator's already sent the car registration back to the computer in Jerusalem, and this squaddy has to keep us talking long enough for the reply to come through. A minute maybe, no more. Bite the bullet, kid. But don't swallow it.

'I'm not sure,' he confessed. 'We're staying in Jerusalem, at the Anani. I just got word from London that my mother's seriously ill, I'm flying home from Lod in the morning. I couldn't sleep, so we decided to go for a drive.'

'Passports?'

Charlie got them from the car, and the soldier thumbed

through them in the torchlight. He paused when he got to Charlie's profession.

'You the kind of director that makes money, or the kind that makes films?'

'Films,' said Charlie.

'Me too,' said the squaddy. 'Though you may not guess it. Six of us here tonight: a university lecturer, a kitchen porter, an electrician, a farmer and a nightclub singer. And me. Whatever else you say about this army, it's not snobbish. What kind of films you make?'

'Documentaries. And you?'

'Drama. Kid's drama.' He gripped the flashlight in his mouth to free his hand, and held it out for Charlie to shake. 'Sammy Folberg.'

'Charlie Kavanagh,' said Charlie, vowing to be honest more often.

'I know,' said Sammy, giving him back his passport. 'You two want some coffee?'

The pick-up had stopped half a mile back, lights off, just out of sight of the checkpoint. Shimon walked on a few yards to get a clear view, leaving the girl in the car. He watched Charlie, Julia and the reservist abandon the Subaru and vanish behind a jeep.

What the shit's going on, he wondered. How the hell you meant to tail a car in the wilderness when it's dark and there's no one else around except you and them? Maybe their documents are out of order. Maybe Kavanagh said something undiplomatic. Who knows. Why the hell are they driving round Judea in the middle of the night anyway, come to that. First he thought they were heading for Jericho, or maybe Allenby Bridge, try and smooth-talk their way into Jordan. Only they wouldn't have made it, not in an Israeli car, not at this hour. When they turned south at Kallia, he thought it must be Eilat, then on to Egypt. Queer way to drive from Jerusalem to Eilat, but it would get you there. He wondered what he was meant to do if they did make a run for it, whether to try and stop them. He could alert the border guards, invent some story, flash his credentials. But what was the point? If they were doing a bunk the operation was screwed up anyway. Better to take them out while he had the chance. Two bodies now would be easier to explain away than the story they'd tell the press if they got away.

He walked back to the pick-up. Tina was asleep, mouth open, red hair pressed flat against the window glass.

'Your shift,' he said. 'This could go on all night.'

Three other members of the patrol were sitting on the rocks smoking. Charlie wondered which was the nightclub singer and which the kitchen porter, but in that light there was no telling. Sammy lifted the canteen off the stove and poured them coffee in tin mugs.

'So what's the film you're making called?'

Charlie looked at Julia. It didn't have a name – they'd talked about it, but come up with nothing. It ought to have a name, very important to know what things are called: until something has a name it has no identity, no life of its own.

'The series is called *The Last Supper*. This one's subtitled "Hero Israel",' said Julia. 'As in "Hear, O Israel".'

'Good title,' said Sammy, and sat down.

Charlie couldn't make out Julia's face in the darkness, but he could tell how she held herself, wrapping herself up in her own limbs, scared. Or maybe just cold. The other three had come across to meet them.

'Who you got here, Sammy?' asked the sergeant, in an accent that wandered between Minsk and Whitechapel.

'Tourists with a bad sense of direction. From Jerusalem. Took the wrong turning coming off Ben Yehuda, got lost in the one-way system.'

The sergeant chuckled and refilled his mug from the canteen. His smile was half gum, wet and pink. Charlie could smell his breath, three parts tobacco to two parts garlic.

'They're TV, taping a programme in Jerusalem,' Sammy explained.

'About what?'

'About Israel,' said Charlie cautiously.

'Na! You can't go making a film about something as vague as that,' objected the sergeant. 'Good films are about something specific.'

He rubbed his nose on the back of his sleeve.

'You reckon?' asked Charlie.

'I reckon. Smaller the subject, better the programme. Not always, but usually. You make a programme about me, or him, then you learn something, and people get interested in us, because there's bits of us they can identify with even if the rest is strange and unfamiliar. But a whole country? Not that this is a whole country, we come from all over the place. Nahariyya's all Germans, Galilee's full of Brits, Beersheba's Moroccans, Nazareth's full of Russians. White Jews, brown Jews, even American negroes. Imagine how much that lot haven't got in common with each other. A very inflammable mixture, unshared experience. You ever read poetry?'

Charlie nodded.

This country's like that pulped fruit juice cocktail you get, twenty different kinds of fruit in it, tastes of everything and nothing. You want to describe the taste of orange juice, or grapefruit, or plum, or pineapple whatever, no problem. But you mix them up and shove them all through a blender, what you get is nothing. All kinds of fruit, but no particular kind. They ought to print it on the flag: Contains Jews of more than one country of origin. Everything and nothing,' he repeated.

'I met the blacks,' said Charlie. 'Down in Dimona. They still there?'

'Could be.'

'Couple of hundred of them, out of Detroit and Chicago, think they're the Lost Tribe of Israel. Black Hebrews, pure negro, dressing up in Old Testament robes and going for walks in the desert. Not very long walks, but they looked great, very Cecil B. de Mille. TV crews queueing up to take their pictures, they were having a wonderful time. Except they thought Dimona was Detroit, and kept slipping back into the old ways, chasing each other with axes and feuding over wives and who was the true prophet. I asked one of them if he really had Jewish blood. "Sure, man," he says. "My people were from Sierra Leone, way up country. And in the old days they used to get missionaries, traders, all sorts of Europeans come up country to see them. Now my people's cannibals, right?" He patted his stomach. "I got Jewish blood, Irish blood, Italian blood, you name it ..."'

They talked for the best part of an hour. For Charlie it was one of those strange, suspended interludes, three in the morning on the shores of the Dead Sea, but somehow no particular time or place. They talked easily, about London and television and soldiering and politics, ancient history, even Charlie's mother. He fetched the whiskey bottle from the car, and they took it in turns to drink, wiping the neck carefully on their sleeves before passing it on. He expected the lecturer and Sammy to be confident and educated, but the farmer and the electrician were too, and the kitchen porter was funny and told stories about the catering trade. The nightclub singer held himself back from the group, maybe through temperament, maybe because he was the radio operator, and needed to keep his mind on the job. Only when the talk came to the West Bank did he break his silence.

'I'm not prejudiced against Arabs,' he announced. 'I just don't like them. That's not prejudice, that's judgement. And it's entirely mutual.'

' "There is no misunderstanding between Jew and Arab, but a natural conflict",' Sammy quoted. 'Jabotinsky, father of Israeli terrorism.'

'I thought that was King Saul,' the nightclub singer objected. 'Listen, you build a new house and you find it has rats, you get rid of the rats. They have a right to be there, same as you, sure. But you live in the house, you don't think like that, you just want rid of the rats. There's plenty of room for them out in the fields.'

The others came and went, disappearing into the rocks to relieve themselves, checking the occasional car. There was no sign of the pick-up.

Eventually Charlie and Julia made a move to go.

'If you want my advice,' said the sergeant, 'forget Jerusalem, go to Eilat. Very nice at this time of year.'

'I'd love to. But I have a plane to catch.'

'Of course.' The soldier gripped him affectionately by the back of the neck. 'I hope all is well.'

Then Charlie decided to chance his luck.

'Listen, I wonder if you could do us a favour?'

'Of course.'

'There's a car following us,' he explained. 'Toyota pick-up, been behind us ever since we left the hotel, must be somewhere back up the road.' He nodded at Julia. 'We think her husband's having us tailed.'

'Ah,' said the sergeant, tapping the side of his nose. 'How long do you need?'

'How long can you give us?'

'Half an hour? Longer if you need it,' said Sammy. 'Enjoy your flight.'

Tina woke Shimon.

'They're going.'

Shimon sat up, stretched, and massaged the crick in his neck.

'What time is it?'

'Gone three.'

'Shit.'

He started the engine and drove slowly down to the checkpoint. Sammy and the sergeant waved him down.

'Where you going?'

'To Eilat,' said Shimon nicely. 'Been up visiting friends in Jerusalem, driving back down overnight to Eilat, the Red Sea Hotel, room three-five-seven. We're tourists ...'

'Out,' said Sammy. 'Both of you.'

12

DAVID BERMANT HAD BEEN awake since five. Even after three weeks in the job he still felt disorientated in the mornings. When he first opened his eyes it took him time to work out where he was, sniffing at the darkness, listening to the dulled sounds of the world outside through the double glazing. He remembered talking to a much-travelled American politician once – Schultz, or maybe Cyrus Vance – who told him his life's ambition was to get hotels to put up signs on their bedroom walls telling you what town you were in, like in railway stations, so that you didn't need to start each day struggling to remember where you were.

Not the kibbutz, he decided. Back in Galilee he'd have got up, turned on the radio, made coffee, showered and shaved, got dressed, walked out on to the terrace and watched the sun rise over the Golan, listened to the first sounds of the settlement starting a new day, doors slamming, animals stirring; seen the lights go on in the milking shed, someone loading the truck for an early run into the vegetable market. Not the kibbutz, not Galilee: this, he decided at last, was Jerusalem, the government flat in Rehavia, neither home nor away. Here, when he woke, he was frightened to even cough in case he disturbed his minders.

The flat was temporary, a few weeks until his official quarters were ready. And it was home of a sort, he supposed: bed and board, and he'd get used to it eventually. Before he became a Minister he'd never bothered with a proper flat in Jerusalem, booking in with friends or at one of the cheaper hotels when he had to stay over in the capital. But now it was different: now he was a senior government Minister. They wanted him somewhere secure.

Rehavia was quiet and green but close to the heart of the New City, near the junction of Ussishkin Street and Ramban Street, an area haunted by the ghosts of old Zionists – Menachim Ussishkin himself, Levi Eshkol, Ephraim Katzir, Golda Meir, Eliezar Sukenik. Not far from Jason's Tomb, which the archae-ologists had discovered by chance in 1956 – he could remember the excitement at the time, the photos in the papers of learned academics from Oxford and Yale pouring over the Roman inscriptions.

He had no real reason to complain about the apartment, which was large and well-appointed and comfortable. What he minded was the staff and the security: the cleaners who weren't cleaners and cooks who weren't cooks, the windows that didn't open, the doors that looked like painted timber but clanged like metal when you knocked on them, the teak-veneered bookcase between his bed and the window that turned out to be made of one-inch steel. The staff did everything for him, whether he wanted them to or not: packed and unpacked his suitcase, made his bed, laid out his pyjamas, and two glasses of water by the bed, one for thirst, the other for his false teeth. Whatever time he woke he'd find his breakfast laid out and ready for him, and a woman in uniform waiting to make him fresh toast and coffee and throw herself between him and any Palestinian assassin who might have made it five flights up the drainpipe. If there'd been a drainpipe, which he was sure there wasn't. These people took no chances.

It was seven before a full bladder forced him to get out of bed and tiptoe to the bathroom. Through an open door he could see Rosa moving stealthily round the kitchen laying the tea tray.

Rosa was his maid. She must have been about twenty-one, dark and pretty, with one of those sensual figures that looked voluptuous at twenty-one but would inflate like a barrage balloon as soon as she'd trapped a bee in her honeypot, found herself a husband. She wore a uniform which wasn't a uniform, more a civil service approximation of what domestic servants should look like, an over-ironed navy skirt down to her calves, a white synthetic blouse, black leather shoes with soft supple soles in case she had to do something in a hurry. But she was pretty, and it even crossed his mind that her official duties might extend beyond domestic chores and security, that the Foreign Minister's other appetites were being provided for by a thoughtful commissariat. But he'd been chaste as a hermit since Ruth's death, and the thought of breaking the habit with this plump chicken-in-gravy seemed almost blasphemous.

Carnal thoughts aside, though, he'd cultivated her assiduously over the weeks, to the point where she'd even talk to him. Her conversation was a disappointment. He already knew more than he wanted to about her hobbies (swimming, badminton, hill-walking); her love-life (a paratrooper called Daniel, nice boy but too interested in football and other girls); and her ambitions (marry Daniel, visit the United States). Her politics came straight from the tabloid press, in at the eyes, out at the mouth, without any apparent contact with her brain. Arabs were incurably 'different' (why wouldn't they be?), West Bank settlers models of self-restraint and moral courage. Israel's neighbours only understood the language of violence.

Rosa didn't call it violence, but 'firmness'. Half the country — more — seemed to think this way nowadays. In the circumstances it was good of her to be so polite to a bigoted old liberal like him. Maybe she was right, maybe his generation was too old, hung up on the values of a different culture and a different time. Out of the mouths of babes and sucklings ... but then in David's experience what came out of the mouths of babes and sucklings was half-digested vomit and burp-gas. 'Making *sefokh*', the Italian Jews used to call it.

Still, at least she hadn't got religion, like so many of her generation: at least she'd risk the wrath of the rabbis to bring him hot refreshments on the Sabbath, even if he didn't want them.

By the time he got back from the bathroom the tea tray was by his bed. David never drank tea, but the moment to say so had passed: the first morning he'd felt it would be rude, and now it was too late, he was condemned to start every day with it. Maybe he could persuade the doctors to say it was bad for his health. But then they might ban coffee too: Morton's fork.

He opened the drawer of his bedside table and took out his

pills, filled the palm of his hand with them, poured himself a cup of tea and swallowed them in a single gulp. Some joke, retiring Libschitz on health grounds. He tried counting up which parts of his own body could still be said to be in real working order, and came to the conclusion there were none. Bowel, spleen, gall bladder, heart, chest, joints, eyes, ears – they put dogs down when they got to this stage. Some people even put their wives down. Fill them up with Brompton's Cocktail, the comforting mixture of opiates and sedatives they give terminal cancer patients, then slip the polythene bag over their head. No marks, no evidence, just the unspeakable pain of watching the last breath of life slip away from someone you love.

'We decided it was time', Chaim had told him when he'd protested he wasn't fit enough for the Foreign Minister's job, 'for the young people to stand down and give the old a chance.'

Very satirical. He looked at his watch: it was almost half-past seven. He drank the rest of the tea, and was shaved and dressed by the time the car called half an hour later to take him to breakfast with Chaim.

They ate in an alcove in the restaurant of the King David Hotel, the closest thing to normal life he could find in this new world of power and position. The nearest officials and minders were a good twenty feet away, snouts in the trough, gorging themselves on strawberries and Scottish smoked salmon at the state's expense. Obsequious waiters hovered unnecessarily with fresh coffee and un-asked for toast. He himself made do with coffee and a pastry, pecking at it nervously like an elderly cockerel, hungry but unsure of himself.

Chaim spoke quietly, discreetly.

'Next week in New York, eh?'

'Next week ...' David repeated in a frustrated whisper. 'I don't mind the UN, it's America that scares the shit out of me. I feel like a fiancé going to be looked over by the bride's parents.'

'It's not like before, David. They're relatively soft these days. Who'd have believed it? American Zionists urging restraint on us.'

'Not all of them. Only the ones who want to be asked to Georgetown cocktail parties.'

'Maybe you are. Maybe Arafat converted to Judaism, maybe the phone system started working, maybe the rabbis opened a Saturday market in Mea Shearim, with pork scratchings on special offer. Or maybe none of you care what I think.'

Chaim moved a bishop.

'Check.'

David blocked him with a pawn: Chaim retreated.

'So what's your conviction?'

'My conviction is that we have to stop messing around, stop all this self-justifying shadow-boxing. Because we haven't much time, things are going from worse to worse than worse. You know the most dangerous thing in politics? The alliance of bigotry and economic self-interest. And that's what's happening on the West Bank. People with no politics move to the West Bank for cheap housing, and suddenly they have politics, the politics of staying put, looking after their investment. Who else wants them there? The bigots, the religious head-bangers, the ones with the ex-directory phone line to Jehova. But the ones who go for money, for cheap land and housing, they're the most dangerous. People will always modify their ideas more willingly than they'll drop their standard of living.'

'Your move,' Chaim reminded him. 'And I still don't know your conviction.'

'Wait. We have to get rid of our colonies, Chaim. Britain had to in the end, France had to, Belgium had to, Holland, Spain, Italy, Portugal. Russia and America are beginning to. Not for moral reasons, for practical reasons. It seemed impossible at the time, economic and strategic suicide, a recipe for mutiny and civil war. In hindsight it seems an entirely obvious thing to have done. Holding on would have been suicide. In a generation we'll be outnumbered inside our own borders, if we haven't gone bankrupt in the meantime. We'll have to choose between a democratic state and a Jewish one. I tell you, Chaim, a few years from now and our problem won't be the Palestinians, it'll be Islamic fundamentalists. That'll be a pretty party, Arab ayatollahs on one side, Jewish ayatollahs on the other. Like something out of Greek mythology, our God against theirs, and may the cruellest man win. It'll go that way, unless there are governments people can have faith in.'

145

'That's your conviction?'

'No, that's my analysis.'

'It doesn't work. It doesn't work because ...'

'I know it doesn't work,' David interrupted. 'It's true, but it doesn't work. It's one thing for the British to get their settlers out of Kenya or Malaya, another for us to withdraw from Judea and Samaria, I know, I'm not that stupid. But it's not *that* different. And what we're doing at the moment doesn't work either – just because one person in an argument's wrong doesn't mean the other person's right. Nor does a problem have to have a solution, for that matter, sitting there waiting to be discovered. Plenty of problems are insoluble.'

'Is that it? Is that what you've been wanting to say all week? The problem is insoluble. Official. That's what you want to tell the UN?'

'No. What I want to say is this: I think what we have to do is be generous to the point of madness. I think we have to make the Palestinians an offer they can't refuse. That's what they did to us in eighty-nine, only we refused it anyway. Out of habit.'

'They'd laugh at you.'

David ran the tips of his fingers over his eyebrows.

'Whose side are you on, Chaim?'

'The same side as always. But I'm sick of this self-righteousness, David, this myth that the old days were so noble. They weren't noble at all. We massacred, we drove people from their homes. Remember Khirbet Azzun? Remember Arab Rubin? Yibna? Zarnuga? Kaukaba? Deir Yassin?'

'Deir Yassin was a reprisal for Gush Etzion. And anyway it wasn't us, it was Irgun, that was Begin.'

'Maybe. All right, forget Deir Yassin. How about Ilaboun? Qibya, in fifty-three ...'

'Qibya was Ariel Sharon, we all know about Sharon.'

'OK, forget Sharon. What about Lod and Ramla? Fifty thousand pushed out by the Harel Brigade. Fifty thousand – that's roughly how many Jewish settlers there are living in the West Bank now. It's as if all the settlers had been shifted out of the Territories, told to start walking, just like that. In heat you wouldn't believe, no water, nothing. When did Gush Emunim ever push out fifty thousand? And Kefar Kassem in fifty-six –'

'Ya ya ya, and they did the same to us, and worse. What are we, schoolchildren? Let's not get into all those arguments.'

'OK. So this offer they can't refuse. Who you going to make it to? Who are Allah's peaceniks?'

'I don't know. I mean to find out.' He moved his queen on to Chaim's baseline. 'Check.'

Chaim counterattacked.

'On guard. So you want peace. What the hell do you think the rest of us want – war? This isn't an argument about objectives, this is about means. You go out and offer them everything, no conditions, no safeguards – what is there left to negotiate about? That way you don't get peace, that way you make them think we're weak. Your knight, David – you really want to give me your knight?'

'I'll look after myself, Chaim. This is every man for himself.' But he moved his knight to safety none the less. 'So you do want me to negotiate with the Arabs?'

'Of course.'

'Bullshit. All you want me to do is make them offers we know they can't accept. Stall, play for time until ... until I don't know what. Until they give up negotiating, I suppose, and start another war. Wars we can handle, it's settlements we are bad at.'

Chaim concentrated on the chess board.

'Maybe so,' he said without looking up. 'Maybe that's why we hired you. And I assume that's why you took the job.'

'I took the job for three reasons.' David numbered them on his fingers. 'One, because I've spent too many years talking and doing nothing. Two, because I'm old and if I don't do something now I never will. And three, because I don't mind if I get fired.'

'OK. But it's a two-way trade. Maybe we move too slow sometimes. But if you move too fast, we all lose.'

'Tell me something,' David asked him. 'Whose idea was it to offer me the job – yours?'

'No, not mine. I'm not sure where it came from.'

'I'll tell you. The Americans. I'm a sop to Washington, that's all. Ritual sacrifice.'

'Being chosen for sacrifice was once considered an honour,' said Chaim. 'People used to queue up for it.'

13

BEERSHEBA, FOR ALL THE biblical grandeur of its name and its civic pretensions as capital of the Negev, is a cheerful mess of a town. It stands on – or a few miles from, depending on your archaeological prejudices – the site of the spring where in Genesis 21. 32, King Abimelech granted Abraham the right to water his flocks. Charlie knew this because he'd read it on the main signpost on the edge of town. You didn't need a sign to see what had gone wrong with modern Beersheba. It was a do-it-yourself, self-assembly city, built from an instruction book clearly intended for another kit. Nothing fitted, nothing was in the right place, huge and vital chunks were missing. It reminded Charlie of one of those post-war cities in Eastern Europe, full of unnecessarily large buildings with too little furniture in them, picked up from Bulgaria or Silesia and dumped down on the edge of the desert.

It used to be an Arab settlement, modestly expanded by the Turks into an administrative outpost to control the wandering Bedouin; liberated by Allenby in 1917, and then left to doze in the sun until 1948. The population at Independence was three thousand: now it was forty times that size, a rambling, chaotic frontier town. Most of the population were Sephardis, Jews from North Africa, for whom the Promised Land turned out to be flowing not with milk and honey but with concrete and cheap cigarettes. Dusty trucks parked in the main streets while their drivers went looking for beer, soldiers in shorts with sun-blistered faces and sand in their hair queued to use the public phones outside the post office, no one wore more than shorts and a T-shirt. Even the teenage girls posing on the sidewalks shared the fashion sense of the panzer brigade, one size fits none. A lot of shops sold hardware, plastic and tin, pipes and ropes, tractor tyres and car parts, and the record shop played Country and Western, Waylon and Willie and the Boys, 'Luckenbach Texas, Ain't Nobody Feeling No Pain', followed by a disco version of Beethoven's 'Ode to joy'.

Charlie and Julia had breakfast at JoJo's KwikSnack café on Ha'azmaut Street. Julia had slept a little in the car, but Charlie had gone right through, knowing that if he once closed his eyes that would be it. Both of them were pale and red-eyed – even stay-pressed, ever-fresh Julia.

At eight in the morning it was already hot. Charlie ordered everything the waiter offered: thin grey coffee, sour bread, processed cheese, chemical jam.

Julia just wanted coffee, and an end to travelling.

'How far are we now?' she asked.

'About eighty clicks from Jerusalem.'

'You have to be at the airport at twelve. At the latest.'

'I know.'

She smiled wearily over the rim of her coffee cup.

'You know something, Charlie? Two days ago I thought I understood you.'

He chewed on his bread and cheese.

'Then what happened?'

'I don't know. You changed.'

'I'll tell you, Julia. Nothing happened to me, except that my mother got ill. It's you who changed. What was the last time you told me you loved me?'

'Last night, I think. On the way out of Jerusalem.'

'Doesn't count: I ordered you to.' He chewed his toast. 'Before that.'

'I don't know.'

'I'll tell you. When we arrived at the Embassy thrash, just before we got out the car. You stuck your tongue in my ear and told me you loved me. Since then: zilch. Cut-off. You stopped having a good time and started worrying about something. Not my mum, not me fucking off for a few days, something else.' Another mouthful of bread, washed down with the acorn coffee.

'Let me give you a theory. What worries you isn't what happens to the film, what worries you is something between you and Harry Greenbaum, some deal I don't know about. Score me out of ten.'

She played with a paper beer-mat, splitting it with her finger-nails, eyes lowered, not looking at him. She's too tired to pretend any more, Charlie decided. Conventional interrogators do it by keeping you on your feet all night in a cell with the lights on: Charlie did it by making you climb steep mountain paths in the Judean wilderness to look at archaeological sites.

'Ten.'

'Promise?'

'Promise. But you mustn't ask me why.'

'Is it to do with us?'

'No. No, not you. Someone else.'

'Nick?'

Her eyes stayed on the beer mat.

'No clues.'

It's Nick, Charlie decided. Nick the Arnold Schwarzenegger Look-Alike she'd had on her arm at Dick and Liz's wedding. Nick who was hard in all the wrong places. He didn't know why, but he was sure. The way someone can mention a name casually two or three times in a week and you know they're having an affair with them.

She'd mentioned Nick again in passing three hours before, at Massada, sitting in the darkness on the edge of Herod's ritual bath, watching the pink line of dawn split the night sky from the Moab hills. Somewhere on the far side of those hills, and a few miles to the south, was Petra, rose-red and half as old as the yarn she'd been spinning him. And yet he'd believed what she'd told him there. It wasn't a story about Harry, or the film, or weddings in Wales: it was about her. The truth, nothing but the truth, but not necessarily the whole truth. However, he was making progress.

She wasn't twenty-six, she was thirty. Her father was a businessman, now dead, a surfeit of long expense-account lunches: her mother a beauty who aged badly. He left her for someone else, then died; she moved to Suffolk and took to the bottle, but not to excess, just as a gentle anaesthetic against reality, a way of forgetting the things she'd meant to do with her life and hadn't. There were three children: Julia, a brother who was a dentist in Leeds (not Australia), and a sister married to a self-sufficient hippy somewhere in the Welsh borders, with a kitchen-full of long-haired children who wiped their ever-running noses on the sleeves of their ankle-length home-knit jumpers. Julia was educated at a liberal-minded co-ed boarding school, lost her virginity at fifteen without enjoying it much, smoked, listened to rock music, acted, played tennis, flirted with boys, learned about clothes and make-up, ski'd in winter, went to France and Tuscany and Greece in the summers. Academically she was bright.

'Or I was good at exams, which isn't necessarily the same, I suppose.' She'd lit another cigarette, the pink line above the Jordan hills bleeding up into the sky like watercolour on wet cartridge paper. 'I always came second, though. If you come first or third people say well done. If you come second they think you should have come first; you're bright but you're not really trying.'

But of course no one wanted her to try: they just wanted her to be herself. At that age, when most people are busy deciding – or being told – who to become, it was made clear to Julia that she needn't become anything other than what she was: a pretty, cheerful, friendly, relaxed, intelligent young woman.

Pretty being the operative word. You can be all the rest, and the world still expects you to *do* something with your talents. Your jokes have to be funny, your observations astute. But not if you're pretty, not if you have long lean legs and a good figure and a graceful neck, and strong shoulders and long fingers and lithe wrists, and bright laughing eyes and healthy blonde hair, and a perfect mouth through which the perfect white teeth show when you smile, which is often. Not if you're Julia Cornwall. You realise that they don't want you to achieve anything in life, they just want you to be what you already are. Or what they think you are. Anything you say is interesting, all your jokes are funny, or if they're not they're charming.

'Do you understand all this, Charlie? I'm not trying to boast, I'm trying to explain.'

Charlie understood. They sat close but not touching.

'This was when you got to University?'

'Then, and after.'

The Moab hills had gained their third dimension now, no longer a silhouette but a battered wall of red sandstone slashed with the dark shadows of the wadis, rising out of the soft early morning mists of the Dead Sea.

'I didn't try to look the way I did,' Julia explained. 'It was just how I was. A lot of women hated me because men hovered round me like moths, and I wasn't even trying. So I lost the friendship of women and had to make do with men. Only the sort of men I liked were terrified to come near me. The ones who had the bottle were shallow and vain. Entertaining, some-times, but shallow, shallow as clingwrap. And they didn't want a friend, they wanted a good-looking lover, someone to be seen with. Or messed around with: a man who can afford to fuck up a pretty woman is reckoned to be someone special. And they didn't mind paying for the privilege – they gave me whatever I wanted. I didn't have to ask, I didn't have to do anything, they just gave me things. Took me out, took me on holiday, took me to stay in expensive hotels, bought me extravagant presents. I had a cheerful, playful nature, I went along with it. Seemed churlish not to. But I felt a fraud, because I wasn't doing anything, I wasn't giving anything back. Not even in bed – bed was OK, but nothing special, I didn't really enjoy it much then.'

She lit another cigarette, blowing the smoke at the view.

'You're not crying, Charlie, you're meant to be crying by now. This is a sad story.'

'Very satisfying, though. I was one of the shy ones who didn't dare talk to people like you.'

'Liar.'

'Snap.'

She gave him a look.

'I'm not lying.'

'I know. I'm sorry, it's the shock of discovering I'm not old enough to be your father. Go on.'

They got up from the bath and walked across to the West Gate, looking down on the Roman ramp. The landscape was very empty, receding lines of hard bare hills stretching away as far as the eye could see.

'That's it, really.' She leaned against the fortress wall. 'Then and since. Everyone else got on with their lives, I stayed the same because that's all anyone expected of me. Anything I wanted I got, just for being me. But there was nothing specific I wanted, nothing anyone wanted me to achieve. All through my twenties. I think you have to be a bit hungry or angry to achieve things – I've never been either. And suddenly I was thirty, unmarried, no kids, none of my relationships had gone anywhere much. And I was convinced that the moment men got past the stage of wanting to look at me, they'd discover I was ordinary. Unless they were married: the married ones seemed safer, in a way. They fancied me because I was free and independent, and they weren't; they hankered after the danger of falling in love, of illicit liaisons. And I learned to push the independent image, because that's what that kind of man wants. The last thing he fantasises about is domesticity, babies, sagging tits and greying hair. So here I am. Deep down I'm not dangerous enough to go crazy over, or domesticated enough to marry. You reach that conclusion about yourself, there doesn't seem much point in anything. Everything's OK, but pointless. Close to the edge of the abyss. What most people do in that situation is marry someone safe and dull and middle-aged, who may not be their Dream Male but will probably be kind and generous and not too demanding.'

'And what does your Dream Male consist of?'

'The usual. Extrovert and quiet, funny and serious, thoughtful and impulsive, gentle and passionate, tolerant and strong-minded, intelligent, modest . . . I haven't a clue, Charlie.'

'And you met him.'

She gave him another look.

'Yes.'

'But you're not with him any more.'

'I don't know.'

'And he's why you're here?'

'No comment.'

'Fair enough.' They got to their feet.

'You know why I brought you here?' Charlie asked her.

153

'Because Massada is a symbol for Israel. But not the symbol they write about in the guide books: it's a symbol of necrophilia. You drive out from Jerusalem through that empty desert, climb a bare, lifeless mountain, and when you get to the top, what do you find? Nothing. A pile of stones, the ruins of some old paranoid's fortress. In the middle of a barren, useless desert. And this is what the Yaakov Tylers aspire to: climb on top of a rock and pull up the drawbridge, shut out the real world, shut out the present, pretend you're still living in the first century AD. Except the Zealots who died here in the first century weren't much concerned with even *that* reality – their heads were further back still, somewhere in the second millennium BC. It's a great trick if you can pull it – no need to worry about your mother dying, or the programme you're meant to be taping in four days' time, or paying the rent, or getting on with your neighbours. It's as if they're all walking backwards. And those guys – the modern zealots – want Israel to be like that, a new Massada, ready and waiting for the apocalypse.'

'You really believe that?' asked Julia.

'Not really. You talk to Walter, or Goliath, or David Bermant, a lot of Israelis, most of the Jews in the diaspora, and you understand how they feel, how much it matters to them to have a country where they don't have to live as strangers. Nothing special, just a place to live, and to get on with their lives. And then you talk to the Settlers. Correction: you don't talk to them, you listen. And it scares the shit out of you.'

They'd reached the edge of the cliff.

'Let's go find some breakfast,' said Charlie.

And they'd taken the Snake Path back down the cliffs to the car park, wondering how they'd ever managed it in the darkness two hours before. Lights were going on in the kibbutz by the cable car terminus, but the café was closed.

And so to Beersheba, by way of Arad, a twisting mountain road across the wilderness.

'How's my jigsaw doing?' she asked, lighting another cigarette.

'Getting there. Still not done, but I'm getting there. Always do the edges first, they're the hardest bit.'

An army truck drove past, scattering dust. She wiped her fingers on the paper table cloth, eyes down.

'Charlie.'

'Yes?'

She looked up, and put her hand on his wrist.

'I'm being stupid. Of course you have to go home. I should be helping you instead of cracking up all over you. We haven't even talked about your mother. Are you worried about her?'

'I should be, but I'm not. One of those emotions you know you should be feeling but don't.' He gripped her hand. 'We should go, we're late.'

At last, at last, she was back. And he realised the truth. Whatever the danger was it wasn't to do with him, he was peripheral. She was the one they were following, she was the one who cried in her sleep. All night he'd been fishing without confronting her, looking for clues, arrogantly assuming he was the crux of the problem. But now she'd said he could go.

He sensed the crisis was still there, but now he could accept it at face value. She had a motive: she was out of her depth, had bitten off more than she could chew, a woman facing a mid-life crisis who had decided to stop going with the flow of fate, decided to turn and swim against the current. What she was frightened of was doing it alone. Now he knew that, he could start to help her. Sooner or later she'd talk about Nick, in her own time. They'd reached that crisis in a relationship, the point where you have to find the courage to admit your vulnerabilities, stop pretending you're superhuman, trust your lover to love you for your faults and weaknesses.

It still didn't explain the jokers in the pick-up, but Charlie was well used to all that, these things were not uncommon in Britain, let alone Israel. All it took was a slight irregularity on your passport, or a policeman's mistaken hunch. On another trip to Israel, filming an innocuous piece of nonsense about the Eurovision Song Contest, he'd gone back to his room at the Hilton one lunchtime to find an engineer fitting a bug to his telephone. 'Sorry, wrong room,' the man told him, as though that explained anything. In Moscow they eavesdropped on all ten thousand foreign residents, twenty-four hours a day. Which meant thirty thousand listeners, working eight-hour shifts, making the operation one of the largest employers in the Soviet Union. Surveillance was a habit, harmless unless you had something to hide. And he had nothing to hide, nothing at all. He leaned over and kissed her on the mouth, and she kissed him back, and smiled a shy smile, back together again. Now he knew she needed help, he could help her.

The road back to Jerusalem was fast, a straight run across the Judaic Highlands, through Hebron and Bethlehem. The traffic was light. It was quarter to ten when Charlie pulled up outside the Anani. The weather had cleared overnight and the air was warm and dry, smelling of pine and petrol. He left Julia in the car while he went to collect his suitcase.

As he by-passed the lounging policemen on his way across the lobby Salam Anani called across to him.

'Mr Kavanagh! We thought you'd gone!'

Salam reached into the pigeon-holes behind the desk and handed him down the two messages.

One was from Vincent, timed at eight that morning, confirming the flight. BA had been bullied into upgrading him to Club Class. That's my boy, Vincent. I wonder who you told them I was. Travel Editor of *The Observer*, probably. Or Carol Thatcher's fiancé.

The second envelope contained a cable from London. Charlie tore it open, fished out the flimsy sheet of telex, read it once, then again, and stuffed it in his pocket.

He went back out to the car park and told Julia the news.

'Betty's OK. Back to square one.'

'Charlie! But that's wonderful!' She was out of the car, arms round him. 'Read it to me!'

'Fractures minor stop,' he intoned wryly, 'No concussion stop absolutely no cause for concern stop no need to break off your trip stop best wishes Dr Patterson.'

He handed her the telegram and gripped her by the waist.

Julia laughed aloud.

'I don't believe it!'

Nor did Charlie. Because there never was a fall, there never were any fractures, or concussion. He'd made it all up.

The original message from London had been real enough. But

by the time he'd phoned the hospital from the Ambassador's study, Betty's crisis had been and gone – a possible coronary that turned out to be nothing of the sort. They'd kept her in overnight and then sent her home to Highgate.

Two years before, when he was still married, he'd had an argument with the first Julia. They were at the end of a miserable, bickering holiday in Scotland, driving across Rannoch Moor on their way back from Ardnamurchan to Glasgow. The row had rumbled all the way up Glencoe, in rain so torrential that the water running off the bare mountains made them look like submarines surfacing in a storm. He had no memory at all of what the argument was about, except that it started as something trivial and escalated until the air in the Renault was poisoned with speechless rage. Julia was driving. They hadn't spoken for five or ten minutes, silently rehearsing their indignation and resentments. Then she'd made a cutting remark. Suddenly Charlie exploded, shouted at her to stop the car, got out, slammed the door and walked off into the bog, gale blowing, shoes full of water, just in order not to be in the car with her any more. It was as if his brain had boiled over.

He had no plan as to what to do next, just a reflex that things couldn't go on like this any longer, that a crisis was called for.

And that was what had happened in the Ambassador's study. The lie had come to him quite spontaneously, spoken before he'd even started to think it through. This time there was no anger, no blind rage, just a primal impulse to bring things to a head. Instead of boiling over his brain had fused. He didn't know what was going on, or why. He'd been drugged with sex and money, and then used for he wasn't sure what. He didn't believe in Harry Greenbaum, or Eric, or their programme. He didn't think the bomb at the Royal Garden was a coincidence. Didn't believe, didn't disbelieve. It could all be paranoia, of course, but he didn't have enough information even to know that. All the initiatives up to now had come from somewhere else. He'd reached a point where he felt blind, completely out of control. He needed to test the system, try and put his finger on what was so odd about this whole scam, see what happened if he derailed Harry Greenbaum's sleek, well-oiled roller coaster for a couple of days.

Dr Patterson was a phoney. And a phoney with an accomplice. Someone didn't want him to leave the country, someone who knew he was about to. He thought back to the night before, wondering who could have set him up. Not a long list: Vincent, Roger, Julia. Joan Willis, from the Consulate. Improbable. And that was all. The facts of the case begin to emerge, Milud.

So much for the poor little pretty-girl with the mid-life crisis.

Why would Harry Greenbaum pick an inexperienced novice like Julia to spend his money? Harry might be many things, but he hadn't struck Charlie as a fool. Maybe they were all in on it – Harry, Eric, Julia, even Walter. Though he doubted if Walter was involved: Walter seemed more like a fellow-victim than a conspirator.

Whatever was going on, it wasn't his business. He was being used. A week ago he'd hardly met these people. Why was he useful to them? What was it they wanted him to do? He went over the schedule in his mind, looking for clues, trying to think laterally. A man cycles across the Swiss/Italian border every day with a sack of rocks over his shoulder: the customs stop him time after time, search his sack, search his clothes, looking for contraband, find nothing. Because what he's smuggling is bicycles. It had to be something like that, something totally mundane.

In the bedroom he was all noisy bonhomie, singing in the shower, proposing toasts with the last of the duty free booze, a model of relieved enthusiasm. Keep up the spirits, keep up the mood. Remember, they think I think something good just happened to me. It was an effort – it was thirty hours since he'd slept, many of them eventful. He wondered if the room was bugged, where the microphone was. No point looking, just assume it's there. Wired into the phone, probably. Julia joined in the celebrations, but it wasn't a terribly convincing performance, more like a prisoner at a Christmas party who'd been given a paper hat and a plastic nose and told to enjoy herself.

' "Tell me who's been polishing the sun",' he serenaded her, ' "Shining up the clouds so grey ..." '

Julia rang Walter, and told him the news. Then Charlie rang the airport and cancelled his reservation.

'Certainly, Sir Charles,' said the British Airways girl in a respectful Home Counties accent. Only a knighthood, Vincent. You disappoint me.

His other calls he needed to make alone, from a clean phone. Julia was by now in the bath.

'Back soon,' he called through the door.

'Where are you going?'

'A surprise.' He'd think of one before he got back.

'Hold on ...'

But he was gone.

He left the Anani by the goods entrance, via a service lift and the laundry, looking cheerfully lost as he bumbled past waiters and chambermaids, until he found himself in a narrow lane lined with refuse bins. No Miss Marble, no blonde athletes. He headed up the lane away from the main road, kept walking until he reached the Nablus road, crossed over to the Sheikh Jarrah filling station, and asked if he could use their payphone. The boy was helpful, and sold him a token.

'With Thank You And Courtesy' said the sign above the petrol pumps. You'd get arrested offering that kind of service in the New City.

Roger wasn't at the Embassy, and the girl on the switchboard wouldn't give him a home number.

'This is Sir Toby Eady,' he explained nicely, 'MEP.'

No one, but no one, knew the names of Euro-MPs.

Still no number, but she offered to ring Roger and give him Charlie's number.

'Difficult,' said Charlie, looking at the blank dial in front of him, 'I'm on the move. Why don't you ring him and ask if it's all right, and I'll call you back?'

Which she did.

Roger was about to leave for lunch.

'Get a pen,' said Charlie, 'and don't ask any questions. There isn't time to explain. I swear it's important.'

He heard a sigh rather like the sea running back over a gravel beach.

'Where are you, Charles?'

'Turn left at the air pump, half-right at the grease-gun, and straight ahead of you you'll see a queue for the phone. I'm the one at the front of the queue, in the kilt. Are you ready?'

'OK. Fire away.'

'I want police records on a Nick Parrish, Brit, probably in his thirties. I want to know when a Julia Cornwall last applied for a passport, and where.''

'The blonde?'

'Correct. And if she's recently registered a Ford Sierra in her own name. And I need to find out from the Americans if they've ever heard of someone called Harry Greenbaum, pharmaceuticals tycoon. Or something called the Harry Greenbaum Foundation. It's a charity, if it exists.'

'Your cheque bounced.'

'Nothing so straightforward.'

'Is that all?'

'For now. It'll take time. It has to be quick, Rog.'

'I'll do what I can. How will I find you?'

'Whistle,' Charlie slipped into a passable Bacall falsetto. 'You know how to whistle, don't you, Roger? You just put your lips together and suck.'

Next he tried Goliath, but all he got was an answering machine.

Back at the Anani he stopped off at the reception and asked to see his bill. It was half-past ten.

'You leaving, Mr Kavanagh?' asked the clerk.

But he just wanted to check his phone calls. Or Julia's, to be more precise. There were three that morning, two local, one to a number in Tel Aviv.

'Can I keep this?'

'Of course.'

He folded the account and stuffed it in his jacket pocket.

Julia was on the balcony, her back to the room, long thin fingers grasping the balustrade. She'd changed into a skirt and blouse, very cool and clean, and put on his fuchsia earrings and a splash of perfume. He handed her a scrap of paper with the biro drawing on it.

'Is this my surprise?'

'Uh huh.'

'What is it?'

'It's a painting. Only the gallery was closed. Terrible country to shop in this – Friday the Muslims shut up shop, Saturday the Jews, Sunday the Christians. You like it?' His voice aped Harry this time, back in the hotel suite in London two long, long weeks ago. 'Take it, Julia, I'd like you to have it. I can always get another.'

She looked at his drawing, turning it through a hundred and eighty degrees, then back again, and smiled a brave smile.

'What's it of?'

'Two old bachelor farmers hoeing a field of melons. Two brothers who live alone together, on the family farm, no electricity or running water and almost no furniture, no curtains or carpets and a single-ring cooker and two tea-cups and one saucepan. And they work the land as their father did, by hand, slow and hard, plodding through the seasons. Very subdued colours, weary grey and soil-brown, with withered green leaves. And away in the background' – he pointed at the paper – 'there's a main road, and a group of racing cyclists in day-glo shorts and shirts, heads down, legs working, hurrying past from one place the brothers have never been to another. And the brothers don't even look up, just keep hoeing. At least that's my reading of it. Oil on canvas, about four foot square. The frame's natural wood.'

Who are you, Julia Cornwall? Why are you doing whatever it is you're doing? Why do I have this feeling that you're not as hateful as I think? Maybe you're not ready to tell me yet. Maybe that's it.

'Are we the brothers or the cyclists?' she asked.

'Both.' He looked out the window at the sunlit city. 'You know those soldiers we met last night? In seventy-eight I was up at Matulla, in the pan-handle between the Golan and Lebanon, the day the Israelis launched Operation Litani. We were filming an artillery unit, firing across the border into Lebanon, at a crusader castle called Beaufort, twenty miles away to the north, where Fatah had holed up in the dungeons. All the might of modern warfare – a hundred and eighty millimetre guns, aircraft, the works, battering away at those crusader fortifications and getting nowhere. The walls are thirty, forty feet thick, shells just bounced off them. The lieutenant in charge of the Israeli guns was a Scotsman, from Glasgow – big Jewish community in Glasgow. He must have been about twenty-five. History graduate from Glasgow University. The subject of his Ph.D. thesis was 'Crusader castles of the Levant', and Beaufort in particular. And here he was a year later supervising the destruction of the bloody place. Archaeologist and artilleryman, preserver and destroyer, victim and oppressor, all the same thing. Olde Kavanagh's Book of Homelie Platitudes, chapter six, page forty-seven.' He fingered his collar. 'We should phone Feinberg and tell him we'll be late.'

'I already did, no problem. He'll see us at twelve. Walter'll meet us there.' She reached up and ran her fingers through his hair. 'Everything's going to be fine, Charlie.'

'Liar.'

A flicker crossed Julia's face.

'What do you mean?'

'The four commonest lies in the world are,' he listed them: ' "The cheque's in the post", "I love you", "The performance will start in three minutes", and "Everything's going to be fine".'

Julia gave him a big, dishonest smile.

'I need to get some cigarettes,' said Charlie. 'I'll be back in a minute.'

He had more calls to make, to England this time. Not the sort of calls you can make from a payphone.

'If you had a friend who thought his telephone was being bugged,' he asked Salam Anani, 'and who wanted to make a very personal call, what would you suggest?'

'In Israel?'

'Of course not. In another country.'

'Ah.' Salam looked at his fingernails. 'It depends. It depends if this someone was being listened to only in his hotel bedroom, or for example on the hotel switchboard, or even at the exchange. In some countries you know they will do all three, just to be certain. And in those countries they even arrange for pay-telephones near the hotel to be – what's the word? – monitored.'

'Suppose,' said Charlie, 'it was all three. And my friend found it difficult to leave his hotel. For personal reasons.'

'Then that would be difficult. If he couldn't get to a telephone then I think it would be necessary for the Mountain to come to Mohammed. So how are you enjoying your stay?'

'Enormously.'

'Good. Please, come with me, I have something I wish to show you. A new toy. My brother gave it to me for my birthday, I've been meaning to try it out for months. In fact I only used it yesterday for the first time.'

'I know,' said Charles. 'I saw you with it.'

'You did?'

Salam took him behind the reception, through a panelled door, into a small whitewashed catacomb containing a desk, two chairs and one of the finest Bokhara rugs Charlie had ever seen. A crucifix hung on the end wall: the Anani's were Christians.

He opened the desk drawer and took out a cordless phone.

'The main unit is here in the office. It has a range I think of sixty metres. Please.'

He handed it to Charlie.

'Just for half an hour or so,' Charlie explained.

'Of course. Any time.'

Dougie Thomas closed his eyes and tried to pretend the shuddering body beneath him wasn't Doreen. Dougie who was Charlie's friend at London Weekend Television, Doreen who was Dougie's Personnel Officer, the one who OK'd his expenses. Doreen was wobble-bottomed, white-bloused and crucifixed, with close-cropped hair, a mole on her upper lips and eyebrows that met in the middle, and knew enough about Dougie's financial misdemeanours to have him thrown out of the company. Which explained his present predicament.

'Douglas!' she cried out with every thrust, as if to remind him she was there, 'Douglas! Douglas! Douglas! DOUGLAS!'

He put one hand across her mouth to muffle her, and used the other to balance his weight against the wall. The chrome and corduroy office sofa rattled under them like a railway truck in a shunting yard. Above them the rain beat against the wide picture window, high up on London Weekend Television's Kent House. Far below on the wet concrete walkways of the South Bank the first of the weekend commuters were hurrying away towards Waterloo station. The door was locked, the office next door empty. He hoped.

'Douglas!' She snatched his hand away from her face. 'Is that good? Harder, oh oh my God, gently, you're hurting me. Move your leg higher. The other one, darling. Further.'

Darling? Help.

Doreen's bra and petticoat were peeled up over her full white breasts, and her tights hung from one ankle. Dougie's pants and trousers lay in a heap at his feet: he still had his shirt and socks on.

He snatched a glance at his watch.

'Take me,' she ordered him, 'take me! Or I'll tell them everything.'

Dougie did what he was told, until the rattling subsided into post-coital silence.

'You're a very experienced virgin, Doreen,' he joked afterwards, urgently lighting a cheroot. She lay across his chest, her hand on his stomach, and told him she loved him, but that he wasn't to worry about it. He worried a great deal.

The phone in the outside office rang twice before switching itself through to the ansaphone. Charlie's voice sounded far away, down the end of a long metal tube.

'Hello, ansaphone, this is Charlie Kavanagh looking for Dougie, rather urgently.'

'There's no one here,' Doreen called back. She bent down, opened Dougie's shirt and kissed him wetly on the nipple.

'Oh yes there is,' said Dougie, and grabbed the phone.

'Dougie?' said Charlie. 'I wonder if you could do me a favour.'

Dougie listened as Charlie talked, scribbling notes. Doreen had her hand between his legs again.

'When do you want all this by, Charlie?'

'The day after tomorrow. We record on Monday.'

'Do you mind who I hire? I could try and get Apple Townsend. But she's expensive.'

'Don't worry about money,' said Charlie. 'Harry's paying.'

14

THE NAMEPLATES ON THE entryphones in Rehavia were heavily studded with Doctors, some of them medical, many not. Danny Feinberg went one better and called himself Professor, which he had been, once. He lived three blocks away from David Bermant, at the end of a quiet tree-lined cul-de-sac leading to a small park with a children's playground. More greenery than you would have thought possible filled the narrow gaps between the four-storey apartment houses and shaded the tiny gardens – pines, date palms, carob and fig. Ivy and clematis hung from the balconies, which also hosted their own miniature forests of pot-plants and shrubs. The street was largely residential, apart from an Institute, a private clinic and a small row of shops on the corner of the main road – a dry cleaner, a hairdresser's, a small polite grocer's selling imported foods, and a modest bank with smoked-glass windows. In the playground a bored *au pair* read a paperback novel on a bench while her solitary charge clambered over the red plastic climbing-frame, and an elderly woman in a fur coat, hands clasped across her bosom, walked her chihuahua along the tarmac path between beds of narcissi and rosemary. All very European: half-close your eyes, forget the palms, and this could be Prague or Vienna. A far cry from the noisy souks and construction sites a mile to the East: no foot patrols here, no Border Police behind their blue and white steel barricades.

Charlie and Julia parked the Subaru under a tree outside Feinberg's apartment. Walter came across to join them, a plastic SoopaFoods carrier bag of papers under his arm.

'Shove off, Jewboy,' said Charlie cheerfully. 'We're closed.'
Walter grinned.

'What about my pound of flesh?'

'The abattoir was shut.' He picked up his papers and got out of the car. 'You can have a slice off Julia if you're really hungry.'

'Thanks and no thanks. Nothing personal, Julia, but it has to be kosher, it's in my contract. Did you bring the Professor's flowers?'

'He's gay?'

'As the Fourth of July.'

'I think I'll wait down here,' said Julia.

'No, we need you for protection.'

Feinberg was a small man, almost completely bald, with a soft black beard that nearly disguised his lack of chin, and a habit of clasping his manicured hands across his chest while he talked. His apartment was on the third floor, tastefully furnished in the Bauhaus style, steel and glass and brightly coloured geometric fabrics. The air smelled of fresh coffee and freesias.

'You know the longest silence known to man?' he joked as he steered them round an angular bronze sculpture that Charlie thought might be a Gaudier-Brzeska. 'It comes after someone asks you what you do and you say "I'm a mathematician." No one knows what to say next.' He'd given up his university post fifteen years before and turned himself into a lawyer. 'Not because of the silence: because of the money. No one can afford to pursue that kind of knowledge any more, not unless there's a practical application. There is, of course, but not in the university.'

These days he applied his legal and mathematical skills to commerce, advising merchant banks and public corporations on risks and probabilities, lending his sober academic credentials to the prospectuses of adventurous property developers and commodity brokers.

Before they started talking he wanted to settle his fee.

'Six hundred dollars,' he announced. 'Not because I need it, but because it's what I think I'm worth. You sell yourself too cheaply, people don't take you seriously. That's one of Bermant's problems: he gives himself away to anyone, so no one values his opinions.'

Charlie looked at Walter, then at Julia.

'Fine,' she said, and filled out a contract form for him. Feinberg put on his glasses, read it through, took a gold fountain pen out of his jacket pocket and signed.

'Who's going to see this programme?' he asked.

'Europe and the States,' said Charlie.

'I should have asked for more.'

He disappeared to the kitchen and returned with coffee and petits fours.

'So what do you want me to ask him?'

Charlie was too tired to remember without consulting his notes. Feinberg's relationship with Bermant was largely professional: the two men had sat together on various public bodies over the years – a board of enquiry into agricultural exports, a committee set up to assess the effectiveness of army education programmes. He was an odd choice, but Walter was keen, and Charlie had trusted his judgement.

'In a sense it's up to you.'

'Ah! Delicious.' Feinberg chuckled and plunged his fists enthusiastically into the pockets of his cotton jacket. 'Let me see. I'd like to ask him about the price of his ideals, the years he spent preaching peace and drawing his army pension. I'd like to ask about the cost of keeping the kibbutz movement alive. And what lessons he draws about the viability of worker-control from the present state of the Histadrut, whether it's a serious labour organisation or a rest-home for failed socialist politicians. I'd be interested to know his views on civil rights in Syria and Jordan, and the place of women in Saudi Arabia. That sort of thing?'

'That'll do fine,' said Charlie.

He wasn't concentrating: his mind was on other things.

It was after one when they left the Professor and went to look at the location for Monday's dinner. Charlie had wanted to do it at the Anani, but Julia vetoed him on the grounds that they'd need somewhere with a kosher kitchen. Instead they'd opted for the Star of David, a modern high-rise hotel on the western edge of New City, one of a colony of new hotels off Sderot Herzl that included the Hilton, the Sonesta and the Ramada. Handy for the Knesset and the Israel museum, but a long hike from the places most tourists would want to visit, a fact that was carefully disguised in the tour brochures by the use of phrases like 'quiet and secluded', and a heavy emphasis on the luxury of the in-house facilities.

The Star of David was light on character, but efficient and on the whole friendly. The General Manager was an Argentinian called Aaron Fluck, famous in Israeli folklore because the State President had once absent-mindedly introduced him to a conference on tourism as Aaron Clunt. Aaron was in his forties. He wore a hotelier's morning suit and a startlingly obvious hairpiece, and was the sort of man to whom nothing was too much trouble until you asked for it. Taking over the main hotel restaurant was out of the question, but in its place he offered them a choice of function suites, each named after an international airport. Air travel was the theme of the Star of David's current décor – last year, before its biennial refurbishment, the hotel had been dedicated to wildlife, with a stuffed bear and a tankful of terrapins in the lobby.

Aaron and his function manager met them in the lobby. Goliath was already there, together with an engineer, a sound supervisor and two lighting men. The ten of them set off on a conducted tour, notepads in hand, weighing up the advantages and disadvantages of the O'Hare and Schipol suites, puzzling over the problems of cable-access and acoustics and power supplies. Visually all the rooms were a disaster, but Charlie reckoned he could get away with most of them by careful set-dressing and atmospheric lighting. Initially they opted for the Gatwick, a square box with fake-wood panelling and a handsome chandelier. But the Gatwick wasn't free until six on Monday evening, too late for the crew to set up. Instead they chose the Sheremetyevo, christened in honour of Israel's cautious *détente* with the Soviet Union. The room was a barn, so big that it could be subdivided into three sections, each large enough to play tennis in. Hard to imagine how a space like that could be transformed into a suitable venue for an intimate soirée, but it would. Choose a corner, add a few pot-plants and paintings and bits of period furniture, install a couple of candles, turn off the overhead lights, add a few of your own, no problem. Or not many.

'Air conditioning,' said the soundman.

'We have it,' said Aaron.

'Off,' said the soundman. 'And I'll need some room-dividers.'

And a comfortable chair. Somehow soundmen always wound up with the best furniture on location: everyone else was off shifting cables, erecting lights, worrying about camera angles and reflective surfaces, and suddenly you turned round and found that sound had built themselves a comfortable little nest right in the middle of the room, comfy chairs, desks, telephones, electric kettles, the lot, just where camera one was meant to go.

Aaron wanted to know about the food.

'I don't suppose you do a De Luxe Meal C for Seven Persons?' asked Charlie.

'I'm sure we can arrange something like that.'

Charlie turned to Walter.

'Any suggestions?'

'A great many. You have a menu?'

'Of course,' said Aaron.

'That's settled then,' said Charlie. 'Walter's in charge of the catering.'

They had lunch in the Star of David's rooftop restaurant, formerly the Eagle's Nest, now the Alcock and Brown. The reservation desk was called Air Traffic Control and the waitresses wore leather flying caps and goggles.

Walter filled Charlie in on the state of his archive searches.

'I hate to raise the ugly question of ethics,' said the researcher through a mouthful of kleftiko, 'but how scrupulous are we being?'

'Explain,' said Charlie.

'Take the wars. If you want footage of a particular battle on a particular day in a particular place, it's going to be difficult. If all you want is guns firing in the desert, it's a lot easier. Same war, different location. Will anyone notice?'

'You were in the army, Walter – you tell me.'

'I don't know much about aircraft or tanks, I'm afraid. Not my area.'

'What was your area?' asked Julia curiously.

Walter looked sheepish.

'Bomb disposal. Still is, I'm afraid. When they remember to call me up. Everyone here stays in the Reserve, they don't let you off until you're fifty.'

'Bomb disposal? You're joking.'

'No. When they first drafted me I tried to get myself discharged on mental grounds, but it didn't work. Catch twenty-two is alive and well in the IDF: if you're sane enough to try for a mental health discharge then you're sane enough to fight. All that happens is they punish you by putting you in explosives. I know how to take the fuse out of a two hundred pound bomb, but I couldn't tell a Merkava tank from a Deux-Chevaux.'

Julia still didn't believe him.

'You really did that?'

'Defused bombs? Sure.'

'Weren't you scared?'

He laughed, and took a sip of beer.

'Of course I was. Bloody terrified. There's no trick, you just have to do it, you don't have any choice. It doesn't get any easier, either. Brown corduroys every time.'

'Shit,' said Charlie.

'Exactly.'

The Jewish Quarter of the Old City is small, maybe five hundred yards square, no bigger than Wembley Stadium, or the Hollywood Bowl. Before Independence it was indistinguishable from the narrow alleys and covered markets of the neighbouring Christian and Moslem quarters – dirty, noisy, overcrowded, not that different from the city which Theodore Herzl visited in 1898.

'When I remember thee in days to come, O Jerusalem,' the founding father of Zionism wrote, 'it will not be with delight. The musty deposits of two thousand years of inhumanity, intolerance and foulness lie in your reeking alleys. If Jerusalem is ever ours, I would begin by cleaning it up. I would tear down the filthy rat-holes, burn all the non-sacred ruins, and put the bazaars elsewhere. Then, retaining as much of the old architectural style as possible, I would build an airy, comfortable, properly sewered, brand new city around the holy places.'

During the War of Independence the Israelis and the Arab Legion took care of most of the tearing down and burning of the Jewish Quarter, and between '49 and '67 the Jordanians finished the job, leaving it ripe for architectural pasteurisation when the Israelis recaptured the Old City during the Six Day War.

Days of hope and glory, those had been. One of the first films Charlie made in Israel had been about the realisation of that Zionist dream, about the loving care with which the new buildings had been slotted in between the restored ruins, the pains the planners had taken to match the scale of the rest of the souk. The scale is right, the design tasteful, but the transition when you cross the divide from the Christian and Moslem quarters is still quite startling. Suddenly everything is tidy, everything is affluent. The narrow honey-stone streets and the cleverly interlocked buildings are improbably clean. There are no street vendors here, no urchins selling postcards, or hawkers with trays of halva or pistacchios, or cramped caverns hung with embroidered shirts and Bedouin dresses. The discreet arcade shops in the Jewish Quarter have plate-glass windows, and cash tills, and fixed prices on their up-market souvenirs and antiques. No crumbling plaster or graffiti on the walls either: just ceramic plaques and Visa and Amex signs; no money changers, just a computerised cash-dispenser outside the United Mizrahi Bank.

'Reminds me of Carcassonne,' said Julia, 'or even Covent Garden.'

'Except there aren't any pubs,' Charlie complained.

The apartments and houses are well designed, unobtrusive, the doors have brass entryphones and wrought-iron lamps, the windows are neat and double-glazed. Fig trees and tamarisk grow against the walls, plants and shrubs decorate the upstairs balconies. And all is quiet: no barkers, no traffic – the streets are too narrow for cars. The Company for the Restoration and Development of the Jewish Quarter has won many awards for its work, and you can understand why.

The main business inside the Quarter is now, as ever, religion. Almost every street and square contains a yeshiva, a school or college where the Orthodox study the Talmud. Yeshiva students, bearded, ringlocked, often dressed in the long black coats and hats of the eighteenth-century Polish *stetl*, can spend a year or a lifetime at their studies: they do no other work, nor are they subject, like other Israeli males, to military conscription. If a living has to be earned, their wives earn it. Thus spake the Lord.

It's a wonderful place for a devout Jew to live and worship, and the houses and apartments fetch equally wonderful prices, often from American immigrants, *olim*. Unseen, New York voices chatter and argue on the shrub-bedecked balconies, and the furniture and kitchen fittings glimpsed through the ground-floor windows are unmistakably North American. Half a mile away Armenians and Arabs hang sheets to air from their garret windows: here it's strictly duvets.

Yaakov Tyler met them at the door with a smile and a bone-cracking handshake and ushered them up the narrow stairs. It was a beautiful house. A spacious living room occupied the second floor, one set of windows giving on to a courtyard containing a fig tree in a stone trough, the other looking out across the ruins of the medieval German Hospice to the Dome of the Rock. The walls were white, the furniture a mix of chrome and black leather. Sacred artifacts lined the glass shelves – a ceremonial ram's horn, a nine-armed Menorah candlestick – and there were many, many books, mostly religion and politics.

Julia and Charlie sat down on the sofa, balancing their coffee cups. Walter perched himself on the edge of a cavernous velvet armchair. Yaakov stayed standing, his back to the window, hands in his trouser pockets.

Charlie apologised for changing their arrangements that morning.

'My mother had a fall,' he explained.

Yaakov looked sympathetic.

'Is she all right?'

'She's fine, thanks.'

Charlie put his coffee cup down on the floor. Yaakov gave his groin another scratch.

'I'm sorry too – about the Royal Garden. It's one thing if they want to blow me up, but they have no business involving people like you. This is not your argument.'

'Do they know who was behind it?' asked Charlie.

Yaakov shrugged.

'What are they calling themselves this week – Holy Jihad, The PFLP, The Revolutionary Palestine Army, Martyrs for the Faith, Black October, Green November, I lose track. People who don't like Jews.' He smiled, picked the coffee-pot up off the occasional table and refilled Julia's cup. 'Scotland Yard picked up two Lebanese students.'

'I heard,' said Charlie.

'I don't know if they've talked yet. We'll know soon enough – if it was them someone will be kidnapped in Beirut shortly, that's usually the way. Cheaper than putting up bail. So who are my co-stars in this movie?'

'No clues I'm afraid,' said Charlie.

The big man chuckled.

'And what would you like me to ask our friend Bermant about?'

'What he stands for, what he represents, how his political vision differs from yours, the place of religion in the State.'

'How long have I got?'

Professionals always ask the same questions. Charlie remembered briefing Sammy Cahn, composer of 'Three Coins in a Fountain', before a chat show once.

'You want me to do the story of how I wrote "Coins"?' asked Cahn. 'I tell it in four versions,' he explained. 'Two minutes, five minutes, seven or eleven minutes. Which do you want?'

Charlie asked for the five, and Cahn brought it within three seconds. Yaakov Tyler was that kind of professional too. What surprised Charlie was how generous the man was towards Bermant. Yaakov didn't agree with him on anything, but thought it vital that Israel tolerate his kind of people. They'd known each other thirty-odd years, served on opposing sides in the Knesset, differed on almost everything. But the anecdotes were almost affectionate, the criticisms muted. It was like listening to a carefully polite obituary.

'When it comes to the point he's as committed to the State as anyone, maybe more than most. It's like a couple deciding about

173

what house to build. They both argue endlessly about which way it should face, how many rooms it should have, how big the kitchen should be, whether they want a garden. But they never doubt they need it – they both need somewhere to live.'

David Bermant and Yaakov Tyler going on air and announcing they were life-long friends and colleagues was frankly the last thing Charlie wanted. There are few worse disasters in television than two antagonists who are booked to slag each other off and arrive in studio only to agree on everything that's put to them. As far as Tyler was concerned the Foreign Minister was a sincere, honest, patriot: their differences were differences of emphasis and interpretation, but not of substance. Areas of obvious disagreement were merely 'complex problems', which could be resolved with a little mutual goodwill. This from a man who explained the Holocaust as God's judgement on the Jews for mingling too freely with the gentile world, who less than a week before, at the Royal Garden, had been breathing fire and brimstone, advocating the expulsion of all Palestinians from *eretz Israel*, proposing a whole sheaf of fundamentalist laws that would exclude Reformed converts from citizenship, threatening to set up an independent Zionist state on the West Bank if the Jerusalem government did any kind of deal with the Arabs. Then – and on every other occasion Charlie had heard him in the past twenty years – he'd spoken and acted like an Ayatollah: today he was a lap-dog.

Charlie tried him on defence, policing, education, economics, social policy: nothing. As a last resort he threw a question on religion, exploring the divide between those Orthodox who, like Tyler, were passionately pro-Zionist and those who condemned the very existence of Israel as a biblical blasphemy. In the yeshivas, in the synagogue discussion-rooms, the *besh medresh*, arguments over such things run for centuries. In this world debates about angels on the head of a pin are regarded as macrocosmic. Tyler, however, treated the question as if he'd been asked about flower arranging.

'In Britain or America,' he replied amiably, 'you have people who believe in all sorts of things. Ideas get discussed, one man believes one thing, another believes another, it's up to the individual to respect the position of his adversary and then decide what he must do. It's not so different here. Except that unlike Britain or America we don't have a secure country to argue about, we have to spend all our time defending our borders against people who want to slit our throats. You know how the Americans worry about Central America? Imagine if Canada was Iran, if Mexico was Libya.'

Charlie nodded, but without much conviction.

'You'd like me to be a little harder, eh?' Yaakov guessed.

'I'm afraid so,' said Charlie.

'A little more argumentative, a little more Jewish. Of course.' He turned to Julia. 'I saw a TV programme in London once, a discussion on what should be done about old Nazis, whether they should still be kept locked up. Ludovic Kennedy, talking to a rabbi in Amsterdam about two old fascists who were in prison there. These were men who had arranged the deaths of tens of thousands of Jews, people they had never even met before. Tens of thousands, can you imagine it? Think of someone you're fond of, and their wife or husband, and their children, and their neighbours, a whole street, the next street, on and on, until it's a large town, all taken away and gassed on the orders of these two collaborators. And these Nazis were unrepentant: if the same situation arose they'd do it all over again. In this situation, said the rabbi, the best thing was to leave them behind bars. And you know what Kennedy said to him? "Don't you think that's a very unChristian attitude, rabbi?" *UnChristian*. To a rabbi. It's true, I saw it with my own eyes.' Tyler chuckled. 'You know what I'd do to them – the Nazi geriatrics? I'd let them out on condition they came and lived here, in Israel. Put them on a kibbutz some place, so they have to sit down to three meals a day with a roomful of yids, have their bodies looked after by Jewish doctors. Heh!'

Time was running out: in half an hour it would be sundown, the start of the Sabbath. Nothing moved in the Jewish Quarter on the Sabbath, least of all men like Yaakov Tyler. The Jewish Quarter on the Sabbath made Stornaway on a wet Sunday look like Las Vegas.

'OK,' Yaakov concluded. 'You want the raging bull. Of course. David and I have had these arguments many times before. Which I presume is why you booked me. No, I don't mean that rudely, I understand. A dialectic. If he's happy with that, so am I. It won't resolve anything, but it may enlighten.'

'What the hell was that about?' Charlie asked as soon as they were outside. 'He's meant to be the Mad Axeman. On that form he'd make a first-class babysitter.'

Julia shrugged her shoulders.

'Who, Yaakov? He'll do all right, won't he?'

For what, Charlie wondered.

15

THE SUN'S SHADOWS WERE moving up the walls of the Quarter towards the Sabbath dusk as they made their way back through the narrow lanes, past the War of Independence Memorial and into the open square in front of the Ramban Synagogue. The square was empty except for a solitary Arab pushing a trolley of boxes and a brace of cats scavenging a small skip of rubbish, hungry to take what they could before the Municipality rushed it away.

'That business of the unChristian rabbi,' said Walter, 'reminded me of a Japanese correspondent who arrived in Cairo, his first posting, and sent home a report saying that the best illustration of the state of Egypt's moral decadence was that no one ate seaweed for breakfast.'

'He only told that story to humiliate us,' said Julia crossly. 'Moral blackmail. It's fifty years ago, Charlie. None of us were even born. What the hell are we supposed to do about it?'

'Make sure it never happens again, I suppose. It's one of those questions that doesn't have an answer. You can argue both ends all night, but in the end it's in your gut. Love, jealousy, revenge, rock and roll – what's there to talk about? Either you feel it or you don't.'

They moved on, under an archway and down a thin alley beside the Wohl Torah Centre, its windows already dark for Sabbath, to the car park at Beit Hasofer, overlooking the City Wall and the Kidron Valley. Beyond, on the far side of the valley, was the Arab village of Silwan, its jumble of flat-roofed houses climbing like broken steps up the steep hillside. Silwan was silent and deserted too, but for another reason. The military curfew had been in force there for three days now, the population confined to their houses while police went from door to door looking for troublemakers, collecting unpaid traffic fines and television licences, impounding property and even vehicles from those who couldn't or wouldn't pay up. Further East the dying sun cast a pink wash over the vast and ancient Jewish cemetery on the slopes of the Mount of Olives, where the dead lay waiting to enter through the Golden Gate on the Day of Judgement.

'You coming to Eilat with us tomorrow?' Charlie asked Walter.

'No such luck. I need to spend some time at the hotel, they want to discuss security and so on. Also I need to talk to Bezeq and the IBA about the landlines.'

'Thanks for today, anyway. Maybe I'll call you in the morning.'

He gave Walter a punch on the shoulder, and the researcher scuttled back into the labyrinth of the Old City.

Julia stood looking at the Arab village.

'Do you ever look at a city and think – all those houses, all those lives, every bit as real as mine?' She spoke quietly, almost a whisper. 'It's like trying to imagine infinity.'

Charlie put his hand on her shoulder and gave her a squeeze. She put her arm round his waist and leaned in towards him.

'Sometimes,' she went on, 'I look at all the bedrooms and wonder what their secrets are, the things they only dare say to each other in bed, when it's dark. Not sexually, but naked and trusting. And all the things that go wrong with people's lives and marriages, all the lives that didn't work out. At least that's what I think when I'm up. When I'm down I think fuck them all, why do they all have it so easy? Do you know that feeling, Charlie – when one moment life is full of profound meaning, then in a flash has no meaning at all? Do you ever get that?'

'Yup.'

'Normally it only happens when I've been on my own a lot. But it's happening all the time now. I don't know why.'

'Fear.'

'Is that it?'

'I don't know. Are you afraid of something?'

Julia nodded, and let go of him. They walked together to the car.

That night they got drunk. Heavy drinking is not an Israeli vice, and the Sabbath Eve is a difficult night to try, but they managed it. They started back at the hotel, whiskeys in their room and then tequilas in the bar, and after that took a taxi to an Indonesian restaurant with a gentile proprietor off Ben Yehuda. They were almost the only guests, hunched over a red-clothed table by the window playing with the candle-wax and eating Ajam Bumbu and Lapies Daging. They were both so tired they were floating. Julia took her shoes off and rubbed her stockinged feet against Charlie's ankle.

Charlie leaned across and grabbed her by the wrists.

'I'm sick of all this good living, Julia. Why don't we run away, just walk out the door, phone your mother to let her know where we're going, get on a bus, make a whole new start.'

'Where would we go, Charlie?'

'Worthing. Croydon. Billericay – what does it matter? As long as it's got a WH Smith and a Boots and a Safeways. I could get a job in the bank, you could stay home getting bored . . .'

He let go of her and sat back in his chair.

'God, but we're lucky. You know that, how lucky we are? You're sitting there trying to look as cheerful as you can but you reckon deep down your problems are awful. Me too. We're a pair of spoiled brats. We have no responsibilities outside ourselves. No children, either of us can walk out on anything tomorrow and it wouldn't matter much. We've got plenty of upper-middle-class confidence, plenty of job qualifications and friends to take us up on them. There, that's my Thought for the Day. What's yours?'

Julia ran a finger round the rim of her wine-glass and lowered her eyes.

'I think you're right, we're lucky,' she said quietly.

'We're lucky, and we're ignorant as pigs,' Charlie went on, pointing his finger at her. Drink was beginning to slur his speech. 'We know less about life than the poor, the uneducated, the homeless. We know nothing, understand nothing, can achieve almost nothing significant with our lives. The best we can do is be kind to each other, and loyal to our friends and families, and cause as little pain as possible. Here endeth the platitudes.' He raised his glass, drank and wiped his lips. 'Shit, I'm exhausted though. I don't think either of us have had a proper night's rest in a week.'

'That's because we keep going to bed.'

'Probably.'

'You seem to thrive on it. Lack of sleep, that is. My mother always told me to beware of men who don't need sleep. Most of the world's evil geniuses made do on three or four hours a night. Hitler, Stalin, Thatcher ...'

'Thatcher's not a man.'

'No. Though a lot of feminists wish she was.'

The waiter brought more wine. Charlie could feel a bloom of cold sweat on his forehead, the drink beginning to hit hard.

'You ever sleep with your ex-wife?' Julia asked him.

'No. The earth moved on, and left no forwarding address.'

'Rubbish, Charlie.' Tiredness and alcohol were loosening her up too. 'Everyone does. I read about it in *Newsweek*, five out of six divorcees subsequently sleep with their ex's. Like clothes you keep in the cupboard for years without wearing them, then you get them out, put them on, remember how awful they are and put them back. Five years later you do the same thing all over again. Everyone has a spare fuck tucked away somewhere for a rainy day.'

'Who's yours?'

'Harry Greenbaum.'

'You're joking, of course.'

'Yes, Charlie. I'm joking.' She reached into her blouse and scratched her armpit. 'I'm not looking for anyone else at the moment. I'm too busy with what I've got.'

He squeezed her foot and lit a cigarette.

Half of him wanted to marry her there and then, the other half wanted to put her on the rack and keep turning the wheel until he got some honest answers.

'You know what I don't understand?'

'What don't you understand, Charlie?'

'Van Morrison's lyrics.'

She laughed and spilled the dregs of her wine across the table.

'That and a bunch of other things,' Charlie continued. 'For example: in what ways do cultures that write from left to right differ from those that write from right to left? Someone set that in an exam once. And: why is Variety called Variety when it's the most unvaried genre in the history of entertainment? That's another. Also,' he drew heavily on his cigarette, 'I don't begin to understand what's going on round here. I don't understand if someone's doing something to you, or if you're doing something to me, or if someone's doing it to both of us. I'm not even sure what it is that's being done, come to that. Does any of this make any sense? Are you as drunk as I am?'

Julia didn't answer, she just gave him a smile. She was looking straight at him, and it seemed to Charlie that she couldn't stop blinking, as though her eyelids were stuttering. But perhaps that was just the drink in him: a lot of things in the restaurant seemed to be behaving strangely, walls waving in the wind, pot-plants melting, noises he couldn't understand. Everything kept moving and staying in the same place at the same time.

'You know what my problem is?' he went on. 'I'm in love with you. When I fall in love with someone I'm out of control. I'm told the experience of having Kavanagh fall in love with you is a bit like having a six-foot cow pat dropped on your head, warm and wet, the shit goes everywhere, suffocates you. And when I'm in love I have no brakes. I have no brakes, and you have no steering. Bloody dangerous combination.'

She was still looking at him, straight in the eyes. He wondered if the pot-plant was melting for her too. And he wondered what she must have been like as a girl – what it must be like to grow up discovering a woman's body rather than a man's. But then the whole world wonders that, what it's like to be the other kind. Mostly they seem to decide men get the better deal.

At last she spoke, quietly, almost under her breath. Either that or Charlie had been talking horribly loudly.

'I love you too. I don't know what to do about it, but I love you Charlie. Can we go home now?'

'Sure.'

He called the waiter and asked for the bill.

'Certainly sir. Small or large?'

Charlie summoned all his concentration and signed the Visa voucher.

'You want a taxi?' asked the waiter.

'No thanks, we'll walk.'

It was maybe a mile to the Anani. He looked at Julia.

'You drunk too?'

'Uh huh.' Now she was standing he could see her rock from side to side as she tried to focus on his face. 'Air'll do us good.'

'Been a long day,' said Charlie. 'What time do we start in the morning?'

'We have to be in Beersheba by noon.'

'*Again*? Haven't we been to Beersheba once already today?'

'That was business, this is pleasure. You have an interview with an agricultural chemist.'

Eric and Tina were alone in the flat in Nayot. Shimon had gone out twenty minutes before, and wasn't due back for an hour.

'You ever been to Miami?' she asked him. 'I have an uncle in Miami who's in real estate. Only he says he's going to move because Miami is all Cubans and Colombians now, no one even speaks English. Which is a joke because apparently he couldn't speak English when he arrived there either.'

'The nearest I've been to Miami,' said Eric, 'is the airport. I stayed a night in a hotel with a swimming pool the size of a bidet and cheap mirrors on the bedroom ceiling. Everything smelled damp, you know that smell, like you're washing a wool sweater. I don't think you'd like Miami, Tina.'

Eric wondered if he should risk anything, a casual touch, a hand on her shoulder to emphasise some point he was making, see what came back at him.

'Fuck your uncle, tell me about yourself,' he suggested.

'I'm a Leo,' she told him.

'What time of day were you born?'

That usually got to them. You don't ask someone what time of day they were born unless you find them an interesting human being. Tina's fingers moved slowly up and down her arm. She wore skin-tight blue-jeans and a loose green short-sleeved blouse and she looked beautiful.

'Three in the morning.'

'Mmmm,' said Eric, nodding thoughtfully. 'What year?'

'I'm twenty-one.'

'Mmmm,' Eric repeated. 'How interesting.'

'Why?'

'Because that means you're astute, thoughtful, independent and strong-willed.'

Tina liked that. She ran her hand through her hair.

'What are you?' she asked.

'Pisces.'

'I guessed you were. Shall we go to bed?'

He hesitated. He wanted her, but he worried about the complications.

'What about Shimon?'

'He wouldn't mind.'

Eric doubted it. This was Shimon's flat, the bed was Shimon's bed. Eric was five foot four and weighed a hundred and ten pounds, Shimon was over six foot and half as heavy again. He didn't fancy getting into anything physical with Shimon, not unless he had a gun.

Fuck it, why not, he decided. But not to bed, people can smell what's been going on in their beds. They made do with the sofa, which was where Eric was sleeping anyway.

'I'd like to go to America,' Tina confessed afterwards as she got back into her jeans. 'Not Miami, somewhere in the wilderness, California or Colorado. Have you really killed people?'

'Maybe.' Eric buttoned up his shirt. 'And you?'

'Oh yes. Of course.'

He looked up. She was straightening her hair out in front of the mirror.

'How?' he asked.

'Drugs and chemicals, mostly. That's how I met Shimon, we were on a job together in Geneva. He's good but he's clumsy. They use me when they want things to be undetectable. Only this time it's meant to be detectable as undetectable, if you know what I mean. What was your favourite crime?'

He thought for a moment.

'The best ones aren't always the big ones. There was a scam up in Albany, long time ago, I was a student, must have been about nineteen. No big deal, but it was a lot of fun. We'd watch the long-stay car park at the airport, spot a family going off on vacation. Soon as their flight was airborne we'd lift their car, drive it back into town, put an ad in the paper for a quick sale. Owner emigrating, all that shit. And sell it to some dumb moose thought he was getting a bargain. Then we'd wait a couple of days and steal it back, drive it out to the airport, leave it where we found it first time round. The original owner gets back from his vacation, car's still there, doesn't even know it's been missing. Your kind of operation, invisible crime. Bliss.'

Shimon got back a little after midnight. His blond hair was cropped and black, and he sported a moustache, full and detachable. Tina giggled when she saw him, but Shimon took these things seriously.

'How do I look?' he asked, preening himself in front of the same mirror Eric had watched himself make love in twenty minutes before.

Tina thought he looked fine. The moustache would need fixing so that the joins didn't show close-up, but otherwise no problem. They got out a photo of Shimon taken two weeks ago, before he went on leave, with his real moustache in place. No one would know the difference. But Eric wasn't happy.

'I don't understand why you did it this way. The man saw you on the first day, right outside his window. You should have pulled out then, put someone else on the job. Instead you chase him half way to Jordan, just to make sure he knows what you look like. All you needed to do was leave a message at his hotel telling him his mum was all right. Which I did while you were off taking part in an identity parade beside the Dead Sea. You didn't even need to tail him in the first place, the woman was with him. That's the whole deal, she can't afford to screw up. Some covert operation this is turning into: one man with two overcoats. Fucking amateur night.'

Shimon unstuck his moustache, put it on the table and turned to face Eric. A hundred and eighty pounds of muscle against a hundred and ten of bone, not a strong proposition. But then he'd just fucked Shimon's girl-friend on Shimon's sofa, and he felt pretty good about that.

'You're right,' said Shimon, 'we do it your way. We fix it so you change flights without telling anyone and show up in the middle of the night with a plastic gun doing Sam Spade impressions, but unfortunately no one gets killed. Not your fault, just bad luck. Then we advertise in the paper for a part-time gumshoe to replace me, interview the applicants, tell them about the job, arrange for them to get on the government security rota. You're right, I'm sorry, next time we'll play it by the book. Fucking smart-ass.'

'Plenty of people could do the job. Inside people – aren't we meant to have friends on the inside? Apart from you, that is.' Then something dawned on Eric. 'Of course. It's money, isn't it. Someone else comes in, you lose your slice. I'm sorry, I take that back about amateur night, there's obviously serious money at stake here.'

'I'm not in it for money. Money's got damn all to do with it.'

'But you get paid?'

'Sure I get paid, what's that got to do with anything? I have expenses.'

'And if you don't do the job you don't get paid?'

'You're the hired hand, you're the one they had to buy in because they needed an American.'

'But I'm right, aren't I? You don't get paid unless you deliver?' Shimon didn't answer.

'Or maybe you're just doing this as a favour?' Eric went on. 'She cooks your supper, you help her knock off the odd politician – is that how it works?'

'You two should get married,' said Tina.

They calmed a little, half-apologised to each other.

'I know the girl can't afford to screw up,' said Shimon, 'but I'm worried.'

He bit the ring-pull off his beer with his teeth. Tina could never understand why he did that, it didn't even look tough, it just looked like he didn't know how to open a can of beer. Bottle-tops, yes: ring-pulls no.

'I think he's playing at something,' Shimon went on. 'I don't know what it is, but I don't trust him.'

'Leave him to me,' said Eric.

That night Charlie had a dream. He was standing on a beach

beside the sea, only the sea wasn't sea, it was something thick and heavy, fruit yoghurt maybe, so that the breakers slurped and slapped as they broke over the sand, only the sand wasn't sand but something soft and fine and treacherous, like icing sugar, or Fuller's Earth. A gale was blowing: clouds raced silently overhead, so that the weather changed by the second, and the sky was bright and clear one moment, slate-grey the next. Charlie stood on top of a steep dune, waiting for someone, impatient, afraid. Far in the distance a figure appeared, walking towards him, not necessarily threatening. A veiled woman – but who? Julia? His mother? The pre-Raphaelite? The other Julia? He strained his eyes, but the face was always in shadow. He could fly if he wanted, step off the dune and walk on air; but the wind was too strong, and each time he tried the gale blew him back inland, away from the beach and the woman. Behind him the land was dry and hard and hostile, a desert running away towards harsh inhospitable mountains. The woman kept walking and he wanted to cry out to her, warn her about the quicksands, but this was a silent movie, no voices. The figure was on the edge of the sand now: another step and she'd be gone. At the last moment before she vanished beneath the sand a gust of wind blew the veil from her face. No woman, but Vincent Fallop, wrapped in a counterpane.

Charlie was awake now. Bloody Vincent. Of course. But where was he?

16

THE MESSAGE WAS WAITING for Charlie and Julia when they came down to breakfast: Mr Lowe had arrived from America yesterday, Friday, and would very much like to see them while he was in town if they had time, though he realised how busy they were. They could contact him at the Hilton, if it wasn't too much trouble. Mr Greenbaum sent best wishes.

'Who the hell is Mr Lowe?' asked Charlie.

'Little Eric,' said Julia. 'You remember Eric?'

'The Earnest Mormon? What's he doing here?'

Julia had no idea. It was a late breakfast, after nine before they even sat down to table. Elsewhere, in Jewish Jerusalem, the faithful were tucking in to cold Sabbath fare. Here at the Anani, Charlie passed up the kippers in favour of Devils On Horseback smeared with Cooper's Oxford marmalade, and a side order of kedgeree. Hangovers always tended to give him an appetite. Julia too was hitting the solids, nose down in the scrambled egg, mainlining on sweet tea, paying for the previous night's excesses. The bloom of freshness which she usually radiated was today heavily dependent on the make-up bag.

'Do you think Harry's here as well?' Charlie wondered. 'Maybe that's what Eric's up to. The big man dropping in to see how his money's being spent. Have you talked to him at all?'

'No need, he said the first he wanted to hear from us was the countdown on the studio clock. I sort of got the impression he might show up on Monday, but I wouldn't count on it. That's his way, he likes to delegate, set up the deal and then stand back and watch it happen.'

Charlie read the *Jerusalem Post*. More trouble in Gaza: kids stone an IDF jeep, army shoots kids. In New York Sotheby's were auctioning a pig on which Andy Warhol had painted a picture. The pig was alive at the time it was painted but like the artist had since passed on. Critics and dealers were keen to find out if a dead work of art was worth more than a living one. A sixty-one-year-old baker in Ramla had gone on hunger strike because the manufacturers of his frost-damaged solar heating system refused to repair it on the grounds that frost in a place like Ramla was an Act of God.

Charlie smiled: he knew there'd be a hunger strike sooner or later. In Israel hunger strikes were the opening gambit in an argument, coming somewhere between having an idea and writing to the local paper about it. Israelis went on hunger strike because their phones were out of order, the garage overcharged them, their neighbour's dog barked too loud. The strikes varied in duration from a couple of hours to forty days, although the longer ones were more by way of a diet: last time Charlie was here two sisters in Zefat had eaten only bread and cheese for a month in protest at a change in the radio schedules; the time before a schoolteacher in Ashdod had given up breakfast and lunch because his estranged wife wouldn't allow him access to the family dog. What a wonderful world.

He poured himself another cup of Twinings and checked his watch.

'What shall we do about Eric?' asked Julia.

'Do we have any choice?'

'I suppose not. I wonder what time he gets in.'

Charlie phoned the Hilton from the bedroom.

'Welcome to Israel. Did I wake you?'

'Not at all, as a matter of fact I was watching the in-house movie,' said Eric.

'At this hour in the morning?'

'Sure. They're showing *Jagged Edge*, seems like a very exciting story.'

'The newspaper editor did it all along,' said Charlie. 'So what are your plans?'

'To be honest I don't have anything fixed the next couple of days, I wondered if maybe I could tag along with you people, learn a bit about the business.'

Charlie covered the mouthpiece with his hand.

'He wants to come with us,' he hissed to Julia.

'Why?'

'To see how a programme gets made. Yes or no?'

Julia shrugged.

'Yes, I suppose. I can't think of a reason why not. Or not one you could use to his face.'

'Shit,' said Charlie. 'I suppose not.'

They picked up Eric from his hotel at half-past ten. Same three-piece suit, same shirt and tie, same haircut, same polite, obsequious manner.

'You're sure I won't be in the way, Mr Kavanagh?'

'No, not at all. And it's Charlie – remember?'

Eric smiled apologetically.

'Sorry, Charlie. I just don't want to be a nuisance.'

'You're welcome. I'm afraid it's not a terribly exciting way to spend a day. Television's a bit like war, ninety-nine parts excruciating boredom to one part panic. You'll need a good book. What brings you here, anyway?'

Eric was in town on business for Mr Greenbaum, some contacts to follow up, avenues to explore. Necessary work, but not too much of it, so he thought he'd teach himself a little about the television business while he was here. If they were sure that was OK.

'We're going on to Eilat tonight, you'll need your suitcase,' Julia told him.

Eric already had an overnight bag, packed and ready.

'Let's get on the road, then,' said Charlie.

Eric perched in the middle of the back seat, leaning forward so that his head was level with theirs, nervous and eager as a spaniel pup.

'How's it been going? Getting what you need?' he asked.

'So far so good,' said Julia.

'We lost half a day,' Charlie explained. 'My mother was ill, we thought I might have to fly back to London.'

'Oh. I'm very sorry to hear that. About your mother I mean. But she's all right?'

'Yes, she's fine,' said Charlie. 'Harry's not coming out?'

'I don't think so, no, Mr Greenbaum's very tied up at the moment.'

They drove south. The roads were quiet, and they made good time across the city, out past the railway station and on to the Bethlehem Road. Charlie turned on the radio.

'People say that life is strange,' croaked Little Stevie Forbert. 'But compared to what?'

The weather was overcast, and a cold wind blew from the North. Two days ago people in the street wore shorts and sandals, today it was anoraks and desert boots. They were on the West Bank now, the housing unmistakably Arab, flat-roofed beneath tall TV aerials, the cars older. Israeli cars have yellow borders to their number plates, those from the Occupied Territories blue, hire-cars an unhappy compromise, yellow and white stripes. In the early days of the *intifada* the stone-throwers concentrated on the yellows, but nowadays they picked on anything that wasn't blue. The Subaru had a large press sticker inside the windscreen in English, Hebrew and Arabic, but even that was no protection, because the security forces had been known to rent hire-cars and pass themselves off as journalists when it suited them. As had some of the Settler vigilantes.

Outside Bethlehem a teenager tossed a half-brick which bounced noisily off the roof, but it wasn't until they reached Hebron that they hit serious trouble, the dying embers of what had been full-scale riot. The night before a woman from the neighbouring Jewish settlement at Qiryat Arba, north-east of the town, claimed that her car had been attacked by stone-throwers and her daughter injured by flying glass. In the small hours, Sabbath or no Sabbath, a convoy of settlers had driven down and set fire to Arab crops and vehicles. Today the army was out in force, fighting running battles with mobs of children and teenagers. There were settlers there too, blue and white Israeli flags fluttering from their car aerials, driving up and down the Arab streets to demonstrate their citizens' rights to be there, the same way Northern Ireland Protestants insist on marching through nationalist areas to remind the Catholics what country they're living in.

'Always Bloody Hebron,' Charlie cursed as a patrol waved them down.

Hebron, where Abraham was buried, and Sarah, and Isaac and Jacob, in the Cave of Machpelah behind the high walls of Haram el-Khalil, sacred to Moslem, Jew and Christian alike; where from the time of the Marmeluke conquests in 1267 no infidel set foot until 1862, when the Prince of Wales was granted a special dispensation by the Turkish Sultan to visit the tomb, and the scene of regular riots and pogroms ever since, most notably in 1929 when the Arabs massacred most of the Jewish population. If you were into confrontation, Hebron was where you moved to, long before the *intifada* came along.

In the distance a bulldozer and a flock of jeeps were gathered round the ruins of two Arab houses, demolished in retaliation for the morning's misdemeanours. The army examined Charlie's papers, and glanced into the back of the car.

'Press?' asked a corporal, pointing unnecessarily at the windscreen.

'Afraid so,' said Julia.

'All this is your fault, you know that?' said the soldier.

'We know,' said Charlie, 'but thanks for reminding us.'

'Just checking,' said the soldier. 'What country you from?'

'Canada.'

'You don't sound Canadian to me. But then Canadians don't sound too Canadian to me either when I come to think of it. Why do you come all this way? Haven't you got any troubles of your own in Canada?'

'We have,' said Charlie, 'but you can't lie about your own troubles, people spot it. It's safer to keep your lies for foreign countries.'

'Get the hell out of here, will you?'

'Have a nice day.'

They were directed on a long lonely diversion round the outskirts of town, the kind of diversion that keeps running out on you in places you don't feel like getting out and asking the way. Julia lit a cigarette for herself and one for Charlie, and Eric stayed very quiet in the back with his knees together and his arms gripped across his chest. Near the Russian Church two stones hit the car, denting the bonnet and cracking a nearside window. Charlie didn't stop to see who threw them. Not a big crack, more of a souvenir, but they were all relieved to be out on the open road again and heading for Beersheba.

'Does that happen a lot?' asked Eric nervously. 'I mean, should we be here?'

'Happens all the time,' said Charlie cheerfully. 'Welcome to Israel. Your first trip, Eric?'

'I was here once before, on a pilgrimage. But it was different then, they weren't throwing things. And we were on a coach, somehow it seems safer on a coach.'

'Maybe we should rent one,' Charlie suggested.

Eric nodded.

'I think you're right, Charlie. I'm sure it's what Mr Greenbaum would want. I'm sure he wouldn't want any of us to get hurt.'

Charlie nodded too.

'I'll fix it when we get back to town.'

Julia gave him a kick on the shins hard enough to make him brake. Eric flinched and leaned forward to look at the road ahead.

'More trouble?'

'Just a pot-hole,' Charlie improvised. 'Tell us about your pilgrimage.'

'You'd really like to hear about it?'

'Really,' said Charlie.

Eli Kaufman had a tin leg, a face like a badly carved children's toy, and a toothless smile that threatened to split his face clean in two. He was seventy-three years old, wore his dentures only when he had to, and favoured knee-length shorts of the kind the British Army abandoned the year the Gold Coast went independent. He'd been a soldier too, but mostly he was a chemist. Not a theoretician, though he knew a lot of theory, but the kind who know instinctively that there must be a way to drip-feed artichokes to grow on bare basalt, if only you could get the mixture in the drip-feed right. In their own way, people like Eli Kaufman had done as much for the security of the

State of Israel as all the sword-rattling colonels and gun-toting generals, the clandestine hit-squads and undercover agents. If Israel was doomed to be Sparta, the least Sparta could do was to try and feed itself. They also serve who grow cabbages in the sand. Expensive business, but worth it.

Eli was forty-one and a reserve captain when he lost his leg, which was why people looked on him as a war casualty. But war had nothing to do with it: he was driving an old MG which skidded off the edge of an unpaved road in the desert south of Dimona, the famous Scorpion Ascent, which links the Machtesh Katan crater with the desolate Valley of Zin.

'Got me out of the bloody army. Cheap at the price.'

Charlie and Julia found him twenty miles south of Beersheba, in the desert, dwarfed by high sandstone cliffs at the entrance to a deep gorge. Eli leaned on his good leg against the bonnet of his dented Land Rover, Charlie stood facing him, while Julia perched on a boulder to his right and Eric took photographs with his Instamatic. A mourning wheatear balanced on a dead thistle, a covey of sand partridges scurried through the rocks, far above them three fan-tailed ravens circled in the thermals. The temperature was in the upper eighties, cool for the desert but a welcome change from the mountain chill of Jerusalem.

Eli's accident happened in 1958. As soon as he was out of hospital he'd moved to Beersheba, bought a bungalow and a second-hand Land Rover, and got himself a job. Later he joined the staff of the Arid Zone Research Institute, from which he retired in 1982. But he didn't stop work: he called himself a consultant, and continued to hire himself out to anyone who'd have him, provided that he could stay in the Negev. The desert was all that mattered to Eli Kaufman. He travelled a lot, though, all over the Third World, advising people on how to grow things in unpromising places.

He'd first got to know David Bermant during the Sinai campaign in 1956. Kaufman was a lieutenant, Bermant a major. The campaign opened on the afternoon of 29 October, when four ancient Israeli Mustang fighters penetrated deep into the desert and destroyed all the Egyptian telephone communications by flying at the wires at a height of twelve feet and cutting them with their propellers. Schoolboy comic stuff. Two hours later a force of four hundred paratroopers landed at the crucial Mitla Pass, a hundred and sixty miles behind the front line and within striking distance of the Suez canal. At first the Egyptians thought it was merely a reprisal raid, but they discovered the truth soon afterwards, when the main Israeli army launched attacks at Themed in the south, along the Mediterranean coastal strip in the north, and at Kusseima in the centre. This was desert warfare at its starkest: the distances were long, lines of communication precarious, intelligence hard to assess, and time of the essence, since much depended on the actions of the British and French at Suez. The UN was liable to intervene at any moment.

Bermant and Kaufman were given the job of harrying Egyptian communications and supplies in the southern Sinai, working behind the Egyptian lines while the main Israeli force advanced down the Gulf of Aqaba towards Sharm El-Sheikh and the Straits of Tiran. It would be hard to imagine worse terrain – bare, saw-toothed, mountainous, deep ravines filled with soft sand and boulders, no water, no paved roads and no air cover. The camel-mounted Egyptian Frontier Force had laid mines in the wadis, and set ambushes in the passes.

'We used to drive goats in front of us to clear the mines,' Eli explained. 'Bermant's Kebabs, we called them. Ridiculous, because we didn't have enough goats, and the few we had were too smart, they knew what we were up to. There we were, so-called élite combat soldiers, nothing to drink, most of us hadn't slept for a week, the temperature at a hundred and ten, in that kind of country, running round the wadis rounding up mutinous goats and trying not to let the Egyptians see us. Not something they teach you about at West Point. Worse than that, I had piles.' He chortled at the memory. 'Not so funny at all at the time. I was the only one who knew about the desert, and all I could concentrate on was the pain in my arse. You ever had piles?'

'Not yet,' said Charlie.

'You will. They're like Toyotas, everyone gets them in the end. These things are very important in war, people forget that. A whole British brigade was lost in Burma in forty-two because some colonel had an abscess in his ear and accidentally blew up the bridge they were meant to be retreating over. The sappers called him up on the radio, asked if he was ready to let the charges off, the poor man was so distracted with pain that he said he didn't give a fig what anyone did. Japanese captured the lot of them. What was I talking about before we got on to piles?'

'Goats,' Julia reminded him.

'Oh yes. The road to Sharm El-Sheikh. Our main job was meant to be reconnaissance. But David decided we might as well try a little sabotage while we were at it. We were a long way ahead of the main brigade – the ninth, under Avraham Yoffe – the man who founded all the nature reserves. Chaim Ezra was with Yoffe too, I think he was a colonel by then. Most of the ninth were reservists, farmers from the valley of Jezreel, up north. Plenty of guts, but not used to the desert. They managed to get themselves ambushed by the Egyptians outside Dahab, nothing serious but they took quite heavy casualties. The Egyptians were a little cocky after that. They're not used to victories, and when they have one it goes to their heads. Not that Dahab was much of a victory – it only lasted a couple of hours. But David saw his chance.

'We came out of the mountains that night, down to the main road, and shot up what we thought was a patrol. Turned out to be a convoy, a couple of hundred men in two-ton trucks moving up to reinforce the front line. The whole lot surrendered on the spot, poor bastards. It was comic, really. There were only thirty of us, but they thought we were a whole division that had landed from the sea. We didn't know what to do. If we broke cover they'd realise how few of us there were. But thank God it was dark. We made them line up in the headlights and take their trousers off – can you talk about that sort of thing on television?'

'I don't see why not,' said Charlie.

'By the way, there's something else I meant to ask you about television,' Eli went on. 'Do you look at the camera when you're talking, or the person you're talking to?'

'The person you're talking to,' Charlie explained. 'Just as though you were having a normal conversation, as natural as possible. Pretend the camera crew isn't there.'

'You want me to be natural, or you want me to act as though

all those people aren't there? I can do either, but not both, you have to tell me which.'

'Then pretend, please.'

Julia produced cans of beer from the Subaru.

'Do you see much of Bermant these days?' asked Charlie.

Kaufman took a long drink from the can before he answered.

'Does anyone?' he said eventually. 'He's a difficult bastard.'

'In what way?'

The old man scratched the back of his neck.

'Same as me, I suppose. Doesn't go in for close friendships. Everyone admires him. As long as I've known him he's never put a foot wrong, said all the right things at the right times, won all his battles, supported all the right causes. When he dies half the country will go to his funeral. He likes that: he likes the idea he's well thought of. But he doesn't have too many friends. Ezra and he have always been quite close, but I think Ruth was the only person who ever got inside him, and he hated her for it. They fought like cats, threw things at each other, very violent relationship.' He took another drink. 'I see him once in a while. He was here last week for an hour or two, on his way somewhere. We go through the ritual of talking about the past, he tells me what's wrong with the country, I go along with it. Nothing personal. That's what I feel about him: nothing personal.'

'Would you say that to his face?' asked Charlie.

Kaufman shook his head.

'Of course not.'

'Tell me about Ruth.'

'Childhood sweetheart, I think they met when they were seventeen or eighteen. And that was it. You know how that happens sometimes? They got twisted together, like bindweed and ivy. Didn't matter that they fought all the time, once they were together there was no separating them. It was funny watching them together, they got so indignant with each other, couldn't believe that the other could be so blind to whatever truth it was they were debating. Then she got stomach cancer. It must be fifteen years ago she died. There was a rumour at the time they'd had a suicide pact, only he broke it. I don't believe it. And no, I won't ask him that to his face either.'

'But you'd asked him about his marriage?' asked Charlie.

Kaufman thought for a minute.

'Perhaps. He'd get very emotional – you mind that?'

'I'm not sure,' said Charlie.

The drive on south to Eilat was breathtaking, a dry moonscape of multicoloured rock, blood-red, black, purple, chocolate, sepia, as far as the eye could see, ringed by ridges of blue-grey mountains stretching away to infinity in the late afternoon light. Apart from the modern settlement at Mizpe Ramon and an occasional army camp there was no habitation, only a few bedouin camped in the wadis.

'That was very interesting about the piles,' said Eric. 'Can you really say things like that on television?'

'You can if you've got a stethoscope on. Not otherwise. We may have to, it's about all he has got to say.'

'Come off it, Charlie. He wasn't that bad,' Julia objected.

'Not bad,' he admitted crossly. 'That's the problem. Tyler spends an hour telling us how much he admires his life-long enemy. The moment Eli says something revealing he backs off like an Italian general. Feinberg was OK, but he's a bit of a joke, Truman Capote in a yarmulke. Freak show time, great cabaret but fuck-all to do with anything. We're making Tact-vision, Julia. Easily digested, no unpleasant odours, shovel it out and cash the cheque. Is that what Harry wants, Eric?'

Eric wasn't sure.

'Cheer up, Charlie,' said Julia.

He took one hand off the wheel and scratched the back of his head.

'I'm sorry. But I want this programme to be different, I want it to be something special.'

'I think that's what Harry wants too,' Eric agreed.

'The programme I've always wanted to make,' Charlie went on, 'is about what powerful people are really afraid of, what they say when they're tired or drunk or in bed with their wives or husbands. The things Maggie Thatcher worries about to Denis. I bet it's not the Official Secrets Act or what the Russians are up to. You know what Idi Amin couldn't stand? Anyone touching his hair. He had to be sedated when he went to the barber, and if he went to bed with a woman he wore a swimming cap. De Gaulle couldn't relieve himself if there was anyone else in the gents, he'd spend an hour in the urinal gazing at the wall-tiles until he was on his own. David Ben Gurion was terrified of talking to strangers: if he was lost someplace he'd drive round all day rather than stop and ask the way.'

'How interesting. How do you know all that?' enquired Eric.

'Sound recordists tell you. People get tense before an interview, and they think sound recordists are neutral, anonymous, someone they can talk to. Sound recordists and make-up artists, confessors to the famous.'

'You should write a book,' Eric told him.

'No one would believe me,' said Charlie.

Betty Kavanagh took the crystal decanter out of the glass-fronted sideboard and poured herself a glass of tonic wine. Betty disapproved of alcohol, but then tonic wine wasn't alcohol, it was medicine – healthy, natural medicine, not some manu-factured chemical full of industrial poisons, and far more thera-peutic than Dr McLennan's horrid little pills. An odd glass or two of tonic wine settled her for the evening, relaxed her, took her mind off the arthritis and blurred the edges of her headaches. She drained the glass, poured herself another, and closed the curtains. Not that anyone could see in her fourth-floor windows, but it was best to be on the safe side.

Only then did she turn on the television. *Neighbours* was Betty's other little secret, not something she wanted people to know about. A lot of people were snotty about soap operas, thought them common. Which they were, but harmless, and quite entertaining in their own way. And Dickens' novels were Victorian soap operas, someone had said on the radio. No one thought Dickens common. If he was common people might even read him.

She was just settling herself down in her armchair when the doorbell went.

'Hello? Mrs Kavanagh?' asked a woman's voice. Probably not a woman at all, Betty decided: probably one of those homo-sexual social workers.

'Who is it?' she demanded, checking that the security chain was in place.

'Mrs Kavanagh?' asked the voice beyond the door.

'I'm not in.'

'Hello?' the voice repeated. 'It's Apple.'

'No one's called Apple,' Betty decided out loud. 'She must have the wrong flat.'

She was half-way back to the sitting room when the bell rang again.

'I phoned you, Mrs Kavanagh. About Charlie.'

So she had, Betty remembered.

'Just a moment, dear.'

She hurried through to the sitting room, turned off the television, put her dirty glass back among the clean ones on the sideboard, lifted a leatherette poetry book off the bookcase and arranged it open beside her chair.

Apple was tall and wide-shouldered and wore expensive boutique clothes, a short black skirt with a thick black belt and a soft leather jacket over a brightly-embroidered blouse. Purple plastic earrings hung from her lobes, and she carried a canvas fisherman's bag instead of a briefcase.

She was terribly friendly.

'Silly of me not to remember your name,' Betty apologised. 'Such an unusual name, Apricot.'

'Apple. It's awful, isn't it!'

They moved through the hall into the sitting room.

'That's a lovely little figure,' Apple said enthusiastically, lifting a porcelain Spanish dancer off the sideboard.

'Do you like it, dear? You're very discerning. Can I get you a cup of coffee?'

'Please.'

It was dark by the time Charlie and Julia and Eric reached the Arava, the great flat-bottomed rift valley which runs south from the Dead Sea to the Gulf of Aqaba and divides Israel from Jordan.

The Sabbath was over at last. Another half an hour and they could see the lights of Eilat ahead; a final army checkpoint and they were driving down the boulevards, past the airport, heading for the centre of town. Except that Eilat didn't have a centre as such. They probably reckoned it didn't need one with a setting like that, ringed by high desert mountains, its shoreline lapped by the clear warm waters of the Gulf of Aqaba – Aqaba, where Lawrence of Arabia finally reached the sea, now a port and resort on the Jordanian side of the border, three miles to the east. Travel five miles south from Eilat on the west shore of the Gulf and you're in Egypt. Fifteen miles south on the Jordanian side and you're in Saudi Arabia.

Eilat was the place Israelis went to get out of Israel without having to leave the country. It only just made it into Israel in the first place: a small army contingent dashed south in the closing days of the War of Independence and ran up a hand-painted star of David over the deserted Jordanian police post to secure the new State an outlet on the Red Sea. There was no town then, and there wasn't much of one now, apart from the hotels, the airstrip and the oil terminal. English tourists came to Eilat, and the Scandinavians, and off-duty UN soldiers from Sinai, to snorkel over the coral reefs and bop in the discos and barbecue their well-oiled bodies in the harsh desert heat.

They found Benny Kimche in the foyer of the Eilat Beach Palace, bronzed and affable, cigar in mouth, smiling like a cat, glad-handing guests and laughing loudly at their little jokes. He was a short man, almost top-heavy, his puffed out chest balancing precariously on thin, athletic, Daks-wrapped legs. With his brass-buttoned blazer and paisley cravat and well-groomed moustache he looked as English as an Indian general.

Benny owned the Eilat Beach Palace and half a dozen other hotels in Israel, as well as a transport company, clothing factories, a fast-food franchise, a mail-order business and a newspaper. He was also a politician, a man of the right, sometime Minister of Transport and Housing. One of the conditions that Labour had laid down for the present coalition was that Benny Kimche was not part of it. Smiles or no smiles.

After they'd done the introductions Charlie and Julia went upstairs to change and unpack. Nice room: pile carpet as thick as a meadow, two queen-size beds, an eight-foot sofa, colour TV with in-house movies (*Care Bears IV*, *Plaza Suite*, *Casablanca*), a mock-mahogany fridge, tasteful prints of the desert on the walls, a bowl of fruit on the dresser. One wall was all glass, giving on to a generous balcony with a miniature palm-tree in a terracotta pot. Charlie got drinks and peanuts from the fridge and they went out on to the balcony to look at the sea. Offshore two tankers lay at anchor, ghostly floodlit giants suspended in the black night. To the east the lights of Aqaba sparkled across the water.

'How the hell do we get rid of Eric?' asked Julia.

'We don't, I suspect. Is he bothering you?'

'I suppose not.'

'I'll think about it,' said Charlie. He helped himself to a drink from the fridge. 'I'm sorry I got moody in the car. I think Kaufman will be fine, I really do.'

'You want him to ask David about his marriage?'

'I really don't know. You start out making a programme about someone and you stay on the surface – you stick to their public image, their political ideas, what they've achieved. And then you see a chink. The reason we're making a programme about him is because he's a politician, that's what makes him important. But listening to Kaufman talk about him and Ruth, that's something else, something personal. None of our business, except that maybe it tells us why he's who he is. The Bermant who argues with his wife, nurses her through cancer, is the same man who stands up at the UN in a couple of days and pontificates about the future of his country. A lot of politicians' wives are alcoholics – did you know that? Their husbands drive them to drink, and then live with the consequences, day after night. Happens to the husbands of women politicians, too. It's like that story about the man who had piles in Burma – who knows how many political decisions are grounded in their authors' private lives? When Kaufman told us about Ruth, I got interested in Bermant for the first time, he became three dimensional.'

'Are you frightened of asking him about it?'

'Of course. The easy thing is to stick to the politics, his career, maybe a bit of general stuff about his childhood, his family background. Beyond that I don't know, I really don't know.'

They waited a quarter of an hour, then went downstairs. It was just after seven: they were due to have dinner with Benny at eight-thirty. Eric was waiting for them in the bar reading *What's On in Eilat.*

'You ever met Benny before?' Julia asked Charlie.

'Years ago. I don't think he'd remember. He's famous for using political interviews to plug his business interests. I wager a thousand dollars he manages to bring in his hotels somewhere in the programme. Ask him about nuclear physics, he'll talk to you about the leisure facilities at the Tiberias Beach Palace – which doesn't have a beach, by the way, he screwed up on the name; seemed a good idea when it was just Tel Aviv and Herzliya and Netanya and here, but a hell of a problem inland. Tiberias is just plausible, at least it's near the Sea of Galilee. Jerusalem's the real bugger, everyone's longing for him to open up a Beach Palace in Jerusalem.'

Eric took a sip of mineral water and put down his glass.

'What would you like him to say, Charlie? I mean, in an ideal world.'

'I'd like him to say David Bermant is a dangerous man. I'd like him to call Bermant an appeaser, the new Chamberlain. I'd like him to say that liberals have always failed to solve ethnic problems because they lack ruthlessness, that only strong governments can cope with minorities – look at what's happening in Russia now the KGB have started going soft on dissent. I'd like him to say that the only way to resolve the Palestinian problem is by war. That's the way it's always been done for the past three thousand years, and it's arrogant of Bermant to think he's any cleverer than his ancestors. I'd like him to rubbish the idea of compromise because the only ultimate compromise on offer is that the Jews get out.'

Eric smiled meekly.

'That all?'

'No, there's more if you want it.'

'And you don't think he'll say any of that?' Eric asked politely.

'Not at all. He'll talk about bargain breaks at the Netanya Beach Palace.'

Eric looked puzzled.

'What makes you think that?'

'Hunch.' Charlie stubbed out his cigarette. 'And the way our luck is going this week.'

They had dinner with Kimche on the terrace, with the lights of the town in the background and a bucket of champagne on the table. Relays of waiters brought food and drink, tray after tray of it, balanced on their shoulders – pasta and salads, smoked cheese, pickled spinach, taramasalata, humous, lobster, prawns, stuffed peppers, dolmades, whitebait, clams, brown olives the size of apricots, aubergines flambéd in brandy, quails' eggs in aspic, and a large, lavishly garnished fish, type unknown.

Benny talked about the old days, his time in Washington with David Bermant buying tanks and aircraft.

'Those were the days,' he said nostalgically. 'The Americans would give us anything. If the government didn't come up with the goods, the market place filled in the gaps. A printer in Baltimore ran up End User certificates if we needed them. David looked after the money and the political lobbies, I did the shopping. He was very good with the Jewish groups – he dreamed up the Sponsor A Tank programme, you could have your name or the name of a loved one etched on the gun turret. And there was a Buy A Bullet scheme for the kids. Quite a double act we made. This was just after sixty-seven – Israel was a hero nation in the States. Very different from now.'

Charlie was looking for clues.

'Was David comfortable in America?'

Benny sucked on his cigar.

'Is he ever comfortable? He didn't socialise a lot. He and Ruth had a house out of town, she wouldn't live in the city, he had to spend a lot of time travelling. They didn't show up a lot on the usual diplomatic circuit. But then she was never much into that life here either. It's an open secret – she held him back professionally, wouldn't mix in the right political circles. Which is why he became a pundit, I think, an armchair politician. Even after he went into the Knesset, she wouldn't let him put the hours in. So he wound up telling us all what to do, never did much himself.'

'What would you do if you were in his shoes now?' Charlie asked.

'If I were in his shoes,' said Benny, 'I would take them off. Just as if I had been Neville Chamberlain, I would have turned round at the airport. David Bermant is an appeaser. Nowadays they call themselves liberals, but it's the same thing.'

Attaboy, Benny: someone's been briefing you. So much for the harmless little Mormon.

Julia was right, Eric would have to go. Or maybe Charlie should go himself. Only he doubted if Julia would come with him.

Tina lay face down on the wide white bed, Shimon astride her, massaging her back. The room was dark, but a soft light spilled in the uncurtained window from the streetlamp outside.

'You really think Julia fancies him?' she asked.

'Why not?' He ran his hands down her pale freckled skin, his fingers shaping her fragile vertebrae. 'They have a lot in common. He likes her, she likes herself too.'

Tina drummed her fingers against the edge of the mattress.

'Seriously.'

'How would I know?'

She rolled over.

'I don't know. Something's wrong, that's all.'

'Like what?'

He looked down at her naked body silhouetted in the yellow light, circling the palms of his hands on the flat of her stomach. Tina lay quite still, eyes open.

'I don't know. I think he knows something. I don't know what, but I think he knows something.'

She pushed herself up on her elbows, and he bent forward and flicked his tongue across her nipples. Soft, unaroused.

'What's the matter with you tonight?'

'Nothing's the matter. I'm just thinking. She doesn't have to do it the way she's doing it. The last way to keep a man under control is to throw yourself all over him. She might at least pretend to play hard to get.'

'They're both doing it exactly the way we want them to. If they do it any other way we take both of them out, here and now. The least hint that anything's going wrong.'

'You sure about that?'

'Certain. That's why Eric's with them.'

His hands moved to her sides, stroking them gently, brushing lightly against her breasts. She reached out and took a tissue and blew her nose.

Shimon sighed. His last night before going back on duty, the last night of his leave.

'I slept with Eric yesterday,' Tina told him.

He took his hands off her and straightened: a sudden, violent motion.

'You did *what*?'

'We screwed. Next door, on the sofa. One of the cushions has a stain on it, I turned it over so you wouldn't see.'

The flat of his fist slammed angrily against the wall.

'Shit.'

Tina stayed still, looking straight at him.

'While you were out fixing your hair. Just out of curiosity.'

'I'll kill him.'

'Why him? Why not me? It was my idea.'

'Bitch.'

As he raised his hand to slap her, she smiled and reached up and gripped his limp penis.

'Go on.'

Shimon's mouth tightened slowly into a thin smile.

'You bitch. You're making this up, aren't you.'

She bared her teeth, allowing the tip of her tongue to show briefly between them.

'That's something you've got to work out for yourself, Shimon.'

And then the phone rang.

Shimon swung round on to the edge of the bed and picked up the receiver. Tina could hear Eric's voice at the far end – too far away to hear what he was saying, close enough to hear who it was.

'Ask him if he fucked me,' she whispered softly in Shimon's free ear.

'Where?' Shimon asked Eric.

Tina licked his lobe, her lips warm and wet.

'Shit,' Shimon repeated. 'When?'

Another pause. She held him from behind, ran the palms of her hands up over his stomach, and started kneading his chest, her breasts pressed against his back. The nipples were hard now.

'Shit,' he repeated for the third time, and put down the phone. 'Kavanagh wants him to go and help Walter with the archive material. Fly up to Jerusalem while they drive, spend the day in the vaults.'

She rested her chin on his shoulder.

'Why doesn't he just say he can't?'

'He needs an excuse. If he says he can't, he has to have something else to do. If he has something else to do he has to go and do it. Either way he leaves them on their own.'

'What are they playing at?'

'He thinks Kavanagh's just being friendly, showing him how the business works.'

'I think they're playing games.'

'You could be right. Or they could simply be looking for a bit of privacy. If they're trying something on, the worst thing to do is feed their suspicions. He has to go along with it. We have to take the risk.'

Tina got up from the bed.

'I think she's told him something.'

'She can't afford to. Anyway, Eric's putting a bug in the car before they leave. We'll know soon enough.'

17

THE SINGLE RUNWAY OF Eilat's little airport is roughly where the main street ought to be, at right angles to the promenade, dividing the beach hotels from the rest of the town climbing up the hill to the west. Overshoot it to the left and you'd land in the foyer of the Galei Eilat hotel; to the right you'd demolish the car-hire offices and sunglasses shops in the Shalom Shopping Centre.

Julia and Charlie walked Eric from the Palace to the terminal after breakfast. It was hot and dry, heading for the upper eighties, a clear blue sky, shimmering sea, the ring of savage red mountains clean and crisp in the morning air. Already the first windsurfers were in the water, the Scandinavian girls unhooking their bikini tops on the beach under the watchful eyes of the off-duty UN soldiers, the ersatz schooners in the port loading up with tourists for their day-cruise down the gulf to Coral Island. Where the beach ran out, in front of the ramshackle Peace Café, hippies and vagrants drank coffee from paper cups and bargained with the foremen from the restaurants and construction firms looking for cheap day labour; no papers, no questions asked. Flocks of buntings infested the palm trees, pigeons pecked at the dry, empty flowerbeds. The shutters were coming up on the tourist boutiques, which sold orange nylon camels with 'I Love Eilat' sun-hats on, and the sort of cheap embroidered shirts that embarrass their wearers' friends for years to come. Not a lot else.

Charlie wore jeans and a white shirt, Julia tight cotton shorts and a loose pink T-shirt, Eric his three-piece suit and a raincoat over his shoulder, to be on the safe side. Nothing too odd about that: in Herzliyya women wore fur coats in the punishing heat of July, in case people thought they didn't own one.

'How will I recognise Walter when I meet him?' asked Eric.

'Hard to put into words, really,' said Charlie. 'He's kind of unique. For example he may have his clothes on inside out. If he hasn't eaten for a while he wilts visibly, like butter left out in the sun. In some lights you could confuse him for a sack of cats with their tails tied together . . .'

Eric stopped nodding and smiled politely.

'And you're sure he won't mind me being there?'

'Not at all.'

The Arkia turboprop was parked next to an army Hercules on the apron, engines already running as the passengers picked up their boarding cards in the tiny flat-roofed terminal.

'We'll ring you at the Hilton when we get to town,' Charlie told Eric as he flustered over his ticket.

'You'll be at the Anani?'

'I think so.'

Julia threw Charlie a curious glance.

'Fine,' said Eric. 'But you'll let me know if your plans change?'

'Of course.'

They stood and watched as the aircraft taxied out. The pilot increased the engine power to a thin whine, and in a moment it was gone, rising steeply and banking to the west to avoid Jordanian airspace.

They walked out of the terminal and stopped at the pedestrian lights on the main road.

'What was that business about the hotel?' Julia asked, slipping her hand through his arm. Charlie lit a cigarette.

'Just a thought. Maybe we should try a change of scene, see if anyone objects.'

'Be careful, Charlie.'

'What about?'

Julia said nothing.

The lights changed, and they crossed to the far pavement.

Vincent Fallop was staying in Tel Aviv, at the Dan Hotel, looking out on the Mediterranean and the long public beach which stretched from the yachting marina at the north end down to the spruced-up remains of the old town of Jaffa to the south. Jaffa used to be an important and picturesque Arab port: these days it served as a combination heritage centre and leisure complex for the Tel Aviv middle class, a place to eat foreign food in cellar restaurants and buy expensive jewellery in perfumed boutiques.

Vincent had had a troublesome morning. Up at seven, which wasn't his style at all; a quick cup of coffee from a reluctant room service, then down to the car park, out with his map and off to Jerusalem. On the way out of the hotel he stopped and told the reception to play dumb on any calls from London. As far as his office was concerned he was sick in bed.

It took him an hour and a half to reach Jerusalem, weaving in and out of the air-conditioned buses and sherut Mercedes taxis, the slow-moving container trucks and low-loaders slung with army tanks across the coastal plain and up the long valley to the capital. Once there it took him another half an hour to find the city's modest domestic airport, which is at Atarot, six miles north, on the Ramallah road.

He parked across the terminal and waited for the Eilat flight to land, his battered Nikon on the passenger seat beside him, the two hundred millimetre lens already screwed in place. This was like old times, staking out pervert scoutmasters and dodgy pyramid-salesmen for the *News of the World*. Not a period of his life that featured too heavily in his current curriculum vitae, but useful skills.

He wondered what the hell Kavanagh was up to. Cryptic phone calls in the small hours, no attempt at conversation, just a set of marching orders. Look out for a skinhead dwarf in a three-piece suit, can't miss him, they only made the one, and stick with him. Don't call me, I'll call you. Trust your old mate Charlie, it's important. Oh, and don't forget your camera. Ping.

Arrogant bastard.

Eric's flight landed on time. The American picked up a cab off the rank, and Vincent set off in pursuit.

It was a little after ten when they reached the city. The dual carriageway split, became a one-way loop, split again, the traffic for the New City heading off right, Jericho to the left. Eric's taxi kept straight on. The road followed the contours of the old Green Line, forked right outside the American Colony, down Shivetei Yisrael and on towards the Old City. When the taxi drove slowly through the Jaffa Gate, Vincent was thirty yards behind.

There was only one way a car could drive through the Old City, along a narrow lane pinched between the city walls and the Armenian Patriarchate. Less a lane than a thin canyon, too narrow to park, too dangerous to let him out of sight. Once Eric was out of the cab and into the Jewish Quarter he'd be irredeemably lost.

Either he already knows I'm following him, Vincent decided, or else he doesn't, and stuck close behind the taxi, flattening monks and tourists against the walls as they made their way south towards Mount Zion, emerging finally into the open at the Beit Hasofer car park. And there they stopped.

Vincent picked up his camera and took aim. The Nikon motordrive gave a shlack-prr-shlack-prr-shlack as Eric got out, paid the driver and stood on the pavement consulting his map. He didn't know where he was going either. Vincent gave him a twenty-yard start and followed him into the Quarter, down alleys, up steps, through arches, bumping into schoolchildren with bags of books on their backs and skullcaps on their heads, into a square with saplings in stone pots and white plastic café furniture under red Marlboro sun-umbrellas; down a vaulted tunnel lined with art galleries and antique shops. An army foot-patrol loitered, guns on shoulders, watching the girls from the shadows, and there were tourists, not a lot, Americans for the most part, and free-lance guides hovering to pounce, and chain-smoking yeshiva students scurrying east towards the Wailing Wall, coat tails flapping, arguing with each other as they walked, avoiding eye-contact, stopping to emphasise a point, scurrying on, their black hats and *stetl* habits dusty and dishevelled, worn not from choice but as a necessary protection, a Jewish raincoat in a world full of gentile vice and carnal temptations.

Eric moved surprisingly fast, stopped twice to check his map, then trotted up a flight of steps and under an arch to a cul-de-sac, a young fig tree on one side, a varnished oak door with wrought-iron fittings on the other. He straightened his tie and pressed the bell.

Vincent had the camera wrapped in a coat, shooting from the hip. He waited until Eric had gone inside before following him into the yard, checked the name on the bell, and looked around for somewhere to wait. It was a hot day, and he was sweating from the exertion.

Charlie and Julia left Eilat at nine. The drive north was the best part of two hundred miles, but it was a good road, and the traffic light, up the arid Arava depression, high desert mountains on either side, running straight for almost a hundred miles along the wide empty valley floor until they reached the salt flats at the southern end of the Dead Sea, ten miles short of Sodom. Julia drove, sunglasses on, elbow out the open window, cruising at seventy, Charlie beside her with his feet up on the dashboard, clipboard on his knees, making notes. For the first hour they hardly spoke, lost in their own preoccupations.

'How much do you need to know?' Julia asked him eventually.

'Mmm?'

'About Harry, about what's going on.'

'Not a lot. And to be honest I'm not that curious. Unless you think I ought to be. I'm with you, I'm getting paid, as far as I know I haven't done anything to upset anyone.' He slid the clipboard on to the floor and lit a cigarette. 'Are there things I should know?'

'Maybe you should know about my father?'

'Which one?'

Julia bit her thumb.

'The real one. His name's Wolfgang. He's seventy-four years old, quite decrepit, smokes too much, doesn't look after himself very well. I don't know how much longer he'll last. Two or three years, maybe.'

'Where does he live?'

'In Ireland. County Waterford, on the River Blackwater, between Youghal and Cappoquin. Beautiful country, very untouched.'

'He's German?'

'Yes, he's German.'

'And your mother?'

'Anna? She's Dutch. Mrs Tiggywinkle. Bakes a lot, wears her hair in a bun. She's quite a lot younger than him, still in her sixties. They have a farmhouse at the end of one of those long boreens with grass growing through the tarmac, and an overgrown garden running down to the water's edge. It's a lovely place, very tranquil. Otters and herons, deer and badgers. Trees all round, oak and beech and Scots pine – it's got some fine woods, the Blackwater valley. Spenser wrote *The Faerie Queen* there, in between persecuting the peasants.'

She pulled out to overtake a truck.

'My father was in Auschwitz.'

'As a prisoner?'

'No. He was SS. He got out after the war, stole someone else's papers, the usual story. Wound up in a Displaced Persons camp in the British Zone, outside Hamburg. Which is where he met my mother.'

'And she didn't know?'

'Still doesn't. They went to Canada first, then to the States, then England, Rhodesia, Singapore, Iraq – all over the world. He's a construction engineer. He worked as a consultant, which meant he could keep moving on, in case someone caught up with him, I suppose. Then when he retired he decided Ireland would be safe. Ireland's full of Germans anyway, no one seems to mind them much.'

'And you?'

'The passport's right. I was born in Calne. My real name's Koeppen. They anglicised it to Cornwall.'

They forked left for Dimona, climbing steeply out of the valley towards the desert plateau.

'Who told you?' asked Charlie.

'Harry Greenbaum. He didn't tell me, he wrote to me. God knows how he found out after all these years. White Manilla envelope sitting on the hemp doormat in Maida Vale one morning. I read it on the bus on the way in to work. "Your father's a Nazi war criminal, RSVP". Or words to that effect. Great way to start your day.'

They reached the top of the escarpment. The road ran straight across the stony desert moonscape: to their left the land opened up into the endless crater of Machtesh Katan, its walls a rainbow of multicoloured rock.

'Do you know what he did in Auschwitz?'

'Only what they've told me. He was very young, you forget how young a lot of people were during the war. You look at nineteen-year-olds nowadays, up on murder or bank-robbery charges and you think – I could never have done that sort of thing when I was nineteen, I wasn't that together, wouldn't have had the nerve. Not that I wouldn't be capable of it, but the circumstances of my life were so different, that's all. Anyway, I'm not apologising, I'm just explaining that he was young. His job was to transfer new arrivals from the station. He rounded them up with dogs and made them take their shoes off and walk barefoot over the jagged hardcore of the railway line for the last seven kilometres to the camp. For no reason, just because he wanted them to. Anyone who fell by the way got shot. Harry sent me a photograph, with a circle drawn round my father's head. Very strange to see your own father in SS uniform, little more than a boy, swagger-stick in hand, Alsatian straining at the leash. But that wasn't all he did, apparently. He was known as Mad Wolf. The British tried him in his absence after the war, Harry sent me the court transcripts as well. That's why I freaked when you gave me Gilbert's book on the Holocaust. I thought you must know too.'

'Could you recognise him in the photograph?'

'Sort of. It's fifty years ago, he's changed a lot. But yes, I could believe it was him.'

'And that's why you're working for Harry?'

'Yes, that's the deal. I don't care much about my father, but I do about my mother. I don't even know what this is about, they just tell me what to do. They also promised me no one would get hurt.'

'Ring your father. He must be used to moving on by now. The pair of them could be on a plane to Paraguay by the time anyone here knows what's happening.'

Her face was very white, her eyes on the road, knuckles gripping the wheel.

'Harry said not to even think of warning him. Anyway it's

academic. Wolf has emphysema. The journey would kill him.'

'What the hell, Julia? He's an old man, his life's almost over, a lot of people would argue he doesn't deserve to be alive anyway. Your life or his, it's not really such a hard choice.'

'I can't, not in cold blood.'

'This isn't in cold blood.' But he understood. 'Have they talked to you since you got here?'

'Not really.'

'But he didn't ask you to do anything specific?'

'Not at all.'

'What about Eric?'

'Not a word.'

'Clever buggers. Do you have any idea at all what they're up to?'

'Not really. I've been trying not to think about it. I don't know but maybe they want to set Bermant up in some way.'

'Do you get the impression that they're working on their own?'

'I don't think so. They seem very well organised. Passports and so on.'

'So what the fuck do we do?'

Julia ran her hand back over through her hair.

'I don't know. We have until Monday to decide, I suppose. Until then we act as normally as we can. Do you think they suspect anything?'

'Whoever they are. Heaven knows. I guess not, or they'd have made a move of some kind.'

Up ahead a gazelle ran across the road and disappeared into the boulders.

'You could go now, I suppose,' Julia said quietly. 'Now you know.'

'Would you come with me?'

'I can't. I have to trust them to keep their word.'

'What would happen if you did?'

'They'd extradite him, I suppose. There's no business like Shoah business. Bring him here, put him on trial, confront him with survivors, probably lock him up for the rest of his life.'

'Very unchristian of them,' said Charlie unkindly. 'But you can see their point.'

'I know. I have no sympathy for him, none. Less than none. And it's not just my mother either, though God knows what would happen to her. She'd have to live with it, I suppose. She's too old to do anything else. She's innocent, but she'd have to live with it. But there's me, too. He's my father after all.'

'You can hardly be blamed for things that happened before you were born.'

'It's not as easy as that.'

'Why not? What have you done?'

'I'm doing something now.'

Her eyes were still looking straight ahead. Up ahead two gazelle crossed the road, stopped on the verge, looked round, and vanished into the rocks. Charlie doubted if she'd even seen them.

'You call this doing something? You don't even know what it is you're doing, you don't even know who you're doing it for. For fuck's sake, Julia.'

'They're Jews. That's all that matters. I have a debt to them.'

'You weren't even born, you said it yourself.'

'I was trying to convince myself. It didn't work.'

'Do you have any idea what they're up to?'

'I don't know, Charlie. I've thought about it. My guess is they want to humiliate Bermant somehow. I don't know how, but I think that's their plan.'

'And you really have no idea who they are?'

'None at all. The only people I've met are Eric and Harry.'

'How about blondie and Miss Marble?'

'They're working for Harry. At least I assume they are. She's called Tina, the boy's Shimon, he followed us down to the Press building on Wednesday morning, gave me a number to call if I was in trouble.'

'And you did?'

'After you got the news from your mother. I phoned from the filling station.'

'You got the number?'

Julia opened her bag and got out her notebook.

'Seven-three-one-nine-four-five.'

'And what about Walter? Did you really find him through the TV station?'

'No, Harry suggested him. But I'm pretty sure he's straight, I think he's in the same boat as us.'

An awful truth dawned on Charlie. This wasn't a game any more; this wasn't the sort of shadow-boxing journalists do with secret policemen, the kind of schoolboy pranks you play in Moscow or Cape Town, safe in the knowledge that head office or the embassy will bale you out if things go wrong. This was the real McCoy. And a complicated McCoy at that, the sort where people get killed, and head offices and embassies aren't a lot of use to you. He'd seen people on trial after revolutions, innocent people who'd always assumed that the police and the courts were there to protect them, the terrible realisation there were no safe assumptions any more, the doomed, astonished despair in their faces.

This time he was sure Julia was telling the truth. It explained what she was doing, why she asked so few questions, and worried so little about what happened. She didn't need to worry, because what happened was someone else's responsibility. She was only a foot-soldier, and foot-soldiers don't question, they just obey, and make the best of it.

But in whose army? Mossad? Shin Beth? Why would the security services want to go into the television industry? They did, of course, but only for practical reasons. M.I.5 had their men in the BBC and ITN, just to keep an ear open, swap information once in a while. But they didn't make programmes. If the Israelis wanted a propaganda film about David Bermant they could make it themselves. Everyone makes propaganda films, and a lot of broadcasting organisations show them, often without revealing their provenance. No, it wasn't the programme itself, not unless Bermant was being set up by his own people. And why would they want to humiliate him? The man had only been in office three weeks. He found it hard to believe this was an official operation. Drug smugglers? There was a time when people used to bring hashish back from North Africa in cans of unexposed film, daring the customs to open the lid and spoil the negative. But not any more. Sniffer dogs and a new generation of X-ray equipment put an end to that. And anyway it seemed a bloody long-winded way to go about running drugs – tracing the daughters of war criminals, hiring TV crews and researchers, then spending a week running round the country interviewing politicians. Much cheaper to buy yourself a trawler.

He didn't have much to go on, and he didn't have a lot of time. Today was Sunday: by tomorrow night it would all be over, the show transmitted.

All he had to go on was the leg-men. Julia, Eric, Harry Greenbaum, Shimon and Tina.

Maybe he should go to the police. And tell them what? He'd been hired by a production company that didn't play by the usual rules. He'd been followed; a couple of times. And? And nothing, he didn't know, had no evidence, unless Dougie or Roger had come up with anything. No one had threatened him, the film was going ahead, his cheque hadn't bounced. Nothing.

Or he could pull out, break his contract. Fly home and forget the whole business, Julia and all. Poor bloody Julia. But there'd be other lovers, other bedrooms, other holiday romances.

There would, but not with Julia. Julia was no holiday romance.

'And what about me?' he asked her.

'That's the complication. That's what I didn't reckon on.'

'Me, or us?'

'Us.'

'Expunge the guilt of the Holocaust, or have an affair with Charlie Kavanagh. Tough choice. You wouldn't think of doing both?'

She gave him a sad smile.

217

'I'd like you to stay, Charlie. Will you?'

'I'm not sure.'

Below him the spools of Eric's tape recorder spun silently, taped to the springs beneath Julia's seat.

18

IT WAS A COLD GREY February morning in London, a wet wind blowing from the north, scattering refuse down the pavements. Dougie Thomas lived in a modest Victorian terrace in what ten years before had been the grimly unfashionable hinterland of north Kilburn. British West Hampstead, the wags used to call it when the Afro-Caribbeans took it over in the sixties and seventies. Not any more. One by one the West Indian and Irish families had been bribed and bullied out, and the humble artisans' dwellings gentrified into bijou middle-class residences. The Ford Cortinas and Vauxhall Vivas had gone, their places at the kerb taken by builders' skips, fun jeeps and German saloons with smoked-glass windows.

Dougie and Apple sat behind bright-green venetian blinds in the comfort of the centrally-heated kitchen, side by side on an expensively recycled church pew, studying the files and photographs laid out between the Sunday papers and the half-empty flagon of Valpolicella on the stripped-pine table. Dougie was fresh from the shower in a blue-denim shirt and chocolate-brown corduroy trousers, wrinkling his bare toes on the warm cork tiles. Apple wore tight white jeans, and a sweatshirt made from a Mexican coffee-sack, her back straight, one leg tucked under her. In the background the weekly Omnibus edition of *The Archers* played on the radio, Mrs Antrobus complaining to Jack Woolley about the price of dog-food.

'Fucking unbelievable,' said Dougie, and handed Apple back the photograph of Charlie Kavanagh. Charlie sitting cross-legged on the cushioned floor of a desert tent, drinking from

what looked like a small brass coffee-cup. On his right sat
Colonel Muammar Qadhafi. Both men were smiling.

'Where did you find it?'

'Camera Press. Filed in Charlie's name.'

'Must be a forgery.'

'Bloody good if it is. And that's only for starters.'

She reached into her fisherman's bag and took out another
reinforced brown envelope. Inside were more pictures of
Charlie – showing off an M-16 outside Sidon, deep in conversation with a PLO delegation in Tunis.

Dougie held the photographs in one hand, picked up his wine
glass in the other and drained it.

'Easy enough to do, I suppose. Call in at the picture agencies,
ask to see the right files, add in a few snaps of your own.'

'They don't have to be forgeries,' said Apple. 'They're all
places he's been to.'

She read off a chronology of Charlie's overseas travel.

'Ten trips to the Middle East. Beirut, Cyprus, Jerusalem,
Baghdad, Damascus, three times to Tripoli, Baghdad again,
Jerusalem again. Twice to East Berlin in eighty-two.' She
thumbed on down the list. 'Havana, Tehran, Moscow. Eleven
visits to Belfast inside two years. His second trip to Libya dated
a week before the IRA's Eksund arms shipment, after which he
went to Dublin and then Derry.'

'So what? The man's a bloody journalist, he's bound to go to
places like that. And all that was years ago. What else?'

She licked her thumb and turned the page of her spiral
notepad.

'Very active politically as a student. International Socialist,
official steward at the Grosvenor Square riot outside the US
Embassy. One conviction for disorderly behaviour. All in his
early twenties. And then he suddenly gave it all up.'

'Of course he did. He stopped being a student and joined the
BBC, bought himself a suit.'

'I believe you, Dougie. I'm not sure a jury would.'

'What's he on trial for?'

'He was at the Royal Garden seminar when they tried to blow
up Yaakov Tyler, left just after the explosion, and then vanished.
His friends think he may have gone to Israel.'

'But no one's accusing him of causing it?'

'No, they're still holding the Lebanese. I don't think the police have any interest in Charlie at the moment. Circumstantially it would look bad for him if they did get interested.'

'Who told you all this?'

'I just treated it as ordinary research. Talked to his mum and some former colleagues, rang some friends at the BBC, looked in the cuttings files, checked out back numbers of the radical press.'

Which was what Charlie had asked Dougie to arrange: hire a researcher, and get her to put together a profile of him. Blind, as though she'd never met him. And find out if anyone else had been doing the same lately. Someone had: and whoever it was had been rewriting Charlie's history as they went along.

'Not just the photos. I got hold of his BBC personal file. Ten pages of it, they're very conscientious about that sort of thing. Deathly boring, like school reports, "Charles has done well this year, but needs to watch his impetuosity." The usual garbage. Except there was a memo in there from someone called The Investigator. The Investigator liaises between the Beeb and the security services. But they fucked it up. The Investigator in question was dead at the time he's meant to have written the memo.'

'How do you know?'

'I rang him up and got his widow instead.'

That was the sort of hunch that made Apple worth two hundred pounds a day, way over the odds for a television researcher.

'And what did the memo say?'

'Nothing specific. Enough to suggest that he was viewed as politically suspect.'

Dougie got up, took a small tin down from the dresser, took out the dope and skins and a wallet of tobacco, and started to roll a joint.

'What else?'

'I went down to the BBC film archive at Brentford to try and suss out how anyone could have got a list of his films. Impossible: they don't file them under directors and producers, only under programmes and subject matter. It would take a month to begin to get together a breakdown.'

'Charlie couldn't figure that either.'

'Right. So it didn't come from the system, it came from a person. His wife. I rang her up and said I was from BBC Copyright, we were updating on residual payments to directors for overseas sales, a lot of money was coming in now because so much old material was getting on to cable and satellite. I couldn't find Charlie, did she have any kind of record of what he'd done. There was a fair bit of money involved. They're still technically married, so I guessed she would be in on any pay out.'

'And?'

'She chewed me off. Because she'd been through his papers ten days ago doing exactly that for someone else from the BBC. She couldn't remember a name.'

'Hey ho,' said Dougie, rolling the tobacco carefully between his fingers.

Apple began tidying up her papers.

'Do you think we should tell the police?'

'I'm not sure. If we don't, I've a suspicion someone else will before very long. Did you take all the photos?'

'And the memo. But there's bound to be more stuff out there when they start looking for it.'

He twisted the end off the joint and lit up.

'I wish the bugger would ring me.'

On the upstairs balcony of the Quarter Café, Vincent picked up his Nikon, left elbow resting on the table top, right hand gripped around the long lens of the Nikon. Schlack-prr-schlack-prr, and quickly back to his newspaper. Yaakov Tyler had more visitors: a boy with a moustache and a thin red-haired girl. Vincent had no idea who they were or if they mattered. He wanted another coffee, but he doubted if his bladder could take it.

Tyler let Tina and Shimon in and took them upstairs.

'Hi, blondie,' said Eric, balanced on the window sill among the brass and copper ornaments, feet dangling.

'Hello, Eric,' said Shimon coldly.

Tyler waved Tina and Shimon towards the black sofa and sat down behind the fat mahogany desk.

'They may be changing hotels,' Eric told them. 'I think the police at the Anani are getting to them.'

'Do you know where they're thinking of moving to?' asked Tina.

'No. They'll leave me a message at the Hilton if they do.'

'If they get here,' said Shimon.

'Don't worry,' said Eric. 'They'll get here.'

'You're sure?'

'Sure.'

'OK.' Yaakov scratched his beard. 'Shimon goes on shift at noon. When do you leave, Eric?'

'I'll fly back tomorrow.'

'Tina will have your money tonight, you can collect it before you go.'

'Thanks.'

'You're sure you're happy?' asked Yaakov.

'Absolutely. Kavanagh's worried about the programme content, the girl's a bit tense, but yes, I'm happy, I think we're in business.'

'Who else have they seen so far?'

'Liel, Kaufman, Feinberg.'

'Are Liel and Kaufman members?' asked Shimon.

'They all are. Liel would do anything for another vase. Kaufman travels a lot to useful places. He's chronically short of funds for his bloody vegetables. And the tin leg's handy, you can carry a lot in a tin leg. He even took a dog through customs in it once. No, they'll do what they're told, it's all in the family.' He got up from the desk. 'But no risks from now on. If you're in any doubt, we abort. No one need know.'

'I think we're in business,' Eric repeated. 'I'll know for sure when I've picked the tape up from the car.' He looked at his watch. 'I'd better go, I'm meant to be with Walter this morning.'

Charlie and Julia reached Jerusalem at noon, and spent an hour and a half with Goliath filming in the New City, knocking off a couple of tapes of moving wallpaper for the opening and closing titles. On Monday evening he'd shoot a short sequence of the guests arriving at the hotel and do a rush edit before the meal started, have it ready to run in live at the start of the programme.

'Every frame a Tretchikoff!' Goliath roared as he picked off the clichés one by one, the faces in the vegetable market, traffic in the Jaffa Road, the walls of the Old City from the terrace of the King David, the quaint, Hassidic families in Mea Shearim. But Charlie's heart wasn't in it. He was wondering whether to go home. He wasn't his girl-friend's father's keeper, it wasn't his war.

He could explain it to Julia tonight, leave it to the last minute so she didn't have time to dither, offer to take her with him, catch a morning flight back to London, take the phone off the hook for a couple of days, catch up on his laundry. It didn't matter what Eric and his mates were up to: the crucial thing was not to be around when it happened.

At least that was what the rational half of his brain told him to do. His emotions were another matter. He could have another try at persuading Julia to come with him, but he didn't know what he'd do if she chose to stay. Or what to do if anyone tried to stop them leaving. He sometimes fantasised about how he'd react to a situation like this, and concluded he'd be the worst kind of coward, go to pieces completely. But in the event he didn't feel scared: he felt angry. Angry at the way they were blackmailing her, angry at being used. Fuck them.

They finished shooting at half one, and adjourned for lunch at an open-air restaurant in the Russian quarter. Sitting in the warm sun Charlie realised that after four days he'd stopped noticing the landscape or the weather. Israel was all around, narrow lanes and low stone pantiled villas behind high walls, the eucalyptus and pines rustling gently in the warm afternoon air, but they could have been anywhere.

'You ever think of leaving this country?' he asked Goliath.

The cameraman tore off a strip of pitta bread.

'You live here you think of little else. Cost of living through the roof, the army calling you up two months a year, politicians raving on like rats in a box, there has to be something else to do with your life. Only if you go it's giving up. People move to the States, get well-paid jobs, they dream of sleeping soundly in their beds knowing no one's about to invade or strap a bomb to the suspension of their car. Only they don't sleep, they stay awake all night staring at the ceiling and feeling guilty. I suppose it's the same for refugees anywhere, except that we're not running away from foreign invaders, we're running away from ourselves. Not our enemies, our enemies we can handle. A lot of things I don't like in this country, a lot I don't like about what's happened to it lately. But I still love it, I still think we could make it better than it is. Besides, there are plenty of compensations, plenty of things you get fond of when you've lived here all your life. It may be a shit hole, but it's our shit hole. Everyone needs a home, the Jews have been living in rented accommodation too long. For me the argument's about what sort of home it should be. No, I'll stay here, Charlie. And you'd do the same.'

After lunch Julia and Charlie had a rendezvous with Walter and Eric at the Israeli Broadcasting Authority, where the researcher had booked an editing suite to put together the main titles and the archive film on Bermant. On the way up from Eilat Charlie had roughed out a commentary, which he recorded on to tape. They then dropped in the pictures to match his words, and added a few sound effects.

The suite was in the basement, an overcrowded and windowless cupboard stacked with monitors and tape machines. A young engineer pressed the buttons while Walter and Charlie selected the sequences. Normally this was a cheering moment in the evolution of a programme, the first time ideas and images came together in concrete form. Looking at the tape running on the monitor it was possible to imagine the finished product, a glimpse of what you were trying to achieve. But Charlie didn't really care, found it hard to summon up much enthusiasm. He wanted to talk to Walter, but he didn't know how.

The engineer stopped to change tapes, and Eric slipped out to the gents.

'Have you met Harry?' Charlie asked the researcher as casually as he could.

'Briefly,' said Walter. 'He was here a couple of weeks ago, rang me up and said he was looking for a researcher. We met for half an hour at the Sheraton, he was interviewing a bunch of us. To be honest I found it hard to take him seriously – he kept talking about his mother. I thought I'd screwed the interview. The next I knew was when Julia phoned me.'

Charlie shot a glance at Julia. For a second she caught his eye, then looked away.

'Was Eric with him?' he asked Walter.

'The midget? Absolutely. Tongue halfway up his arse.'

So how come Eric had to ask him what Walter looked like, Charlie wondered.

Walter looked nervously towards the door. A moment later Eric reappeared.

Charlie went back to the dope-sheets.

'You staying at your sister's?' he asked Walter.

'No such luck. She threw me out this morning. Nothing personal, but my habits get on her nerves somewhat. Maybe I'll buy her a present, see if she can put up with me for another couple of days.'

'Is she married?'

'No, she's waiting till she meets the wrong man. She's had a lot of problems, my father's death hit her very hard.'

'Sarah Kaplan said she'd been at Kefar Sharon for a time.'

'That's right. She was a little sick in the head, she spent a lot of time in mental hospitals after dad died. Then she met a lawyer on the bus one day, fellow called Gerry Nowitz, a quiet, shy little man. Gerry fell in love with her, he didn't see her as a problem at all. She moved in with him. They had a flat in Tel Aviv, a block in from the sea. And gradually she started to get better. She even got a job, helping out in a health food shop. Gerry was as gentle as a lamb. He trusted her completely. But he was away a lot, and she got bored. She started seeing other men. It's a long story, I'll try to keep it brief. You don't mind me telling you all this stuff?'

'Not at all. It's a relief to talk about real people for a change.'

They paused for a moment while the editor spooled through and showed them more footage – tanks in the Sinai sand-dunes in '56; aircraft overhead in the distance.

'Come in after the shot of the road,' Charlie told him. 'There's a milepost there, someone might know where it was.'

Walter took a sip of coffee.

226

'Gerry didn't seem to mind her sleeping around,' he continued, 'but she minded, she hated herself for what she was doing, and yet she kept doing it. She had another breakdown. They took her into hospital and gave her drugs and elec-trotherapy. I've got nothing in principle against either – if your body's ill you think nothing of taking a pill if you think it'll make you better, and there seems to me no reason why the same shouldn't go for the mind. But they turned her into a zombie. This was still in Tel Aviv, another private clinic. Eventually she begged to be taken away, and I gave in. The army gave me compassionate leave. I hitched down from Metulla on a Thurs-day, and picked her up in a taxi. I had no idea what I was going to do. We still had the flat in Herzliyya, so I took her there. I had to be back up on the border on Monday morning: my aunt was away in America at the time. And then I thought of Sarah.'

'And she got better?'

'More or less,' said Walter. 'Better enough to be called up. She was in the army to start off with. They put her behind a desk in the pay corps. And then they transferred her to intel-ligence. It's funny, she loved that. Being a spy married perfectly with her two best skills, deceit and fantasy. She's also very interested in the mechanics of death – she was the one who found my father.'

'This was with Mossad?'

'You tell me. I think so. It's hard to know how much of what she tells you is the truth and how much is wish-fulfilment. Certainly she travelled a lot. She worked under cover as a nurse at a French field hospital in Beirut for a while, an American journalist friend ran into her there. And I got postcards some-times, from Switzerland and Sweden. You know those terrible comedy cards, the kind people stick up behind bars? "You don't have to be mad to work here, but it sure helps." '

'And what does she do now?'

'Not a lot. She finished her service a couple of months ago, she's looking for work. She wants to write kids' books. More fantasy, I suppose. You got any nuts in your family?'

'Afraid not,' said Charlie, dunking his cigarette in the remains of his vendomat coffee. 'They're all a lot duller than that.'

'I had an aunt,' Eric offered, 'who thought she was Ella

227

Fitzgerald. People kept telling her Ella Fitzgerald was black, she used to say "Keep race out of this, will you?" '

The editor offered them more shots, a convoy of Egyptian troops driving through the desert, waving cheerfully at the camera as they passed.

'I thought we could use that for the business with Kaufman, the ambush by the Red Sea,' Walter suggested.

'Where's the sea?' asked Charlie.

Walter shrugged his shoulders.

'Tide's out, I guess.'

'You mind if we break for a few minutes?' asked the editor. 'I have to make some calls.'

'Fine by me,' said Charlie.

'Is there a chemist anywhere round here?' asked Eric.

'Top of the road,' said the editor.

'You feeling OK, Eric?' asked Julia.

'Fine. Just my gut's playing up. I think it must have been something I ate at the hotel last night. Have either of you had any trouble?'

They hadn't. He picked up his briefcase.

'I'll be back in five minutes.'

It took Eric a couple of minutes to find the Subaru, parked at the back of the building among the dustbins and builders' skips. The lock took him under ten seconds. He reached in beneath the driver's seat and untaped the recorder. German made, a miniature Uher, no bigger than a cigarette box. A true work of art, which is what made Uher the soundman's stock-in-trade. He slipped it into his pocket, and closed the car door.

Walter waited until he was alone with Charlie and Julia.

'Tell me something, Charlie, do you believe this programme's for real?'

'What do you mean?'

'I don't know. Don't get me wrong, I'm not complaining. Someone pays you good money to do a job, doesn't ask you to break the law or sleep with them, then that's fine by me. Also I've enjoyed meeting the two of you. But there's a lot of odd things happening.'

'Like what?'

'I don't know. Little things. I'm being followed.'

'Us too,' said Charlie. 'I thought maybe they were fans.'

'Red-headed girl and a big blond gorilla?'

'That's right. Drive a Toyota pick-up.'

'Shimon and Tina,' said Julia.

'Yeah, I checked them out,' said Walter.

'You did?'

'You drive as slowly as I do, you notice these things. I got an army friend to run their car registration through the police computer. He's called Shimon Heilman. He's a spook, works for the government. I got my sister to run a check on him too. Shin Beth. They don't call them that, they call them security liaison personnel, but that's what he does.'

'He works for Harry and Eric,' said Julia.

Walter looked at her.

'How do you know that?'

'I asked him.'

'You did? And he didn't seem embarrassed?'

'Not particularly.'

'According to the records he's on leave at the moment. Busman's holiday, maybe. What's he doing working for Harry?'

'I don't know. Keeping an eye on us three, I suppose.'

'He's keeping an eye on Julia,' said Charlie. 'Harry's blackmailing her.'

Julia shot him a look.

'You serious?' asked Walter.

'Absolutely.'

'To do what?'

'Make the programme.'

'Why does he need to do that?'

'I don't know, Walter,' said Julia.

'This blackmail, it's something you can't afford to ignore?'

'Absolutely.'

'It's not something she's done,' Charlie explained, 'it's to protect someone else.'

'So the programme gets made come what may?'

'I suppose it has to.'

'You could go to the police,' Walter suggested.

'If I go to the police,' said Julia carefully, 'I have to tell them everything. I can't do that. Don't ask me why, but I can't.'

'Shit.' He ran his hands through his hair. 'So you keep going whatever happens?'

'I don't have much choice,' said Julia.

The three of them sat for a while, not talking, listening to the hum of the machinery.

'I'll tell you what I think,' Walter said eventually. 'It's nothing to do with any of us. Two possibilities, either they want to do something to humiliate David Bermant. Live on TV, all over Europe and the States. Or none of that matters either, and the whole thing's to do with dirty money.'

'Explain,' said Julia.

'This country's awash with dirty money, looking for a laundry. Films and TV are a great laundry. Pay for the production with dirty money here in Israel, the profits come out clean. Better than that, they get tax breaks too. Happens all the time.'

'Whose money?'

'You tell me. But it's not that stupid an idea. Set the whole thing up so it looks as if it's coming from Britain or America. English producer with a clean record, established director with respectable credentials – you seen the budget for this show?'

Julia shook her head.

'No, just a cheque-book.'

'I bet the budget's huge. I bet on Harry Greenbaum's books this little number is costing – what, quarter of a million bucks? For what? I don't know how much you two get paid, but even if they pay way over the odds it's not a lot, they only need you for a couple of weeks. Plus a couple of air fares, my salary, a hire car, rent a room in the Star of David and an OB for the day. What are we talking about, fifty grand? Most of which they pay here in local currency. The profits are in dollars or pounds or marks. The fifty grand they write off against tax. So anything they get abroad is cream off the cake. You know how I reckon they got Global Village and the other boys to take this rubbish sight unseen? They offered it at a bargain price. They wave your c.v. under their noses, and Bermant's name, and then tell them they can have it cheap. The main US networks wouldn't take it, not in a million years, not without a pilot. Nor would the BBC, or ITV, or ZDF. But Global Village don't work like that, they pump out shit, ten-year-old Australian soaps and wall-to-wall game shows, with the odd bit of serious programming once in a while to give them a thin veneer of respectability. Cable and satellite's the same. Someone comes along and offers them a bit of live current affairs on the cheap, they'd jump at it. But cheap to them is free dollars as far as our boys are concerned.' He scratched his head again. 'Or it might be Bermant they're after. Or both.'

A door slammed in the corridor outside.

'I suppose,' said Walter, 'we just keep going. Why worry? We're being paid.'

'You do something for me?' Charlie asked him. 'Have another word with your sister. See if she can peel another layer off the onion.'

They finished the edit at five.

'You two doing anything this evening?' Charlie asked Walter and Eric.

'I thought I might go shopping,' said Eric. 'There's a shop on Ben Yehuda sells Israeli Special Forces T-shirts, "Mess with us and we'll make chopped liver of you". I thought I might get one for Harry, he likes that sort of thing.'

'How about a meal after?' Charlie suggested.

'Sure.'

'And you, Walter?'

'This is free food?'

'Absolutely. Mention David Bermant along the way and we may even pay you overtime as well.'

'Charlie, sometimes I find you quite irresistible,' said Walter. 'Where?'

'You name it.'

'You like Turkish? There's a place on Devrech Hevron, near the railway station. They keep a suit of armour by the bar, you can't miss it.'

'What time?'

Charlie was due to meet Vincent at seven.

'Half-eight?'

*

Charlie and Julia drove back to the Anani to pick up their bags. Charlie had no particular reason to move now, except that the more unpredictable he was, the more confusion he hoped he'd be creating. And the Anani was part of something that was over now, a lost idyll.

In its place he chose the Majestic, next door to the King's hotel, on the corner of Ramban and Keren Hayesod, across from the Sheraton Plaza. The period in question was the nineteen fifties, and the clientele uniformly ethnocentric, conservative Jews from Western Europe and the United States – family parties from North London in town for their son's bar mitzvah, elderly uncles and aunts from Ohio attending a niece's wedding. This was the heartland of Judaism in New Jerusalem, next door to the Great Synagogue, just down the road from the Jewish Agency.

The Majestic had plenty of staff, mostly friendly, and customers with very firm views on life.

'Regular tuna salad, and *no* lemon juice, you got that? Absolutely no lemon juice. You want to write that down?'

'Someone took my room key.' Not 'I've lost my room key,' or 'has anyone found my room key?': 'Someone took it.'

'That's my taxi.'

'It's not your taxi, it's the driver's taxi.'

Charlie loved all that stuff, and the lookalike faces: Dustin Hoffman behind the reception desk, Tony Perkins as the hall porter, Jean-Paul Sartre collecting his room key, an elderly Bette Davis knitting ferociously on an upright chair in the souvenir shop.

They checked in and took the lift to the fourth floor, and walked down the high wide corridor to their room. A generous box, recently refurbished, with a view on to the Centre for Conservative Judaism, the Baha'i B'rith World Centre, and Sapir Furs, Leather Remodelling and Repairs. Muffled sounds of traffic rose from the road below.

'You've been here before?' Julia asked.

'Of course. I rather like it. Staying in a place like this reminds you what country you're in. Journalists don't know much, but they know about hotels – hotels, restaurants and airlines. And

PRs' children, you get to be quite expert on their children and holidays.'

'It makes me feel very foreign.'

'So it should. You're in a foreign country.' He dumped his suitcase on the bed. 'The British know fuck-all about Jews, absolutely fuck-all, except that they circumcise their sons, they don't eat pork, they have a thing about their mothers and they drop out of Bible class at the end of the Old Testament. And they get persecuted. That's about it, really. Yes, they're foreign. So is everyone else.'

'Sorry,' said Julia.

'Me too,' said Charlie. 'Did you mind me telling Walter?'

She put her hold-all on the bed.

'I don't mind anything much any more, Charlie. No, in a way I'm glad. I think he's in the same boat we are, I think they're using him too. I suppose we'll find out soon enough if he's on the other side.'

She opened the bag and took out her cigarettes. Watching her, Charlie realised her hands were shaking.

'Are you all right?'

'Yes. I mean no, of course I'm not all right.'

'We can still go home.'

'I know, I've been thinking about that.'

He offered her a light. She lit her cigarette and inhaled.

'I'm scared, Charlie. I don't know if I can handle tomorrow.'

'What about Mad Wolf?'

'I've been thinking about that too. I suppose we could warn him.'

'I already suggested that, you said it wouldn't work.'

'We could try.'

'Then let's get out while we can. I'll phone the airport.'

'Wait. Suppose Walter's right, suppose it's just a scam, a way of moving money around. Suppose there really is a quarter of a million dollars floating on this deal. Whoever set it up isn't about to take any risks, they'll have taken precautions. Hell, I wish I knew what was going on.'

'We should get out of here, Julia. The only reason I haven't gone already is because I didn't think you'd come too.'

'That's really why you stayed?'

'Of course.'

She put her arms round him.

'I'm sorry about all this, Charlie. I thought – I don't know what I thought. Yes, let's go home.' She kissed him. 'I love you.'

Charlie held her very close. She was a strong woman, but she felt very frail in his arms.

'I love you too.'

'Do you think we could get a flight out tomorrow?'

He picked up the phone. All the lines to the airport were busy. While he was waiting he thumbed through his address book and found Roger Hogarth's number.

Julia sat beside him on the bed.

'What will we do when we get back?' she asked him.

'Hold on a moment,' said Charlie. 'I just want to find out what we're leaving behind.'

Roger came on the line.

'No Harry Greenbaum Foundation. Or not under that name. No Harry Greenbaum either, or not one that the American Pharmaceutical Association have heard of. Julia Cornwall doesn't own a car. The police have no interest past or present in a Nick Parrish.'

'Oh,' said Charlie.

'But they are looking for Ms Cornwall. Her flat was flooded out – the neighbour upstairs left his bath running. The landlord let himself in. Not much damage, but a lot else. I don't know if she's told you, but your girl-friend appears to keep Semtex in her fridge.'

'You're joking.'

'I'm not.'

Charlie felt ill.

'Do they know where she is?'

'Not yet. I wanted to ask you about that. They were a little curious to know why I was phoning in the first place.'

'What did you tell them?'

'I was vague. But I have a message to ring them back. Someone's putting two and two together.'

'Tell them it's a security matter with diplomatic overtones, ask them to leave it alone for a couple of days.'

'Commercial attachés don't have a lot to do with security, Charlie.'

'Do it, or I'll tell them about your pretty little Bulgarian waiter – what was his name? The one with the Russian wife.'

'Fuck off. And he wasn't Bulgarian, he was Polish.'

'Two days, that's all I need.'

'I'll do what I can.'

And then he phoned Dougie, and heard his news.

'Do a couple more things for me, will you?' he asked when Dougie had finished. 'Check out a missing Nazi called Wolfgang Koeppen. Simon Wiesenthal's lot in Vienna should know. And get the spare keys to Monmouth Place from Betty, and have a look round.'

'What am I looking for?'

'The new me.'

Charlie and Julia weren't going home any more: they weren't going anywhere.

19

DAVID BERMANT DIDN'T KNOW what to make of his new body-guard. They all seemed the same to him, these sons of Sparta: correct, anonymous, terribly conscientious. And so bloody healthy. They hardly bothered to introduce themselves any more, and he found it hard to remember which ones he'd met before and which ones he hadn't.

This one he was pretty sure was new. The first time he'd even noticed him was at lunch, a dreary but necessary affair at the Moriah Hotel to welcome a delegation of American fund-raisers. You had to hand it to these people: year in year out they rounded up cheques, lobbied Capitol Hill, canvassed for *olim*, wrote countless letters to *Time* magazine and the *Washington Post*. Even if their rhetoric was a little strong at times, they deserved their thanks, and a photo of them shaking hands with the Foreign Minister to take home and display on their pianos.

They sat at white-clothed circular tables decorated with car-nations in pink porcelain vases, and ate a predictable banquet served with military precision, soup and salads, chicken and cheesecake decorated with irradiated strawberries, two bottles of sweet Carmel wine and a jug of iced apple juice to each table. David sat with the wife of a Seattle real-estate broker on his right, a junior Congressman on his left, the one a hardliner, the other nervously concerned about the effect Israeli Army tactics on the West Bank were having on US public opinion. Not a bad conversation. Then came a long and impassioned speech from a New York lawyer, some of which he agreed with; a few words from himself, carefully written for him by his staff at the Foreign

Ministry, and then much exchanging of plaques and mementos, a lot of handshaking, and a quick bolt to the limousine. The new man was waiting with the rear door open.

'Do I know you?' David asked him as they drove off up the broad avenue of Keren Hayesod.

'No, sir.'

'You new?'

'No, sir, I've been with the service two years.'

And that was all.

David had other problems on his mind. His New York speech was ready. Not his speech: they'd handed it to him, pre-written. He'd objected, they'd shrugged their shoulders. He'd argued it in Cabinet, tried to insert a few words of compromise, suggested how the nuances could be shifted a little, just a little, if only for cosmetic purposes. To no avail. Even his Labour Party colleagues had said nothing. Afterwards Chaim had soothed him, explaining the difficulties, the problems he'd had getting the damn thing toned down in the first place. The arguments had already been had. David demanded a meeting of the Party Executive, Chaim said it was a waste of time. David threatened to resign, and bring the government down with him if he could.

'You know what that would mean?' Chaim had explained. 'Another general election. The Party can't afford it. And we'd be taken to the cleaners.'

'Not a bad thought, with the state of our laundry.'

'Don't jest, David. Look at the polls.'

'I've looked at them. They don't seem that bad to me. And what if we lose? Is that the end of the world? The longer we hang on, the less credibility we have. It's like eighty-eight all over again.'

'You're not a politician, David. You have to take my word for it. An election now would be a catastrophe.'

And that was where they'd left it, because David needed time to consider his position. If he resigned, they'd find someone else to make the speech. Chaim himself would probably do it if there was no one else. And he understood Chaim's position. They were both Social Democrats at heart, and Social Democrats had had a short life expectancy in recent years. All the western leaders he admired – Willy Brandt, Olaf Palme, Roy Jenkins, even Jimmy Carter – where were they all now? A terrible advertisement for men of principle.

The oldest argument in politics, whether to resign or hold on in, do what you can, because if you go they'll replace you with someone worse.

Charlie sat on the bed and watched Julia getting changed. There's no justice in the world. Some people come out of the egg looking like Walter Eitan and some come out looking like Julia Cornwall. She was unashamed but unaffected by her beauty. He supposed if you had a body like that you came to take it for granted, the breasts were just breasts, the legs just legs, that was the way your hair fell naturally, that was the shape of your cheekbones, the down on your neck: you'd never know what it was like to be any different.

She sat down on the bed beside him and pulled on her knickers.

'What are we seeing Vincent for, by the way?'

'Didn't I tell you? He's on the payroll now.'

'Vincent?'

'Every dog has his day.'

Vincent was waiting for them in a downstairs bar off Hillel Street. Low lighting, stone floor, candles on scrubbed wooden tables, half a dozen young Israelis drinking in corners. The sounds of Boney M came from the jukebox.

A broad-beamed Australian waitress with bad skin and a toothy smile brought them beers while Charlie opened the FastFoto envelope and looked at the pictures.

'Any use to you, old boy?' asked Vincent.

'I'm afraid so,' said Charlie.

He looked at the pictures one by one, then handed them to Julia. Vincent leaned forward and lit his cheroot on the candle.

'Are you two going to inform me what's going on round here?'

'I would if I knew. The girl's a foot-soldier of some kind, she followed us half-way to Amman the other evening. I don't know who the boy with her is, she was with a blond before. The flat belongs to Yaakov Tyler.'

'Didn't someone try to kill Tyler in London just the other day?'

'I did,' said Charlie. 'Or, rather, that's what it looks like.'

'You serious?'

'Absolutely.' Charlie put the photos back in the envelope. 'What time did you take these?'

'Mid morning. He stayed about twenty minutes, then he grabbed another cab. Afraid I lost him after that. You need two on a job like that.'

'They call that over-manning these days, Vincent. Ma Thatcher put a stop to all that.'

Funny bugger, Kavanagh, Vincent reflected. Like all those college boys, beaming confidence, knows all about claret and poetry, wears clothes that look as if they've been in the family three generations, tweed jackets marinaded in mulligatawny soup, brogues you could bath a spaniel in. And tennis shoes, and lived-in jeans that somehow kept their shape. Their trick was never to own anything new, so that the rest of the world couldn't pop out to the shops and buy the same rig off the peg. Ordinary people would get thrown out of pubs if they dressed like that, but for the Charlie Kavanaghs it was a badge of class.

Class was all they needed: an old corduroy jacket, an Oxbridge degree – preferably nothing too good – the right Voice, and you could walk into any job you wanted. Vincent had to do it all from the ground up: teaboy on the *Wolverhampton Express and Star*, cub reporter on the *Birmingham Post*, chasing ambulances, describing starlets' wedding frocks, drinking with boorish policemen – bloody years of it, until you got a job in London on the *Mail* or the *Express*; and when you finally did the job security could be measured in hours. All you lived by was your ability to deliver the goods. If you didn't, you were dead. Television was different; in television the Kavanaghs of this world weren't hired because they delivered, they were hired because they were who they were, clones of the men who hired them – personnel officers who didn't go to Oxbridge but hired people who had because they'd always wanted to themselves. If things went badly wrong, if anyone really screwed up, took to the bottle, stuck their freckled fingers in the till, then they might

239

be shifted sideways, made Deputy Head of Special Projects, put in charge of the Scottish Agricultural Unit, sent off to Brunei to help the Sultan set up a radio station. But not real work, that was all strictly lifestyle stuff, thirty grand a year, good pension, your own parking place and regular drinks with the Channel Controller.

For the real work they recruited disreputable mercenaries like Vincent Fallop. Then they paired them off together: an Oxbridge producer to do the social graces, and an ex-Fleet Street hack to do the graft, doorstep the villains, make the unpleasant phone calls, tell the half-truths that got you into places you needed to get into. In return for which the Oxbridge boys got promoted, and the hacks got underpaid, had their expenses scrutinised by teams of puritanical clerks in Burton's suits, and got invited to nice dinner parties by producers anxious to show off their rough-trade colleagues to banking and barrister friends, the way the aristocracy parade head gamekeepers in front of their house-guests. A character, terribly good at the job, but not a Serious Person.

Fuck the lot of them.

But of course that wasn't the whole story. There were good times, and friendships of a sort inside them, and with time some of the hacks had become a bit gentrified, and some of the Oxbridge boys turned out to be tolerable journalists, once they'd been on the job a year or two.

Kavanagh had never been much of a journalist. Too easy going, not enough anger or hunger in him. But he wasn't pompous, didn't drop you in the shit, and he didn't push either his ego or his career too hard, which is probably why he never really made the grade. He took the trouble to ring or drop you a line if you'd done something he admired. And he was disrespectful to Management, always a healthy sign.

'Shall we tell him?' Charlie asked Julia.

Julia looked as pale as a nun and tense as a trigger, hair tied back at the neck, fingers playing with the cuff of her blouse. Charlie was going to have to relax her somehow before they met the others. She shrugged her shoulders.

Charlie started in at the beginning.

240

Later they drove across town to the restaurant, up the hill from the Cinematheque, facing Mount Zion and the still-curfewed Arab village of Silwan. Rough stone walls, wine-red carpet, a fish-tank, silk flowers on the tables and the imitation suit of crusader armour on a velvet plinth beside the bar.

There was no sign of Walter or Eric, or any other customers: the place was empty.

'Lucky we booked,' said Vincent facetiously.

The patron advanced across the floor towards them like an opera singer.

'Hallo! Deutsch, no?'

'No,' said Charlie.

'Français? American?'

'English.'

'Ah! English, of course, How do you do! Bottoms up, mate! Please, a seat. What would you like?'

'We're waiting for friends,' Charlie explained. 'But some wine would be nice.'

'Any particular wine?'

'Wet,' said Vincent.

They waited half an hour for Walter and Eric, and then decided to order anyway.

'A wise move,' the patron informed them. ' "A man who waits for his friend is a man without a friend." It's an old Turkish saying.'

'Very true,' said Vincent. 'Do you have any more?'

'Turkish sayings? Of course. How long do you have?'

'My plane leaves tomorrow lunchtime.'

'It's too short, you must come back when you're not so rushed.'

'Just one more?'

'OK. "When the olive-blossom is green, Mustaffa must look to his grapefruit trees." '

'Brilliant.' Vincent nodded appreciatively. 'What does it mean?'

'It means: if you like to order my tongue is loose and my pen is sharp and ready.'

'Fire away.'

'I recommend squids, very fresh.'

They shook their heads.

'No? OK. Kebab? Fish? Qashda?'

'What kind of fish?' asked Charlie.

The patron searched for a word, tried drawing in the air with his hands, gave up.

'Just a fish, fried fish. Or grilled.'

'And what's qashda?'

'Qashda? You don't know qashda?'

He was dumbstruck. Everyone knows what qashda is.

'Try it, is very good. From the unborn goat, I can particularly recommend.'

Julia opted for the steak.

'Ah. To be fairly honest with you, madam, the steak today is not so good, it is a little, er, plump. Fat.'

She looked at the menu.

'Lamb?'

He shook his head.

'Meat balls?'

'Perhaps, excuse me, I'll have to ask.'

He asked. There were no meat balls; or chicken; or stuffed vine leaves.

'Kebab,' said Vincent and Charlie in unison.

'Me too,' said Julia.

'And to start? We have dried fish,' he mimed each item with his fingers, 'tarama, also yoghurt, with no additions, natural ship's yoghurt; eggplant and cumbercue salad – you know how it's done, in salt and fish oils, delicious, I recommend. Also curd cheeses, humous, dried-in-the-sun beef – and squid, excellent squid.'

They ordered humous.

'And more wine,' Vincent suggested, 'with as many additions as you want.'

A waiter arrived with cutlery and four slices of grey bread. The patron followed him with three thimbles of brandy on a brass tray.

'From my family's vineyards in Anatolia, I think you like.'

'You're very kind,' said Julia.

'Over one hundred years old, I swear to God.'

'Small for its age,' said Charlie, examining the glass.

'I'm sorry?'

'Nothing, it's an old joke.'

Anything for a joke, anything to keep the spirits up. The main problem of the evening was going to be keeping up appearances, allaying Eric's suspicions. When he finally got here. Charlie took a chile and bit off the tip.

'By the way, I forgot to tell you. Someone put a tape recorder in the car. On the way back from Eilat. Eric, I presume. I found it when I was looking for my cigarettes.'

'Jesus,' said Julia. 'What did you do with it?'

'I wiped it, and left it for him. With luck he'll think the machine wasn't working. But they must have been suspicious to put it there in the first place.'

And then they arrived, and the double-bluff began. Charlie introduced Vincent to the man he'd been tailing all day.

'You new to this business?' Vincent asked Eric.

'Absolutely, Mr Fallop.'

'But he's a quick learner,' Charlie congratulated him.

'Thank you,' said Eric with a self-effacing smile.

'If you want to learn to be a TV producer, son,' said Vincent, 'the best thing to do is to get someone to make a film about you. That way you really learn how the business works.'

For a moment Charlie thought he caught a slight tension round Eric's eyes, but then he was looking for it, just as he knew Eric was watching him.

Walter ordered a double portion of qashda, and Eric made do with a limp seafood salad. Vincent took the waiter aside for a quiet word. Outside the window an army flare burst brightly over Silwan, and they could hear the distant sounds of sirens.

'I still think that's the film we should have been making,' said Charlie, nodding at the Arab village. 'Ordinary people, people caught up in events beyond their control. Not politicians. Politicians have choices.'

'Come back and make it next time,' said Walter. 'This problem isn't about to go away. Suggest it to Harry.'

Eric asked Charlie if he was still worried about the content of the programme.

'You always worry,' said Charlie cheerfully. 'Or if you don't, should. It changes by the day, one moment you think you're sitting on a masterpiece, the next you think it's a disaster. Thank heavens we're going out live. With live shows you worry before you shoot, and then that's that, nothing you can do about it. Filming documentary is far worse. You have all the worry before you shoot, and then when that's over you start worrying all over again. You get a dazzling interviewee, take the stuff home and look at it, and find he's said nothing. You film on a spectacular location, and the feeling of the place is so strong when you're there that you forget to take the really obvious pictures that show what it's like. And you can be so busy concentrating on practical things that you forget about the detail, too. Little things make all the difference. The expression on someone's face before they answer a question, the landscape, little things that people who don't know much about your subject can identify with.

'Did you notice the way Benny Kimche signalled to his staff during dinner last night?' asked Julia. 'He didn't need to say anything, you just know what he was like.'

'Sure. Except that once you get to film him, you forget about that stuff. You've had such hassle getting someone to agree to talk in the first place that it's easy to be lazy once you've got him, just sit him behind a desk and let him talk. People behind desks feel comfortable. Some desks tell you things about their owners, but mostly they're anonymous, the man might as well be on the radio. You only do it because you can control what's happening in an office, nothing distracting's going on, or if it is you can do it again. You can't ask people to eat a meal again. If we'd been filming Benny and he'd said things in the wrong order, I'd have wound up editing him so what he was saying made sense but the meal wouldn't. First time you see him he's eating pudding, five minutes later he's starting his soup.'

'Do people really notice those things?'

'They do in the business. I don't think Joe Public does, not shot by shot. But if odd things are happening in the background all the time there's a cumulative effect, he senses something's amiss.'

'Pompous bullshit,' Vincent interrupted in mid-mouthful. 'Don't listen to him. The simple rule is that if what's happening

244

is interesting you don't have a problem. If what's happening is boring, then your attention wanders. You ever see a movie called *Bullitt*? Steve McQueen, great movie. There's a famous car chase across San Francisco, McQueen versus the psychopath. Cars bouncing all over the shop, hubcaps falling off. McQueen's car has four wheels. Watch carefully, and you see six different hubcaps fall off. At the end of the chase the psychopath's car hits a gas station and the whole lot blows up. Only it doesn't: they could only do one take and the stunt driver missed the building; the gas station blew up but if you know what to look for you can see the car speeding happily away across the field in the background. You ever meet anyone who noticed?'

'Is that really true?' asked Eric.

Vincent refilled his own wine-glass.

'McQueen told me himself.'

'You met him?'

'If you call interviewing people meeting them. Twenty minutes on a hotel sofa with ten PR's hovering on the edge of frame telling you what questions not to ask while he plugs his next picture.'

'You must meet a lot of interesting people in your job, Vincent.'

No, Eric. Most of them are like you. Vincent turned to Walter.

'You're Moses Azeff's son, aren't you?'

Walter nodded.

'You knew him?'

'I met him. Bit like Steve McQueen, I'm afraid, I remember him but I doubt he'd have remembered me. He committed suicide, didn't he?'

Walter put down his glass.

'Who told you that?'

'I can't remember.'

'They called it a heart attack.'

'I'm sorry. I'm sorry whichever it was. He always struck me as a decent man, if that doesn't sound too pompous.'

'Not at all,' said Walter. 'He was, I think.'

'Didn't he and David Bermant have some kind of a row?'

Walter took a mouthful of qashda.

'Not a row, really. My father's business got into trouble, Bermant was involved in the Commission of Enquiry.'

'And what was the business?' asked Eric.

'Military uniforms – the police, army, air force, whatever was wanted. Dad and Chaim Ezra set it up, years ago. It started out as a patriotic venture – at that time we were importing almost all our uniforms. The customer supplied the designs, they bought in the cloth, and put the cutting and making up out to contract. All over the place. Several kibbutz were involved, which my father liked: it seemed an ideal industry for a country like this, something that could be done away from cities, in the villages and moshavs.'

'This was for the IDF?'

'Of course, but they also exported – Western Europe, the States, the Third World. You can't go wrong in the Third World: every time there's a coup the incoming regime wants new uniforms. They even sold to Arab countries – I remember as a kid, during the Yom Kippur war, Chaim coming to see us and chuckling because he said all four armies were wearing our trousers. The patriotic factor didn't seem to worry him: we were going to win the war anyway, so we might as well take some money off them while we were at it.'

Across the valley a flare went off, illuminating the hillside opposite and the flat-roofed houses of Silwan. The army was taking its curfew duties seriously.

'So what went wrong?' Charlie asked Walter.

'Business took a dive when Likud got into power in seventy-nine. There weren't as many friendly people in high places any more, I suppose. The IDF switched its orders elsewhere. Inflation was going through the roof, interest rates were high, a lot of businesses got into trouble. They started having to lay people off. But Dad wasn't too worried about it to start with. As far as we knew he'd never taken much money out of the company, always ploughed his share of the profits back into the business. He assumed there must be plenty of assets to carry them over. But there weren't. And then the rumours started in the press, hints that funds had gone missing. Dad was quite well known as a politician by then, a tribune of the liberal left, campaigning for the homeless, sitting on civil rights committees, you name

246

it. And now he was about to be revealed as a bent capitalist. It was a big company: the government set up a committee of enquiry. David Bermant chaired it. There was a big scene between my father and Chaim one evening. They stayed up half the night. I don't know what Chaim said, but he finally left at about three, my mother heard the car go. Dad came up to the bedroom to see her, and told her he was going for a walk. They found his body in the morning, hanging from a beam in the garage.

'Most of it never came out. Bermant's committee was dissolved: tasteless to hound the dead. There was a big funeral – Begin was there, and Peres, and Rabin. My mother wouldn't let Arik Sharon come, she put her foot down at that. I was only seventeen at the time, and Tina was fourteen.'

'And what did Chaim have to say about it all?'

'Nothing, really. He was very good to us afterwards, made sure we were all right. He got the doctor to fix the death certificate so that it looked like a heart attack – that way we collected the life insurance.'

'What year are we talking about?' asked Charlie.

'Lots of years. It started in about sixty-five, I think. My father died three years ago.'

'What a terrible story,' said Eric.

At that moment the waiter returned with Vincent's champagne.

'It's Julia's birthday,' he announced.

Charlie prayed that she'd have time to absorb the news before their eyes were on her. She managed a blush and a smile.

'Vincent, really!' she reproached him.

'Twenty-seven today,' said Charlie.

Or was it thirty-one?

'Speech,' Vincent demanded. 'Or perhaps you'd rather give us a song?'

'It's really your birthday?' asked Walter.

'I'm afraid so.'

'Wait!'

He was on his feet. The restaurant was by now half-full, mostly quiet tourist couples whispering over their kebabs.

Walter headed for the sweet trolley and purloined a gâteau. Charlie collected up candles from the other tables. Vincent sang 'When you said you loved only me, Maggie', and would have sung more if he'd been let. Eric allowed a silk rose to be inserted behind his ear, and Walter gathered up the other customers for an impromptu display of folk dancing, the kind that exposes the damp patches under your armpits. The patron smiled, adding invisible extras to the bill. And Julia smiled too, mostly with love for Charlie.

Eric found the celebrations hard to take. There was something he didn't trust about Vincent. And he was worried about Charlie. The tape in the Subaru had been blank. Not like a Uher to jam like that.

And he worried about Vincent. Nothing suspicious, just a hunch. A hunch, and a half-remembered face from the Old City that morning.

Charlie was right: Vincent was getting rusty.

20

VINCENT REMEMBERED THE car engine stalling, and after that he didn't remember much at all. He'd driven less than half a mile from the restaurant.

'Bloody hire cars,' he cursed.

And then he saw Eric's face through the glass. He was half-way out of the car, bleary with drink, when the little man reached up on tiptoe and hit him on the back of the neck, a clean, well-judged blow. After that all was darkness.

The next thing he knew he was indoors, in a kitchen, propped in an upright chair with his head slumped on the table in front of him. A modern kitchen, green fitted cupboards and beige formica worktops, an electric clock and a framed poster of alpine skiers above the stainless steel sink. A white Chinese paper lampshade hung from the ceiling. His mouth was gagged, his wrists tied behind his back. Eric was perched on the table edge opposite him, fiddling with a pistol. Shimon was making coffee. No Tina. There was music playing from a radio cassette, sounded like Barry Manilow. To drown the screams, he supposed.

Eric put down the gun, got up and loosened Vincent's gag. Vincent felt the sweat running from him, down his face, under his arms, moistening his underwear.

'I say, you wouldn't have an aspirin would you, old boy?' he asked. 'I seem to have a hangover.'

Eric allowed himself a thin smile.

'Tell us about you and Charlie Kavanagh.'

'He's a friend.'

They know I know, Vincent deduced. I don't know how they know, but they know. They must have seen me with the camera, I suppose. His head ached, but he felt terribly sober.

'That's all?'

'We used to work together, a long time ago.' He nodded towards the pistol on the table. 'That's a P-38, isn't it? Czech. Very popular in Italy, Alberto Moro was shot with one, I seem to remember. One in every three Americans owns a gun, only one in nine owns a passport, did you know that? At least I think that's the figure. You are American, aren't you?'

Bloody Kavanagh. I should be home in England, lying in bed in the green glow of the clock radio, listening to the Islington traffic and trying to get to sleep. Round about now I'd take a pill, switch on the World Service, wait for the sleeper to close my brain down for the night.

'Your friend Charlie's in trouble,' said Shimon.

'Makes two of us.'

'No, you're not. Not yet.'

'Of course I'm not, how stupid of me.'

Shimon picked up his coffee mug and sat down at the end of the table.

'I'm sorry about the violence. We didn't know how else to do it.'

God, what a cliché. Hard man Eric, nine-guy Shimon. If you could call Shimon a nice guy, which he doubted.

'By the age of seventeen,' Vincent told them, 'a child will have seen sixteen thousand deaths on television, I read that somewhere too. How did you fix the car? Sugar in the tank? Handkerchief up the exhaust? We did that to the art master at school one time. Mr Murphy, a nice man, came from Dundee or somewhere. But weak. The weak ones are irresistible, I'm afraid. Remember that, Eric – if you can't kick a man when he's down, you'll never have the balls to kick him when he's on his feet.'

He glanced across at Shimon in time to see a quick smile cross his face. Shimon was enjoying this.

'What did Charlie tell you about the programme?' asked Eric.

'A doddle. Yes, that was the word he used: a doddle. Milk and two sugars please.'

Maybe they don't know, maybe it's all a bluff.

'Apart from that?'

'He said the trouble with working in Israel was the food, a week of steamed chicken and gefilte fish and his appetite packed in completely. He said he couldn't understand how a race which was so obsessed with healthy eating complained so much about its bowels. Which reminds me, I need the toilet. You're all welcome to come along, but I do need the toilet. Must have been the bloody qashda.'

'Later,' Shimon said quietly.

'Later may be too late. Listen – I'll do you a deal. I get to shit, and afterwards you get to hang me upside down and carve your initials on my bum. You can't say fairer than that.'

Shimon shook his head sadly.

'This isn't a game, Mr Fallop: there's a war going on in this country at the moment. Last week, a gang of Palestinian teenagers stopped a school bus outside Ramallah, opened the front door and threw in a petrol bomb. The week before three fedayeen were caught in a rubber boat off Nahariyya with twelve pounds of Semtex explosives and the plans of a synagogue in their rucksacks.'

'I know there's a bloody war going on. I just got wounded in it. One moment I'm driving along minding my own business and the next someone hits me over the head, trusses me up like Tom Kitten and takes me off to see their kitchen. It's a nice kitchen, very well laid out, and I've seen it now, and I'd like to go home. In the meantime I need to use the toilet.'

Shimon sighed.

'I'm sorry, Vincent. We need to know what Charlie told you this evening.'

'*You're* sorry? How do you think *I* feel?'

Eric got up and walked round the table, so that he was standing directly behind Vincent. He pressed his knuckle against the base of his nose.

'Mmm,' Vincent protested. 'That's nice. Harder, and a little to the left, that's right. I suppose a fuck's out of the question?'

The other fist struck him a hard dull blow at the bottom of his ribcage. Vincent gasped.

'OK, OK, let's get on with it. You want me to tell you

251

something. I've seen the movies, I know the script: I can make things easy for myself, or you can do it the hard way. The problem is I haven't the remotest bloody idea what you want to know.'

Shimon allowed himself another smile.

'What are you doing in Jerusalem?' Eric hissed.

'Sightseeing. Looking for the Lost Ark, doing my Christmas shopping.' He twisted his head round. 'Come on, Eric old boy, it's in the script. I make a wisecrack and you slap me across the face.'

Eric jerked the chair back. Vincent's face hit the table as he fell forward. He felt the blood trickle from his nose, and sniffed.

'Good, very good son. Now, you keep thumping me until I pass out. Try the kidneys, apparently that usually works. Though to be honest I've never been too sure where my kidneys are. Round the back somewhere, I think. Start at the arse and work your way up.'

Eric lifted him by the hair and put him back in his seat.

'What did you tell him about Bermant and Azeff?'

Oh God, Vincent realised. There may even be some logic in all this.

'Now this is tricky,' he told them. 'What I'm meant to do is give you my name and number and then shut up. You hit me again, I do the same. Only I don't have a number. I could make one up, I suppose. Either that, or I confess. You write down what I say, only you write it in Hebrew. Then you give it to me to sign. And because it's in Hebrew I can't read a word of what I've confessed to. Some fellow in the Dan Hotel told me that's how it's done in Gaza. Clever stuff.'

He knew they were going to kill him. They had to: they couldn't go lifting people off the street, beating them up, and then letting them go again. What have the following in common: Charlie Kavanagh, David Bermant, Moses Azeff, Chaim Ezra, Yaakov Tyler and a skinhead midget called Eric? Answer: none of them have yet played for Arsenal. If there was a real answer it was lost somewhere in the wastepaper basket of his memory, crumpled, torn up, mixed in with ten thousand other names. In the BBC he'd have rung News Information, asked them to send up the cuttings file. You don't need a memory when you have News Information at the end of a telephone, the brain can get on with more practical things.

No, he had no idea what the hell cause it was he was dying for, who these people were. Twelve hours ago he'd never even met them. Like all the important transitions in life it was so bloody random – you happen to be in Israel, happen to run into an old colleague who probably lives two miles away from you in London but neither of you have taken the trouble to see each other in five years; you get drunk with him and his girl-friend, help him out with a few pictures, and before you know it: bang, out you go feet first, exit stage left with a cheap wreath from the NUJ on your coffin. Greater love hath no man than this, that he lay down his life for Charlie Kavanagh's girl-friend's father.

He realised that Shimon was talking to him.

'Sorry, old boy. Come again?'

'It's very important that you tell us anything Charlie and Julia may have said to you today.'

'Important for who?'

'For everyone.'

'I'm going as fast as I can,' Vincent apologised. 'You have to give me some clues. Is it a book or a film?'

'Hopeless,' said Eric.

'No,' said Shimon. 'But getting that way.'

This was the moment his life was meant to flash before his eyes, but it was just a blur, nothing much there. Born, grew up, ate, slept, had a few jars, kept his head above water, more or less. RIP. Pretty meaningless stuff.

Shimon opened the fridge door and got out a syringe.

' "Had I been cloven not crested, my lords," ' Vincent proclaimed, ' "thou would'st have treated me thus!" Queen Elizabeth The First. Only she was cloven, she had the other problem. What's in the syringe?'

'Tongue-loosener. It'll help relax you, take away the pain.'

'Couldn't I have a Scotch instead?'

'Eric doesn't approve of alcohol, he thinks it harms the body.'

'Quite right, Eric. Don't drink, don't smoke, don't mess with women and if you don't live another fifty years it'll feel like it.

That's what Bob Hope used to say. Or was it Archie Andrews? Listen, if you're not going to kill me you'd better get me a bed pan.'

Charlie and Julia lay on their backs in the darkened hotel room, heads on adjoining pillows, looking at the ceiling.

The trouble with not being able to sleep in a hotel room is that there's nowhere to go that doesn't involve getting dressed, nowhere to prowl, no kitchen downstairs, no domestic tasks to burn up the energy. A hotel room in the middle of the night can be a blissful limbo or a prison cell. Television is the only known antidote, and both the IBA and the Jordanians had long since closed down for the night. The Majestic wasn't the sort of hotel that went in for in-house videos.

Charlie sat up and hunted the bedside table for his cigarettes, lit up and handed one to Julia.

'I don't think it's the money,' she said quietly. 'I think it's Bermant. Just suppose it is, suppose they plan to knock him off. Why?'

'I've spent a lot of time wondering about that.' The tip of Charlie's cigarette glowed in the darkness as he inhaled. 'To pull Labour back in line, I suppose. Show how impossible it is to try and do deals with the Arabs. It would shock the hell out of the Americans.'

'And where does Yaakov Tyler fit in?'

A shaft of orange street-light cut across the room, catching the drifts of grey cigarette smoke that hung like mist in the still, airless room.

'We don't even know for sure that he does. What have we got – Vincent's photos. All they prove is that Eric went to see Yaakov – what's so criminal about that? A three-year-old could come up with a credible explanation.'

Charlie stubbed his cigarette and turned on the light.

'We know from Vincent's photos that Yaakov Tyler's involved,' said Julia. 'Eric went to see him, so did Tina and Shimon. So it's not official, it's a cowboy operation.'

'The trouble with this bloody country is you can't separate out the citizens from the state. Practically every man and woman in Israel has been in the armed services at some point or other,

254

and most of them still are for months of the year. Most politicians are ex-colonels and majors, half the cabinet's done time on the intelligence payroll. You can't isolate the politics of the State from the politics of the military and the intelligence services, you never know what's official and what isn't. Israel doesn't have a foreign policy, or an economic policy, or a social policy: it has a defence policy. Full stop. Everything else is incidental. They can't afford to do otherwise. The politicians tell Shin Beth or Mossad what they want achieved, and leave the details to the professionals. Nothing unusual about that, every government in the world does the same. Only there are more professionals here, and more to be done, that's all. And because there are more professionals there's a lot of skilled labour around – mercenaries, anti-terrorist specialists, arms experts, free lancers. Some of them still in official positions, some of them not. This could be a Mossad operation, because it involves foreigners. Or it could be domestic, Shin Beth. Or it could be neither.'

'But we know it's Yaakov,' Julia repeated.

'True. Or we know he's involved.' Charlie pulled back the blanket and swung his legs over the side of the bed. 'And he has a motive, or at least I could have a guess at one. You know what land costs in this country nowadays?'

'I haven't a clue.'

'Plenty, particularly if it's near the cities. Whereas land on the West Bank costs next to nothing. Depends who you buy it from – if you have friends in the right places, it costs you literally nothing, the government gives it away. Most of it's not worth much, either – rock and sand, even the goats complain. But there's a lot you can do with rock and sand. If it's near Jerusalem, you can build towns on it, cheap housing for commuters. If it's in the Jordan valley it's not rock and sand at all, it's fields. Imagine what you could do with a place like Jericho if you put your mind to it. There's a speech of Yaakov's in the cuttings about what he'd do with Jericho. He wants to rebuild it the way they rebuilt the Jewish Quarter in Jerusalem, rebuild the walls, make a resort out of it, bring in some industry and hi-tech agribusiness. The only trouble is, the land doesn't belong to him, or not yet. He's half-way there.'

'And Bermant wants to hand it all back to the Palestinians?'

'He's been saying so for twenty-five years. Only now he's in a position to do something about it.'

'They won't let him.'

'Of course they won't. But he's in the way. And suppose a famous moderate like that got knocked off by the Palestinians now, what would that do?'

'Ruin everything the PLO have been trying to do for the past five years.'

'Which is not something they are likely to do themselves of course. But there are plenty of other groups in the Arab world who'd love to see them come a cropper.'

'OK. Six out of ten for motive. But how are they meant to get close enough to do it?'

'They're not. They're going to hire someone to do the job.'

'You serious about this, Charlie?'

'Why not? If they use us, it looks as if it's the West's fault. Charlie Kavanagh and Julia Cornwall, international terrorists, spoiled children of European liberalism. The Brits will feel guilty about it, Jewish fellow travellers in the diaspora will stop moaning about Israeli violence on the West Bank and come back into the fold. And the waverers here will come back into line. People expect the Palestinians to be violent, and they understand why – they're a victim race. Kicked out of their homeland, stuck in refugee camps, fucked around by their Arab neighbours. Who can blame them if they get a bit carried away from time to time? But a sane, educated Englishman and his girl-friend, that's different. And we're not even nutters, we're cold and calculating middle-class ideologues.'

'Except that we're not,' said Julia without too much conviction.

'Don't tell me, tell the jury. No one's going to believe us – they've had plenty of time to smear incriminating evidence around the place. We only know what we've found, there's bound to be more. Maybe you're right, maybe we should make a run for it. But where? Believe me, I've thought about it. I suppose we could get on a day trip to Egypt and not come back. Gets us out of Israel, but not much more. The best we could hope for would be to find our way to Libya or Iraq, I suppose.

You fancy settling down in Baghdad or Tripoli for the rest of your life?'

Julia watched him cross the room and collect up his clothes. She didn't dare ask what he was doing. Half of her wanted him to go, get out, find somewhere safe. The other half just wanted to be with him whatever happened.

'Where are you going, Charlie?' she whispered finally.

'Out.'

She lay and watched him getting dressed, pulling on his underpants, collecting a shirt from the wardrobe, scratching his buttocks as he looked around for his trousers. Happens in a billion bedrooms every day, a woman watches a man get dressed, a man watches a woman, such a mundane thing. Sometimes you want them to go out the door and walk under a truck, and sometimes you're overcome with tenderness to the point of pain. She looked at Charlie and suddenly wanted to be ordinary with him, do the dull habitual things that her self-image abhorred, do them week after week, month after month, sink back into the daily habits of life, stop trying to be all the things she'd encouraged the world to think she was. Normally there came a point in her relationships when she tried to picture a common future, and that was when the relationship failed, no matter how in love she was or how happy she felt at the time. She not only loved Charlie, she wanted to grow old with this thick-set, hairy-chested, unambitious, quick-to-sweat, tousle-haired, middle-aged career failure. It felt a curiously cold, objective decision, coming not from her emotions or even her brain. But she wanted it desperately.

Some hope: this was it, he was going. Who could blame him?

'Charlie,' she said.

He was dressed now, one foot balanced on the upright chair in front of the dressing table as he tied the lace of his gym shoe. He looked up.

'Can I come with you?' she asked.

She wanted him to stay, she wanted him to go.

'You don't even know where I'm going.'

'I'd like to come anyway.'

She wanted to go with him because she couldn't bear it if he walked out that door and didn't come back. If he got run down by a drunken driver. Or if he went to the airport and argued or charmed his way on to the first flight out in the morning.

Charlie smiled. But then he would, wouldn't he.

'I'd like it too, Julia. But you can't.'

'Why not?'

'They'd think we'd both done a bunk.'

'Are you taking the car?'

'I'm not sure.'

She started to get out of bed.

'Are you coming back?'

She was standing now, very naked, wondering whether to put on her kimono.

'Guess.'

His tired, pale face smiled at her through the freckles. But then it would, wouldn't it.

Julia started to cry.

'For God's sake, woman,' said Charlie, and put his arm gently round her waist. 'Of course I'm bloody coming back.'

21

DAVID KNEW REHAVIA'S DAWN chorus by heart now. At five-past six the elderly Polish violinist in the flat upstairs padded across David's ceiling to the bathroom, coughed, spat, lowered the lavatory seat and turned on the hot-water geyser. At six-fifteen the metal garage door across the street rattled open and Yitzak Stern, the argumentative construction engineer who lived on the ground floor of number thirty-eight, got into his ageing bullnose Volvo, started the ignition, drove out into the road, left the car door open with the radio on while he got out to close the garage door and then motored off down the hill towards Jabotinsky. Ten minutes later Argov the grocer arrived to open up his basement delicatessen and began stacking his vegetable crates on the pavement. And on it went, louder and louder as the day began, doors slamming, shutters opening, baths running, arguments starting, Mrs Smolenskin repri-manding her dog, Dr and Mrs Rosenman's young twins playing on the balcony while they waited for someone to get them breakfast.

David had never spoken to most of these people, but he knew who they were because his minders told him. Not just the names, but their politics, the state of their marriages, how they were getting on in their careers. Obsessive little Mr Argov, for example, had a once-a-week liaison with a spinster school-teacher at her flat in Kiryat Aryeh. The Szczupaks who lived on the third floor of number twenty-seven had a daughter in a mental institution (paranoid schizophrenia, prognosis not good) and a student son who was active in the Peace movement. The

Polish violinist had not, as he claimed, studied at the Warsaw Conservatoire, but in provincial Bydgoszcz.

David slept little these days, four hours at most. Sometimes he read – biographies, Russian novels, political journals; and sometimes he propped himself up on the pillows and wrote notes and observations, reminders to himself, letters to old friends in the diaspora, most of whom he hadn't seen in twenty years.

Shortly before seven the noises came closer to home, Rosa moving in the kitchen, the tinkling of cup on saucer, the padded click of the fridge door, footsteps in the hall, then a knock on his door, as usual rather louder than he thought necessary.

Good Morning Minister, Good Morning Rosa, the buckle of your brassiere shows like a carbuncle through the back of your blouse, even I could find it in the dark with my bony freckled old-man's fingers. If the paratrooper hadn't got there first.

I'm glad I please you Minister, but don't forget I'm still a virgin.

I never forget it, Rosa, and when you finally decide to open your thighs they will drown the world in sweet, sweet honey.

Honey enough for everyone, Mr Bermant.

I know, Rosa, but I'm an old man and I can no longer swim as strongly as once I did.

And yet you still tingle and harden when you smell my perfume bending over your bed with the tea tray in the mornings.

Cheap scent, my child, a chemical approximation of roses, with a heavy hint of lavender.

It's all I can afford.

I could buy you better.

You disgust me, Minister.

Not as much as I disgust myself.

She put the tray on his bedside table, pulled back the curtains on the damp grey morning, and withdrew. David waited until she was back in the kitchen before pouring the tea into the waterlogged busy lizzie by the window, taking care to leave a little in the cup. Then he showered and shaved, counted out his fist-full of pills and swallowed them in a single wincing gulp.

At eight he phoned Ezra from his study.

'I'll go to New York, Chaim, and I'll make the speech. But I can't promise it'll be your speech.'

'What the hell does that mean?'

'It means I'm thinking about it. I could lie, I could say I'll do exactly what you all want. But I haven't decided. Which means you can take the risk, or you can sack me.'

There was a pause at the far end of the line. Which was what David expected: dismissing the new Foreign Minister at a time like this would be difficult.

'Is this official?' asked Chaim eventually.

'No, this is friend to friend. As far as the rest are concerned I'm going. I just wanted to warn you.'

'Can I see the other speech?'

'No.'

Another pause. He could picture Chaim drumming his fingers, scratching his ear, clicking his teeth as he weighed the news.

'Has anyone else seen it?'

'No.'

'You can't do this, David. You're where you are because the elected government appointed you. When you accept the job you accept collective responsibility, we all do.'

David looked out the window as he listened, at the buntings in the ivy, the starlings on the TV aerials, the cats stalking among the shrubs. Jerusalem seethed with cats, a symbol of something but he could never quite decide what.

'Na, Chaim. That's bullshit, and you know it.'

'It's not bullshit. If you get up in the United Nations and make a speech which doesn't reflect the policies of your own government, all you achieve is chaos. Worse than chaos, you make your country look stupid.'

'It's what they do to us. One moment a Syrian minister's in London or Washington waving olive branches, the next he's on Damascus radio preaching genocide. Mondays Arafat embraces the Pope, Tuesdays he's cracking jokes with hijackers and letter-bombers. Different strokes for different folks. It's called diplomacy, I think.'

'You'll make a fool of yourself if you do it.'

'Maybe I will. Maybe we should make fools of ourselves more often.'

Chaim sighed.

'Do as you wish, David. I won't try and stop you. But I'd like to see you anyway. Not in Cabinet, just the two of us.'

'It's a busy week. We have the English TV jokers tonight. Maybe we can talk afterwards.'

'I'd like that,' said Chaim.

The Deputy Prime Minister put down the receiver and shrugged his shoulders at Yaakov Tyler, sitting opposite him in an upright chair, a cup of coffee on his knee.

'He intends making a different speech,' said Chaim wearily. 'As if it mattered.'

Yaakov sipped his coffee and wiped his lips on the back of his hand.

'You know what the doctors say about him? They say he has maybe a month to live, not more.'

'I know,' said Chaim. 'That's the only reason I'm prepared to go along with this nonsense.'

'You change your mind, Chaim, I could have you in prison inside a week,' said Yaakov. 'On more charges than I care to mention.'

'And I you,' said Chaim. 'And the rest of them.'

'I know, that's why we make such an unbeatable team.' ·

'Don't remove food from the restaurant', said a printed sign on the wall above the queue for the breakfast buffet in the Majestic's dining room. No one among the busy crowd of guests was paying much notice. Hard boiled eggs vanished into jacket pockets, pots of yoghurt into shirt fronts, cheese slices were slipped inside folded newspapers. Directly in front of Julia a stout and well-upholstered woman in a fashion beret and high heels picked over the fruit basket, selected a pear, dropped it in her handbag, changed her mind, put back the pear and stole a grapefruit instead.

Julia helped herself to a bowl of cream cheese and a plate of salad and found an empty table in the corner. No sign of Charlie. It was eight-fifteen, and they were due to meet the crew at the Star of David at nine.

Breakfast at the Majestic was a seething, garrulous obstacle course, a mêlée of couples and family parties arguing and jostling their way through the tables, stealing each other's toast from the squeaking chrome conveyor-belt by the door, waylaying each other's waiters, helping themselves to milk-jugs and sugar bowls while their neighbours' backs were turned. Julia couldn't believe that the simple business of eating a meal could generate so much heated debate, that these people could find so much to complain about so early in the morning.

'Young man!' an elderly, unshaven Englishman in a tweed jacket, a tartan shirt and an embroidered velvet skullcap called out to the waiter who was pouring Julia her coffee. The waiter was far from young, well into his fifties.

'One moment, sir.'

The Englishman leaned over and caught the waiter by the hem of his jacket and pulled him backwards towards his table.

'Three friends are going to sit down beside me here,' he instructed him, pointing at the empty seats. 'You understand? Three people. They need cutlery, plates, napkins. To eat off,' he explained.

The waiter abandoned Julia and began assembling handfuls of crockery. She looked sadly at her half-cup of coffee, wondered whether to join battle, decided against it.

To her left an American woman was complaining to a friend about bedding.

'Twice we've asked for more blankets and pillows.'

'You found the extra pillows in the cupboard?'

'Yes, I found them, they give you two spare, I need at least three, Jo needs another. In fact he needs more.'

'You can never have too many pillows,' said her friend, holding her saucer to her chin as she drank.

Still no sign of Charlie.

The Englishman's geriatric friends had arrived: a senile Sid James with a pencil moustache, a voice like Enoch Powell and a blazer with a not very credible RAF crest on the pocket; a George Burns in yellow check golf trousers; and a Lyndon Johnson in drag, average age maybe seventy-five. All wore thick pebble spectacles and carried glass bowls of prunes.

'They have to stop the music, Art. I can't eat to that music,' complained LBJ, waving her spoon towards the tannoy speaker, out of which came the sound of an accordion combo playing

Yiddish medleys to the accompaniment of a dull, repetitive drum machine.

'You're right,' said Sid, doing nothing to stop it.

Julia reached into the pocket of her blouse, took out Eric's typewritten note, and read it again. The American had been called home in a hurry, was taking the morning flight to New York, apologised for not having time to say goodbye.

Odd that Eric should use a typewriter. She folded the note, put it back in her blouse, and tried to eat her salad, but she had no appetite.

'Waiter!' A young woman in black with bad skin and a lot of gold round her neck and wrists waved a herbal teabag in the air. 'I need hot water.'

Come on Kavanagh. It was twenty-five to nine. Julia's eyes were on the entrance.

A smiling corpulent American in a yellow dressing gown, velvet slippers and a skullcap wandered in with a child in silk pyjamas.

'Mamma's over there, sweetheart,' he told the child loudly. 'Tell her Uncle Reuben's gone back to bed.'

And then behind them she saw Charlie, cheerful and smiling, bag on shoulder, still wearing the clothes he'd left in six hours earlier. He was beside her before she had time to stand up, arm on her shoulder, bending down and giving her a weary kiss on the cheek.

'Where have you been?'

'I'll tell you later.' He put his bag down and looked over at the buffet. 'How do you get a coffee round here?'

'Take your clothes off and scream,' Julia suggested.

Behind him two primly dressed English boys in prep-school shorts and ties and jackets posed for their mother's camera.

'Straighten your skullcap, Simon.'

Charlie sat down.

'What time are we meeting the crew?' he asked.

'Nine. We have twenty minutes.'

'Shit.'

'Walter's meeting us there.'

'And Eric?'

'No Eric.'

She showed him the note.

'This hot water's too hot to drink,' complained the girl with the teabag.

'I'm sorry, I thought you asked for it hot, madam,' the waiter apologised.

'Not that hot.'

'I'll take it,' said Charlie, picking a sachet of Nescafé from the bowl in front of him and pouring the powder into a cup. The waiter topped it up for him.

'Hold on, that's *my* water!'

The waiter shrugged his shoulders.

'I thought you didn't want it.'

'Of course I wanted it, I just wanted it cooler. You do something for me?'

'Yes ma'am.'

'Get me the restaurant manager?'

'I am the manager, madam.'

'OK. Then get me a real waiter, will you?'

Charlie put milk in his coffee, helped himself to a teaspoon of Julia's cream cheese, and examined Eric's note.

'So that's the end of the Mormon?'

'I suppose so.'

'Do you know what I find odd? Harry. Where is he? How come he never calls us?' He gulped down his coffee. 'We should go. I need to change.'

'Aren't you going to tell me where you've been?'

'Not now, there isn't time.'

Julia didn't know why, but she didn't mind, wasn't even that curious. She loved Charlie, loved his optimism and energy, but it was all hopeless. There was no way all this could end well. But at least it would end with Charlie.

The car was parked on the pavement outside the hotel. Not the Subaru, but a battered Ford Escort with Israeli plates.

'Borrowed,' he explained.

The weather in Tel Aviv was warm, a clear sky and gentle wind blowing in over the flat blue Mediterranean. The temperature was in the low seventies, a pleasant June day in England, and a full ten degrees higher than Jerusalem. But the long flat beaches were almost deserted. No one swam in Tel Aviv at this time of year, not even the tourists. There were joggers, though, and seagulls scavenging the flotsam offshore, and a few guests from the high-rise hotels taking their morning constitutionals on the municipally cleansed sand.

Roger trotted heavily along the beach in his nylon tracksuit and size twelve trainers. He found it hard to be fond of the city. Tel Aviv reminded him of those Greek and Roman towns – Salamis, Caesarea – whose centres have been washed away into the sea, leaving only suburbs behind. But then that was what Tel Aviv was, an overgrown suburb, always had been, from the day in 1909 when a group of Jews from Jaffa bought a sand-dune on the outskirts of town and set about turning it into a garden city. Within five years the population increased twenty-fold: by Independence it was a quarter of a million, today it was half as big again, a breeze-block city built on sand, and built in a hurry. Dust and concrete, ersatz boulevards and scorched parks: one of those characterless twentieth-century conurbations whose tourist literature is reduced to praising the municipal wax museum and the tallest office block in the Levant. Some garden city.

An army helicopter flew in along the coast. Roger panted his way up on to the promenade, changed out of his tracksuit, locked it in the boot of his car and walked a block inland to the embassy. Since 1967 Israel has looked on Jerusalem as its capital, but as far as the diplomatic community is concerned nothing has changed. Jerusalem is still half Jordanian: and the embassies are still in Tel Aviv.

Roger's phone was already ringing when he reached his office. It was just after nine, two hours ahead of London. But Scotland Yard's anti-terrorist squad were no respecters of the clock.

The Yard wanted Kavanagh, and they wanted him fast.

This was merely a courtesy call. In a couple of hours the Israelis would be informed: a cable was on its way to the embassy through the proper channels. By the end of the day there'd be a full-blown extradition request. Unless of course the Israelis had things of their own they wanted to talk to Charlie about.

'Are there charges?' asked Roger.

There would be once forensic had finished with Monmouth Place. The Yard had shown his photo round the staff of the Royal Garden, and sourced the two and a half thousand pounds paid into his bank account on a Syrian bank bond. Harry Greenbaum's body, or the body of someone calling themselves Harry Greenbaum, had been discovered when maintenance men drained the filter beds at the Hounslow reservoirs earlier in the week, and identified from a photofit in the *Evening Standard* by the head waiter at the Hilton.

Roger didn't know where Charlie was. Or why Charlie had wanted to know about Harry's car.

He didn't know where he was, but he'd find him.

One reason TV people call each other mate and love and darling is that on a busy day a studio can contain upwards of forty engineers and technicians and cameramen. The following day there's a new shift and forty more names to remember, and it's thought more polite to call someone Mate than to call them by the wrong name. (The other reason that TV people call each other mate and love and darling, of course, is that the business is riddled with pretentious poseurs who want to give the impression that they once worked in the theatre. The theatre, regardless of content, being considered a creative profession, as opposed to television, which is commercial. *Puss in Boots* at the Golders Green Hippodrome is art, *The Singing Detective* or *King Lear* on the box is not.)

Names were going to be a problem today, Charlie decided as he glanced around the thirty busy strangers in the Sheremetyevo suite. He didn't even know what the Hebrew for mate was. Goliath introduced him to the cameramen, most of whom seemed to be called either Zak or Tony, then the sound supervisor and the floor manager, who weighed close on three hundred pounds and answered to the nickname Titch. That one Charlie reckoned he could remember, but he wrote it down in biro on the palm of his hand just in case. Finally he met Louella the make-up lady. Louella was from Chadron, Nebraska, and from the way Goliath introduced her he guessed their relationship was not confined to business.

'They have Jews in Chadron, Nebraska?' Charlie asked her.

'Not any more.' Louella gave him a big smile. 'We left.'

Across the room Aaron Fluck was supervising the decorations, the most obvious of which was a six-foot square Star of David Hotel sign on the wall behind the dinner table.

'No,' said Charlie.

'No?' said Aaron sadly.

'Absolutely not.'

'How much is all this costing us?' Charlie asked Julia.

'You really want to know?'

'No.'

They found Walter going over the menu with the catering manager.

'How may strawberries in a portion?'

'Enough.'

'Make it more. And where do your artichokes come from?'

'The Jezreel valley.'

'At this time of year?'

The manager shrugged his shoulders.

'How's it going?' asked Charlie.

Walter grinned.

'We're getting there. Did you know Bermant's a vegetarian?'

'That's what we hire researchers for,' said Julia. 'Any other problems?'

There weren't. Walter had spoken to all the guests, arranged transport for them, and make-up, and a side-room for drinks before the recording. Security had already done an initial check on the Sheremetyevo, and Bermant and Ezra's people would be over in the afternoon to liaise with them and check over the rooms and equipment. The crew, guests, and necessary hotel staff would be issued with passes, and no one else allowed anywhere near the suite. Even those with passes would be routinely searched every time they came and went.

Charlie took Walter out into the corridor.

'Did you get a chance to talk to your sister?'

Walter looked over his shoulder to see no one was listening.

'She doesn't know anything we don't know, Charlie. Except that our friend Shimon has been off work for the past two weeks, he clocks on again today. But she's had a word with Chaim Ezra's security people, she has friends there.'

268

'What are they going to do?'

'Make sure nothing happens. And if those guys say nothing's going to happen, nothing happens. They'll search the hotel, and then they'll search it again. They'll make sure no one gets anywhere near the shoot unless they know who they are. If someone asks you to strip naked and stand on your head, do what he says. These guys know orifices you didn't know you had. All the crew are being re-vetted. Already they want us to change the soundman, he has a brother who's done time for selling IDF small-arms on the side. Maybe we'll lose more people before the end of the day.'

'But they think we should go ahead?'

Walter smiled.

'Of course. This is Israel, we have our reputation to consider.'

They moved aside to let through a rigger with a coil of cable.

'Have they told Ezra?' Charlie asked when he'd gone.

'No. Not the man himself. They don't think there's any need.'

'Will you do something for me, Walter?'

'Not tonight I'm afraid, Charlie. My period just started.'

'If anything happens tonight, keep an eye on Julia.'

Walter put his hand on Charlie's shoulder and gave him a squeeze.

'Nothing's going to happen. But if it does, yeah, I'll make sure she's OK.'

'Thanks.'

'For nothing.'

They went back through into the Sheremetyevo.

'So what do you want us to do?' asked Charlie.

'Fuck off,' said Walter. 'Unless you want to help with the gazpacho.'

It was almost noon: less than seven hours to go.

Charlie felt like a walk.

22

HARRY GREENBAUM'S WASN'T THE only body to turn up unexpectedly. At eight that morning a stray dog had found Vincent and Eric in a concrete waste pipe on a construction site off the new Jericho road, not far from a bus stop where early morning commuters from Giv'at Shapira were queuing up for the ride into Jerusalem. Eric had a P-38 bullet in his brain: Vincent was thought at first to have died of natural causes, until a sharp-eyed policeman noticed the bruise-mark of the syringe on his fore-arm. Estimated time of death was some time in the small hours. There were two heel-shaped furrows in the dry red earth where Vincent had been dragged to the pipe from a car, but a dark stain in the dry red earth suggested that Eric had been shot close to where they found him. The initial police theory was that he'd been moving Vincent's body at the time.

They also found Vincent's car, parked out of sight in a refuse-filled wadi on the side of French Hill, less than a quarter of a mile away. Tracing it involved no more than a phone call to Hertz in Tel Aviv. There was a notebook in the door pocket of the Renault. Charlie's name and hotel phone number were among half a dozen scribbled in biro on the cover, in between an escort agency in Tel Aviv and British Airways reservations. No surname, just Charlie.

There were no obvious clues as to Eric's identity, but they'd find out soon enough.

'Who did you borrow the car off?' Julia asked curiously.

Charlie gave her an enigmatic smile.

'From each according to his ability, to each according to his needs.' He patted the Escort's bonnet. 'I haven't met the owner yet.'

They parked in Bloomfield Parade, and strolled over to the Rob Van Tricht Garden, perched on the rim of the Hinnom Valley, looking out across the pantiled rooftops of Mishkenot Sha'ananim to the Sultan's Pool and the walls of the old City. 'This garden was created', said a stone-carved sign, 'by Jill and Mendel Kaplan, South Africa, in memory of our friend.' Narrow stone paths twisted in and out among the olive trees and rose-mary shrubs and boulders fringed with narcissi and low wax-leafed desert flowers, and symmetrical rows of ornamental green and purple cabbage circled the trees, partly obscuring the black plastic irrigation pipes that ran like snakes through the plants.

'The Dwellings of Tranquillity,' said Charlie, pointing at the rooftops below them. 'Built in the eighteen sixties, the first Jewish settlements outside the City Walls. Dangerous place to live in those days.' He pointed across to the cedar and pine-covered slopes of Mount Zion. 'And that's where the Canaanites used to throw virgins off the cliffs before a battle.'

'I'm afraid I'm not much use to you on that score, Charlie,' said Julia.

They reached a simple stone wall with a wooden rest behind it. 'Sidney's Bench', said the plaque, 'In Honour of Lord Bernstein, a dear friend of Jerusalem, on his 90th birthday, 30 Jan 89.'

Charlie sat down.

'If I wind up dead this week, Julia, I want you to erect a monument in the foyer of the Sheraton Plaza Hotel and dedicate it to The Unknown Smiler. I love this country, I love its people and its energy and its obsessions. But I miss the smiles. Have you ever met a happy Israeli? There must be some, but they keep them off the streets. The best you hope for is wry resignation.'

'Happiness is a gentile aberration, Charlie. You're looking for seaweed for breakfast. Being Jewish isn't about being happy. I'm not even sure that being British or American or Irish is about being happy, and we've got a lot more to be happy about. Anyway, who says you're going to wind up dead?'

'No one. And I don't intend to.'

She looked very beautiful in the soft sunshine. Exhaustion had stripped all artifice from her face, so that her expression flickered from the innocence of a child to the weariness of old age.

Charlie snapped off a twig of rosemary and twisted it in his fingers.

'Suppose someone really did want to kill David Bermant. Suppose there was a motive. Suppose Yaakov Tyler or whoever thought that assassinating a liberal Foreign Minister might have a purpose. Sober up the peaceniks, pull the Americans back into line. I can sort of buy that. It doesn't solve anything, but when a war goes on long enough people give up the idea of solving problems, they come to terms with the concept of insolubility and just get on with the fighting, battle by battle: they know no one can win. What's important is not losing, and making sure the enemy feels the pain. Ulster's like that, and Beirut – they're not fighting over ideas any more, they're fighting about religion and race, neither of which are winnable arguments. Knocking off Bermant stirs the pot up again. But if all they want to do is kill him, why involve the rest of us? Why not just do it? God knows there are enough firearms lying around the place. That's what I don't understand, where you and me and Harry Greenbaum fit in.'

'You really think they're going to kill him?' asked Julia.

'I think they're going to try.'

A cat stalked the flowerbeds, and twenty yards away an old man in a raincoat kicked a football to his grandson. From below in the valley came the muffled sounds of buses and taxis climbing the hillside opposite towards the Jaffa Gate. Further up the park a crocodile of schoolchildren sang their way towards the Montefiore Windmill. On Mount Zion a church clock struck the quarter. Lutheran chimes: Mount Zion plays host to the protestant sects who arrived too late to claim their share of the sacred sites inside the walls.

'Are you scared, Charlie?' Julia asked.

'I don't know. I'm not used to this sort of thing, it's too unreal. No, strangely enough I'm not. Are you?'

'I'm like you, I'm past being scared. Where did you go last night, by the way?'

'You really want to know? I went back to Kefar Sharon. I went to see Sarah Kaplan.'

Tina was alone in the flat. At two o'clock she turned on the radio and spent a peaceful hour in the bedroom doing yoga, letting her mind flow gently through her body, emptying her brain of conscious thought, her skinny body naked except for her white cotton knickers. Then she rubbed herself all over with herbal oils, got dressed, brushed out her hair, and was half-way out the door when the phone went.

Shimon spoke quietly, almost in a whisper, as though he was calling from someone's office.

'Haven't you gone yet?' he hissed.

Tina sighed.

'You have called Jerusalem zero-treble two-seven-four-seven-one. I'm afraid I can't take your call at the moment, I've popped out to deliver a package of illegal substances to the Star of David Hotel. If you have any more asinine questions please leave them after the explosion. Of course I've gone, Shimon. Where the fuck are you?'

'Outside the Knesset. In the car, I can't talk now.'

'In whose car?'

'Bermant's. He's due out any minute. I have to go.'

Tina had had enough of Shimon. Two hundred pounds of ersatz muscle in search of a new mother to abuse. Two hundred pounds, an IQ in the low nineties and the decision-making talents of a blind sheep. She'd never met a man who was so inept at decisions. Give him a script and he was fine, but anything that required thought and he went to pieces. If you told him to swim to Rome and strangle the Pope he'd do it without a moment's hesitation, just give him a length of rope and a bathing costume, take him to the beach and point him towards Italy. But offer him a tray of chocolates and he'd go into an interminable slow-motion panic trying to decide which one to take. Once this was over that would be that. As far as Tina was concerned four weeks living with a man was anyway as much as any woman could be expected to endure. After four weeks they stopped buying you flowers and started farting in the bedroom.

Shimon had a good body, though: she'd miss that.

She let herself out of the flat, hurried downstairs and round the corner to the shops. She stopped off briefly at the supermarket, navigating her way between the racks of imported food towards the vegetables. Self-reliant Israel imported things other countries didn't know they exported: Irish crispbread, Canadian herb-teas, Norwegian paper tissues, Belgian cocktail biscuits. She shopped here every day, even knew the checkout girls' names. Every day they treated her as a total stranger, refused her cheques, ignored her requests for carrier bags, sent her to the back of the queue if an item was unpriced. Nothing personal: in this country the customer – any customer – was always wrong.

Golda behind the till looked angrily at Tina's twenty shekel note and shook her head.

'Exact money only.'

'Since when?'

'Since now.'

'Sometimes,' the New Zealand *olim* in the queue behind her said drily, 'the charm can be overwhelming.'

Tina bought a newspaper, dropped in briefly to the pharmacy, walked up Yehuda Burla and cut through the campus of the Hebrew University to the Star of David.

'I'm with the TV crew,' she told the security man outside the hotel entrance.

'You have a pass?'

Tina had a pass. The searcher asked her to open her handbag.

'You know something?' said Tina. 'I don't think you guys are looking for terrorists, I think you're voyeurs. I think you like to find out what women keep in their handbags.'

He picked out a small blue box.

'What's this?'

Tina opened the box. Inside was a chrome clip holding a mesh-covered metal ball the size of an acorn.

'It's a Sony personal microphone.'

'They make them that small?'

'Looks like it,' said Tina. 'You want to run your hands over me while you're at it? Ten shekels a minute, cash in advance.'

*

274

Chief Superintendent Levin pushed his way to the front of the queue at the Majestic's reception and asked the Orson Welles lookalike behind the desk if he had any Charlies staying in the hotel.

'Many,' beamed the fat man. His chins wobbled like blancmange at his little joke.

'What?' said the policeman irritably.

'It's an English expression,' Orson explained. 'A Charlie is a fool.'

'Very entertaining,' said Levin. 'You heard the one about the wobblebottom hotel clerk who fell out with the policeman and got cut up and used as traffic cones?'

'No,' said Orson, reaching for a pen. 'Tell it to me, my nephew collects these things.'

'You should see a doctor,' the policeman sighed.

'A lot of people tell me that,' Orson chuckled as he got out the registration cards. 'So this Charlie is a Charlie someone, or a someone Charlie?'

'We don't know.'

'I see. And it's a man or a woman?'

'We don't know that either.'

'You gonna be long?' asked the woman at the head of the queue behind Levin wearily. 'Only I'm seventy-nine years old and I'd like to see my bedroom before I die.'

They went through the registration cards one by one. There were three possible candidates: Horowitz, Ben-Dor, and Kavanagh. They found Horowitz in the coffee shop eating cream pastries with his elderly mother. He turned out to be a balding and argumentative New York attorney who took strong exception to being accosted by the police in a public place.

'What is this? You have a warrant?'

'No,' said Levin politely. 'We just want to ask you a few questions.'

'Speak up,' shouted Horowitz. 'Make sure the whole hotel can hear. What do you want to question me about – espionage? Rape? Child abuse? No – don't tell me yet, let me open the windows, there may be people out in the street who can't hear you.'

The Chief Superintendent sighed.

275

'There's been a murder, Mr Horowitz. We're trying to trace colleagues of one of the deceased. We're told one of them is called Charles and is a guest in this hotel. We don't know his surname.'

'Murder?' The lawyer hit his forehead with the palm of his hand. 'I look like a murderer?'

His mother took a half-eaten slice of cake out of her mouth and put it on the side of her plate.

'Don't even talk to them until you have an attorney, Charles.'

'I am an attorney, mother. I should talk to myself?'

'No dear, people might get the wrong impression.'

Horowitz had never heard of Vincent Fallop.

Ben-Dor was neither Charlie nor Ben-Dor, but an adulterous dentist from Haifa called Rafael Nesvisky travelling under an alias. His wife thought he was at a conference in Tiberias. They found him to their mutual embarrassment in flagrante with his mistress in room 405.

Which only left Charlie Kavanagh. Kavanagh, according to the night porter, had left the hotel in the small hours, around the time Vincent and Eric had been left on French Hill.

'All we need to do now,' said the Chief Superintendent, 'is find the bastard. Do you know his car number?'

Orson checked Charlie's registration card and read out the number of the Subaru.

It was now half-past three. The pace at the Star of David was hotting up: engineers and technicians swarmed over the car park and the Sheremetyevo suite rigging lights and laying cables.

Walter was in the hotel kitchens, jacket off and sleeves rolled up, supervising the dinner preparations.

'No! You cut them like that the seeds fall out. Here, give me the knife.'

Goliath was at his elbow, camera on his shoulder, taking close-ups of the Yemeni chef slicing into a sharon fruit with a soft-steel knife. Overhead a sparks stood on the counter adjusting a sun-gun; behind him among the fridges Julia took shot notes on her clipboard. Charlie was putting together a montage for the opening titles, food intercut with the guests arriving and scenes of rioting in the occupied territories.

Goliath swung the Betacam round on to Walter.

'Heh! You keep my face out of this!' said the researcher.

'Which do you reckon's his best profile?' Goliath asked Charlie.

'He hasn't got one.'

'What is all this for?' asked the Yemeni.

'*Midnight Cowboy Two*,' Walter explained. 'I'm the Jon Voight character, I work as a kitchen porter in a fast-food joint in Zefat making kosher blintzes, then one day I decide to stuff the job, throw my phylacteries in the bin, take the bus to Tiberias and become a rent-boy. Only what I don't know is that there are no homosexuals in Israel. I run into Yaakov Tyler, who plays Rizzo the Yiddisher hustler. Tyler suggests we team up and invade Syria, bring about a thousand years of love and peace and make a few shekels on the side while we're at it.'

'Cut,' said Charlie.

They moved upstairs to the Sheremetyevo. The set was in place, the electricians rigging the last of the lights. Aaron Fluck and the function manager were personally polishing the cutlery.

'Hi Charlie,' said Titch.

'Hello, Tiny,' said Charlie. 'We ready for a camera rehearsal yet?'

'Why not?'

The control scanner was in a Fiat truck parked by the kitchen entrance and connected to the Sheremetyevo by a spaghetti of cables which ran up the outside of the building and in a third-floor window. Inside the truck was cramped: a line of monitors stacked on industrial shelving, three portable tape machines, a homemade bench with a padded vinyl covering and a mixing desk. Charlie would be doing his own mixing, punching between the output of the four cameras on the monitors.

There was just room on the bench for three of them: Charlie, a technical manager, and Julia, who would keep check of timings and warn cameramen when their shot was about to be used. Sound had their own van parked alongside. A talk-back system linked the scanner with the sound supervisor, the cameramen and floor manager upstairs: the director's desk microphone fed directly into everyone else's headphones. Anyone who wanted to speak back could do so at the flick of a switch. The technical manager had left a list of cameramen's names ready beside the desk mike: Goliath on camera one, Tony J. on two, Tony R. on three, Zak on four. Charlie would be OK, provided he didn't have to put faces to them.

Directing television discussions is a bit like rally driving, all reflexes and nerve. The director has to decide which camera to cut to, anticipate, decide again, guess who's about to talk next, watch the listeners for their reactions. It's a curiously demanding but mindless job, like air-traffic control, requiring concentration and nerve but little in the way of creativity. In the end what matters is having a focused camera and a working microphone on whoever's speaking, the rest is icing on the cake. Once you've been doing it a while your conscious mind switches off altogether, so that you can listen intensely, word by word, to an hour long discussion, hit every cut and reaction on the button, and discover at the end that you have absolutely no idea what's been said or by whom. Doesn't matter: the content's for the producer to worry about. Unless you're both producing and directing, when life becomes more complicated.

But Charlie wasn't too worried – this was a job he knew backwards. If it came to that.

He lined up the cameras on the dinner table, and began talking the cameramen through their shots. The two Tonys covered the guests, Zak stayed on Bermant, Goliath offered a wide shot and anything else that took his fancy. They spent half an hour playing around, moving bits of set and vases of flowers around to fit in with the shots. Then Charlie released the cameras for a technical line-up.

Chief Superintendent Levin was making progress, but not a lot. A thorough search of Charlie and Julia's room had revealed no clue as to where they were or what they were up to, no passports or notebooks or travel documents. Charlie had taken his research with him to the location.

But by now they knew of Julia's existence, and who Eric was, or who he claimed to be. And shortly before half-past four airport police found the Subaru wheel-clamped on the verge outside the hire-car pound on the fringes of Ben Gurion International.

'Damn,' said Levin. 'How long has it been there?'

'Since this morning. The Avis clerk says it was there when he arrived at eight.'

'Run Kavanagh's name against the airline passenger lists,' instructed the Chief Superintendent. 'Fast. And while you're at it check if they did a switch, talk to the coach drivers, see if anyone picked them up off the taxi rank, any way they could have doubled back. And,' he added as an afterthought, 'find out if any vehicles were stolen round that time.'

'Done it already, Sam,' said his airport colleague. 'Nineteen eighty-three Ford Escort belonging to a cleaner, went missing about eight this morning.'

At home in the Old City, Yaakov Tyler waited for the last of his colleagues. There were four men gathered in the apartment: Tyler, Liel, Feinberg, and Kimche, with Kaufman still to come. Ezra would meet them at the hotel.

Benny Kimche stood at the window smoking a cigar and looking out towards the Wailing Wall.

'You catch the riot?' he asked Yaakov.

There'd been a disturbance at the Wall that afternoon. In the late eighties the Chief Rabbinate had caved in to ultra-Orthodox pressure and imposed a ban on women singing or raising their voices in prayer, on the grounds that the sound of female voices is lascivious. Worship at the Wall is sexually segregated: men to the left, women to the right, with a metal guard rail between. That afternoon a group of male *haredi* hard-liners had imagined they heard singing coming from the equally devout women across the barrier, and had responded by throwing abuse and then chairs at the offending party. The police were powerless to intervene: the Wailing Wall was a protected zone under the direct administration of the Religious Affairs Ministry, which in turn was under the control of the National Religious Party and the Chief Rabbinate. It took an hour before the necessary authorisation arrived, and by that stage the riot had reached such proportions that tear gas had to be used. The *haredi* contingent wrapped their prayer shawls over their mouths and noses, picked up the canisters and threw them back at the police. By the time order was restored sixteen people had been taken to hospital, and arrests made. Not that anyone would be charged.

'These people are getting hard to control,' said Kimche.

'Do they need to be controlled?' Yaakov chuckled. 'In the old days it was thought sinful to extinguish the fire in your own hearth.'

Despite the air conditioning the atmosphere was thick with cigarette smoke. Danny Feinberg was seated on the sofa, Reuven Liel examining a Persian spice box on the mantelpiece. This was a meeting of old friends – an alliance of interests that went back over twenty-five years. Tyler was the moving force, the one who kept a watchful eye on the rest, making sure that none of them became too ambitious or overstepped the marks of caution, reminding them discreetly of the fat file of documents he kept in his safe, with copies in a numbered vault at the Bank Leumi and instructions with a neutral lawyer in case he himself should meet with a less than accidental death. Not that any of them needed keeping in line: this was a marriage of mutual convenience, of favours done and returned. Rotary Clubs and Freemasons work on much the same basis, helping each other out in times of need: problems with the tax authorities and obstructive government departments, sons in the army anxious for promotion, matters that would be embarrassing if they made the press. Or that's how it began, a group of friends meeting for lunch once a month to talk about life and old times, do a little business, complain about the state of the country. There had been others, too: some had died, others withdrawn, their lips sealed by the knowledge of what lay in Yaakov's safe.

With time the favours became projects. Liel was posted to Washington, and found himself with access to confidential information on Israel's arms-procurement plans, information which could be put to lucrative use on Wall Street by a man of Danny Feinberg's financial acumen. Liel's access to antiquities also married in with Eli Kaufman's overseas shipments of fruit and vegetables: a smuggled Roman statue or a Byzantine vase fetched top dollars in Paris or London, enough to finance Kaufman's increasingly expensive research projects. When Benny Kimche came up with a plan to export Israeli detergent to Saudi Arabia and the Gulf via a re-labelling operation in Cyprus, Chaim

Ezra's political connections oiled the necessary wheels. Political sympathisers in North America regularly sent Yaakov Tyler large sums of money to advance the cause of *Eretz Israel*, far more than Tyler thought the cause needed. Kimche helped him launder the cash back into hard Western currencies for deposit in the banks of Luxembourg and Lichtenstein. These things began when none of them were men of much power or influence: the scale of their activities had grown with their careers.

If there was a rationalisation behind their activities, it was a belief that what was good for committed Israelis like them must be good for the country too – the argument of Business all down the ages, and this after all was business. But nowhere had politics, patriotism and the turning of a dishonest penny found such perfect harmony as in the matter of developing the West Bank. Charlie had guessed right: colonisation of the West Bank meant housing, construction, land speculation and, it seemed increasingly likely, mineral exploitation. As long as the West Bank stayed in the right hands. The plot to kill David Bermant had upgraded a comfortable conspiracy into a Cause, one which justified hiring in outside help.

The original plan had been for a straightforward assassination, arranged to maximise outrage in the outside world. Tina had been recruited with the idea of setting up Bermant for one of the more militant Palestinian groups in Lebanon. It was Tina who had come up with the idea for the TV programme. Many of the group had their reservations, but Tyler loved it. Hard to imagine anything more dramatic than a man dying in close-up on television. The major networks might be squeamish and make do with a still frame, but the cable and satellite boys would use every second, again and again. Like that footage of the Saigon police-chief blowing the VC prisoner's brains out with his pistol, the world could never get enough of it.

'And afterwards?' asked Benny. 'What happens to Kavanagh and the girl?'

'What do you think?' said Yaakov. 'Two terrorists caught in the act – you think the security men walk over and have a quiet word with them, invite them to come down the station and answer a few questions?'

'Depends on your security men,' said Feinberg. 'You have anyone in particular in mind?'

Yaakov stubbed out his cigarette.

'Very much so.'

The doorbell rang: Eli Kaufman had arrived. It was time to leave.

'It's best if we get there separately,' said Yaakov.

23

WALTER EMERGED FROM THE hotel kitchens at seven, just in
time to force a comb through his hair, put on a tie, and position
himself in reception to meet the guests. Charlie had broken the
crew for an hour at six, and they were beginning to drift back
in to the hotel. The recording was due to start in half an hour.

Goliath and his assistant were setting up by the door to film
the arrivals.

'Who comes up with all this stuff?' Walter asked the cameraman, pointing at a twelve-foot scale model of the Spirit of St
Louis hanging above the hall porter's desk. 'I mean, it must
be quite an industry, dreaming up new junk for hotels and
restaurants and so on. You been to that gothic wine-bar in Jaffa?
At least I think it's gothic – big fibreglass arches and stained-
glass windows and a wishing-well with a thatched roof in real
straw. Not badly done, if you forget the aesthetics. Shit, but
well-cooked shit, they know what they're doing, must have
been to art school somewhere along the way. Spend four years
learning to appreciate the finer points of Cimabue's technique,
and then apply the lessons to papier mâché palm-trees and
polystyrene camels.'

'Maybe that's all Cimabue was doing,' Goliath suggested.
'Old man Medici calls him in and asks for thirty virgins picking
grapes on his dining room ceiling, he doesn't want them good
he wants them ready for the Pope's visit next Thursday. Maybe
the only difference is that Cimabue was better at it. How's the
cooking going?'

'A bit special,' said Walter.

Charlie was upstairs with Julia sneaking a whiskey in the side-room they'd set aside for hospitality. He glanced at his watch nervously.

'Half an hour to go.'

'Has it occurred to you we may be making this whole thing up, Charlie?' asked Julia. She refilled her glass from the row of bottles on the side-table.

'It has and we're not,' said Charlie.

And then the phone in the corner rang.

'Charlie?'

The voice was disguised.

'Who's that?' asked Charlie.

'Listen, don't talk. If you know who I am, don't say.'

Handkerchief over the receiver job, Charlie decided. Roger Hogarth was the only person he knew who still owned a handkerchief.

'Fire away.'

'First, there's a warrant out for you from London. Secondly, Vincent Fallop was found dead at breakfast time, someone injected him with a horse-size dose of heroin and dumped him on a building site. They found another body with him, an American called Eric Lowe, if that means anything to you. Bullet in the back of the head. There's a watch out for you at the airport, and I guess they'll have covered Allenby Bridge and the Egyptian border by now. God knows why they haven't found you yet, but they can't be far off. I don't know what the hell you're up to, Charlie. But good luck.'

And then Roger hung up.

Poor bloody Vincent. But there wasn't time for remorse, yet.

David Bermant had left the Foreign Ministry at half-past five and been driven back to Rehavia to change. He tried for a slightly casual look – black suit trousers, short at the ankle, with a white shirt with a long broad pointed collar that stretched halfway across his shoulders, and a new pair of thick-soled brown shoes. In a vague sort of way he was looking forward to the dinner. All you had to do on television was talk, and talking was never a problem. There were people who argued that his whole career had been built on talk.

It had been a wretched day, the worst mix of formal functions and office hysteria. A Mossad agent had been arrested in Holland and charged with the killing of a Lebanese academic in Amsterdam. The Dutch were terribly self-righteous about these things, summoning in the ambassador and threatening expulsions. Two left-wing Israeli politicians – one of them a grizzled war hero of spotless credentials – had turned up in Tripoli talking to the PLO. A trade and technology deal with Brazil was going dodgy. Intelligence reports suggested that a Palestinian peace initiative was being prepared to coincide with his UN speech at the end of the week, and the Americans were putting the screws on for a positive response. Between which he'd welcomed a delegation of English fund-raisers, spoken at a lunch for the Foreign Press, and given an interview to CBS. He was getting too old for this game.

He checked his clothes in the wardrobe mirror and fumbled in his case for more pills: his angina was giving him trouble, and even the exertion of bending down to tie up his shoes left him breathless.

Downstairs Shimon slouched on the bonnet of the Mercedes like a TV cop, keeping a watchful and unnecessary eye on the upright citizens of Rehavia.

Yaakov Tyler pushed his way through the glass doors of the Star of David like a wrestler entering the ring and advanced through the line of security men into the lobby. Goliath bent over his camera and started shooting as Walter advanced to meet him.

'Long time no see, Walter,' bellowed the rabbi. 'How's your sister?'

'Crazy as ever,' said Walter. 'But earning a living. Come on up.'

Reuven Liel arrived two minutes later, then Danny Feinberg. Walter escorted them to the hospitality room, where an air-hostess in a short skirt relieved them of their coats.

'What a bunch of rogues,' Yaakov joked as Kaufman and Kimche joined them. 'Beware of Reuven,' he warned Julia conspiratorially. 'Half a glass of wine and he starts to cry and sing Polish songs.'

'Step outside, Tyler,' the ex-ambassador chuckled. 'Let's settle this thing once and for all.'

'No conferring,' Charlie warned them.

'Perish the thought,' said Yaakov.

'I'm his lawyer, it's my right to confer,' Feinberg objected.

The hostess hovered, offering drinks.

'Martini, please,' said Benny. 'Dry.'

'Dry?' she asked tentatively.

'Very dry. Like James Bond.'

The girl was new, first day on the job. Where she came from no one drank dry Martinis: they drank beer, whiskey, cherry brandy, wine maybe – but not Martini. She withdrew to the bar, examined the bottles, poured an inch of Martini into a glass, added an inch of gin, looked along the line of bottles again, picked out the dry sherry and topped the glass up to the rim. Charlie watched in amazement.

Chaim Ezra had arrived, accompanied by two aides.

'Do you know everyone?' asked Julia, and immediately wished she hadn't.

'Only too well,' said the Deputy Prime Minister.

Kaufman took Charlie to one side.

'About his marriage. How far do you want to go?'

'Just ask him about it in general terms,' Charlie told him. 'Nothing too personal. If you're happy with that.'

'You know what I heard, Danny?' Kimche poked his glass towards Feinberg. 'I heard that in New York scientists have started using lawyers instead of rats in their experiments. First, there are more of them: second, there's less danger of getting attached to them.'

Feinberg scratched his neck with the back of his hand.

'You write this stuff yourself, Benny, or you get them out of a book?'

'I got one for you too, Chaim,' Benny Kimche continued. 'The Swiss apply to the Israelis for permission to post a naval attaché to Tel Aviv. The Israelis object. "How come you need a naval attaché when Switzerland doesn't have a navy?" they say. "What's the problem?" reply the Swiss. "After all, Israel has no money but it doesn't stop you having a Minister of Finance."'

'Same book,' complained Feinberg. 'Tell me, Benny, you ever read bedside stories to your grandchildren?'

'Of course.'

'Who falls asleep first?'

Yaakov buttonholed Walter.

'We start eating at the same time the programme starts?'

'No, you have one course to get going, talk about anything you want. The cue to start asking him questions is the Tournedos Rossini. I'd like you to put the first question, if that's OK.'

'Sure.'

It was time to go to make-up. The assistant floor manager gathered them up and led them off down the corridor.

Goliath was on the phone for Charlie. The cameraman was in the lobby, waiting to get a shot of the Foreign Minister's arrival.

'How much longer do you want me to hold on? Time's getting tight, I ought to be setting up upstairs.'

'Give him another couple of minutes.'

Outside the window the sun was sinking like an outsize orange into the Jerusalem Forest.

Charlie went through into the Sheremetyevo for a last look at the set, double checked the seating plan, had a friendly word with the sparks, checked his shots with the camera crew. Security were there too, watching who came in and out. Four of them, suited and broad-shouldered, another three down in the reception. Four more with Ezra made eleven, plus whoever came with Bermant. Ironic to be a murder suspect in a room full of plain clothes coppers. A moment to savour in days to come, if there were going to be any days to come. He even introduced himself to them, explained about the programme, what was going to happen and when. None of them seemed very worried or even interested. They were being thorough, but they were just going through the motions: another routine day, trailing round after government ministers and digging into people's handbags.

Quarter of an hour to go, and still no sign of Bermant.

Charlie smelled Julia's perfume behind him.

'I love you,' she whispered.

He leaned back so that their bodies touched.

'You're a fool, Julia. But I love you too,' he whispered. 'Whatever happens stick close.'

Shimon and Bermant were stuck in the traffic. A container truck had jack-knifed at Kiryat Wolfson, where the four-lane highway from the north meets Ramban and Ruppin, a mile from the hotel. The roads were blocked in all directions. Cars tailed back east on Ramban as far as the Spanish Consulate. The sun was almost gone, throwing long shadows through the trees. Overhead pigeons and starlings darted across the darkening sky.

David felt a pain in his chest.

'Don't worry, sir. I'll sort this out,' promised Shimon, opening the door of the Mercedes.

'You'll do what?' asked David.

'Sort it out, sir.'

David couldn't contain his curiosity.

'How?'

Shimon looked at the queue of stationary cars and hesitated. They should have had a police escort. Chaim Ezra had a police escort, the Prime Minister had a police escort. The only reason Bermant didn't was because he refused to have one. Driving round Jerusalem without an escort to clear your way was like going for a walk in a thunderstorm without an umbrella.

'I could phone in for a helicopter, sir.'

The man was clearly mad. They were a mile from the hotel: they could walk it in the time it took to bring in a chopper. Even if there was somewhere for the chopper to land, which there wasn't.

'It doesn't matter,' said David. 'It's only a television programme, so what if we're a little late. TV people always keep everyone else waiting, I don't see why we shouldn't return the compliment once in a while, just call in and let them know we've been held up.'

Aaron Fluck and his assistant were fussing over the chefs in the hotel kitchens when Walter pushed through the swing doors.

'How's it going?'

Aaron smiled weakly.

'I'm praying, Mr Azeff.'

Walter wanted to know who would be serving the food, and the manager introduced him to the two waiters. Both wore Battle of Britain flying suits.

'No!'

'No?' said Aaron sadly.

'A thousand times no. This is in danger of turning into a Bunuel movie. Six politicians sit round a table talking about international diplomacy when a man in a flying suit walks in carrying a side of beef.'

'Just the goggles?'

'White shirts, black trousers, dinner jackets if you want. No goggles, no parachute harness, no water wings.'

'How long have we got?'

'As long as it takes, Aaron. Say two minutes. Meanwhile show me the food.'

The manager led him through the kitchens.

The last sliver of the sun's orange globe sank behind the hills to the west. Shimon switched on his sidelights. The traffic on Ramban was beginning to move at last. David reached into his pocket and took out another pill. The pains in his chest were getting worse. A policeman on point duty recognised the Mercedes and beckoned them through. Once across the junction the road was clear, up Ruppin, past the Knesset and the Prime Minister's office, a left at Sderot Herzl and they were almost there.

Charlie was in the scanner, checking that the landlines were working. To his right the engineer was talking to satellite control rooms in London and New York. He checked his watch: dinner was due to start in ten minutes: they went on air in half an hour. He hurried out of the van and crossed the car park to the lobby to meet the Foreign Minister.

Walter too was back on station, brushing a fresh fall of dandruff off the shoulders of his suit.

'You nervous?' The researcher asked.

'Are you?'

'Should I be?'

'You tell me. Anyway, we're on autopilot now. Roller-skating down the Eiger. I don't really believe it's happening. You've done a good job, though, Walter.'

Walter blushed and scratched the top of his head.

'Oh shucks, Charlie. I don't know what to say.'

Charlie laughed.

'Save it for the judge.' He slapped him on the back. 'Good luck, kid.'

Bermant's limousine swept in under the canopy.

'Thanks,' said Walter with sudden sincerity. 'I've enjoyed it, I really have. Good luck to you too.'

Shimon was out of the car before it stopped. More TV cop stuff. A hotel flunky hurried to open the door, two more security men took up their positions on either side of him. Bermant gathered up his briefcase and stepped out on to the hotel steps. Goliath had his camera on his shoulder, his right hand adjusting the focus.

'Here we go,' said Walter.

But Charlie's eyes were on Shimon, trying to place the face.

I know him, and I don't know him.

Bermant was inside now, looking around for his reception committee. The pill was working: he felt better, the chest pains gone. Charlie stepped forward to greet him.

'Foreign Minister, how do you do. I'm Charlie Kavanagh.'

'I'm sorry we're late,' said Bermant. 'I hope the food isn't ruined.'

Vincent's photo. But not just that, there was another memory.

'Not at all.'

They walked across the foyer towards the lift.

'You know Walter Azeff?'

'Of course.'

Julia met them at the third floor, shook hands and guided them down the corridor towards the make-up room.

'Do I get to meet my guests beforehand?' David asked.

'I'm afraid not. It's meant to be a surprise.'

Charlie and Julia left him in make-up with Walter.

'This is Shimon, by the way.' The Foreign Minister gestured towards his guard. 'Maybe you could use him as a wine-waiter.'

'Aaron Fluck would kill me,' said Charlie cheerfully.

Shimon, of course. Forget the moustache, forget the hair. Of course.

Shimon offered them a nervous smile. Julia glanced across at Charlie. There was panic in her eyes.

They left Bermant in make-up, Julia to collect the other guests, Charlie to go back down to the scanner.

'Five minutes!' Titch shouted from the Sheremetyevo. 'Cameras to opening positions.'

'I'll see you downstairs,' he told Julia. 'Make it quick.'

As he turned to go Shimon put his arm on Charlie's shoulder.

'Can I watch from the control room?'

Charlie hesitated.

'Sure, why not? It's very cramped down there, you may have to watch through the door.'

'No problem. If it's OK by you.'

'Sure. Go down with Julia, she'll show you the way.'

Shimon glanced round at Julia's retreating figure.

'Isn't it simpler if I come with you?'

'No,' said Charlie.

24

Tina made herself a glass of carrot juice and drank it slowly, swilling each mouthful carefully round her gums to let her saliva dissolve in the sweet liquid: that way the vitamins and nutrients are all absorbed when they reach the bowel. Then she took a sheet of kitchen roll and wiped the orange stain carefully off her lips, pulled on a sweat-shirt and a light bomber jacket, and picked up her motor cycle helmet from the hall. Almost as an afterthought she tucked the P-38 into the waist-band of her jeans.

Her Honda 250, chained to the railings outside the flat, started first kick. It took her less than five minutes to drive through the park, past the floodlit Knesset and the darkened windows of the Prime Minister's office. Half-way up David Wolfsohn she pulled off the road up a slight rise on to a patch of scrub overlooking the Star of David, and parked the bike among the trees. She checked her watch: it was twenty-five past seven.

Charlie and the sound supervisor arrived at the lift at the same moment.

'Nervous?' asked the soundman.

Charlie thought for a moment.

'Terrified. Don't tell anyone. And you?'

'One of the security guys trod on Bermant's microphone just now.'

'Any damage?'

'We were lucky, it was fine. But I've hidden a desk mike in the flower bowl to be on the safe side.'

Julia showed the guests to their places.

'Do we get to see the menu?' asked Yaakov as he settled in to his seat.

'Apparently Bermant's bringing a loaf and a few fishes,' joked Feinberg, unwrapping his napkin. 'Right now he's out back turning the wine into water.'

All around them lighting men made final adjustments, the sound crew checked mikes, Louella gave Feinberg's dome a final dusting of talcum powder.

Walter appeared at the door.

'Who's looking after Bermant?' hissed Julia.

'I am. But I wanted to check the food.'

'You're mad.'

'Three minutes,' shouted Titch.

Julia made a dash for the lift, pressed the button, looked despairingly at the indicator, and decided to take the back stairs. Shimon was close behind.

'I heard about Vincent and Eric,' she panted as they tore down the concrete steps. 'Is that what you have in mind for the rest of us?'

'Relax,' said Shimon. 'It's not you we're after.'

They'd reached the ground floor, through carpet-covered doors and out into the lobby. A tour group was booking in at the reception desk. They steered their way through the piles of suitcases towards the exit.

'Where's Tina?' asked Julia. As if she cared.

'It's her night off. Mondays she always goes to see her astrologer.'

Julia stopped.

'That what she tells you? You poor dumb fool.'

She pushed through the glass doors, out into the car park. It was dark now, the hotel white and starkly ugly in the floodlights. A crescent moon hung over the northern horizon; bats flickered through the pine trees.

Charlie was already in the scanner, seated at the control desk, talking into the microphone. Julia slid in beside him. Shimon stayed outside, watching through the open door. He felt inside his pocket and checked the small black transmitter. It had a range of half a mile, easily enough to reach the Sheremetyevo.

Then he put his other hand inside his jacket and loosened the clip on his shoulder holster.

The floor manager's voice came over the talk-back speaker.

'One minute, studio.'

'Stand by the waiters, Titch,' said Charlie. 'You happy in sound?'

'Roger.'

'Is Bermant ready?'

'Almost.'

'First on camera one,' said Julia. 'Stand by camera three.'

Charlie looked at her in amazement.

'Where the hell did you learn all that from?'

'My father used to be a vision mixer.'

She gave him a bitter-sweet smile.

'OK,' said Charlie into the mike. 'Get ready to bring Bermant in. We'll treat it for real from now on in, but we don't go live for another ten minutes. When we do, there's thirty seconds of opening titles, then another two minutes of compilation on tape, then we come to the studio. Out words on tape,' he checked his notes, 'are "... at the United Nations in New York." We'll count you out of it.'

A disembodied voice crackled out of a speaker.

'Hallo, Jerusalem. London here.'

'Hallo London,' said Charlie. 'You have sound and pictures?'

'Yup. Can you give us bars and tone?'

The engineer pushed a switch and the monitors changed to vertical colour bars to allow London to check the colour alignments.

'You getting that, London?'

'Fine. Give us another thirty seconds.'

'How's the weather in England?' asked Charlie.

'Eighty in the shade.'

'Liar. What happened in the Arsenal-Newcastle match?'

'Newcastle won three two after extra time. Could you take the reds down a little?'

The engineer adjusted the vision output.

'OK, let's have Bermant, Titch,' Charlie said.

David Bermant paused at the open door.

'I booked a table for seven,' he said wryly. 'In the name of Jehovah. Good evening, Chaim, hallo Benny, Yaakov.'

He took his seat at the end of the table. Louella moved in with a comb and powder puff. Someone else clipped a personal mike on to the lapel of the Foreign Minister's jacket.

'Could you give us a few words to test for level, sir?' Titch asked him.

'You want me to talk? What would you like me to say?'

'Could you tell us what you had for breakfast?'

'You sound like a bloody doctor,' said David. 'Grapefuit and toast. Dry toast. That do you?'

'That's fine.'

The waiters brought in the first course: gravlax salmon and strawberries, arranged in nests of knitted chives and watercress, surrounded by a circle of peeled grapes and asparagus. Bermant was a vegetarian, but he didn't mind fish.

'So what are you bastards going to ask me about?' the Foreign Minister asked the company. 'Let's have some ground rules, shall we? No politics, no sex, no religion.'

'Sounds like it's going to be a short programme, David,' said Kaufman, chewing on his gravlax.

Outside in the scanner, Charlie leaned in to the microphone.

'Goliath, give me a big wide, will you? We'll rehearse the opening mix.'

His fingers fidgeted with the faders and buttons.

'OK, now go in tight on Bermant. Right. When the opening compilation finishes, I'll mix to you, then pull wide to show the whole group. Then I'll take close-ups on two, three, and four, round the group, which gives you time to get back in on the talent again. Looser shot this time, cut him at the breast pocket. Titch, could you confirm with Yaakov Tyler that he'll ask the first question?'

'Check,' said the floor manager.

Charlie looked up at the clock.

'Is that time right?' he asked the technical manager.

'To a tenth of a second.'

They had two minutes to air. Charlie put his fingers on the mixer faders, ready to go. Julia passed him a cigarette.

*

'How personal are you going to get?' David asked his guests. They looked at each other.

'How personal do you want us?' asked Feinberg.

'Up to you.' David put down his knife and fork and put his hand inside his jacket. The pains were coming back. 'Though I'm not sure how interested the outside world would be in my private life. Such as it is.'

Kaufman took a sip of wine, and put down his glass.

'The producer wants me to ask you about Ruth's death.'

'Shit,' said Charlie. 'The lying bastard.'

Behind him Shimon felt into his pocket and put his hand on the transmitter.

'One minute,' said Julia.

'Standing by,' Titch confirmed over the talk-back.

Charlie lit another cigarette.

'We're ready to go, London. Stand by on opening titles, stand by sound. Good luck everyone.'

The van was suddenly very quiet. The time you worry isn't when the jungle drums start: it's when they stop.

'Thirty seconds,' said Julia.

At ten seconds Charlie cued the titles. The centre monitor flickered, settled, and a clock appeared, its hand ticking mechanically through the seconds.

'Five-' said Julia, leaning in to the desk mike, 'four-three-two-one – on air. We're on tape for two minutes seven seconds.'

The music of Richard Strauss boomed through the speakers, and images of Jerusalem appeared on the screen, intercut with shots of rioting on the West Bank, Bermant at the rostrum in the Knesset, Walter in the kitchens, PLO leaders shaking hands with European premiers in Brussels. Charlie drummed his fingers on the desk in time to the music. A caption appeared, 'The Greenbaum Corporation Presents', superimposed on a wide shot of the Old City. The shot changed, and a second caption appeared, 'The Last Supper'. The music reached a climax; another cut, this time to Goliath's footage of Bermant arriving at the hotel; the picture froze, and the final title, *Hero Israel?* revealed itself across the Foreign Minister's chest. Charlie had added the question mark at the last minute.

'Heh, you spelled that wrong,' hissed Shimon.

'Get to fuck,' said Charlie.

The tape was still running. Charlie winced at the sound of his own voice narrating Bermant's life story over the archive footage.

'Thirty seconds to studio,' said Julia. 'Camera one first on Bermant.'

Goliath's camera was locked off on a wide shot.

'Can I see your opening shot, camera one?' asked Charlie.

The camera didn't move. Shimon put his hand in his pocket.

'Tight on Bermant, Goliath,' Charlie repeated urgently.

'Twenty seconds left on tape.'

'Where the hell's camera one?'

Titch's voice came over the talkback.

'He's gone, Charlie.'

'He's what?'

'He's not here.'

'Coming to studio,' said Julia. 'Ten-nine-eight-seven-'

And then the fire alarm went off.

The panic was simultaneous. Upstairs in the Sheremetyevo the security men grabbed their walkie-talkies, shouting to make themselves heard above the sirens. Titch went white, recovered himself, and started giving orders.

'Don't use the lifts!'

Already the corridor was full of retreating bodies stampeding towards the staircase. In the middle of them Aaron Fluck stood like a rock in a stream, shaking his head.

'Leave the equipment!' bellowed the technical manager.

'What the hell's going on?' Chaim Ezra asked his bodyguard.

'Bomb scare, sir.'

'Bomb scare or bomb?'

'We're not sure.'

David Bermant was on his feet.

'Where's Shimon? That's the way with bodyguards, there's never one around when you need one.'

Walter was beside him, shaking.

'We should get out, Foreign Minister.'

By now the suite was almost empty, chairs up-turned, food trolleys abandoned. The last of the electricians grabbed two bottles of claret and stuffed them inside his jacket. At the head of the table Titch stood like a captain on the bridge of a sinking ship, surveying the scene.

Yaakov Tyler and Danny Feinberg took the steps two at a time.

'Was this planned, Yaakov?'

'Not by me it wasn't.'

And then came the first explosion: a dull crack, a flash of flame and then a pall of black smoke pouring out from the kitchen entrance.

In the darkness outside the hotel the crowd had gathered in the flower beds. The last stragglers hurried out of the lobby. A beanpole Canadian in Bermuda pants and a skullcap tried to push his way back towards the entrance.

'I got to get to my room. There's two thousand dollars worth of Nikon up there.'

'Take the insurance and buy a Canon,' said the Star of David's function manager.

A second explosion erupted at the back of the hotel.

'I tell you what that is,' announced the function manager to no one in particular. 'Petrol bombs is what that is. Amateur stuff.'

'Seems pretty damn effective to me,' said the Canadian.

'Ah, but you know what they say – Noah's Ark was built by amateurs, the Titanic was built by professionals.'

Shimon stood transfixed on the tarmac. Charlie and Julia were beside him. Then Shimon took out his gun.

'Shouldn't you be looking after Bermant?' asked Charlie, pointing towards the bent figure of the Foreign Minister sitting on the grass thirty yards away in front of the hotel.

Goliath hit Shimon square across the back of the skull with a stage brace. Shimon sank to the ground.

The cameraman was out of breath.

'Sorry about the bangs, boss, best I could manage. I had to make do with petrol. Is everyone out safely?'

'I reckon. Where the hell's Walter?'

A warm dry wind fanned the flames. The smoke was thicker now, billowing in black clouds out of the ground floor. From inside the building came the crackle of timber and glass: the fire was spreading fast. In the distance Charlie could hear sirens.

He looked around for Walter's face in the crowd.

'Over there!' shouted Julia. 'Walter!'

Walter's mind was somewhere else entirely.

They ran through the shrubs towards him. At the last minute he turned and saw them.

'We need your car, Walter,' Charlie improvised.

The researcher looked at them blankly, and turned back to the fire. Finally he spoke.

'I wonder who did it? An architectural aesthete, probably. Provisional Wing of the Civic Trust. Pity about the model aeroplanes, I know a children's home in Petah Tiqwa that could have used them.'

'For God's sake, man!'

Walter didn't move. He was in shock.

A fireball erupted in the kitchens, and then a succession of minor explosions.

'That would be the butane cylinders,' said Goliath. 'Followed by the wine store. Here, grab these.'

He handed Charlie a fistful of red dye-capsules, the kind make-up artists use to simulate gunshot wounds. Make-up artists like Louella, Julia guessed. Then the cameraman disappeared into the darkness. He had Shimon's pistol in his hand.

Charlie handed Julia two capsules.

'When you hear a shot, break them. Doesn't matter where – over your neck, stomach, take your choice.'

There were police everywhere now, forcing the onlookers further back up the darkened hillside behind the hotel. Someone was giving orders through a loud hailer. Across the car park Charlie saw Chaim and David being bundled into their cars. As the Mercedes reached the exit three fire engines turned the corner of Sderot Herzl, sirens screaming, lights flashing. Close behind them was an ambulance.

Six gunshots sounded in quick succession.

'Get down!'

Walter stood transfixed. Charlie took a breath, thought of Vincent and landed his fist square and hard in the researcher's stomach. Walter slumped to his knees.

Charlie fell with him, smearing mock blood all over the researcher's face as the three of them writhed on the ground.

It took the police half a minute to reach them. Goliath was there too, holding on to his shoulder and wincing with pain. A red stain seeped slowly through his shirt.

'He's over there,' Goliath shouted at a sergeant, 'in the bushes.'

'You badly hurt?'

At that moment the ambulance arrived, a Dodge van in the colours of the American Red Magdam, donated to the people of Israel by John and Sarah Lloyd-Wallace of Chicago, Illinois. Behind the wheel was Ruth Kaplan; beside her sat the gate-keeper from Kefar Sharon in a white paramedic's jacket and trousers.

'Get them out of here!' yelled the sergeant, pointing at Charlie and Julia.

Sarah and the gatekeeper were already running stretchers out the back of the ambulance. Charlie gripped his stomach. Julia started to scream. Walter lay very quiet, hardly breathing. A moment later they were inside.

'You need a doctor?' a policeman shouted through the window.

'I am a doctor,' said the gatekeeper.

Sarah gunned the engine. As they turned the corner out onto the road the Star of David's ballroom roof caved in.

'Fucking beautiful!' whispered Goliath. 'And I haven't even got my camera.'

They drove at speed, siren on and lights flashing, north up Herzl towards the main Tel Aviv road. For a while none of them spoke. Charlie got a packet of cigarettes out of his pocket and handed them round.

Sarah pulled back the glass partition.

'You'd better stay wounded for the moment, there may be road blocks. Any real injuries back there?'

'No,' said Charlie. 'Except Walter. I may have hit him harder than I meant.'

'You all right, Walter?' Sarah asked.

Walter said nothing.

'He's fine,' said Goliath. He bent over the researcher. 'You try anything now, kid, I break your legs. Nothing personal, just don't try to be clever. We've had enough of that for one evening.'

'Where did you get the ambulance in the end?' Charlie asked Sarah.

'Borrowed from the Ezrat Nashim Hospital, out by the Har Menuhot cemetery. You know Lev, by the way?' She nodded towards the paramedic. 'He has a cousin works as an ambulance driver. Foolishly left the keys in the ignition when he went to have dinner.'

'You planned this?' asked Julia.

'More or less,' said Charlie.

As they approached the Tel Aviv highway Sarah glanced in her mirror, turned off the siren, indicated left and cut up a side-road towards Giv'at Sha'ul, the last of the modern hill-top suburbs before Jerusalem ended and the forest began. In front the mountains were silhouetted against the aquamarine of the night sky; behind lay the lights of the city. A black column of smoke from the Star of David was just visible in the darkness.

'Anyone care to tell me what the hell's going on?' asked Julia.

'Ask Walter,' said Charlie.

25

WALTER OFFERED NO RESISTANCE as they walked him across the grass to Sarah Kaplan's bungalow. The only thing he'd said on the drive down was sorry. He was sorry about Vincent, and Jo Bellini, the actor who'd played Harry Greenbaum at the Hilton in London. Eric liked to get rid of witnesses as he went along.

'And who killed Vincent?' asked Charlie.

That was Eric too, Eric and Shimon. Shimon said it was an accident: they got the wrong syringe.

And Eric?

That was Tina – she didn't approve of what had happened to Vincent. Shimon was still needed, but not Eric.

Tina was Walter's sister.

Now Walter sat in the nylon-upholstered armchair in Sarah's little living room, hands on his stomach, eyes on the square of cheap carpet in front of him. Charlie perched on the arm of the sofa opposite. It was a small room, the same size as Liel's, only without the antiques. In fact Sarah had few possessions: a shelf of books, a radio, two cheap reproductions on the wall, a Chagall and a Vermeer. Her vintage Uzi sub-machine-gun, the most ubiquitous of Israeli artifacts, yellow-green paint flaking off its butt, hung among the coats on the pegs in the corridor which ran from the front door to the bathroom. There were children's paintings from the kindergarten on a noticeboard beside the sink. Icons of Israel: the machine-gun and the kindergarten.

'I told you about my father and Ezra, didn't I?' said Walter without looking up.

'Yes,' said Charlie.

'My father was too busy with his political work to have much time for commerce. Chaim looked after the business – he's always found time for making money. It's the commonest story in the world, two partners, one naïve, the other's greedy. Dad signed the books, not much more. He didn't need to involve himself day to day: the business seemed very successful. Except that Chaim had creamed off every penny.'

Next door in the tiny kitchen the kettle whistled. Sarah was making tea and sandwiches.

'And your father had signed all the papers?'

'Exactly. But it was worse than that. Chaim had been using the company as a front. All manner of dodgy deals had gone through the books – arms sales, unsecured loans to Chaim's friends, God knows what else. But mostly it was a money laundry, a way of turning money from the black economy into legitimate cash. None of us knew any of this at that stage, none of us had looked at the company books.'

'What happened to the company?'

'It was taken over by Benny Kimche.'

Sarah brought in a pot of herb tea. Charlie took a sip, winced, and put down his cup.

'Is your mother still alive?' asked Julia.

'No, she lasted about a year. We were OK for money, Chaim made sure of that too. And Dad carried a lot of insurance, a quarter of a million dollars. My mother had a stroke the following spring, died in May. Tina and I inherited half each. Then Tina had her first breakdown. I was just about to go into the army. I hired an accountant to go over the books of the company again. It took him two years, and in the end he handed me the results and told me to get on with my life and forget the whole business. But he'd done a good job: I had the names. Ezra, Liel, Tyler, Feinberg, Kaufman and Kimche.'

'Who did you tell?'

'No one. I wanted to wait until Tina was well enough to talk to her about it.'

Out of the corner of his eye Charlie could see Julia sitting on the floor in the corner, legs crossed, back straight against the wall. She'd smoked without stopping since they arrived, stubbing one cigarette out half-finished and straight away lighting up another. He desperately wanted to be alone with her.

'I'm sorry,' said Walter. 'It's very stuffy in here. Can we open a window?'

'We'll take a break.'

Charlie got up, went over to the door and stepped out on to the balcony. More geraniums in rusting tubs, more weather-beaten garden furniture. It was a clear night, bright with stars. An almost full moon hung like a silver shilling above the black outline of the mountains to the East. The air smelled of pine and tamarisk, lightly perfumed with cow dung from the cattle sheds.

Julia joined him.

'I'd kill for a whiskey,' Charlie complained. 'The most you ever get offered on a kibbutz is a beer, and then only one. Served in a tooth mug, and it has to last you all evening. That or bloody herb tea.'

She was standing close beside him, so that their hands touched.

'How did you find out about Walter?'

'You remember in Eilat, Eric asked us what Walter looked like? Walter said he'd met Eric before, with Harry. One of them had to be lying. I assumed it was Eric, and then I started to wonder. And Walter then told us about his father. The same people – Bermant, Ezra. I needed to talk to someone who knew what had happened, so I came and saw Sarah last night. That's when I found out who Tina was. And that she was working for Tyler.'

Julia slipped her arm into his, and they went back inside.

'What did Tina do when finally you told her?' Charlie asked Walter.

'Went to see Yaakov and asked for a job. He knew about her intelligence background, and asked her what she had in mind. She said she blamed Bermant for dad's death. To cut a long story short, she sold him the idea of 'The Last Supper', said she'd finance the programme herself out of the insurance money. Suited Tyler to a tee, revolution on the cheap. Neither of you were meant to get hurt, by the way,' said Walter apologetically. 'We needed someone who was known here, someone who wouldn't attract too much attention, a name that was already on the books. Then Tina came across your file in the Government Press Office. We picked you because you were dull, Charlie. And you'd made films in Israel before. She had friends in the embassy in London, and they checked you out.'

'And what about Julia?'

'Tyler's idea. Not the first time they've used that trick – they have files on ex-Nazis all over the place. Off-the-peg blackmail. Harry Greenbaum came from Tina. She was very proud of the Harry business.'

'And you didn't mind what happened to us?'

'Nothing was going to happen to you. That was all a sham. Nothing happened to Bermant, either. That was all for Yaakov's benefit. He thought Bermant got the chop, you two were shot by Shimon trying to escape. Case closed. In fact it was meant to happen the other way round, you got out OK, the rest of them copped it.'

'How did Tyler think Bermant was going to die?'

'Death by microphone. Yaakov loved the idea of old loud-mouth Bermant killed by a mike. He said it was the twentieth century equivalent of falling on your sword. You know those Sony personal mikes, the ones you clip on your tie? Tina had one rigged so that it injected you with poison, the same system the Bulgarians used with the umbrella. Fires a microscopic poison pellet into you. Beautiful piece of engineering: it still worked as a microphone. Shimon had a transmitter: the moment we went live on air he'd set it off. Tina dropped the mike off at the hotel this afternoon, and Shimon did the switch. Only she gave him an ordinary mike instead.'

'Bloody complicated way to kill someone,' said Julia.

'I know. Intelligence people are like that, they tend to get a bit carried away. Professional pride, I suppose.'

'But your technique was more traditional.'

'Old as the hills. Poison again, but nothing fancy, hydrocyanic acid. All over the entrecotes. Bermant's a vegetarian, he was safe.' Walter allowed himself another little smile. 'You have to admit it, Charlie – six fatal seizures in the middle of dinner would have made great television.'

'We only had four cameras,' Goliath objected.

'Yeah. But you could have done some cut-aways later.'

'You're mad.'

'I'm coming to that conclusion myself. No madder than Tyler, though. No madder than the border police who get Palestinians to climb live electricity pylons at gun-point to take down PLO flags. No madder than Assad or Habbash or Qadhafi either, come to that. Or Thatcher, or George Bush. I'm sorry I involved all of you, though. And I'm sorry it ended like this.'

Charlie was wrong about the beer. Sarah disappeared back into the kitchen and returned with a jug of sickly home-made plum wine. She poured the wine into green glass thimbles and passed them round. Walter asked if he could use the bathroom.

Tina had kept her distance from the ambulance on the drive down from Jerusalem. Partly out of discretion, but also because by the time they'd turned off the main Tel Aviv highway at Emmaus she'd had a pretty shrewd idea where they were going. She stopped half a mile short of Kefar Sharon, and watched the ambulance drive in through the gates. Then she dismounted, hid the Honda in a ditch, and set off on foot across the fields.

There were few signs of life in the kibbutz. A single floodlight picked out the main gate, and thin lines of street-lamps lit up the pathways between the chalets. Away from the settlement the landscape was in darkness: far to the west the lights of a car moved across the black empty plain. A Hercules flew in low overhead, red tail-light flashing, and vanished across the low hills towards the air base.

She knew her path well, moving fast across a field of spring wheat, then skirting a stand of eucalyptus trees and following a rough track north towards the barns, where a side gate led down to the ponds where the cattle watered. The high perimeter fence, a relic from the days when the Jordanian border ran a mile to the east, now offered no more than a symbolic barrier, and the rusting padlock on the cattle gate hung idly open.

She paused for a moment, listening to the cattle moving

restlessly in their stalls, a dog barking, distant sounds of a radio playing Mozart, then slipped through the gate and up the rise towards Sarah's bungalow. The curtains were drawn, but she could hear voices inside, first Goliath, then Charlie, then Sarah. Lev had taken the ambulance back to Jerusalem, but Sarah's ancient Renault 4 was parked in under the tamarisk tree. Tina inched her way along the wall until she reached the veranda, where a triangle of yellow light spilled out the half-open door on to the grass. She reached her arm round the jamb and unhooked Sarah's Uzi from the pegs.

Walter came back into the room and sat down again.

'Me too, I'm afraid,' said Charlie, and headed for the bathroom.

'So what do you do now?' Walter asked Goliath.

'Give ourselves up, I suppose. Negotiate a peaceful surrender.'

Outside in the darkness Tina weighed her options. Two men and two women, plus Walter. Goliath would be the problem: the big man knew how to handle himself, and he could be armed. The others she wasn't sure about.

'You do something, Rafi?' she hear Walter ask Goliath. 'After this is over, go to my flat. There are papers there, all the shit on Tyler and Ezra and friends. I put them in sandwich boxes in the freezer, seemed like the sort of place no one would look. There are a lot of important people involved, it may suit everyone if the paperwork goes missing. Make copies, hold on to the originals. You do that for me?'

'Sure,' said Goliath. 'You got a key for me?'

'Under next door's mat. We have an arrangement, they keep theirs under mine, and vice versa.'

Charlie washed his hands, dried them on the towel on the back of the door, and walked out into the corridor.

Tina was facing him, the Uzi pointed straight at his chest. She put her finger to her lips, and motioned him past her towards the sitting room. The gun moved to the small of his back, so that as they entered the room he was between her and Goliath.

'Hallo, Tina,' said Sarah.

'Hallo, Sarah.' With her spare hand Tina pulled the P-38 out of her waistband and handed it to Walter. 'Sorry to gatecrash your party.'

'You fire either of those things,' said Goliath quietly, 'you'll have the whole kibbutz here inside a minute.'

'Try me,' said Tina.

No one took up her invitation.

'Listen, Walter . . .' Charlie started to say.

'In the bathroom, all of you,' Tina interrupted. 'Except you.' She singled out Julia. 'You come with us. We need some insurance.'

Charlie looked at Julia.

'Move!' Walter hissed.

Sarah got up, and Charlie and Goliath followed her through. The bathroom was too small for a bath: just a toilet, a washbasin, a glass shelf and a corroded chrome showerhead dripping into a plastic tray in one corner. The window was a narrow rectangle on the wall above the sink, too small to be any use in an escape. Sarah sat on the lavatory, Goliath crouched in the shower tray, while Charlie stood with his back to the wall.

Tina waited in the doorway, holding the Uzi in front of her.

'Car keys, please, Sarah.'

Sarah reached in her pocket and handed her the keys. Tina took them in her spare hand, and then passed them back to her brother. Walter was standing in the corridor, one hand covering Julia with the P-38, a length of washing-line in the other.

'You want me to tie them, Tina?'

'Why not?'

And then the phone rang.

For a fraction of a second Tina looked away. Charlie threw all his weight against the back of the door, slamming it violently against her hand. Julia winced at the crack of breaking fingers. And then Tina started to scream. Goliath was on top of her now.

Walter looked at Julia.

'Run for it, Walter,' she said softly.

He backed away down the corridor, still covering her with

308

the gun, then disappeared into the darkness. There was a brief silence, then the sound of the Renault starting up.

Charlie had the Uzi now, and was running towards the door. He reached the veranda and raised the machine-gun to his shoulder. His thumb slipped off the safety catch, hesitated, then lowered the gun.

'Let him go, Charlie,' said Julia. 'This isn't our war.'

Sarah joined them on the step.

'Phone call for you, Charlie. Someone called Roger Hogarth.'

26

Looking back afterwards, Charlie had little clear memory of the events of the next twelve hours. He remembered Roger Hogarth and Chief Superintendent Levin's midnight arrival at Kefar Sharon, the convoys of blue and white police vehicles, the doctor sedating Tina on Sarah's sofa. Some time in the small hours Roger drove Charlie, Julia and Goliath under escort back to the national police headquarters in north Jerusalem.

And then the serious questioning began – the who, where and when, the drawing up of statements and signing of depositions. Roger had already negotiated a deal with Levin on the minor matter of Charlie's theft of the Ford Escort, and that aside Charlie and Julia didn't seem to have done anything too illegal. But the cameraman was another matter.

'You're not going to charge Goliath, are you?' Charlie asked as he prepared to sign his statement.

'Arson and assault,' said the Chief Superintendent.

Charlie put down his pen.

'Are you serious?'

'I don't have a lot of choice. If he pleads guilty he might get off with a suspended sentence.'

'The streets of this city are crammed with jaywalkers and TV licence evaders, Superintendent. Haven't the police got anything better to do than molest ordinary decent arsonists?'

'This is no laughing matter,' said Levin wearily.

'You're bloody right it isn't,' said Charlie angrily. 'What evidence have you got against him?'

'A burned-down hotel and a security man with a broken collar-bone for starters.'

'Shimon's collar-bone got broken? You should give whoever did it an Olympic Medal. And who saw all this happen?'

Levin sighed.

'You did.'

'Did I?'

'Of course.'

Charlie lined up the sheets of his statement along the edge of the table and lit his cigarette lighter, holding the flame midway between his papers and his cigarette.

'OK, I'll tell you what I saw. I saw Shimon trip over a kerbstone. And I saw the fire. Started in the hotel kitchen, didn't it?'

Levin's eyes were on the lighter.

'Which is where most fires start,' Charlie continued. 'It's an offence in this country to let your chip pan go up in smoke?'

'It's an offence to obstruct the police, Mr Kavanagh.'

Charlie lit his cigarette and inhaled.

'You don't need me to obstruct you. What time did you start looking for me on Monday – eight in the morning? Nine, maybe. Takes you eleven hours to find a man who's spent most of the day in a hotel full of policemen and secret service. Bloody brilliant.'

Levin blushed.

'These things are difficult, we work in different departments.'

'Don't tell me, tell the Press. In the meantime if you want any documents signing, lay off Goliath and tell your forensic people to stop looking for petrol cans in what's left of the kitchen. It's a deal?'

The policeman thought for a moment.

'It's a deal,' he said eventually.

It was six in the morning by the time they left.

'That's it?' Charlie yawned as Levin led them down the long corridor to the main entrance.

'That's it. As far as I'm concerned.' The Chief Superintendent put his hand on Charlie's shoulder. 'Enjoy the rest of your stay.'

And then the bedlam began. There must have been a hundred

journalists gathered on the steps, an orchestra of pizzicato reporters clamouring to be heard above the rumbling timpani of Nikons and Hasselblads in the cold grey light of dawn. Charlie had his arm round Julia, the two of them too tired to feel or think anything very much.

'Charlie! Charlie!'

Charlie reluctantly let go of Julia and turned to face the crowd of reporters.

'I suppose you're wondering why I asked you all here this morning . . .' he began.

'Give Miss Cornwall a kiss, will you Charlie?' interrupted a photographer.

'Would you kiss a man who's smoked eighty cigarettes and been up all night?' Charlie shouted back.

'Let's get out of here,' said Julia.

Roger steered them through the crowd to his car. Goliath got in the front of the Rover beside Roger, Charlie and Julia in the back. The police waved them out onto the main road.

When they reached the Jaffa Gate Goliath asked to be dropped off.

'You do me a favour, kid?' he asked Charlie. 'Next time you get a simple one-day shoot, lose my number. You want to film Beirut, Tehran, mafiosi, Colombian drug barons, I'm free. Talking heads at the Star of David, you're on your own.'

'Get the fuck out of here, will you?' said Charlie.

Julia leaned forward and gave the cameraman a kiss.

'Goodbye, Goliath.'

'Shalom, Julia. And remember, not until he marries you.'

Roger drove them back to the Majestic, but the press were waiting for them there too.

'Drive on,' said Charlie.

'Where to?'

Anywhere. Hong Kong, Fiji, Mexico, Tierra Del Fuego — anywhere but England. Half of Charlie craved the dull, comfortable familiarity of London: ordinary life, waking up, making coffee, going to work, a world where blocked sinks and noisy neighbours and overdue phone bills passed for real problems. But the rest of him was scared of facing that world again, scared of what Julia would think of his mundane, messy little life there.

He turned to look at her. She looked utterly exhausted, emotionally naked, all the artifice gone from her face.

'Where do you fancy? There's a Yemeni restaurant in the Russian quarter does an early breakfast, then we could head up the coast to Caesarea and relax on the beach for a couple of days. Or Cyprus, I've got a mate on the *Observer* has a villa he never uses outside Paphos . . .'

She gave him a weary smile.

'Couldn't we just go home, Charlie?'